Interplanetaries

Uranus, *by Clark Ashton Smith.*

INTERPLANETARIES

The Complete Interplanetary Tales
of Clark Ashton Smith

Edited by Ronald S. Hilger

Hippocampus Press

New York

Published by Hippocampus Press
P.O. Box 641, New York, NY 10156.
www.hippocampuspress.com

Cover illustration and design © 2023 by Jason Van Hollander and
Randy Broecker.
Title design on front cover by Daniel V. Sauer, dansauerdesign.com
Hippocampus Press logo designed by Anastasia Damianakos.

First Paperback Edition
1 3 5 7 9 8 6 4 2

ISBN 978-1-61498-418-4 (paperback)
ISBN 978-1-61498-425-2 (ebook)

CONTENTS

DISCOVERING A WILD MARS

Nathan Ballingrud

I remember a summer evening when I was small. School was out, my dad was cooking burgers and hot dogs on the grill, and the world was an open vault of possibility. I was lying on the grass, breathing in the smell of the cookout, feeling the warm breeze, staring into the sky as it opened its shutters. The sun was failing, turning the sky a deep-ocean blue. The moon, just a pale chalky smudge a moment ago, began to burn with a white radiance that sent electricity through my body.

A few stars were out: a small bright scattering. One of them was pink.

I pointed it out to my dad.

"That's Mars," he said, taking a moment to stare at it with me.

Mars, I thought.

Mars.

The word was an incantation, conjuring a host of wonders in my mind. An alien world so close I could see it with my naked eye. A place no human being had ever been except through imagination.

By this time I had already been there once myself. I'd watched *The Martian Chronicles* television series, based on Ray Bradbury's beautiful stories, so I had some idea of the ancient, haunted cities to be found there. I had visions of families and shopkeepers trying to live ordinary lives surrounded by the deep strangeness of someone else's world, defined by strange customs, languages, and architecture. Visions I took to heart and would deploy in my own work many years later.

The Mars I knew was austere, melancholy, and quiet.

But staring up at that glaring red star that evening, I had the sense there was something more. Something vital and very much alive.

The more I learned of Mars as I grew older, however, the less that seemed to be the case. Science scoured it of romance. It was still lovely, but lovely like a relic from an archaeological dig, lovely in the distant way of the moon. It was a place that rejected the idea of human cities, really only suitable for satellites and rovers. A place for machines to take grayscale photographs of rocks and sand.

To a more scientifically inclined mind than my own, still a land of wonders. But it lost something for me. Mars had drifted into the realm of the mundane. But I barely noticed; somewhere in that time I had become an adult, that dismal stage where, if you're not careful, so much of the romance of life slips away. I was not careful. I'd surrendered Bradbury for the realists, and I became for a time a gray soul in a gray world.

I found Clark Ashton Smith later than most, I think. I was in my thirties, feeling my way back into the literature of the fantastic, rediscovering the pulp writers of the early twentieth century. I caught up on Lovecraft and Robert E. Howard, and I kept coming across the name of a third writer, always mentioned in their company. CAS, as he was often abbreviated, apparently had a polarizing style: lush, dense, forested with esoteric vocabulary. "You'll need a dictionary," I was often warned, not always with approval.

Reading Clark Ashton Smith was like being pulled into childhood all over again. Not because the writing is unsophisticated—it is decidedly not. CAS's vocabulary is every bit as robust as promised, and the advice to have a dictionary to hand is good. It was because reading CAS is like tapping a vein of raw, wild imagination. These stories are volcanic, the pressure of beauty, strangeness, and excitement bursting through the crust and geysering skyward. I was overwhelmed by it, even shocked. I withdrew from him at first, deciding the stories were *too* wild, *too* kinetic. I withdrew, for a time, to tamer pastures.

But I'd gotten a taste of it. CAS's prose and his abundant imagination loomed over everything else I was reading, a distant mountain draped in wonders. I began to feel its lack in everything else.

Two stories cracked him open for me. The first was "The Colossus of Ylourgne," which does not concern this present volume, so I'll only mention it here and recommend it as one of my favorite works of fantasy of all time. The second was "The Vaults of Yoh-Vombis," which you will find herein. This was the story in which I rediscovered Mars.

Here, humans have begun to settle on Mars, but what haunts the red planet is still very much alive. The Martians, who call themselves Aihai, tell stories of an ancient, abandoned city called Yoh-Vombis, which human explorers take it upon themselves to investigate. What they find lurking beneath that ruin is pure horror, a muscular darkness that uncoils like a serpent and threatens not only the hapless protagonists but everything yet alive on Mars.

This story exemplifies the true genius of CAS: the unshackled imagination, the embracing of pulp excess, and the wanton mixture of science fiction, fantasy, and horror into a concoction more potent than any of them individually. Smith wrote three stories set on this particular version of Mars (another, unrelated Martian story, "Seedling of Mars," is also included here with the others), but he did not restrict himself to the red planet when venturing into the cosmos. Of particular note are the two stories set on Xiccarph, an entirely imagined alien world, ringed with four moons and itself orbiting a three-star system.

In the Xiccarph stories, unlike the others, we follow a single protagonist: a sorcerer-scientist called Maal Dweb, who is so all-powerful he is a figure of fear and godlike power to the villagers around him, whose vast intellect makes him susceptible to dangerous bouts of ennui. These stories, with their entangling of far-future science and magic, prefigure the more famous tales of Jack Vance and Gene Wolfe. CAS, famous for his story-cycles (the tales of Averoigne and Zothique being the most well-known) appears to have been starting another one on Xiccarph. What distinguishes it from the others is that "The Maze of the Enchanter" and "The Flower-Women" both center upon a single character, instead of merely a place. It would have been interesting to see CAS develop Maal Dweb over time as he toyed with godhood in his alien milieu, to see how he might have expanded a single character and how he might have played with the confusion of science and sorcery—but it was not to be. He put his pen down shortly after finishing them, and there were no more to come.

We're left to imagine. And I think that's appropriate.

What lingers for me, after finishing any story from Clark Ashton Smith, is the same residue of dream I feel when waking up, filmy wisps of ornamented language that drift pleasantly through my imagination for hours. The prose is essential to the effect. I've seen it described as a barrier, but I don't think that's accurate. Rather, it's a membrane between the mundane world and the strange places CAS wishes to take you. It would be inappropriate to encounter the strange cities of these alien worlds—or the far-future Earth in Zothique, the fable-haunted forests of French Averoigne—in simple, prosaic language. The high-reaching vocabulary is a foundational ingredient. Without it, you would simply be reading words on a page; with it, you are the subject of sorcery.

We began with Mars, so we'll close with it too. Here we have our narrator recounting his first sight of Yoh-Vombis, the infamous ruined city he had been warned against visiting.

"I have seen the hoary, sky-confronting walls of Macchu Pichu amid the desolate Andes, and the teocallis that are buried in the Mexican jungles. And I have seen the frozen, giant-builded battlements of Uogam on the glacial tundras of the nightward hemisphere of Venus. But these were as things of yesteryear, bearing at least the memory or the intimation of life, compared with the awesome and lethiferous antiquity, the cycle-enduring doom of a petrified sterility, that seemed to invest Yoh-Vombis. . . . [H]ere, in this place of eternal bareness and solitude, it seemed that life could never have been. The stark, eroded stones were things that might have been reared by the toil of the dead, to house the monstrous ghouls and demons of primal desolation."

This is incantatory, thrilling prose. Here is the wild Mars I sought as a boy, delivered at last. And here is a wild, dark cosmos, bristling with beauty, threat, and excitement, told in the language of spells.

A sorcerer's vernacular.

Introduction

Clark Ashton Smith considered himself first and foremost a poet, but is largely remembered today for his fantasy and horror stories first published in the iconic pulp magazine *Weird Tales*. What is often overlooked, however, is the pioneering influence of his contributions to the emerging genre of science fiction, many of which appeared in such magazines as *Wonder Stories* and *Amazing Stories*. Smith's prose often defied classification, frequently blending aspects of horror, fantasy, and science fiction, resulting in hybrid stories of "dark fantasy" or "science fantasy." Several examples of these hybrid tales are included in this collection, which is essentially an expanded version of *Xiccarph*, edited by Lin Carter for the Ballantine Adult Fantasy series in 1972. The title "Interplanetaries" was coined by Smith for use in the table of contents of his first hardcover collection *Out of Space and Time*, and was chosen for this book to distinguish it from this well-known predecessor. As Carter points out in his introduction "Other Stars and Skies," the Martian tale "The Vaults of Yoh-Vombis" is primarily a horror story set in a science fictional setting, with a plot heavily influenced by the "lost world" subgenre. "The Maze of the Enchanter" also combines elements of horror, science fiction, and heroic fantasy, all in a setting that has no connection whatsoever to either humanity or the Earth.

Another subgenre Smith was fond of is sometimes referred to as "green horror" and deals with carnivorous, parasitic, often semi-sentient plants. A prime example of this comes from "The Immeasurable Horror," in which Smith describes in grotesque detail the sinister attributes of the Venusian flora.

I'm almost afraid to describe some of those plants. The overlooming palm-ferns with their poddy fronds of unwholesome mauve were bad enough. But the smaller things that grew beneath them, or sprouted from their boles and joints! Half of them were unspeakably parasitic; and many were plainly sarcophagous. There were bell-shaped flowers the size of wine-barrels that dripped a paralyzing fluid on anything that passed beneath them; and the carcasses of flying lizards and strange legless mammals were rotting in a circle about each of them, with the tips of new flowers starting from the putrefaction in which they had been seeded. There were vegetable webs in which squirming things had been caught—webs that were like a tangle of green, hairy ropes. There were broad, low-lying masses of fungoid white and yellow, that yielded like a bog to suck in the unwary creatures that had trodden upon them. And there were orchids of madly grotesque types that rooted themselves only in the bodies of living animals; so that many of the fauna we saw were adorned with floral parasites.

Other examples of green horror may be found throughout Smith's interplanetary tales. "Vulthoom" involves an alien floral being possessing incredible longevity and psychic powers, along with a blossom of a crystalline mineral variety that produces a narcotic fragrance that produces vivid hallucinations of otherworldly forests and singing vegetation, not to mention an immediate addiction. The maze of Maal Dweb is filled with many lethal varieties of vegetation guarding the palace of the enchanter, and the Flower-Women are themselves a sentient form of floral vampires who lure their unwary admirers to a swift and horrible doom by means of an enticing siren song. The *Voorqual* from "The Demon of the Flower" is an ancient bulb-type flower inhabited by some omnipotent Demon who is older than the world of Lophai in which he resides. This tale is also notable for being an expanded version of the prose-poem "The Flower-Devil," which Smith included in *Ebony and Crystal,* published in 1922 by the Auburn Journal Press. The text for this story comes from an early manuscript Smith gave to his lady-friend Genevieve Sully and includes some excised material, including this beautifully poetic opening: "Lying one summer night below the stars, when the Milky Way was spanning the sapphire zenith, and the wind had fallen asleep in the high, somber pines, I heard this tale as a whispering borne from strange worlds beyond the Scorpion."

The interplanetary tales of Clark Ashton Smith include three thematically connected series: The Martian, Xiccarph, and Volmar series. The Martian stories consist of "Vulthoom," "The Dweller in the Gulf," and "The Vaults of Yoh-Vombis." Although not connected to the other three, "Seedling of Mars" is obviously another story set on Mars. These Martian tales are among the most popular of Smith's interplanetary stories, and "The Vaults of Yoh-Vombis" is widely considered one of his best, possibly even an influence for the wildly popular *Alien* movies. "Seedling of Mars" represents yet another example of a sentient plant as well as a very rare case of collaboration, wherein Smith completes a story synopses written by a winner of a contest sponsored by Hugo Gernsback and David Lasser in the Spring 1931 issue of *Wonder Stories Quarterly*. While the collaboration itself was minimal, Smith writes in an August 1931 letter to H. P. Lovecraft, "I received a letter from the *Wonder Stories* editor, enclosing a plot that had taken second prize in the *Quarterly*'s plot contest . . . asking me to make a story out of it. The plot, called 'The Martian,' by one E. M. Johnston of Ontario, was pretty good, so the job wasn't so disagreeable as it sounds . . . it ought to be a pretty fair scientifictional opus."

The Xiccarph tales probably represent the beginnings of another story cycle connected by characters, setting, and so on. As noted by Lin Carter, "Smith wrote only two stories laid on the planet Xiccarph, and only three tales laid on Mars are known to me; why Smith did not produce more tales in these interesting settings is yet another small mystery." The two tales of the omnipotent sorcerer-scientist represent some of Smith's best efforts in prose, fleshing out fully both the atmosphere and setting, as well as the characters themselves. The setting of Xiccarph is distinguished by having no earthly connection and may represent his desire to create a "Hyperborea beyond Hyperborea" in which he allows his imagination to express itself fully without any restrictions or ties to the Earth. On 9 January 1930, Smith wrote to Lovecraft:

> I, too, am capable of observation; but I am far happier when I can create *everything* in a story, including the milieu. This is why I do best in work like "Satampra Zeiros." Maybe I haven't enough love for, or interest in, real places, to invest them with the atmosphere that I achieve in something purely imaginary.

The text for "The Maze of the Enchanter" (as well as all the tales included in this volume) follows the revised and corrected texts prepared by Scott Connors and myself, and was taken from *The Double Shadow and Other Fantasies,* a pamphlet Smith self-published through the Auburn Journal Press in 1933, retaining the original text rather than the subsequent edited version that appears in both *Weird Tales* and the Arkham House volume *Lost Worlds* under the title "The Maze of Maal Dweb."

The Volmar series consists of three lengthy tales written at the suggestion of *Wonder Stories* editor David Lasser, who, after receiving and accepting the first Volmar tale, "Marooned in Andromeda," wrote to Smith proposing "a series of tales about the same crew of characters and their adventures on different planets." Smith proceeded to write two more Volmar stories, "The Red World of Polaris" and "A Captivity in Serpens," also beginning and abandoning a third, "The Ocean-World of Alioth," before giving up altogether. While the Volmar tales are not often considered to be among Smith's best work, it is interesting to note that this series very closely anticipates the incredibly successful and lucrative "Star Trek" series, movies, et al. Could Captain Volmar and the *Alcyone* be the original inspiration behind Captain Kirk and the *Enterprise?* While it is certainly possible that Smith's original concept may have had some influence that eventually reached Gene Roddenberry, we will probably never get a definitive answer to this intriguing question.

Together, the Volmar tales add up to more than 125 pages, far too long to include in this collection; fortunately, the Volmar series has already appeared in book form as *Red World of Polaris* (Night Shade Books, 2003). There are a few other Smith stories that could also be described as interplanetary that are not included here, and some tough editorial choices had to be made in order to present a collection that contains not only the best, but also the most thematically compatible stories. Never fear, faithful reader, when the stars are right we may yet find a home for such great CAS tales as "The City of the Singing Flame," "A Star-Change," "The Eternal World," etc. Moreover, the omission of these tales has allowed such often-overlooked tales as "Seedling of Mars," "The Immeasurable Horror," "The Immortals of Mercury," "The God of the Asteroid," and "Phoenix" to be included herein. I have no doubt that the many avid acolytes of Klarkash-Ton will greatly appreciate these extraterrestrial examples of Smith's unexcelled imagination.

*   *   *

Smith's outré figurines are much sought after by collectors. His illustrations are not less impressive. It is worth mentioning that the cover artists for this book, Randy Broecker and Jason Van Hollander, tried to incorporate some of Smith's unique imagery and have given him equal credit for this thoughtful posthumous collaboration.

—RONALD S. HILGER

TO THE DAEMON

Tell me many tales, O benign maleficent daemon, but tell me none that I have ever heard or have even dreamt of otherwise than obscurely or infrequently. Nay, tell me not of anything that lies between the bourns of time or the limits of space; for I am a little weary of all recorded years and charted lands; and the isles that are westward of Cathay, and the sunset realms of Ind, are not remote enough to be made the abiding-place of my conceptions; and Atlantis itself is over-new for my thoughts to sojourn there, and Mu itself has gazed upon the sun in aeons that are too recent.

Tell me many tales, but let them be of things that are past the lore of legend and of which there are no myths in our world or any world adjoining. Tell me, if you will, of the years when the moon was young, with siren-rippled seas and mountains that were zoned with flowers from base to summit; tell me of the planets grey with eld, of the worlds whereon no mortal astronomer has ever looked, and whose mystic heavens and horizons have given pause to visionaries. Tell me of the vaster blossoms within whose cradling chalices a woman could sleep; of the seas of fire that beat on strands of ever-during ice; of perfumes that can give eternal slumber in a breath; of eyeless titans that dwell in Uranus, and beings that wander in the green light of the twin suns of azure and orange. Tell me tales of inconceivable fear and unimaginable love, in orbs whereto our sun is a nameless star, or unto which its rays have never reached.

VULTHOOM

To a cursory observer, it might have seemed that Bob Haines and Paul Septimus Chanler had little enough in common, other than the predicament of being stranded without funds on an alien world.

Haines, the third assistant pilot of an ether-liner, had been charged with insubordination by his superiors, and had been left behind in Ignarh, the commercial metropolis of Mars, and the port of all space-traffic. The charge against him was wholly a matter of personal spite; but so far, Haines had not succeeded in finding a new berth; and the month's salary paid to him at parting had been devoured with appalling swiftness by the piratic rates of the *Tellurian Hotel*.

Chanler, a professional writer of interplanetary fiction, had made a voyage to Mars with the laudable desire of fortifying his imaginative talent by a solid groundwork of observation and experience. Being over-sanguine, and a poor arithmetician, he had started on this ambitious journey without proper funds. His money had given out after a few weeks; and fresh supplies, expected from his publisher, had not yet arrived.

The two men, apart from their misfortunes, shared an illimitable curiosity concerning all things Martian. Their thirst for the exotic, their proclivity for wandering into places usually avoided by terrestrials, had drawn them together in spite of obvious differences of temperament and training, and had made them fast friends.

Trying to forget their worries, they had spent the past day in the queerly piled and huddled maze of old Ignarh, called by the Martians Ignar-Vath, on the eastern side of the great Yahan Canal. Returning at the sunset hour, and following the estrade of purple marble beside the water, they had nearly reached the mile-long bridge that would take them back to the modern city, Ignar-Luth, in which were the terrestrial consulates and shipping-offices and hotels.

It was the Martian hour of worship, when the Aihais gather in their roofless temples to implore the return of the passing sun. Like the throbbing of feverish metal pulses, a sound of ceaseless and innumerable gongs punctured the thin air. The incredibly crooked streets were almost empty; and only a few barges, with immense rhomboidal sails of mauve and scarlet, crawled to and fro on the waters of somber green.

The light waned with visible swiftness behind the top-heavy towers and pagoda-angled pyramids of Ignar-Luth. It failed upon the sluggish canal, like a reflection of copper on opaque enamel. The chill of the coming night began to pervade the shadows of the huge solar gnomons that lined the shore at frequent intervals. The querulous clangors of the gongs died suddenly in Ignar-Vath, and left a weirdly whispering silence. The strange buildings of the immemorial city bulked enormous, with a few saffron and unwinking lights, upon a sky of blackish emerald that was already thronged with icy stars.

A medley of untraceable exotic odors was wafted through the twilight. The perfume was redolent of alien mystery, and it thrilled and troubled the earth-men, who became silent as they approached the bridge, feeling the oppression of eerie strangeness that gathered from all sides in the thickening gloom. More deeply than in daylight, they apprehended the muffled breathings and hidden, tortuous movements of a life forever inscrutable to the children of other planets. The void between Earth and Mars had been traversed; but who could cross the evolutionary gulf between Earth-man and Martian?

The people were friendly enough in their taciturn way: they had tolerated the intrusion of terrestrials, had permitted commerce between the worlds. Their languages had been mastered, their history studied, by terrene savants. But it seemed that there could be no real interchange of ideas. Their civilization had grown old in diverse complexity before the foundering of Lemuria; its sciences, arts, religions, were hoary with inconceivable age; and even the simplest customs, as well as the traits of the Martian psychology, were the fruit of alien forces and conditions.

At that moment, faced with the precariousness of their situation, the threat of long or permanent exile, Haines and Chanler felt an actual terror of the unknown world that surrounded them with its measureless antiquity.

They quickened their paces. The wide pavement that bordered the canal was seemingly deserted; and the light, railless bridge itself was guarded only by the ten colossal statues of Martian heroes, five on each side, that loomed in war-like attitudes before the beginning of the first aerial span.

The earth-men were somewhat startled when a living figure, little less gigantic than the carven images, detached itself from their deepening shadows and came forward with mighty strides.

The figure, nearly ten feet in height, was taller by a full yard than the average Aihai, but presented the familiar conformation of massively bulging chest and bony, many-angled limbs. The head was featured with high-flaring ears and pit-like nostrils that narrowed and expanded visibly in the twilight. The eyes were sunken in profound orbits, and were wholly invisible, save for tiny reddish sparks that appeared to burn suspended in the sockets of a skull. According to native custom, this bizarre personage was altogether nude; but a kind of circlet around the neck—a flat wire of curiously beaten silver—indicated that he was the servant of some noble lord.

Haines and Chanler were astounded, for they had never before seen a Martian of such prodigious stature. The apparition, it was plain, desired to intercept them. He paused before them on the pavement of blockless marble. They were even more amazed by the weirdly booming voice, reverberant as that of some enormous frog, with which he began to address them. In spite of the interminably guttural tones, the heavy slurring of certain vowels and consonants, they realized that the words were those of human language.

"My master summons you," bellowed the colossus. "Your plight is known to him. He will help you liberally, in return for a certain assistance which you can render him. Come with me."

"This sounds peremptory," murmured Haines. "Shall we go? Probably it's some charitable Aihai prince, who has gotten wind of our reduced circumstances. However, they don't usually go out of their way to befriend terrestrials. Wonder what the game is?"

"I suggest that we follow the guide," said Chanler, eagerly. "His proposition sounds like the first chapter of a thriller. And we'll never know what it's all about unless we go."

"All right," said Haines, to the towering giant. "Lead us to your master." From his smattering of Martian etiquette, he knew that it was not permissible to ask questions. The identity of the person who had summoned them, and his motive, were barred from inquiry by common politeness; though the peremptory invitation itself could have been easily declined without giving offense.

With strides that were moderated to match those of the earth-men, the colossus led them away from the hero-guarded bridge and into the greenish-purple gloom that had inundated Ignar-Vath. Beyond the pavement, an alley yawned like a high-mouthed cavern between light-less mansions and warehouses whose broad balconies and jutting roofs were almost conterminous in mid-air. The alley was deserted; and the Aihai moved like an overgrown shadow through the dusk and paused shadow-like in a deep and lofty doorway. Halting at his heels, Chanler and Haines were aware of a shrill metallic stridor, made by the opening of the door, which, like all Martian doors, was drawn upward in the manner of a medieval portcullis. Their guide was silhouetted on the saf-fron light that poured from bosses of radio-active mineral set in the walls and roof of a circular ante-chamber. He preceded them, according to custom; and following, they saw that the room was unoccupied. The door descended behind them without apparent agency or manipulation.

To Chanler, gazing about the windowless chamber, whose inner door was also grimly shut, there came the indefinable alarm that is sometimes felt in a closed space. Under the circumstances, there seemed to be no reason to apprehend danger or treachery; but all at once, he was filled with a nervous unease and a wild longing to escape.

Haines, on his part, was wondering rather perplexedly why the inner door was closed and why the master of the house had not already appeared to receive them. Somehow, the house impressed him as being uninhabited: there was something empty and desolate in the silence that surrounded them.

The Aihai, standing in the center of the bare, unfurnished room, had faced about as if to address the earth-men. His eyes glowered inscrutably from their deep orbits; his mouth opened, showing double rows of snaggy teeth. But no sound appeared to issue from his moving lips; and the notes that he emitted must have belonged to that scale of overtones, beyond human audition, of which the Martian voice is capable. No doubt the mechanism of the door had been actuated by similar overtones; and now, as if in response, the entire floor of the chamber, wrought of dark, seamless metal, began to descend slowly, as if dropping into a great pit. Haines and Chanler, startled, saw the saffron lights receding above them. They, together with the giant, were going down into shadow and darkness, in a broad circular shaft. There was a ceaseless grating and shrieking of metal, setting their teeth on edge with its insupportable pitch.

Like a narrowing cluster of yellow stars, the lights grew dim and small above them. Still their descent continued; and they could no longer discern each other's faces, or the face of the Aihai, in the ebon blackness through which they fell. Haines and Chanler were beset by a thousand doubts and suspicions, and they began to wonder if they had been somewhat rash in accepting the Aihai's invitation.

"Where are you taking us?" said Haines bluntly. "Does your master live underground?"

"We go to my master," replied the Martian with cryptic finality. "He awaits you."

The cluster of lights had become a single star, had dwindled and faded as if in the night of infinity. There was a sense of irredeemable depth, as if they had gone down to the very core of that alien world. The strangeness of their situation filled the earth-men with increasing disquiet. They had committed themselves to a clueless mystery that began to savor of menace and peril. Nothing was to be learned from their conductor. No retreat was possible—and they were both weaponless. They could not conceive the purpose of their descent, but more and more it assumed a sinister aspect.

The strident shrieking of metal slowed and sank to a sullen whine. The earth-men were dazzled by the ruddy brilliance that broke upon them through a circle of slender pillars that had replaced the walls of the shaft. An instant more, while they went down through the flooding light, and then the floor beneath them became stationary. They saw that it was now part of the floor of a great cavern lit by crimson hemispheres embedded in the roof. The cavern was circular, with passages that ramified from it in every direction, like the spokes of a wheel from the hub. Many Martians, no less gigantic than the guide, were passing swiftly to and fro, as if intent on enigmatic errands. The strange, muted clangors and thunder-like rumblings of hidden machinery throbbed in the air, vibrated in the shaken floor.

"What do you suppose we've gotten into?" murmured Chanler. "We must be many miles below the surface. I've never heard of anything like this, except in some of the old Aihai myths. This place might be Ravormos, the Martian underworld, where Vulthoom, the evil god, is supposed to lie asleep for a thousand years amid his worshippers."

The guide had overheard him. "You have come to Ravormos," he boomed portentously. "Vulthoom is awake, and will not sleep again for another thousand years. It is he that has summoned you; and I take you now to the chamber of audience."

Haines and Chanler, dumbfounded beyond measure, followed the Martian from the strange elevator toward one of the ramifying passages.

"There must be some sort of foolery on foot," muttered Haines. "I've heard of Vulthoom, too, but he's a mere superstition, like Satan. The up-to-date Martians don't believe in him nowadays; though I have heard that there is still a sort of devil-cult among the pariahs and low-castes. I'll wager that some noble is trying to stage a revolution against the reigning emperor, Cykor, and has established his quarters underground."

"That sounds reasonable," Chanler agreed. "A revolutionist might call himself Vulthoom: the trick would be true to the Aihai psychology. They have a taste for high-sounding metaphors and fantastic titles."

Both became silent, feeling a sort of awe before the vastness of the cavern-world whose litten corridors reached away on every hand. The surmises they had voiced began to appear inadequate: the improbable was verified, the fabulous had become the factual, and was engulfing them more and more. The far, mysterious clangors, it seemed, were of preternormal origin; the hurrying giants who passed athwart the chamber with unknown burdens conveyed a sense of supernatural activity and enterprise. Haines and Chanler were both tall and stalwart, but they felt themselves shrinking into mere pygmies when they saw that none of the Martians about them was less than nine or ten feet in height. Some were closer to eleven, and all were muscled in proportion. Their faces bore a look of immense, mummy-like age, incongruous with their agility and vigor. They seemed oblivious of the earth-men, their deeply shadowed eyes preoccupied with some ulterior vision.

Haines and Chanler were led along a corridor from whose arched roof the red hemispheres, doubtless formed of artificially radio-active metal, glared down at intervals like imprisoned suns. Leaping from step to step, they descended a flight of giant stairs, with the Martian striding easily before them. He paused at the open portals of a chamber hewn, like all the others, in the dark and basic adamantine stone.

"Enter," he said, and withdrew his bulk to let them pass.

The chamber was small but lofty, its roof rising like the interior of a spire. Its floor and walls were stained by the bloody violet beams of a single hemisphere orb far up in the narrowing dome. The place was vacant, and furnished only with a curious tripod of black metal, fixed in the center of the floor. The tripod bore an oval block of crystal, and from this block, as if from a frozen pool, a frozen flower lifted, opening petals of smooth, heavy ivory that received a rosy tinge from the strange light. Block, flower, tripod, it seemed, were the parts of a piece of sculpture.

Crossing the threshold, the earth-men became instantly aware that the throbbing thunders and cave-reverberant clangors had ebbed away in profound silence. It was as if they had entered a sanctuary from which all sound was excluded by a mystic barrier. The portals remained open behind them. Their guide, apparently, had withdrawn. But, somehow, they felt that they were not alone, and it seemed that hidden eyes were peering upon them from the blank walls.

Perturbed and puzzled, they stared at the pale flower, noting the seven tongue-like petals that curled softly outward from a perforated heart like a small censer. Chanler began to wonder if it were really a carving, or an actual flower that had been mineralized through Martian chemistry. Then, startlingly, a voice appeared to issue from the blossom: a voice incredibly sweet, clear and sonorous, whose tones, perfectly articulate, were neither those of Aihai nor earth-man.

"I, who speak, am the entity known as Vulthoom," said the voice. "Be not surprised, or frightened: it is my desire to befriend you in return for a consideration which, I hope, you will not find impossible or overly difficult. First of all, however, I must explain certain matters that perplex you.

"No doubt you have heard the popular legends concerning me, and have dismissed them as mere superstitions. Like all myths, they are partly true and partly false. I am neither god nor demon, but a being who came to Mars from another universe in former cycles. Though I am not immortal, my span of life is far longer than that of any creatures evolved by the worlds of your solar system. I am governed by alien biologic laws, with periods of alternate slumber and wakefulness that involve centuries. It is virtually true, as the Aihais believe, that I sleep for a thousand years and remain conscious continually for another thousand.

"At a time when your ancestors were still the blood-brothers of the ape, I fled from my own world to this intercosmic exile, banished by implacable foes. The Martians say that I fell from heaven like a fiery meteor; and the myth interprets the descent of my ether-ship. I found a matured civilization, immensely inferior, however, to that from which I came; and I was regarded with mingled awe and hostility. The kings and hierarchs of the planet would have driven me away; but I gathered a few adherents, arming them with weapons superior to those of Martian science; and after a great war, I established myself firmly and gained other followers. I did not care to conquer Mars, but withdrew to this cavern-world in which I have dwelt ever since with my adherents. On these, for their faithfulness, I conferred a longevity that is almost equal to my own. To ensure this longevity, I have also given them the gift of a slumber corresponding to mine. They sleep and wake with me.

"We have maintained this order of existence for many ages. Seldom have I meddled in the doings of the surface-dwellers. They, however, have converted me into an evil god or spirit; though evil, to me, is a word without meaning.

"I am the possessor of many senses and faculties unknown to you or to the Martians. My perceptions, at will, can be extended over large areas of space, or even time. Thus I learned your predicament; and I have called you here with the hope of obtaining your consent to a certain plan. To be brief, I have grown weary of Mars, a senile world that draws near to death; and I wish to establish myself in a younger planet. The Earth would serve my purpose well. Even now, my followers are building the new ether-ship in which I propose to make the voyage.

"I do not wish to repeat the experience of my arrival in Mars by landing among a people ignorant of me and perhaps universally hostile. You, being earth-men, could prepare many of your fellows for my coming, could gather proselytes to serve me. Your reward—and theirs—would be the elixir of longevity. And I have many other gifts . . . the precious gems and metals that you prize so highly. Also, there are the Flowers, whose perfume is more seductive and persuasive than all else. Inhaling that perfume, you will deem that even gold is worthless in comparison . . . and having breathed it, you, and all others of your kind, will serve me gladly."

The voice ended, leaving a vibration that thrilled the nerves of the listeners for some moments. It was like the cessation of a sweet, bewitching music with overtones of evil scarcely to be detected above the subtle melody. It bemused the senses of Haines and Chanler, lulling their astonishment into a sort of dreamy acceptance of the voice and its declarations.

Chanler made an effort to throw off the enchantment.

"Where are you?" he said. "And how are we to know that you have told us the truth? Your offer is too strange, too incredible, to be accepted hastily."

"I am near you," said the voice, "but I do not choose, at this time to reveal myself. The proof of all that I have stated, however, will be revealed to you in due course. I can make allowance for your incredulity. Before you is one of the flowers of which I have spoken. It is not, as you have perhaps surmised, a work of sculpture, but it is an antholite, or fossil blossom, brought, with others of the same kind, from the world to which I am native. Though scentless at ordinary temperatures, it yields a perfume under the application of heat. As to the perfume . . . you must judge for yourselves."

The air of the chamber had been neither warm nor cold. Now, the earth-men were conscious of a change, as if hidden fires had been ignited. The warmth seemed to issue from the metal tripod and the block of crystal, beating upon Haines and Chanler like the radiation of some invisible tropic sun. It became ardent but not insupportable. At the same time, insidiously, the terrestrials began to perceive the perfume, which was like nothing they had ever inhaled. An elusive thread of otherworld sweetness, it curled about their nostrils, deepening slowly but acceleratively to a spicy flood, and seeming to mix, in some paradoxical manner, a pleasant coolness as of foliage-shaded air with the fervent heat.

Chanler was more vividly affected than Haines by the curious hallucinations that followed; though, apart from this differing degree of verisimilitude, their impressions were oddly alike. It seemed to Chanler, all at once, that the perfume was no longer wholly alien to him, but was something that he had remembered from other times and places. He tried to recall the circumstances of this prior familiarity, and his recollections, drawn up as if from the sealed reservoirs of an old existence, took the form of an actual scene that replaced the cavern-chamber about him. Haines was no part of this scene, but had disappeared from his ken, and the roof and walls had vanished, giving place to an open forest of fern-like trees. Their slim, pearly boles and tender frondage swam in a luminous glory, like an Eden filled with the primal daybreak. The trees were tall, but taller still than they were the Flowers that poured down from waving censers of carnal white an overwhelming and voluptuous perfume.

Chanler felt an indescribable ecstasy. It seemed that he had gone back to the fountains of time in the first world, and had drawn into himself inexhaustible life, youth and vigor from the glorious light and fragrance that had steeped his senses to their last nerve.

The ecstasy heightened, and he heard a singing that appeared to emanate from the mouths of the blossoms: a singing as of houris, that turned his blood to a golden philtre-brew. In the delirium of his faculties, the sound was identified with the blossoms' odor. It rose in giddying rapture insuppressible; and he thought that the very flowers soared like flames, and the trees aspired toward them, and he himself was a blown fire that towered with the singing to attain some ultimate pinnacle of delight. The whole world swept upward in a tide of exaltation, and it seemed that the singing turned to articulate sound, and Chanler heard the words, "I am Vulthoom, and thou art mine from the beginning of worlds, and shalt be mine until the end. . . ."

He awoke under circumstances that might almost have been a continuation of the visionary imagery he had beheld under the influence of the perfume. He lay on a bed of short, curling grass the color of verd-antique, with enormous tiger-hued blossoms leaning about him, and a soft brilliance as of amber sunset filling his eyes between the trailing boughs of strange, crimson-fruited trees. Tardily, as he grew cognizant of his surroundings, he realized that the voice of Haines had awakened him, and saw that Haines was sitting near at hand on the curious sward.

"Say, aren't you ever coming out of it?" Chanler heard the crisp query as if through a film of dreams. His thoughts were bewildered, and his memories were oddly mixed with the pseudo-recollections, drawn as if from other lives, that had risen before him in his delirium. It was hard to disentangle the false from the real; but sanity returned to him by degrees; and with it came a feeling of profound exhaustion and nerve-weariness, which warned him that he had sojourned in the spurious paradise of a potent drug.

"Where are we now? and how did we get here?" he asked.

"As far as I can tell," returned Haines, "we're in a sort of underground garden—a horticultural annex of Ravormos. Some of those big Aihais must have brought us here after we succumbed to the perfume. I resisted the influence longer than you did; and I remember hearing the voice of Vulthoom as I went under. The voice said that he would give us forty-eight hours, terrestrial time, in which to think over his proposition. If we accept, he'll send us back to Ignarh with a fabulous sum of money—and a supply of those narcotic flowers."

Chanler was now fully awake. He and Haines proceeded to discuss their situation, but were unable to arrive at any definite conclusion. The whole affair was no less baffling than extraordinary. An unknown entity, naming himself after the Martian Devil, had invited them to become his terrestrial agents or emissaries. Apart from the spreading of a propaganda designed to facilitate his advent on Earth, they were to introduce an alien drug that was no less powerful than morphine, cocaine, or marihuana—and, in all likelihood, no less pernicious.

"What if we refuse?" said Chanler.

"Vulthoom said that it would be impossible to let us return, in that case. But he didn't specify our fate—merely hinted that it would be an unpleasant one."

"Well, Haines, we've got to think our way out of this, if we can."

"I'm afraid that thinking won't help us much. We must be many miles below the surface of Mars, and the mechanism of the elevators, in all probability, is something that no earth-man could ever learn."

Before Chanler could offer any comment, one of the giant Aihais appeared among the trees, carrying two of the curious Martian utensils known as *kulpai*. These were large platters of semi-metallic earthenware, fitted with removable cups and rotatory carafes, in which an entire meal of liquids and solids could be served. The Aihai set the platters on the ground before Haines and Chanler, and then waited, immobile and inscrutable. The earth-men, conscious of a ravening hunger, addressed themselves to the foodstuffs, which had been moulded or cut into various geometric forms. Though possibly of synthetic origin, the foods were delicious, and the earth-men consumed them to the last cone and lozenge, and washed them down with a vinous garnet-colored liquor from the carafes.

When they had finished, their attendant spoke for the first time.

"It is the will of Vulthoom that you should wander throughout

Ravormos and behold the wonders of the caverns. You are at liberty to roam alone and unattended; or, if you prefer, I shall serve you as a guide. My name is Ta-Vho-Shai, and I am ready to answer any questions that you ask. Also, you may dismiss me at will."

Haines and Chanler, after a brief discussion, decided to accept this offer of ciceronage. They followed the Aihai through the garden, whose extent was hard to determine because of the misty amber luminance that filled it as if with radiant atoms, giving the impression of unbounded space. The light, they learned from Ta-Vho-Shai, was emitted by the lofty roof and walls beneath the action of an electromagnetic force of wave-length shorter even than the cosmic rays; and it possessed all the essential qualities of sunlight.

The garden was composed of weird plants and blossoms, many of which were exotic to Mars, and had perhaps been imported from the alien solar system to which Vulthoom was native. Some of the flowers were enormous mats of petals, like a hundred orchids joined into one. There were cruciform trees, hung with fantastically long and variegated leaves that resembled heraldic pennons or scrolls of cryptic writing; and others were branched and fruited in outlandish ways.

Beyond the garden, they entered a world of open passages and chambered caverns, some of which were filled with machinery or with storage-vats and urns. In others, immense ingots of precious and semi-precious metals were piled, and gigantic coffers spilled their flashing, hundred-colored gems as if to tempt the earth-men.

Most of the machines were in action, though untended, and Haines and Chanler were told that they could run in this manner for centuries or millenaries. Their operation was inexplicable even to Haines with his expert knowledge of mechanics. Vulthoom and his people had gone beyond the spectrum, and beyond the audible vibrations of sound, and had compelled the hidden forces of the universe to appear and obey them.

Everywhere there was a loud beating as of metal pulses, a mutter as of prisoned Afrits and servile iron titans. Valves opened and shut with a harsh clangor. There were rooms pillared with strident dynamos; and others where groups of mysteriously levitated spheres were spinning silently, like suns and planets in the void of space.

They climbed a flight of stairs, colossal as the steps of the pyramid of Cheops, to a higher level. Haines, in a dream-like fashion, seemed to remember descending these stairs, and thought they were now nearing the chamber in which he and Chanler had been interviewed by the hidden entity, Vulthoom. He was not sure, however; and Ta-Vho-Shai led them through a series of vast rooms that appeared to serve the purpose of laboratories. In most of these, there were age-old colossi, bending like alchemists over furnaces that burned with cold fire, and retorts that fumed with queer threads and ropes of vapor. One room was untenanted, and was furnished with no apparatus, other than three great bottles of clear, uncolored glass, taller than a tall man, and having somewhat the form of Roman amphorae. To all appearances the bottles were empty; but they were closed with double-handed stoppers that a human being could scarcely have lifted.

"What are these bottles?" Chanler asked the guide.

"They are the Bottles of Sleep," said the Aihai, with the solemn and sententious air of a lecturer. "Each of them is filled with a rare, invisible gas. When the time comes for the thousand-year slumber of Vulthoom, the gases are released; and, mingling, they pervade the atmosphere of Ravormos, even to the lowest cavern, inducing sleep for a similar period in us who serve Vulthoom. Time no longer exists; and eons are no more than instants for the sleepers; and they awaken only at the hour of Vulthoom's awakening."

Haines and Chanler, filled with curiosity, were prompted to ask many questions, but most of these were answered vaguely and ambiguously by Ta-Vho-Shai, who seemed eager to continue his ciceronage through other and ulterior parts of Ravormos. He could tell them nothing about the chemical nature of the gases; and Vulthoom himself, if the veracity of Ta-Vho-Shai could be trusted, was a mystery even to his own followers, most of whom had never beheld him in person.

Ta-Vho-Shai conducted the earth-men from the room of bottles, and down a long straight cavern, wholly deserted, where a rumbling and pounding as of innumerable engines came to meet them. The sound broke upon them like a Niagara of evil thunders when they emerged finally in a sort of pillared gallery that surrounded a mile-wide gulf illumined by the terrible flaring of tongued fires that rose incessantly from its depths.

It was as if they looked down into some infernal circle of angry light and tortured shadow. Far beneath, they saw a colossal structure of curved and glittering girders, like the strangely articulated bones of a metal behemoth outstretched along the bottom of the pit. Around it, furnaces belched like the flaming mouths of dragons; tremendous cranes went up and down perpetually with a motion as of long-necked plesiosaurs; and the figures of giants, red as laboring demons, moved through the sinister glare.

"They build the ether-ship in which Vulthoom will voyage to the Earth," said Ta-Vho-Shai. "When all is ready, the ship will blast its way to the surface by means of atomic disintegrators. The very stone will melt before it like vapor. Ignar-Luth, which lies directly above, will be consumed as if the central fires of the planet had broken loose."

Haines and Chanler, appalled, could offer no rejoinder. More and more they were stunned by the mystery and magnitude, the terror and menace, of this unsuspected cavern-world. Here, they felt, a malign Power, armed with untold arcana of science, was plotting some baleful conquest; a doom that might involve the peopled worlds of the system was being incubated in secrecy and darkness. They, it seemed, were helpless to escape and give warning, and their own fate was shadowed by insoluble gloom.

A gust of hot, metallic vapor, mounting from the abyss, burned corrosively in their nostrils as they peered from the gallery's verge. Ill and giddy, they drew back.

"What lies beyond this gulf?" Chanler inquired, when his sickness had passed.

"The gallery leads to other caverns, little used, which conduct on the dry bed of an ancient underground river. This river-bed, running for many miles, emerges in a sunken desert far below sea-level, and lying to the west of Ignarh."

The earth-men started at this information, which seemed to offer them a possible avenue of escape. Both, however, thought it well to dissemble their interest. Pretending fatigue, they asked the Aihai to lead them to some chamber in which they could rest awhile and could discuss at leisure the proposition of Vulthoom.

Ta-Vho-Shai, professing himself at their service in all ways, took them to a small room beyond the laboratories. It was a sort of bed-chamber, with two tiers of couches along the walls. These couches, from their length, were evidently designed to accommodate the giant Martians. Here Haines and Chanler were left alone by Ta-Vho-Shai who had tacitly inferred that his presence was no longer needed.

"Well," said Chanler, "it looks as if there were a chance of escape if we can only reach that river bed. I took careful note of the corridors we followed on our return from the gallery. It should be easy enough—unless we are being watched without our knowledge."

"The only trouble is, it's too easy. . . . But anyway, we can try. Anything would be better than waiting around like this. After what we've seen and heard, I'm beginning to believe that Vulthoom really is the Devil—even though he doesn't claim to be."

"Those ten-foot Aihais give me the creeps," said Chanler. "I can readily believe they are a million years old, or thereabouts. Enormous longevity would account for their size and stature. Most animals that survive beyond the normal term of years become gigantic; and it stands to reason that these Martian men would develop in a similar fashion."

It was a simple matter to retrace their route to the pillared gallery that encircled the great abyss. For most of the distance, they had only to follow a main corridor; and the sound of the rumbling engineries alone would have guided them. They met no one in the passages; and the Aihais that they saw through open portals in laboratory rooms were deeply intent on enigmatic chemistries.

"I don't like this," muttered Haines. "It's too good to be true."

"I'm not so sure of that. Perhaps it simply hasn't occurred to Vulthoom and his followers that we might try to escape. After all, we know nothing about their psychology."

Keeping close to the inner wall, behind the thick pillars, they followed the long, slowly winding gallery on the right hand. It was lit only by the shuddering reflection of the tall flames in the pit below. Moving thus, they were hidden from the view of the laboring giants, if any of these had happened to look upward. Poisonous vapors were blown toward them at intervals, and they felt the hellish heat of the furnaces; and the clangors of welding, the thunder of obscure machineries, beat upon them as they went with reverberations that were like hammer-blows.

By degrees they rounded the gulf, and came at last to its further side, where the gallery curved backward in its return toward the entrance corridor. Here, in the shadows, they discerned the unlit mouth of a large cavern that radiated from the gallery.

This cavern, they surmised, would lead them toward the sunken river-bed of which Ta-Vho-Shai had spoken. Haines, luckily, carried a small pocket-flash, and he turned its ray into the cavern, revealing a straight corridor with numerous minor intersections. Night and silence seemed to swallow them at a gulp, and the clangors of the toiling Titans were quickly and mysteriously muted as they hurried along the empty hall.

The roof of the corridor was fitted with metal hemispheres, now dark and rayless, that had formerly served to illumine it in the same fashion as the other halls of Ravormos. A fine dust was stirred by the feet of the earth-men as they fled; and soon the air grew chill and thin, losing the mild and somewhat humid warmth of the central caverns. It was plain, as Ta-Vho-Shai had told them, that these outer passages were seldom used or visited.

It seemed that they went on for a mile or more in that Tartarean corridor. Then the walls began to straighten, the floor roughened and fell steeply. There were no more cross-passages, and hope quickened in the earth-men as they saw plainly that they had gone beyond the artificial caverns into a natural tunnel. The tunnel soon widened, and its floor became a series of shelf-formations. By means of these, they descended into a profound abyss that was obviously the river-channel of which Ta-Vho-Shai had told them.

The small flashlight barely sufficed to reveal the full extent of this underground waterway, in which there was no longer even a trickle of its prehistoric flood. The bottom, deeply eroded, and riffled with sharp boulders, was more than a hundred yards wide; and the roof arched into gloom irresoluble. Exploring the bottom tentatively for a little distance, Haines and Chanler determined by its gradual falling the direction in which the stream had flowed. Following this downward course, they set out resolutely, praying that they would find no impassable barriers, no precipices of former cataracts to impede or prevent their egress in the desert. Apart from the danger of pursuit, they apprehended no other difficulties than these.

The obscure windings of the bottom brought them first to one side and then to the other as they groped along. In places the cavern widened, and they came to far-recessive beaches, terraced, and marked by the ebbing waters. High up on some of the beaches, there were singular formations resembling a type of mammoth fungi grown in caverns beneath the modern canals. These formations, in the shape of Herculean clubs, arose often to a height of three feet or more. Haines, impressed by their metallic sparkling beneath the light as he flashed it upon them, conceived a curious idea. Though Chanler protested against the delay, he climbed the shelving to examine a group of them more closely, and found, as he had suspected, that they were not living growths, but were petrified and heavily impregnated with minerals. He tried to break one of them loose, but it resisted all his tugging. However, by hammering it with a loose fragment of stone, he succeeded in fracturing the base of the club, and it toppled over with an iron tinkling. The thing was very heavy, with a mace-like swelling at the upper end, and would make a substantial weapon in case of need. He broke off a second club for Chandler; and thus armed, they resumed their flight.

It was impossible to calculate the distance that they covered. The channel turned and twisted, it pitched abruptly in places, and was often broken into ledges that glittered with alien ores or were stained with weirdly brilliant oxides of azure, vermilion and yellow. The men floundered ankle-deep in pits of sable sand, or climbed laboriously over dam-like barricades of rusty boulders, huge as piled menhirs. Ever and anon, they found themselves listening feverishly for any sound that would betoken pursuit. But silence brimmed the Cimmerian channel, troubled only by the clatter and crunch of their own footsteps.

At last, with incredulous eyes, they saw before them the dawning of a pale light in the further depths. Arch by dismal arch, like the throat of Avernus lit by nether fires, the enormous cavern became visible. For one exultant moment, they thought that they were nearing the channel mouth; but the light grew with an eerie and startling brilliance, like the flaming of furnaces rather than sunshine falling into a cave. Implacable, it crept along the walls and bottom and dimmed the ineffectual beam of Haines' torch as it fell on the dazzled earth-men.

Ominous, incomprehensible, the light seemed to watch and threaten. They stood amazed and hesitant, not knowing whether to go on or retreat. Then, from the flaming air, a voice spoke as if in gentle reproof: the sweet, sonorous voice of Vulthoom.

"Go back as you came, O Earthlings. None may leave Ravormos without my knowledge or against my will. Behold! I have sent my Guardians to escort you."

The lit air had been empty to all seeming, and the river-bed was peopled only by the grotesque masses and squat shadows of boulders. Now, with the ceasing of the voice, Haines and Chanler saw before them, at a distance of ten feet, the instant apparition of two creatures that were comparable to nothing in the whole known zoology of Mars or Earth.

They rose from the rocky bottom to the height of giraffes, with shortish legs that were vaguely similar to those of Chinese dragons, and elongated spiral necks like the middle coils of great anacondas. Their heads were triple-faced, and they might have been the trimurti of some infernal world. It seemed that each face was eyeless, with tongue-shapen flames issuing voluminously from deep orbits beneath the slanted brows. Flames also poured in a ceaseless vomit from the gaping gargoyle mouths. From the head of each monster a triple comb of vermilion flared aloft in sharp serrations, glowing terribly; and both of them were bearded with crimson scrolls. Their necks and arching spines were fringed with sword-long blades that diminished into rows of daggers on the tapering tails; and their whole bodies, as well as this fearsome armament, appeared to burn and smoulder as if they had just issued from a fiery furnace.

A palpable heat emanated from these hellish chimeras, and the earth-men retreated hastily before the flying splotches, like the blown tatters of a conflagration, that broke loose from their ever-jetting eye-flames and mouth-flames.

"My God! These monsters are supernatural!" cried Chanler, shaken and appalled.

Haines, though palpably startled, was inclined to a more orthodox explanation. "There must be some sort of television behind this," he maintained. "Though I can't imagine how it's possible to project three-dimensional images, and also create the sensation of heat. . . . I had an idea, somehow, that our escape was being watched."

He picked up a heavy fragment of metallic stone and heaved it at one of the glowing chimeras. Aimed unerringly, the fragment struck the frontal brow of the monster, and seemed to explode in a shower of sparks at the moment of impact. The creature flared and swelled prodigiously, and a fiery hissing became audible. Haines and Chanler were driven back by a wave of scorching heat; and their wardens followed them pace by pace on the rough bottom. Abandoning all hope of escape, they returned toward Ravormos, dogged at the same unvarying distance by the monsters as they toiled through yielding sand and over the ledges and riffles.

Reaching the point where they had descended into the river-channel, they found its upper stretches guarded by two more of these terrific dragons. There was no other recourse than to climb the lofty shelves into the acclivitous tunnel. Weary with their long flight, and enervated by a dull despair, they found themselves again in the outer hall, with two of their guardians now preceding them like an escort of infernal honor. Both were stunned by a realization of the awful and mysterious powers of Vulthoom; and even Haines had become silent, though his brain was still busy with a futile and desperate probing. Chanler, more sensitive, suffered all the chills and terrors that his literary imagination could inflict upon him under the circumstances.

They came at length to the columned gallery that circled the vast abyss. Midway in this gallery, the chimeras who preceded the earthmen turned upon them suddenly with a fearsome belching of flames; and, as they paused in their intimidation, the two behind continued to advance toward them with a hissing as of Satanic salamanders. In that narrowing space, the heat was like a furnace-blast, and the columns afforded no shelter. From the gulf below, where the Martian titans toiled perpetually, a stupefying thunder rose to assail them at the same time; and noxious fumes were blown toward them in writhing coils.

"Looks as if they are going to drive us into the gulf," Haines panted as he sought to draw breath in the fiery air. He and Chanler reeled before the looming monsters, and even as he spoke, two more of these hellish apparitions flamed into being at the gallery's verge, as if they had risen from the gulf to render impossible that fatal plunge which alone could have offered an escape from the others.

Half swooning, the earth-men were dimly aware of a change in the menacing chimeras. The flaming bodies dulled and shrank and darkened, the heat lessened, the fires died down in the mouths and eye-pits. At the same time, the creatures drew closer, fawning loathsomely, and revealing whitish tongues and eyeballs of jet.

The tongues seemed to divide . . . they grew paler . . . they were like flower-petals that Haines and Chanler had seen somewhere, at a former time. The breath of the chimeras, like a soft gale, was upon the faces of the earth-men . . . and the breath was a cool and spicy perfume that they had known before . . . the narcotic perfume that had overcome them following their audience with the hidden master of Ravormos. . . . Moment by moment, the monsters turned to prodigious blossoms; the pillars of the gallery became gigantic trees in a glamour of primal dawn; the thunders of the pit were lulled to a far-off sighing as of gentle seas on Edenic shores. The teeming terrors of Ravormos, the threat of a shadowy doom, were as things that had never been. Haines and Chanler, oblivious, were lost in the paradise of the unknown drug. . . .

Haines, awakening darkly, found that he lay on the stone floor in the circling colonnade. He was alone, and the fiery chimeras had vanished. The shadows of his opiate swoon were roughly dissipated by the clangors that still mounted from the neighboring gulf. With growing consternation and horror, he recalled everything that had happened.

He arose giddily to his feet, peering about in the semi-twilight of the gallery for some trace of his companion. The petrified fungus-club that Chanler had carried, as well as his own weapon, were lying where they had fallen from the fingers of the overpowered men. But Chanler was gone; and Haines shouted aloud with no other response than had the eerily prolonged echoes of the deep arcade.

Impelled by an urgent feeling that he must find Chanler without delay, he recovered his heavy mace and started along the gallery. It seemed that the weapon could be of little use against the preternatural servants of Vulthoom; but somehow, the metallic weight of the bludgeon was a thing that reassured him.

Nearing the great corridor that ran to the core of Ravormos, Haines was overjoyed when he saw Chanler coming to meet him. Before he could call out a cheery greeting, he heard Chanler's voice:

"Hello, Bob, this is my first televisual appearance in tri-dimensional form. Pretty good, isn't it? I'm in the private laboratory of Vulthoom, and Vulthoom has persuaded me to accept his proposition. As soon as you've made up your mind to do likewise, we'll return to Ignarh with full instructions regarding our terrestrial mission, and funds amounting to a million dollars each. Think it over, and you'll see that there's nothing else to do. When you've decided to join us, follow the main corridor through Ravormos, and Ta-Vho-Shai will meet you and bring you into the laboratory."

At the conclusion of this astounding speech, the figure of Chanler, without seeming to wait for any reply from Haines, stepped lightly to the gallery's verge and floated out among the wreathing vapors. There, smiling upon Haines, it vanished like a phantom.

To say that Haines was thunderstruck would be putting it feebly indeed. In all verisimilitude, the figure and voice had been those of the flesh-and-blood Chanler. He felt an eery chill before the thaumaturgy of Vulthoom, which could bring about a projection so veridical as to deceive him in this manner. He was shocked and horrified beyond measure by Chanler's capitulation; but somehow, it did not occur to him that any imposture had been practiced.

"That devil has gotten him," thought Haines. "But I'd never have believed it. I didn't think he was that kind of a fellow at all."

Sorrow, anger, bafflement and amazement filled him alternately as he strode along the gallery; nor, as he entered the inner hall, was he able to decide on any clearly effective course of action. To yield, as Chanler had avowedly done, was unthinkably repugnant to him. If he could see Chanler again, perhaps he could persuade him to change his mind and resume an unflinching opposition to the alien entity. It was a degradation, and a treason to humankind, for any earth-man to lend himself to the more than doubtful schemes of Vulthoom. Apart from the projected invasion of Earth, and the spread of the strange, subtle narcotic, there was the ruthless destruction of Ignar-Luth that would occur when Vulthoom's ether-vessel should blast its way to the planet's surface. It was his duty, and Chanler's, to prevent all this if prevention were humanly possible. Somehow, they—or he alone if necessary—must stem the cavern-incubated menace. Bluntly honest himself, there was no thought of temporizing even for an instant.

Still carrying the mineraloid club, he strode on for several minutes, his brain preoccupied with the dire problem but powerless to arrive at any solution. Through a habit of observation more or less automatic with the veteran space-pilot, he peered through the doorways of the various rooms that he passed, where the cupels and retorts of a foreign chemistry were tended by age-old colossi. Then, without premeditation, he came to the deserted room in which were the three mighty receptacles that Ta-Vho-Shai had called the Bottles of Sleep. He remembered what the Aihai had said concerning their contents.

In a flash of desperate inspiration, Haines boldly entered the room, hoping that he was not under the surveillance of Vulthoom at the moment. There was no time for reflection or other delay, if he were to execute the audacious plan that had occurred to him.

Taller than his head, with the swelling contours of great amphorae and seemingly empty, the Bottles glimmered in the still light. Like the phantom of a bulbous giant, he saw his own distorted image in the upward-curving glass as he neared the foremost one.

There was but one thought, one resolution, in his mind. Whatever the cost, he must smash the Bottles, whose released gases would pervade Ravormos and plunge the followers of Vulthoom—if not Vulthoom himself—into a thousand-year term of slumber. He and Chanler, no doubt, would be doomed to share the slumber; and for them, unfortified by the secret elixir of immortality, there would be in all likelihood no awakening. But under the circumstances it was better so; and, by the sacrifice, a thousand years of grace would be accorded to the two planets. Now was his opportunity, and it seemed improbable that there would ever be another one.

He lifted the petrified fungus-mace, he swung it back in a swift arc, and struck with all his strength at the bellying glass. There was a gong-like clangor, sonorous and prolonged, and radiating cracks appeared from top to bottom of the huge receptacle. At the second blow, it broke inward with a shrill, appalling sound that was almost an articulate shriek, and Haines' face was fanned for an instant by a cool breath, gentle as a woman's sigh.

Holding his breath to avoid the inhalation of the gas, he turned to the next Bottle. It shattered at the first stroke, and again he felt a soft sighing, that followed upon the cleavage.

A voice of thunder seemed to fill the room as he raised his weapon to assail the third Bottle: "Fool! you have doomed yourself and your fellow earth-man by this deed." The last words mingled with the crash of Haines' final stroke. A tomb-like silence followed, and the far-off, muted rumble of engineries seemed to ebb and recede before it. The earth-man stared for a moment at the riven Bottles, and then, dropping the useless remnant of his mace, which had been shattered into several fragments, he fled from the chamber.

Drawn by the noise of breakage, a number of Aihais had appeared in the hall. They were running about in an aimless, unconcerted manner, like mummies impelled by a failing galvanism. None of them tried to intercept the earth-man.

Whether the slumber induced by the gases would be slow or swift in its coming, Haines could not surmise. The air of the caverns was unchanged as far as he could tell: there was no odor, no perceptible effect on his breathing. But already, as he ran, he felt a slight drowsiness, and a thin veil appeared to weave itself on all his senses. It seemed that faint vapors were forming in the corridor, and there was a touch of insubstantiality in the very walls.

His flight was without definite goal or purpose. Like a dreamer in a dream, he felt little surprise when he found himself lifted from the floor and borne along through mid-air in an inexplicable levitation. It was as if he were caught in a rushing stream, or were carried on invisible clouds. The doors of a hundred secret rooms, the mouths of a hundred mysterious halls, flew swiftly past him, and he saw in brief glimpses the colossi that lurched and nodded with the ever-spreading slumber as they went to and fro on strange errands. Then, dimly, he saw that he had entered the high-vaulted room that enshrined the fossil flower on its tripod of crystal and black metal. A door opened in the seamless stone of the further wall as he hurtled toward it. An instant more, while he seemed to fall downward through a nether chamber beyond, among prodigious masses of unnamable machines, upon a revolving disk that droned infernally; then he was deposited on his feet, with the whole chamber righting itself about him, and the disk towering before him. The disk had now ceased to revolve, but the air still throbbed with its hellish vibration. The place was like a mechanical nightmare, but amid its confusion of glittering coils and dynamos, Haines beheld the form of Chanler, lashed upright with metal cords to a rack-like frame. Near him, in a still and standing posture, was the giant Ta-Vho-Shai; and immediately in front of him, there reclined an incredible thing whose further portions and members wound away to an indefinite distance amid the thronged machinery.

Somehow, the thing was like a gigantic plant, with innumerable roots, pale and swollen, that ramified from a bulbular bole. This bole, half-hidden from view, was topped with a vermilion cup like a monstrous blossom; and from the cup there grew an elfin figure, pearly-hued, and formed with exquisite beauty and symmetry; a figure that turned its Lilliputian face toward Haines and spoke in the sounding voice of Vulthoom:

"You have conquered for the time, but I bear no rancor toward you. I blame my own carelessness."

To Haines, the voice was like a far-off thunder heard by one who is half-asleep. With halting effort, lurching as if he were about to fall, he made his way toward Chanler. Wan and haggard, with a look that puzzled Haines dimly, Chanler gazed upon him from the metal frame without speaking.

"I . . . smashed the Bottles," Haines heard his own voice with a feeling of drowsy unreality. "It seemed the only thing to do . . . since you had gone over to Vulthoom."

"But I hadn't consented," Chanler replied slowly. "It was all a deception . . . to trick you into consenting. . . . And they were torturing me because I wouldn't give in." Chanler's voice trailed away, and it seemed that he could say no more. Subtly, the pain and haggardness began to fade from his features, as if erased by the gradual oncoming of slumber.

Haines, laboriously trying to comprehend through his own drowsiness, perceived an evil-looking instrument, like a many-pointed metal goad, which drooped from the fingers of Ta-Vho-Shai. From the arc of needle-like tips, there fell a ceaseless torrent of electric sparks. The bosom of Chanler's shirt had been torn open, and his skin was stippled with tiny blue-black marks from chin to diaphragm—marks that formed a diabolic pattern. Haines felt a vague, unreal horror.

Through the Lethe that closed upon his senses more and more, he became aware that Vulthoom had spoken; and after an interval, it seemed that he understood the meaning of the words. "All my methods of persuasion have failed; but it matters little. I shall yield myself to slumber, though I could remain awake if I wished, defying the gases through my superior science and vital power. We shall all sleep soundly

. . . and a thousand years are no more than a single night to my follow-ers and me. For you, whose life-term is so brief, they will become—eternity. Soon I shall awaken and resume my plans of conquest . . . and you, who dared to interfere, will lie beside me then as a little dust . . . and the dust will be swept away."

The voice ended, and it seemed that the elfin being began to nod in the monstrous vermilion cup. Haines and Chanler saw each other with growing, wavering dimness, as if through a grey mist that had ris-en between them. There was silence everywhere, as if the Tartarean engineries had fallen still, and the titans had ceased their labor. Chanler relaxed on the torture-frame, and his eyelids drooped. Haines tottered, fell, and lay motionless. Ta-Vho-Shai, still clutching his sinister instru-ment, reposed like a mummied giant. Slumber, like a silent sea, had filled the caverns of Ravormos.

THE DWELLER IN THE GULF

S welling and towering swiftly, like a genie loosed from one of Solomon's bottles, the cloud rose on the planet's rim. A rusty and colossal column, it strode above the dead plain, through a sky that was dark as the brine of desert seas that have ebbed down to desert pools.

"Looks like a blithering sandstorm," commented Maspic.

"It can't very well be anything else," agreed Bellman rather curtly. "Any other kind of storm is unheard of in these regions. It's the sort of hell-twister that the Aihais call the *zoorth*—and it's coming our way, too. I move that we start looking for shelter. I've been caught in the *zoorth* before, and I don't recommend a lungful of that ferruginous dust."

"There's a cave in the old river bank, to the right," said Chivers, the third member of the party, who had been searching the desert with restless, falconlike eyes.

The trio of earth-men, hard-bitten adventurers who disdained the services of Martian guides, had started five days before from the outpost of Ahoom, into the uninhabited region called the Chaur. Here, in the beds of great rivers that had not flowed for cycles, it was rumored that the pale, platinum-like gold of Mars could be found lying in heaps, like so much salt. If fortune were propitious, their years of somewhat unwilling exile on the red planet would soon be at an end. They had been warned against the Chaur, and had heard some queer tales in Ahoom regarding the reasons why former prospectors had not returned. But danger, no matter how dire or exotic, was merely a part of their daily routine. With a fair chance of unlimited gold at the journey's end they would have gone down through Hinnom.

Their food-supplies and water-barrels were carried on the backs of three of those curious mammals called *vortlups*, which, with their elongated legs and necks, and horny-plated bodies, might seemingly have been some fabulous combination of llama and saurian. These animals, though extravagantly ugly, were tame and obedient, and were well adapted to desert travel, being able to go without water for months at a time.

For the past two days they had followed the mile-wide course of a nameless ancient river, winding among hills that had dwindled to mere hummocks through aeons of exfoliation. They had found nothing but worn boulders, pebbles and fine rusty sand. Heretofore the sky had been silent and stirless; and nothing moved on the river-bottom, whose stones were bare even of dead lichen. The malignant column of the *zoorth*, twisting and swelling toward them, was the first sign of animation they had discerned in that lifeless land.

Prodding their *vortlups* with the iron-pointed goads which alone could elicit any increase of speed from these sluggish monsters, the earth-men started off toward the cavern-mouth descried by Chivers. It was perhaps a third of a mile distant, and was high up in the shelving shore.

The *zoorth* had blotted out the sun ere they reached the bottom of the ancient slope, and they moved through a sinister twilight that was colored like dried blood. The *vortlups*, protesting with unearthly bellows, began to climb the beach, which was marked off in a series of more or less regular steps that indicated the slow recession of its olden waters. The column of sand, rising and whirling formidably, had reached the opposite bank when they came to the cavern.

This cavern was in the face of a low cliff of iron-veined rock. The entrance had crumbled down in heaps of ferro-oxide and dark basaltic dust, but was large enough to admit with ease the earth-men and their laden beasts of burden. Darkness, heavy as if with a weaving of black webs, clogged the interior. They could form no idea of the cave's dimensions till Bellman got out an electric torch from his bale of belongings and turned its prying beam into the shadows.

The torch served merely to reveal the beginnings of a chamber of indeterminate size that ran backward into night, widening gradually, with a floor that was worn smooth as if by vanished waters.

The opening had grown dark with the onset of the *zoorth*. A weird moaning as of baffled demons filled the ears of the explorers, and particles of atomlike sand were blown in upon them, stinging their hands and faces like powdered adamant.

"The storm will last for half an hour, at least," said Bellman. "Shall we go on into the cave? Probably we won't find anything of much interest or value. But the exploration will serve to kill time. And we might happen on a few violet rubies or amber-yellow sapphires, such as are sometimes discovered in these desert caverns. You two had better bring along your torches also, and flash them on the walls and ground as we go."

His companions thought the suggestion worth following. The *vortlups*, wholly insensible to the blowing sand in their scaly mail, were left behind near the entrance. Chivers, Bellman and Maspic, with their torch-beams tearing a clotted gloom that had perhaps never known the intrusion of light in all its former cycles, went on into the widening cave.

The place was bare, with the death-like emptiness of some long-deserted catacomb. Its rusted floor and walls returned no gleam or sparkle to the playing lights. It sloped downward at an easy gradient and the sides were water-marked at a height of six or seven feet. No doubt it had been in earlier aeons the channel of an underground offshoot from the river. It had been swept clean of all detritus, and was like the interior of some Cyclopean conduit that might give upon a sub-Martian Erebus.

None of the three adventurers was overly imaginative or prone to nervousness. But all were beset by certain odd impressions. Behind the arras of cryptic silence, time and again, they seemed to hear a faint whisper, like the sigh of sunken seas far down at some hemispheric depth. The air was tinged with a slight and doubtful dankness, and they felt the stirring of an almost imperceptible draft upon their faces. Oddest of all was the hint of a nameless odor, reminding them both of animal dens and the peculiar smell of Martian dwellings.

"Do you suppose we'll encounter any kind of life?" said Maspic, sniffing the air dubiously.

"Not likely." Bellman dismissed the query with his usual curtness. "Even the wild *vortlups* avoid the Chaur."

"But there's certainly a touch of dampness in the air," persisted Maspic. "That means water, somewhere; and if there is water, there may be life also—perhaps of a dangerous kind."

"We've got our revolvers," said Bellman. "But I doubt if we'll need them—as long as we don't meet any rival gold-hunters from the Earth," he added cynically.

"Listen." The semi-whisper came from Chivers. "Do you fellows hear anything?"

All three had paused. Somewhere in the gloom ahead, they heard a prolonged, equivocal noise that baffled the ear with incongruous elements. It was a sharp rustling and rattling as of metal dragged over rock; and also it was somehow like the smacking of myriad wet, enormous mouths. Anon it receded and died out at a level that was seemingly far below.

"That's queer." Bellman seemed to make a reluctant admission.

"What is it?" queried Chivers. "One of the millipedal underground monsters, half a mile long, that the Martians tell about?"

"You've been hearing too many native fairy-tales," reproved Bellman. "No terrestrial has ever seen anything of that kind. Many deep-lying caverns on Mars have been thoroughly explored; but those in desert regions, such as the Chaur, were devoid of life. I can't imagine what could have made that noise; but, in the interests of science, I'd like to go on and find out."

"I'm beginning to feel creepy," said Maspic. "But I'm game if you others are."

Without further argument or comment, the three continued their advance into the cave. They had been walking at a fair gait for fifteen minutes, and were now at least half a mile from the entrance. The floor was steepening, as if it had been the bed of a torrent. Also, the conformation of the walls had changed: on either hand there were high shelves of metallic stone and columnated recesses which the flashed rays of the torches could not always fathom.

The air had grown heavier, the dampness unmistakable. There was a breath of stagnant ancient waters. That other smell, as of wild beasts and Aihai dwellings, also tainted the gloom with its clinging fetor.

Bellman was leading the way. Suddenly his torch revealed the verge of a precipice, where the olden channel ended sheerly and the shelves and walls pitched away on each side into incalculable space. Going to the very edge, he dipped his pencil of light adown the abyss, disclosing only the vertical cliff that fell at his feet into darkness with no apparent bottom. The beam also failed to reach the further shore of the gulf, which might have been many leagues in extent.

"Looks as if we had found the original jumping-off place," observed Chivers. Looking about, he secured a loose lump of rock the size of a small boulder, which he hurled as far out as he could into the abysm. The earth-men listened for the sound of its fall; but several minutes went by, and there was no echo from the black profound.

Bellman started to examine the broken-off ledges on either side of the channel's terminus. To the right he discerned a downward-sloping shelf that skirted the abyss, running for an uncertain distance. Its beginning was little higher than the channel-bed, and was readily accessible by means of a stair-like formation. The shelf was two yards wide; and its gentle inclination, its remarkable evenness and regularity conveyed the idea of an ancient road hewn in the face of the cliff. It was overhung by the wall, as if by the sharply sundered half of a high arcade.

"There's our road to Hades," said Bellman. "And the downgrade is easy enough at that."

"Facilis decensus Avernus," agreed Maspic. "But what's the use of going further?" said Maspic. "I, for one, have had enough darkness already. And if we were to find anything by going on, it would be valueless—or unpleasant."

Bellman hesitated. "Maybe you're right. But I'd like to follow that ledge far enough to get some idea of the magnitude of the gulf. You and Chivers can wait here, if you're afraid."

Chivers and Maspic, apparently, were unwilling to avow whatever trepidation they might have felt. They followed Bellman along the shelf, hugging the inner wall. Bellman, however, strode carelessly on the verge, often flashing his torch into the vastitude that engulfed its feeble beam.

More and more, through its uniform breadth, inclination and smoothness, and the demi-arch of cliff above, the shelf impressed the earth-men as being an artificial road. But who could have made and used it? In what forgotten ages and for what enigmatic purpose had it been designed? The imagination of the terrestrials failed before the stupendous gulfs of Martian antiquity that yawned in such tenebrous queries.

Bellman thought that the wall curved inward upon itself by slow degrees. No doubt they would round the entire abyss in time by following the road. Perhaps it wound in a slow, tremendous spiral, ever downward, about and about, to the very bowels of Mars.

He and the others were awed into lengthening intervals of silence. They were horribly startled, when, as they went on, they heard in the depths beneath the same peculiar long-drawn sound or combination of sounds which they had heard in the outer cavern. It suggested other images now: the rustling was a file-like scraping; the soft, methodical, myriad smacking was vaguely similar to the noise made by some enormous creature that withdraws its feet from a quagmire.

The sound was inexplicable, terrifying. Part of its terror lay in an implication of *remoteness*, which appeared to signalize the enormity of its cause, and to emphasize the profundity of the abysm. Heard in that planetary pit beneath a lifeless desert it astonished—and shocked. Even Bellman, intrepid heretofore, began to succumb to the formless horror that rose up like an emanation from the night.

The noise grew fainter and ceased at length, giving somehow the idea that its maker had gone directly down on the perpendicular wall into nether reaches of the gulf.

"Shall we go back?" inquired Chivers.

"We might as well," assented Bellman without demur. "It would take all eternity to explore this place anyway."

They started to retrace their way along the ledge. All three, with that extra-tactile sense which warns of the approach of hidden danger, were now troubled and alert. Though the gulf had grown silent once more with that withdrawal of the strange noise, they somehow felt that they were not alone. Whence the peril would come, or in what shape, they could not surmise; but they felt an alarm that was almost panic. Tacitly, none of them mentioned it; nor did they discuss the eerie mystery on which they had stumbled in a manner so fortuitous.

Maspic was a little ahead of the others now. They had covered at least half of the distance to the old cavern-channel, when his torch, playing for twenty feet ahead on the path, illumined an array of whitish figures, three abreast, that blocked the way. The flashlights of Bellman and Chivers, coming close behind, brought out with hideous clearness the vanward limbs and faces of the throng, but could not determine its number.

The creatures, who stood perfectly motionless and silent, as if awaiting the earth-men, were generically similar to the Aihais or Martian natives. They seemed, however, to represent an extremely degraded and aberrant type, and the fungus-like pallor of their bodies denoted many ages of underground life. They were smaller too, than full-grown Aihais, being, on the average, about five feet tall. They possessed the enormous open nostrils, the flaring ears, the barrel chests and lanky limbs of the Martians—but all of them were eyeless. In the faces of some, there were faint, rudimentary slits where the eyes should have been; in the faces of others, there were deep and empty orbits that suggested a removal of the eyeballs.

"Lord! what a ghastly crew!" cried Maspic. "Where do they come from? and what do they want?"

"Can't imagine," said Bellman. "But our situation is somewhat ticklish—unless they are friendly. They must have been hiding on the shelves in the cavern above when we entered."

Stepping boldly forward, ahead of Maspic, he addressed the creatures in the guttural Aihai tongue, many of whose vocables are scarcely to be articulated by an earth-man. Some of the people stirred uneasily, and emitted shrill, cheeping sounds that bore little likeness to the Martian language. It was plain that they could not understand Bellman. Sign-language, by reason of their blindness, would have been equally useless.

Bellman drew his revolver, enjoining the others to follow suit. "We've got to get through them somehow," he said. "And if they won't let us pass without interference"—the click of a cocked hammer served to finish the sentence.

As if the metallic sound had been an awaited signal the press of blind white beings sprang into sudden motion and surged forward upon the terrestrials. It was like the onset of automatons—an irresistible striding of machines, concerted and methodical, beneath the direction of a hidden power.

Bellman pulled his trigger, once, twice, thrice, at a point-blank range. It was impossible to miss; but the bullets were futile as pebbles flung at the spate of an onrushing torrent. The eyeless beings did not waver, though two of them began to bleed the yellowish-red fluid that serves the Martians for blood. The foremost of them, unwounded, and moving with diabolical sureness, caught Bellman's arm with long, four-jointed fingers, and jerked the revolver from his grasp before he could press the trigger again. Curiously enough, the creature did not try to deprive him of his torch, which he now carried in his left hand; and he saw the steely flash of the Colt, as it hurtled down into darkness and space from the hand of the Martian. Then the fungus-white bodies, milling horribly on the narrow road, were all about him, pressing so closely that there was no room for effectual resistance. Chivers and Maspic, after firing a few shots, were also deprived of their weapons, but, through an uncanny discrimination, were permitted to retain their flashlights.

The entire episode had been a matter of moments. There was only a brief slackening of the onward motion of the throng, two of whose members had been shot down by Chivers and Maspic and then hurled expeditiously into the gulf by their fellows. The foremost ranks, opening deftly, included the earth-men and forced them to turn backward. Then, tightly caught in a moving vice of bodies, they were borne resistlessly along. Handicapped by the fear of dropping their torches, they could do nothing against the nightmare torrent. Rushing with dreadful strides on a path that led ever deeper into the abyss, and able to see only the lit backs and members of the creatures before them, they became a part of that eyeless and cryptic army.

Behind them, there seemed to be scores of the Martians, driving them on implacably. After awhile, their plight began to paralyze their faculties. It seemed that they moved no longer with human steps, but with the swift and automatic stalking of the clammy *things* that pressed about them. Thought, volition, even terror, were numbed by the unearthly rhythm of those abyssward-beating feet. Constrained by this, and by a sense of utter unreality, they spoke only at long intervals, and then in monosyllables that appeared to have lost all proper meaning, like the speech of machines. The blind people were wholly silent—there was no sound, except that of a myriad, eternal padding on the stone.

On, on they went, through ebon hours that belonged to no diurnal period. Slowly, tortuously, the road curved inward, as if it were coiled about the interior of a blind and cosmic Babel. The earth-men felt that they must have circled the abyss many times in that terrific spiral; but the distance they had gone, and the actual extent of the stupefying gulf, were inconceivable.

Except for their torches, the night was absolute, unchangeable. It was older than the sun, it had brooded there through all past aeons. It accumulated above them like a monstrous burden; it yawned frightfully beneath. From it, the strengthening stench of stagnant waters rose. But still there was no sound, other than the soft and measured thud of marching feet that descended into a bottomless Abaddon.

Somewhere, as if after the lapse of nocturnal ages, the pitward rushing had ceased. Bellman, Chivers and Maspic felt the pressure of crowded bodies relax; felt that they were standing still, while their brains continued to beat the unhuman measure of that terrible descent.

Reason—and horror—returned to them slowly. Bellman lifted his flashlight, and the circling ray recovered the throng of Martians, many of whom were dispersing in a huge cavern where the gulf-circling road had now ended. Others of the beings remained, however, as if to keep guard over the earth-men. They quivered alertly at Bellman's movements as if aware of them through an unknown sense.

Close at hand, on the right, the level floor ended abruptly; and stepping to the verge, Bellman saw that the cavern was an open chamber in the perpendicular wall. Far, far below in the blackness, a phosphorescent glimmer played to and fro, like noctilucae on an underworld ocean. A slow, fetid wind blew upon him; and he heard the weird sighing of waters about the sunken cliffs: waters that had ebbed through untold cycles, during the planet's desiccation.

He turned giddily away. His companions were examining the cave's interior. It seemed that the place was of artificial origin; for, darting here and there, the torch-beams brought out enormous columnations lined with deeply graven bas-reliefs. Who had carved them or when, were problems no less insoluble than the origin of the cliff-hewn road. Their details were obscene as the visions of madness; they shocked the eye like a violent blow, conveying an extra-human evil, a bottomless malignity, in the passing moment of disclosure.

The cave was indeed of stupendous extent, running far back in the cliff, and with numerous exits, giving, no doubt, on further ramifications. The beams of the flashlights half dislodged the flapping shadows of shelved recesses; caught the salients of far walls that climbed and beetled into inaccessible gloom; played on the creatures that went to and fro like monstrous living fungi; gave a brief visual existence to the pale and polyp-like plants that clung noisomely to the nighted stone.

The place was overpowering, it oppressed the senses, crushed the brain. The very stone was like an embodiment of darkness; and light and vision were ephemeral intruders in this demesne of the blind. Somehow, the earth-men were weighed down by a conviction that escape was impossible. A strange lethargy claimed them. They did not even discuss their situation, but stood listless and silent.

Anon, from the filthy gloom, a number of the Martians reappeared. With the same suggestion of controlled automatism that had marked all their actions, they gathered about the men once more, and urged them into the yawning cavern.

Step by step, the three were borne along in that weird and leprous procession. The obscene columns multiplied, the cave deepened before them with endless vistas, like a revelation of foul things that drowse at the nadir of night. Faintly at first, but more strongly as they went on, there came to them an insidious feeling of somnolence, such as might have been caused by mephitical effluvia. They rebelled against it, for the drowsiness was somehow dark and evil. It grew heavier upon them—and then they came to the core of the horror.

Between the thick and seemingly topless pillars, the floor ascended in an altar of seven oblique and pyramidal tiers. On the top, there squatted an image of pale metal: a thing no larger than a hare, but monstrous beyond all imagining.

The Martians crowded about the earth-men. One of them took Bellman by the arm, as if urging him to climb the altar. With the slow steps of a dreamer, he mounted the sloping tiers, and Chivers and Maspic followed.

The image resembled nothing they had ever seen on the red planet—or elsewhere. It was carven of whitish gold, and it represented a humped animal with a smooth and overhanging carapace from beneath which its head and members issued in tortoise fashion. The head was venomously flat, triangular—and eyeless. From the drooping corners of the cruelly slitted mouth, two long proboscides curved upward, hollow and cuplike at the ends. The thing was furnished with a series of short legs, issuing at uniform intervals from under the carapace, and a curious double tail was coiled and braided beneath its crouching body. The feet were round, and had the shape of small, inverted goblets.

Unclean and bestial as a figment of some atavistic madness, the eidolon seemed to drowse on the altar. It troubled the mind with a slow, insidious horror; it assailed the senses with an emanating stupor, an effluence as of primal worlds before the creation of light, where life might teem and raven slothfully in the blind ooze.

Dimly the earth-men saw that the altar swarmed with the blind Martians, who were crowding past them about the image. As if in some fantastic ritual of touch, these creatures were fondling the eidolon with their lank fingers, were tracing its loathsome outlines. Upon their brutal faces a narcotic ecstasy was imprinted. Compelled like sleepers in some abhorrent dream, Bellman, Chivers and Maspic followed their example.

The thing was cold to the touch, and clammy as if it had lain recently in a bed of slime. But it seemed to live, to throb and swell under their finger-tips. From it, in heavy, ceaseless waves, a dark vibration surged: an opiate power that clouded the eyes; that poured its baleful slumber into the blood.

With senses that swam in a strange darkness, they were vaguely aware of the pressure of thronging bodies that displaced them at the altar-summit. Anon, certain of these, recoiling as if satiate with the drug-like effluence, bore them along the oblique tiers to the cavern-floor. Still retaining their torches in nerveless fingers, they saw that the place teemed with the white people, who had gathered for that unholy ceremony. Through blackening blurs of shadow, the men watched them as they seethed up and down on the pyramid like a leprous, living frieze.

Chivers and Maspic, yielding first to the influence, slid to the floor in utter sopor. But Bellman, more resistant, seemed to fall and drift through a world of lightless dreams. His sensations were anomalous, unfamiliar to the last degree. Everywhere there was a brooding, *palpable* Power for which he could find no visual image: a Power that exhaled a miasmal slumber. In those dreams, by insensible gradations, forgetting the last glimmer of his human self, he somehow identified himself with the eyeless people; he lived and moved as they, in profound caverns, on nighted roads. And yet he was something else: an Entity without name that ruled over the blind and was worshipped by them; a thing that dwelt in the ancient putrescent waters, in the nether deep, and came forth at intervals to raven unspeakably. In that duality of being, he sated himself at blind feasts—and was also devoured. With all this, like a third element of identity, the eidolon was associated: but only a tactile sense, and not as an optic memory. There was no light any-where—and not even the recollection of light.

Whether he passed from these obscure nightmares into dreamless slumber, he could not know. His awakening, dark and lethargic, was like a continuation of the dreams at first. Then, opening his sodden lids, he saw the shaft of light that lay on the floor from his fallen torch. The light poured against something that he could not recognize in his drugged awareness. Yet it troubled him, and a dawning horror touched his faculties into life.

By degrees, it came to him that the thing he saw was the half-eaten body of one of the eyeless troglodytes. Some of the members were missing; and the remainder was gnawed even to the curiously articulated bones.

Bellman rose unsteadily and looked about with eyes that still held a web-like blurring of shadow. Chivers and Maspic lay beside him in heavy stupor; and along the cavern and upon the seven-tiered altar were sprawled the devotees of the somnific image.

His other senses began to awake from their lethargy, and he thought that he heard a noise that was somehow familiar: a sharp slithering, together with a measured sucking. The sound withdrew among the massy pillars, beyond the sleeping bodies. A smell as of rotten water tinged the air, and he saw that there were many curious rings of wetness on the stone, such as might be made by the rims of inverted cups. Preserving the order of footprints, they led away from the half-devoured Martian, into the shadows of that outer cave which verged upon the abyss; the direction in which the queer noise had passed, sinking now to inaudibility.

In Bellman's mind a mad terror rose and struggled with the spell that still benumbed him. He stooped down above Maspic and Chivers, and shook them roughly in turn, till they opened their eyes and began to protest with drowsy murmurs.

"Get up, damn you," he admonished them. "If we're ever to escape from this hell-hole, now's the time."

By dint of many oaths and objurgations and much muscular effort, he succeeded in getting his companions to their feet. Lurching drunkenly, they followed Bellman among the sprawled Martians, away from the pyramid on which the eidolon of white gold still brooded in malign somnolence above its worshippers.

A clouding heaviness hung upon Bellman; but somehow there was a relaxation of the opiate spell. He felt a revival of volition and a great desire to escape from the gulf and from all that dwelt in its darkness. The others, more deeply enslaved by the drowsy power, accepted his leadership and guidance in a numb, brute-like fashion.

He felt sure that he could retrace the route by which they had approached the altar. This, it seemed, was also the course that had been taken by the maker of the ring-like marks of fetid wetness. Wandering on amid the repugnantly carven columns for what seemed an enormous distance, they came at last to the sheer verge: that portico of the black Tartarus, from which they could look down on its ultimate gulf. Far beneath, on those putrefying waters, the phosphorescence ran in widening circles, as if troubled by the plunge of a heavy body. To the very edge, at their feet, the watery rings were imprinted on the rock.

They turned away, Bellman, shuddering with half-memories of his blind dreams, and the terror of his awakening, found at the cave's corner the beginning of that upward road which skirted the abyss: the road that would take them back to the lost sun.

At his injunction, Maspic and Chivers turned off their flashlights to conserve the batteries. It was doubtful how much longer these would last; and light was their prime necessity. His own torch would serve for the three till it became exhausted.

There was no sound or stirring of life from that cave of lightless sleep where the Martians lay about the narcotizing image. But a fear such as he had never felt in all his adventurings caused Bellman to sicken and turn faint as he listened at its threshold.

The gulf, too, was silent; and the circles of phosphor had ceased to widen on the waters. Yet somehow the silence was a thing that clogged the senses, retarded the limbs. It rose up around Bellman like the clutching slime of some nethermost pit, in which he must drown. With dragging effort he began the ascent, hauling, cursing and kicking his companions till they responded like drowsy animals.

It was a climb through Limbo, an ascent from nadir through darkness that seemed palpable and viscid. On and up they toiled, along the monotonous, imperceptibly winding grade where all measure of distance was lost, and time was meted only by the repetition of eternal steps. The night lowered before Bellman's feeble shaft of light; it closed behind like an all-engulfing sea, relentless and patient; biding its time till the torch should go out.

Looking over the verge at intervals, Bellman saw the gradual fading of the phosphorescence in the depths. Fantastic images rose in his mind, it was like the last glimmering of hell-fire in some extinct inferno; like the drowning of nebulae in voids beneath the universe. He felt the giddiness of one who looks down upon infinite space . . . Anon there was only blackness; and he knew by this token the awful distance they had climbed.

The minor urges of hunger, thirst, fatigue, had been trod under by the fear that impelled him. From Maspic and Chivers, very slowly, the clogging stupor lifted, and they too were conscious of an adumbration of terror vast as the night itself. The blows and kicks and objurgations of Bellman were no longer needed to drive them on.

Evil, ancient, soporous, the night hung about them. It was like the thick and fetid fur of bats: a material thing that choked the lungs, that deadened all the senses. It was silent as the slumber of dead worlds . . . But out of that silence, after the lapse of apparent years, a twofold and familiar sound arose and overtook the fugitives: the sound of something that slithered over stone far down in the abyss: the sucking noise of a creature that withdrew its feet as if from a quagmire. Inexplicable, and arousing mad, incongruous ideas, like a sound heard in delirium, it quickened the earth-men's terror into sudden frenzy,

"God! what is it?" breathed Bellman. He seemed to remember sightless things, abhorrent, *palpable* shapes of primal night, that were no legitimate part of human recollection. His dreams and his nightmare awakening in the cave—the white eidolon—the half-eaten troglodyte of the nether cliffs—the rings of wetness, leading toward the gulf—all returned like the figments of a teeming madness, all to assail him on that terrible road midway between the underworld sea and the surface of Mars.

His question was answered only by a continuation of the noise. It seemed to grow louder—to ascend the wall beneath. Maspic and Chivers, snapping on their lights, began to run with frantic leaps; and Bellman, losing his last remnant of control, followed suit.

It was a race with unknown horror. Above the labored beating of their hearts, the measured thudding of their feet, the men still heard that sinister, unaccountable sound. They seemed to race on through leagues of blackness; and yet the noise drew nearer, climbing below them, as if its maker were a thing that walked on the sheer cliff.

Now the sound was appallingly close—and a little ahead. It ceased abruptly. The running lights of Maspic and Chivers, who moved abreast, discovered the crouching thing that filled the two-yard shelf from side to side.

Hardened adventurers though they were, the men would have shrieked aloud with hysteria, or would have hurled themselves from the precipice, if the sight had not induced a kind of catalepsy. It was as if the pale idol of the pyramid, swollen to mammoth proportions, and loathsomely alive, had come up from the abyss and was squatting before them!

Here, plainly, was the creature that had served as a model for that atrocious image. The humped, enormous carapace, vaguely recalling the armor of the glyptodon, shone with a luster as of wet white gold. The eyeless head, alert but somnolent, was thrust forward on a neck that arched obscenely. A dozen or more of short legs, with goblet-shapen feet, protruded slantwise beneath the overhanging shell. The two proboscides, yard-long, with cupped ends, arose from the corners of the cruelly slitted mouth and waved slowly in air toward the earth-men.

The thing, it seemed, was old as that dying planet; an unknown form of primal life that had dwelt always in the caverned waters. Before it, the faculties of the earth-men were drugged by an evil stupor, such as they had felt before the eidolon. They stood with their flashlights playing full on the Terror; and they could not move nor cry out when it reared suddenly erect, revealing its ridged belly and the queer double tail that slithered and rustled metallically on the rock. Its numerous feet, beheld in this posture, were hollow and chalice-like, and they oozed with mephitic wetness. No doubt they served for suction-pads, enabling it to walk on a perpendicular surface.

Inconceivably swift and sure in all its motions, with short strides on its hindmost legs, levered by the tail, the monster came forward on the helpless men. Unerringly the two proboscides curved over, and their ends came down on Chivers' eyes as he stood with lifted face. They rested there, covering the entire sockets—for a moment only. Then there was an agonizing scream, as the hollow tips were withdrawn with a sweeping movement lithe and vigorous as the lashing of serpents.

Chivers swayed slowly, nodding his head, and twisting about in half-narcotised pain. Maspic, standing at his side, saw in a dull and dream-like manner the gaping orbits from which the eyes were gone. It was the last thing that he ever saw. At that instant the monster turned from Chivers, and the terrible cups dripping with blood and fetor, descended on Maspic's own eyes.

Bellman, who had paused close behind the others, comprehended what was occurring like one who witnesses the abominations of a nightmare but is powerless to intervene or flee. He saw the movements of the cupped members, he heard the single atrocious cry that was wrung from Chivers, and the swiftly ensuing scream of Maspic. Then, above the heads of his fellows, who still held their useless torches in rigid fingers, the proboscides came toward him. . . .

With blood rilling heavily upon their faces, with the somnolent, vigilant, implacable and eyeless Shape at their heels, herding them on, restraining them when they tottered at the brink, the three began their second descent of the road that went down forever to a night-bound Avernus.

THE VAULTS OF YOH-VOMBIS

Preface

As an interne in the terrestrial hospital at Ignarh, I had charge of the singular case of Rodney Severn, the one surviving member of the Octave Expedition to Yoh-Vombis, and took down the following story from his dictation. Severn had been brought to the hospital by the Martian guides of the Expedition. He was suffering from a horribly lacerated and inflamed condition of the scalp and brow, and was wildly delirious part of the time and had to be held down in his bed during recurrent seizures of a mania whose violence was doubly inexplicable in view of his extreme debility.

The lacerations, as will be learned from the story, were mainly self-inflicted. They were mingled with numerous small round wounds, easily distinguished from the knife-slashes, and arranged in regular circles, through which an unknown poison had been injected into Severn's scalp. The causation of these wounds was difficult to explain; unless one were to believe that Severn's story was true, and was no mere figment of his illness. Speaking for myself, in the light of what afterwards occurred, I feel that I have no other recourse than to believe it. There are strange things on the red planet; and I can only second the wish that was expressed by the doomed archaeologist in regard to future explorations.

The night after he finished telling me his story, while another doctor than myself was supposedly on duty, Severn managed to escape from the hospital, doubtless in one of the strange seizures at which I have hinted: a most astonishing thing, for he had seemed weaker than ever after the long strain of his terrible narrative, and his demise had been hourly expected. More astonishing still, his bare footsteps were found in the desert, going toward Yoh-Vombis, till they vanished in the path of a light sand-storm; but no trace of Severn himself has yet been discovered.

The Narrative of Rodney Severn

If the doctors are correct in their prognostication, I have only a few Martian hours of life remaining to me. In those hours I shall endeavor to relate, as a warning to others who might follow in our footsteps, the singular and frightful happenings that terminated our researches among the ruins of Yoh-Vombis. Somehow, even in my extremity, I shall contrive to tell the story; since there is no one else to do it. But the telling will be toilsome and broken; and after I am done, the madness will recur, and several men will restrain me, lest I should leave the hospital and return across many desert leagues to those abominable vaults beneath the compulsion of the malignant and malevolent virus which is permeating my brain. Perhaps death will release me from that abhorrent control, which would urge me down to bottomless underworld warrens of terror for which the saner planets of the solar system can have no analogue. I say *perhaps* . . . for, remembering what I have seen, I am not sure that even death will end my bondage . . .

There were eight of us, professional archaeologists with more or less terrene and interplanetary experience, who set forth with native guides from Ignarh, the commercial metropolis of Mars, to inspect that ancient, aeon-deserted city. Allan Octave, our official leader, held his primacy by virtue of knowing more about Martian archaeology than any other Terrestrial on the planet; and others of the party, such as William Harper and Jonas Halgren, had been associated with him in many of his previous researches. I, Rodney Severn, was more of a newcomer, having spent but a few months on Mars; and the greater part of my own ultra-terrene delvings had been confined to Venus.

I had often heard of Yoh-Vombis, in a vague and legendary sort of manner, and never at first hand. Even the ubiquitous Octave had never seen it. Builded by an extinct people whose history has been lost in the latter, decadent eras of the planet, it remains a dim and fascinating riddle whose solution has never been approached ... and which, I trust, may endure forevermore unsolved by man. Certainly I hope that no one will ever follow in our steps ...

Contrary to the impression we had received from Martian stories, we found that the semi-fabulous ruins lay at no great distance from Ignarh with its terrestrial colony and consulates. The nude, spongy-chested natives had spoken deterringly of vast deserts filled with ever-swirling sand-storms, through which we must pass to reach Yoh-Vombis; and in spite of our munificent offers of payment, it had been difficult to secure guides for the journey. We had provisioned ourselves amply and had prepared for all emergencies that might eventuate during a long trip. Therefore, we were pleased as well as surprised when we came to the ruins after seven hours of plodding across the flat, treeless, orange-yellow desolation to the south-west of Ignarh. On account of the lesser gravity, the journey was far less tiring than one who is unfamiliar with Martian conditions might expect. But because of the thin, Himalaya-like air, and the possible strain on our hearts, we had been careful not to hasten.

Our coming to Yoh-Vombis was sudden and spectacular. Climbing the low slope of a league-long elevation of bare and deeply eroded stone, we saw before us the shattered walls of our destination, whose highest tower was notching the small, remote sun that glared in stifled crimson through the floating haze of fine sand. For a little, we thought that the domeless, three-angled towers and broken-down monoliths were those of some unlegended city, other than the one we sought. But the disposition of the ruins, which lay in a sort of arc for almost the entire extent of the low and gneissic elevation, together with the type of architecture, soon convinced us that we had found our goal.

No other ancient city on Mars had been laid out in that manner; and the strange, many-terraced buttresses of the thick walls, like the stairways of forgotten Anakim, were peculiar to the prehistoric race that had built Yoh-Vombis. Moreover, Yoh-Vombis was the one remaining example of this architecture, aside from a few fragments in the neighborhood of Ignarh, which we had previously examined.

I have seen the hoary, sky-confronting walls of Macchu Pichu amid the desolate Andes, and the teocallis that are buried in the Mexican jungles. And I have seen the frozen, giant-builded battlements of Uogam on the glacial tundras of the nightward hemisphere of Venus. But these were as things of yesteryear, bearing at least the memory or the intimation of life, compared with the awesome and lethiferous antiquity, the cycle-enduring doom of a petrified sterility, that seemed to invest Yoh-Vombis. The whole region was far from the life-giving canals beyond whose environs even the more noxious flora and fauna are seldom found; and we had seen no living thing since our departure from Ignarh. But here, in this place of eternal bareness and solitude, it seemed that life could never have been. The stark, eroded stones were things that might have been reared by the toil of the dead, to house the monstrous ghouls and demons of primal desolation.

I think we all received the same impression as we stood staring in silence while the pale, sanies-like sunset fell on the dark and megalithic ruins. I remember gasping a little, in an air that seemed to have been touched by the irrespirable chill of death; and I heard the same sharp, laborious intake of breath from others of our party.

"That place is deader than an Egyptian morgue," observed Harper.

"Certainly it is far more ancient." Octave assented. "According to the most reliable legends, the Yorhis, who built Yoh-Vombis, were wiped out by the present ruling race at least forty thousand years ago.

"There's a story, isn't there," said Harper, "that the last remnant of the Yorhis was destroyed by some unknown agency—something too horrible and outré to be mentioned even in a myth?"

"Of course, I've heard that legend," agreed Octave. "Maybe we'll find evidence among the ruins, to prove or disprove it. The Yorhis may have been cleaned out by some terrible epidemic, such as the Yashta pestilence, which was a kind of green mould that ate all the bones of the body, starting with the teeth and nails. But we needn't be afraid of getting it, if there are any mummies in Yoh-Vombis—the bacteria will all be dead as their victims, after so many cycles of planetary desiccation. Anyway, there ought to be a lot for us to learn. The Aihais have always been more or less shy of the place. Few have ever visited it: and none, as far as I can find, have made a thorough examination of the ruins."

The sun had gone down with uncanny swiftness, as if it had disappeared through some sort of prestidigitation rather than the normal process of setting. We felt the instant chill of the blue-green twilight: and the ether above us was like a huge, transparent dome of sunless ice, shot with a million bleak sparklings that were the stars. We donned the coats and helmets of Martian fur, which must always be worn at night; and going on to westward of the walls, we established our camp in their lee, so that we might be sheltered a little from the *jaar,* that cruel desert wind that always blows from the east before dawn. Then, lighting the alcohol lamps that had been brought along for cooking purposes, we huddled around them while the evening meal was prepared and eaten.

Afterwards, for comfort rather than because of weariness, we retired early to our sleeping-bags; and the two Aihais, our guides, wrapped themselves in the cerement-like folds of grey *bassa*-cloth which are all the protection their leathery skins appear to require even in sub-zero temperatures.

Even in my thick, double-lined bag, I still felt the rigor of the night air; and I am sure it was this, rather than anything else, which kept me awake for a long while and rendered my eventual slumber somewhat restless and broken. Of course, the strangeness of our situation, and the weird proximity of those aeonian walls and towers may in some measure have contributed to my unrest. But at any rate, I was not troubled by even the least presentiment of alarm or danger; and I should have laughed at the idea that anything of peril could lurk in Yoh-Vombis, amid whose undreamable and stupefying antiquities the very phantoms of its dead must long since have faded into nothingness.

I remember little, however, except the feeling of interminable duration that often marks a shallow and interrupted sleep. I recall the marrow-piercing wind that moaned above us toward midnight, and the sand that stung my face like a fine hail as it passed, blowing from desert to immemorial desert; and I recall the still, inflexible stars that grew dim for awhile with that fleeing ancient dust. Then the wind went by; and I drowsed again, with starts of semi-wakefulness. At last, in one of these, I knew vaguely that the small twin moons, Phobos and Deimos, had risen and were making huge and spectral shadows with the ruins and were casting an ashen glimmer on the shrouded forms of my companions.

I must have been half-asleep; for the memory of that which I saw is doubtful as any dream. I watched beneath drooping lids the tiny moons that had topped the domeless triangular towers; and I saw the far-flung shadows that almost touched the bodies of my fellow-archaeologists.

The whole scene was locked in a petrific stillness; and none of the sleepers stirred. Then, as my lids were about to close, I received an impression of movement in the frozen gloom; and it seemed to me that a portion of the foremost shadow had detached itself and was crawling toward Octave, who lay nearer to the ruins than we others.

Even through my heavy lethargy, I was disturbed by a warning of something unnatural and perhaps ominous. I started to sit up; and even as I moved, the shadowy object, whatever it was, drew back and became merged once more in the greater shadow. Its vanishment startled me into full wakefulness; and yet I could not be sure that I had actually seen the thing. In that brief, final glimpse, it had seemed like a roughly circular piece of cloth or leather, dark and crumpled, and twelve or fourteen inches in diameter, that ran along the ground with the doubling movement of an inch-worm, causing it to fold and unfold in a startling manner as it went.

I did not go to sleep again for nearly an hour; and if it had not been for the extreme cold, I should doubtless have gotten up to investigate and make sure whether I had really beheld an object of such bizarre nature or had merely dreamt it. I lay staring at the deep ebon shadow in which it had disappeared, while a series of fanciful wonderings followed each other in antic procession through my mind. Even then, though somewhat perturbed, I was not aware of any actual fear or intuition of possible menace. And more and more I began to convince myself that the thing was too unlikely and fantastical to have been anything but the figment of a dream. And at last I nodded off into light slumber.

The chill, demoniac sighing of the *jaar* across the jagged walls awoke me, and I saw that the faint moonlight had received the hueless accession of early dawn. We all arose, and prepared our breakfast with fingers that grew numb in spite of the spirit-lamps. Then, shivering, we ate, while the sun leapt over the horizon like a juggler's ball. Enormous, gaunt, without gradations of shadow or luminosity, the ruins beetled before us in the thin light, like the mausolea of primordial giants, that abide from darkness-eaten aeons to confront the last dawn of an expiring orb.

My queer visual experience during the night had taken on more than ever a fantasmagoric unreality; and I gave it no more than a passing thought and did not speak of it to the others. But, even as the faint, distorted shadows of slumber often tinge one's waking hours, it may have contributed to the nameless mood in which I found myself: a mood in which I felt the unhuman alienage of our surroundings and the black, fathomless antiquity of the ruins like an almost unbearable oppression. The feeling seemed to be made of a million spectral adumbrations that oozed unseen but palpable from the great, unearthly architecture; that weighed upon me like tomb-born incubi, but were void of form and meaning such as could be comprehended by human thought. I appeared to move, not in the open air, but in the smothering gloom of sealed sepulchral vaults; to choke with a death-fraught atmosphere, with the miasmata of aeon-old corruption.

My companions were all eager to explore the ruins; and of course it was impossible for me to even mention the apparently absurd and baseless shadows of my mood. Human beings on other worlds than their own are often subject to nervous and psychic symptoms of this sort, engendered by the unfamiliar forces, the novel radiations of their environment. But, as we approached the buildings in our preliminary tour of examination, I lagged behind the others, seized by a paralyzing panic that left me unable to move or breathe for a few moments. A dark, freezing clamminess seemed to pervade my brain and muscles and suspend their inmost working. Then it lifted; and I was free to go on and follow the others.

Strangely, as it seemed, the two Martians refused to accompany us. Stolid and taciturn, they gave no explicit reason; but evidently nothing would induce them to enter Yoh-Vombis. Whether or not they were afraid of the ruins, we were unable to determine: their enigmatic faces, with the small oblique eyes and huge, flaring nostrils, betrayed neither fear nor any other emotion intelligible to man. In reply to our questions, they merely said that no Aihai had set foot among the ruins for ages. Apparently there was some mysterious tabu in connection with the place.

For equipment in that preliminary tour, we took along only a crowbar and two picks. Our other tools, and some cartridges of high explosives, we left at our camp, to be used later if necessary, after we had surveyed the ground. One or two of us owned automatics: but these also were left behind; for it seemed absurd to imagine that any form of life would be encountered among the ruins.

Octave was visibly excited as we began our inspection, and maintained a running-fire of exclamatory comment. The rest of us were subdued and silent; and I think that my own feeling, in a measure, was shared by many of the others. It was impossible to shake off the somber awe and wonder that fell upon us from those megalithic stones.

I have no time to describe the ruins minutely, but must hasten on with my story. There is much that I could not describe anyway; for the main area of the city was destined to remain unexplored.

We went on for some distance among the triangular, terraced buildings, following the zig-zag streets that conformed to this peculiar architecture. Most of the towers were more or less dilapidated; and everywhere we saw the deep erosion wrought by cycles of blowing wind and sand, which, in many cases, had worn into roundness the sharp angles of the mighty walls. We entered some of the towers through high, narrow doorways, but found utter emptiness within. Whatever they had contained in the way of furnishings must long ago have crumbled into dust; and the dust had been blown away by the searching desert gales. On some of the outer walls, there was evidence of carving or lettering; but all of it was so worn down and obliterated by time that we could trace only a few fragmentary outlines, of which we could make nothing.

At length we came to a wide thoroughfare, which ended in the wall of a vast terrace, several hundred yards long by perhaps forty in height, on which the central buildings were grouped like a sort of citadel or acropolis. A flight of broken steps, designed for longer limbs than those of men or even the gangling modern Martians, afforded access to the terrace, which had seemingly been hewn from the plateau itself.

Pausing, we decided to defer our investigation of the higher buildings, which, being more exposed than the others, were doubly ruinous and dilapidated, and in all likelihood would offer little for our trouble. Octave had begun to voice his disappointment over our failure to find anything in the nature of artifacts or carvings that would throw light on the history of Yoh-Vombis.

Then, a little to the right of the stairway, we perceived an entrance in the main wall, half-choked with ancient debris. Behind the heap of detritus, we found the beginning of a downward flight of steps. Darkness poured from the opening like a visible flood, noisome and musty with primordial stagnancies of decay; and we could see nothing below the first steps, which gave the appearance of being suspended over a black gulf.

Octave and myself and several others had brought along electric torches, in case we should need them in our explorations. It had occurred to us that there might be subterranean vaults or catacombs in Yoh-Vombis, even as in the latter-day cities of Mars, which are often more extensive underground than above; and such vaults would be the likeliest place in which to look for vestiges of the Yorhi civilization.

Throwing his torch-beam into the abyss, Octave began to descend the stairs. His eager voice called us to follow.

Again, for an instant, the unknown, irrational panic froze my faculties, and I hesitated while the others pressed forward behind me. Then, as before, the terror passed; and I wondered at myself for being overcome by anything so absurd and unfounded. I followed Octave down the steps, and the others came trooping after me.

At the bottom of the high, awkward steps, we found ourselves in a long and roomy vault, like a subterranean hallway. Its floor was deep with siftings of immemorial dust; and in places there were heaps of a coarse grey powder, such as might be left by the decomposition of certain fungi that grow in the Martian catacombs, under the canals. Such fungi, at one time, might conceivably have existed in Yoh-Vombis; but, owing to the prolonged and excessive dehydration, they must have died out long ago. Nothing, surely, not even a fungus, could have lived in those arid vaults for many aeons past.

The air was singularly heavy, as if the lees of an ancient atmos-

phere, less tenuous than that of Mars today, had settled down and remained in that stagnant darkness. It was harder to breathe than the
outer air; it was filled with unknown effluvia; and the light dust arose
before us at every step, diffusing a faintness of bygone corruption, like
the dust of powdered mummies.

At the end of the vault, before a strait and lofty doorway our
torches revealed an immense shallow urn or pan, supported on short
cube-shaped legs, and wrought from a dull blackish-green material
which suggested some bizarre alloy of metal and porcelain. The thing
was about four feet across, with a thick rim adorned by writhing inde-
cipherable figures, deeply etched as if by acid. In the bottom of the
bowl we perceived a deposit of dark and cinder-like fragments, which
gave off a slight but disagreeable pungence, like the phantom of some
more powerful odor. Octave, bending over the rim began to cough
and sneeze as he inhaled it.

"That stuff, whatever it was, must have been a pretty strong fumi-
gant," he observed. "The people of Yoh-Vombis may have used it to
disinfect the vaults."

The doorway beyond the shallow urn admitted us to a larger
chamber, whose floor was comparatively free of dust. We found that
the dark stone beneath our feet was marked off in multiform geometric patterns, traced with ochreous ore, amid which, as in Egyptian cartouches, hieroglyphics and highly formalized drawings were enclosed.
We could make little from most of them; but the figures in many were
doubtless designed to represent the Yorhis themselves. Like the Aihais,
they were tall and angular, with great bellows-like chests; and they were
depicted as possessing a supplementary third arm, which issued from
the bosom; a characteristic which, in vestigial form, sometimes occurs
among the Aihais. The ears and nostrils, as far as we could judge, were
not so huge and flaring as those of the modern Martians. All of these
Yorhis were represented as being nude; but in one of the cartouches,
done in a far hastier style than the others, we perceived two figures

whose high, conical craniums were wrapped in what seemed to be a sort of turban, which they were about to remove or adjust. The artist seemed to have laid a peculiar emphasis on the odd gesture with which the sinuous, four-jointed fingers were plucking at these head-dresses; and the whole posture was unexplainably contorted.

From the second vault, passages ramified in all directions, leading to a veritable warren of catacombs. Here, enormous pot-bellied urns of the same material as the fumigating-pan, but taller than a man's head and fitted with angular-handled stoppers, were ranged in solemn rows along the walls, leaving scant room for two of us to walk abreast. When we succeeded in removing one of the huge stoppers, we saw that the jar was filled to the rim with ashes and charred fragments of bone. Doubtless (as is still the Martian custom) the Yorhis had stored the cremated remains of whole families in single urns.

Even Octave became silent as we went on; and a sort of meditative awe seemed to replace his former excitement. We others, I think, were utterly weighed down to a man by the solid gloom of a concept-defying antiquity, into which it seemed that we were going further and further at every step.

The shadows fluttered before us like the monstrous and misshapen wings of phantom bats. There was nothing anywhere but the atom-like dust of ages, and the jars that held the ashes of a long-extinct people. But, clinging to the high roof in one of the further vaults, I saw a dark and corrugated patch of circular form, like a withered fungus. It was impossible to reach the thing; and we went on after peering at it with many futile conjectures. Oddly enough, I failed to remember at that moment the crumpled, shadowy object I had seen or dreamt the night before.

I have no idea how far we had gone, when we came to the last vault; but it seemed that we had been wandering for ages in that forgotten underworld. The air was growing fouler and more irrespirable, with a thick, sodden quality, as if from a sediment of material rottenness; and we had about decided to turn back. Then, without warning, at the end of a long, urn-lined catacomb, we found ourselves confronted by a blank wall.

Here, we came upon one of the strangest and most mystifying of our discoveries—a mummified and incredibly desiccated figure, standing erect against the wall. It was more than seven feet in height, of a brown, bituminous color, and was wholly nude except for a sort of black cowl that covered the upper head and drooped down at the sides in wrinkled folds. From the three arms, and general contour, it was plainly one of the ancient Yorhis—perhaps the sole member of this race whose body had remained intact.

We all felt an inexpressible thrill at the sheer age of this shrivelled thing, which, in the dry air of the vault, had endured through all the historic and geologic vicissitudes of the planet, to provide a visible link with lost cycles.

Then, as we peered closer with our torches, we saw *why* the mummy had maintained an upright position. At ankles, knees, waist, shoulders and neck it was shackled to the wall by heavy metal bands, so deeply eaten and embrowned with a sort of rust that we had failed to distinguish them at first sight in the shadow. The strange cowl on the head, when closelier studied, continued to baffle us. It was covered with a fine, mould-like pile, unclean and dusty as ancient cobwebs. Something about it, I know not what, was abhorrent and revolting.

"By Jove! this is a real find!" ejaculated Octave, as he thrust his torch into the mummified face, where shadows moved like living things in the pit-deep hollows of the eyes and the huge triple nostrils and wide ears that flared upward beneath the cowl.

Still lifting the torch, he put out his free hand and touched the body very lightly. Tentative as the touch had been, the lower part of the barrel-like torso, the legs, the hands and forearms all seemed to dissolve into powder, leaving the head and upper body and arms still hanging in their metal fetters. The progress of decay had been queerly unequal, for the remnant portions gave no sign of disintegration.

Octave cried out in dismay, and then began to cough and sneeze, as the cloud of brown powder, floating with airy lightness, enveloped him. We others all stepped back to avoid the powder. Then, above the spreading cloud, I saw an unbelievable thing. The black cowl on the mummy's head began to curl and twitch upward at the corners, it writhed with a verminous motion, it fell from the withered cranium, seeming to fold and unfold convulsively in mid-air as it fell. Then it dropped on the bare head of Octave who, in his disconcertment at the crumbling of the mummy, had remained standing close to the wall. At that instant, in a start of profound terror, I remembered the thing that had inched itself from the shadows of Yoh-Vombis in the light of the twin moons, and had drawn back like a figment of slumber at my first waking movement.

Cleaving closely as a tightened cloth, the thing enfolded Octave's hair and brow and eyes, and he shrieked wildly, with incoherent pleas for help, and tore with frantic fingers at the cowl, but failed to loosen it. Then his cries began to mount in a mad crescendo of agony, as if beneath some instrument of infernal torture; and he danced and capered blindly about the vault, eluding us with strange celerity as we all sprang forward in an effort to reach him and release him from his weird incumbrance. The whole happening was mysterious as a nightmare; but the thing that had fallen on his head was plainly some unclassified form of Martian life, which, contrary to all the known laws of science, had survived in those primordial catacombs. We must rescue him from its clutches if we could.

We tried to close in on the frenzied figure of our chief—which, in the far from roomy space between the last urns and the wall, should have been an easy matter. But, darting away, in a manner doubly incomprehensible because of his blindfolded condition, he circled about us and ran past, to disappear among the urns toward the outer labyrinth of intersecting catacombs.

"My God! What has happened to him?" cried Harper. "The man acts as if he were possessed."

There was obviously no time for a discussion of the enigma, and we all followed Octave as speedily as our astonishment would permit. We had lost sight of him in the darkness, and when we came to the first division of the vaults, we were doubtful as to which passage he had taken, till we heard a shrill scream, several times repeated, in a cat-acomb on the extreme left. There was a weird, unearthly quality in those screams, which may have been due to the long-stagnant air or the peculiar acoustics of the ramifying caverns. But somehow I could not imagine them as issuing from human lips—at least not from those of a living man. They seemed to contain a soulless, mechanical agony, as if they had been wrung from a devil-driven corpse.

Thrusting our torches before us into the lurching, fleeing shadows, we raced along between rows of mighty urns. The screaming had died away in sepulchral silence; but far off we heard the light and muffled thud of running feet. We followed in headlong pursuit; but, gasping painfully in the vitiated, miasmal air, we were soon compelled to slacken our pace without coming in sight of Octave. Very faintly, and further away than ever, like the tomb-swallowed steps of a phantom, we heard his vanishing footfalls. Then they ceased; and we heard nothing, except our own convulsive breathing, and the blood that throbbed in our temple-veins like steadily beaten drums of alarm.

We went on, dividing our party into three contingents when we came to a triple branching of the caverns. Harper and Halgren and myself took the middle passage; and after we had gone on for an endless interval without finding any trace of Octave, and had threaded our way through recesses piled to the roof with colossal urns that must have held the ashes of a hundred generations, we came out in the huge chamber with the geometric floor-designs. Here, very shortly, we were joined by the others, who had likewise failed to locate our missing leader.

It would be useless to detail our renewed and hour-long search of the myriad vaults, many of which we had not hitherto explored. All were empty, as far as any sign of life was concerned. I remember passing once more through the vault in which I had seen the dark, rounded patch on the ceiling, and noting with a shudder that the patch was gone. It was a miracle that we did not lose ourselves in that underworld maze; but at last we came back to the final catacomb in which we had found the shackled mummy.

We heard a measured and recurrent clangor as we neared the place—a most alarming and mystifying sound under the circumstances. It was like the hammering of ghouls on some forgotten mausoleum. When we drew nearer, the beams of our torches revealed a sight that was no less unexplainable than unexpected. A human figure, with its back toward us and the head concealed by a swollen black object that had the size and form of a sofa cushion, was standing near the remains of the mummy and was striking at the wall with a pointed metal bar. How long Octave had been there, and where he had found the bar, we could not know. But the blank wall had crumbled away beneath his furious blows, leaving on the floor a pile of cement-like fragments; and a small, narrow door, of the same ambiguous material as the cinerary urns and the fumigating-pan, had been laid bare.

Amazed, uncertain, inexpressibly bewildered, we were all incapable of action or volition at that moment. The whole business was too fantastic and too horrifying, and it was plain that Octave had been overcome by some sort of madness. I, for one, felt the violent upsurge of sudden nausea when I had identified the loathsomely bloated thing that clung to Octave's head and drooped in obscene tumescence on his neck. I did not dare to surmise the causation of its bloating.

Before any of us could recover our faculties, Octave flung aside the metal bar and began to fumble for something in the wall. It must have been a hidden spring; though how he could have known its location or existence is beyond all legitimate conjecture. With a dull, hideous grating, the uncovered door swung inward, thick and ponderous as a mausolean slab, leaving an aperture from which the nether midnight seemed to well like a flood of aeon-buried foulness. Somehow, at that instant, our electric torches appeared to flicker and grow dim; and we all breathed a suffocating fetor, like a draft from inner worlds of immemorial putrescence.

Octave had turned toward us now, and he stood in an idle posture before the open door, like one who has finished some ordained task. I was the first of our party to throw off the paralyzing spell; and pulling out a clasp-knife—the only semblance of a weapon which I carried—I ran over to him. He moved back, but not quickly enough to evade me, when I stabbed with the four-inch blade at the black, turgescent mass that enveloped his whole upper head and hung down upon his eyes.

What the thing was, I should prefer not to imagine—if it were possible to imagine. It was formless as a great slug, with neither head nor tail nor apparent organs—an unclean, puffy, leathery thing, covered with that fine, mould-like fur of which I have spoken. The knife tore into it as if through rotten parchment, making a long gash, and the horror appeared to collapse like a broken bladder. Out of it there gushed a sickening torrent of human blood, mingled with dark, filiated masses that may have been half-dissolved hair, and floating gelatinous lumps like molten bone, and shreds of a curdy white substance. At the same time, Octave began to stagger, and went down at full length on the floor. Disturbed by his fall, the mummy-dust arose about him in a curling cloud, beneath which he lay mortally still.

Conquering my revulsion, and choking with the dust, I bent over him and tore the flaccid, oozing horror from his head. It came with unexpected ease, as if I had removed a limp rag: but I wish to God that I had let it remain. Beneath, there was no longer a human cranium, for all had been eaten away, even to the eyebrows, and the half-devoured brain was laid bare as I lifted the cowl-like object. I dropped the unnamable thing from fingers that had grown suddenly nerveless, and it turned over as it fell, revealing on the nether side many rows of pinkish suckers, arranged in circles about a pallid disk that was covered with nerve-like filaments, suggesting a sort of plexus.

My companions had pressed forward behind me; but, for an appreciable interval, no one spoke.

"How long do you suppose he has been dead?" It was Halgren who whispered the awful question, which we had all been asking ourselves. Apparently no one felt able or willing to answer it; and we could only stare in horrible, timeless fascination at Octave.

At length I made an effort to avert my gaze; and turning at random, I saw the remnants of the shackled mummy, and noted for the first time, with mechanical, unreal horror, the half-eaten condition of the withered head. From this, my gaze was diverted to the newly opened door at one side, without perceiving for a moment what had drawn my attention. Then, startled, I beheld beneath my torch, far down beyond the door, as it in some nether pit, a seething, multitudinous, worm-like movement of crawling shadows. They seemed to boil up in the darkness; and then, over the broad threshold of the vault, there poured the verminous vanguard of a countless army: things that were kindred to the monstrous, diabolic leech I had torn from Octave's eaten head. Some were thin and flat, like writhing, doubling disks of cloth or leather, and others were more or less poddy, and crawled with glutted slowness. What they had found to feed on in the sealed, eternal midnight I do not know; and I pray that I never shall know.

I sprang back and away from them, electrified with terror, sick with loathing, and the black army inched itself unendingly with nightmare swiftness from the unsealed abyss, like the nauseous vomit of horror-sated hells. As it poured toward us, burying Octave's body from sight in a writhing wave, I saw a stir of life from the seemingly dead thing I had cast aside, and saw the loathly struggle which it made to right itself and join the others.

But neither I nor my companions could endure to look longer. We turned and ran between the mighty rows of urns, with the slithering mass of demon leeches close upon us, and scattered in blind panic when we came to the first division of the vaults. Heedless of each other or of anything but the urgency of flight, we plunged into the ramifying passages at random. Behind me, I heard someone stumble and go down, with a curse that mounted to an insane shrieking; but I knew that if I halted and went back, it would be only to invite the same baleful doom that had overtaken the hindmost of our party.

Still clutching the electric torch and my open clasp-knife, I ran along a minor passage which, I seemed to remember, would conduct with more or less directness upon the large outer vault with the painted floor. Here I found myself alone. The others had kept to the main catacombs; and I heard far off a muffled babel of mad cries, as if several of them had been seized by their pursuers.

It seemed that I must have been mistaken about the direction of the passage; for it turned and twisted in an unfamiliar manner, with many intersections, and I soon found that I was lost in the black labyrinth, where the dust had lain unstirred by living feet for inestimable generations. The cinerary warren had grown still once more; and I heard my own frenzied panting, loud and stertorous as that of a Titan in the dead silence.

Suddenly, as I went on, my torch disclosed a human figure coming toward me in the gloom. Before I could master my startlement, the figure had passed me with long, machine-like strides, as if returning to the inner vaults. I think it was Harper, since the height and build were about right for him; but I am not altogether sure, for the eyes and upper head were muffled by a dark, inflated cowl, and the pale lips locked as if in a silence of tetanic torture—or death. Whoever he was, he had dropped his torch; and he was running blindfold, in utter darkness, beneath the impulsion of that unearthly vampirism, to seek the very fountain-head of the unloosed horror. I knew that he was beyond human help; and I did not even dream of trying to stop him.

Trembling violently, I resumed my flight, and was passed by two more of our party, stalking by with mechanical swiftness and sureness, and cowled with those Satanic leeches. The others must have returned by way of the main passages; for I did not meet them; and was never to see them again.

The remainder of my flight is a blur of pandemonian terror. Once more, after thinking that I was near the outer cavern, I found myself astray, and fled through a ranged eternity of monstrous urns, in vaults that must have extended for an unknown distance beyond our explorations. It seemed that I had gone on for years; and my lungs were choking with the aeon-dead air, and my legs were ready to crumble beneath me, when I saw far off a tiny point of blessed daylight. I ran toward it, with all the terrors of the alien darkness crowding behind me, and accursed shadows flittering before, and saw that the vault ended in a low, ruinous entrance, littered by rubble on which there fell an arc of thin sunshine.

It was another entrance than the one by which we had penetrated this lethal underworld. I was within a dozen feet of the opening when, without sound or other intimation, something dropped upon my head from the roof above, blinding me instantly and closing upon me like a tautened net. My brow and scalp, at the same time, were shot through with a million needle-like pangs—a manifold, ever-growing agony that seemed to pierce the very bone and converge from all sides upon my inmost brain.

The terror and suffering of that moment were worse than aught which the hells of earthly madness or delirium could ever contain. I felt the foul, vampiric clutch of an atrocious death—and of more than death.

I believe that I dropped the torch: but the fingers of my right hand had still retained the open knife. Instinctively—since I was hardly capable of conscious volition—I raised the knife and slashed blindly, again and again, many times, at the thing that had fastened its deadly folds upon me. The blade must have gone through and through the clinging monstrosity, to gash my own flesh in a score of places; but I did not feel the pain of those wounds in the million-throbbing torment that possessed me.

At last I saw light, and saw that a black strip, loosened from above my eyes and dripping with my own blood, was hanging down my cheek. It writhed a little, even as it hung, and I ripped it away, and ripped the other remnants of the thing, tatter by oozing, bloody tatter, from off my brow and head. Then I staggered toward the entrance; and the wan light turned to a far, receding, dancing flame before me as I lurched and fell outside the cavern—a flame that fled like the last star of creation above the yawning, sliding chaos and oblivion into which I descended. . . .

I am told that my unconsciousness was of brief duration. I came to myself, with the cryptic faces of the two Martian guides bending over me. My head was full of lancinating pains, and half-remembered terrors closed upon my mind like the shadows of mustering harpies. I rolled over, and looked back toward the cavern-mouth, from which the Martians, after finding me, had seemingly dragged me for some little distance. The mouth was under the terraced angle of an outer building, and within sight of our camp.

I stared at the black opening with hideous fascination, and descried a shadowy stirring in the gloom—the writhing, verminous movement of things that pressed forward from the darkness but did not emerge into the light. Doubtless they could not endure the sun, those creatures of ultramundane night and cycle-sealed corruption.

It was then that the ultimate horror, the beginning madness, came upon me. Amid my crawling revulsion, my nausea-prompted desire to flee from that seething cavern-mouth, there rose an abhorrently conflicting impulse to return; to thread my backward way through all the catacombs, as the others had done; to go down where never men save they, the inconceivably doomed and accursed, had ever gone; to seek beneath that damnable compulsion a nether world that human thought can never picture. There was a black light, a soundless calling, in the vaults of my brain: the implanted summons of the Thing, like a permeating and sorcerous poison. It lured me to the subterranean door that was walled up by the dying people of Yoh-Vombis, to immure those hellish and immortal leeches, those dark parasites that engraft their own abominable life on the half-eaten brains of the dead. It called me to the depths beyond, where dwell the noisome, necromantic Ones, of whom the leeches, with all their powers of vampirism and diabolism, are but the merest minions. . . .

It was only the two Aihais who prevented me from going back. I struggled, I fought them insanely as they strove to retard me with their spongy arms; but I must have been pretty thoroughly exhausted from all the superhuman adventures of the day; and I went down once more, after a little, into fathomless nothingness, from which I floated out at long intervals, to realize that I was being carried across the desert toward Ignarh.

Well, that is all my story. I have tried to tell it fully and coherently, at a cost that would be unimaginable to the sane . . . . to tell it before the madness falls upon me again, as it will very soon—as it is doing now. . . . . Yes, I have told my story . . . and you have written it all out, haven't you? Now I must go back to Yoh-Vombis—back across the desert and down through all the catacombs to the vaster vaults beneath. Something is in my brain, that commands me and will direct me . . . I tell you, I must go. . . . .

SEEDLING OF MARS

It was in the fall of 1947, three days prior to the annual football game between Stanford and the University of California, that the strange visitor from outer space landed at noon in the middle of the huge stadium at Berkeley where the game was to be held.

Descending with peculiar deliberation, it was seen and pointed out by multitudes of people in the towns that border on San Francisco Bay, in Berkeley, Oakland, Alameda, and San Francisco itself. Gleaming with a fiery, copperish-golden light, it floated down from the cloudless autumn azure, dropping in a sort of slow spiral above the stadium. It was utterly unlike any known type of aircraft, and was nearly a hundred feet in length.

The general shape was ovoid, and also more or less angular, with a surface divided into scores of variant planes, and with many diamond ports of purplish material different from that of which the body was constructed. Even at first glance, it suggested the inventive genius and workmanship of some alien world, of a people whose ideas of mechanical symmetry have been conditioned by evolutionary necessities and sense-faculties divergent from ours.

However, when the queer vessel had come to rest in the amphitheater, many conflicting theories regarding its origin and the purpose of its descent were promulgated in the Bay cities. There were those who feared the invasion of some foreign foe, and who thought that the odd ship was the harbinger of a long-plotted attack from the Russian and Chinese Soviets, or even from Germany, whose intentions were still suspected. And many of those who postulated an ultra-planetary origin were also apprehensive, deeming that the visitant was perhaps hostile, and might mark the beginning of some terrible incursion from outer worlds.

In the meanwhile, utterly silent and immobile and without sign of life or occupancy, the vessel reposed in the stadium, where staring crowds began to gather about it. These crowds, however, were soon dispersed by order of the civic authorities, since the nature and intentions of the stranger were alike doubtful and undeclared. The stadium was closed to the public; and, in case of inimical manifestations, machine-guns were mounted on the higher seats with a company of Marines in attendance, and bombing-planes hovered in readiness to drop their lethal freight on the shining, coppery bulk.

The intensest interest was felt by the whole scientific fraternity, and a large group of professors, of chemists, metallurgists, astronomers, astrophysicists and biologists was organized to visit and examine the unknown object. When, on the afternoon following its landing, the local observatories issued a bulletin saying that the vessel had been sighted approaching the earth from translunar space on the previous night, the fact of its non-terrestrial genesis became established beyond dispute in the eyes of most; and controversy reigned as to whether it had come from Venus, Mars, Mercury, or one of the superior planets; or whether, perhaps, it was a wanderer from another solar system than our own.

But of course the nearer planets were favored in this dispute by the majority, especially Mars; for, as nearly as those who had watched it could determine, the line of the vessel's approach would have formed a trajectory with the red planet.

All that day, while argument seethed, while extras with luridly speculative and fantastic headlines were issued by the local papers as well as by the press of the whole civilized world; while public sentiment was divided between apprehension and curiosity, and the guarding Marines and aviators continued to watch for signs of possible hostility, the unidentified vessel maintained its initial stillness and silence.

Telescopes and glasses were trained upon it from the hills above the stadium; but even these disclosed little regarding its character. Those who studied it saw that the numerous ports were made of a vitreous material, more or less transparent; but nothing stirred behind them; and the glimpses of queer machinery which they afforded in the ship's interior were meaningless to the watchers. One port, larger than the rest, was believed to be a sort of door or man-hole; but no one came to open it; and behind it was a weird array of motionless rods and coils and pistons, which debarred the vision from further view.

Doubtless, it was thought, the occupants were no less cautious of their alien milieu than the people of the Bay region were suspicious of the vessel. Perhaps they feared to reveal themselves to human eyes; perhaps they were doubtful of the terrene atmosphere and its effect upon themselves; or perhaps they were merely lying in wait and planning some devilish outburst with unconceived weapons or engineries of destruction.

Apart from the fears felt by some, and the wonderment and speculation of others, a third division of public sentiment soon began to crystallize. In collegiate circles and among sport-lovers, the feeling was that the strange vessel had taken an unwarrantable liberty in preempting the stadium, especially at a time so near to the forthcoming athletic event. A petition for its removal was circulated, and presented to the city authorities. The great metallic hull, it was felt, no matter whence it had come or why, should not be allowed to interfere with anything so sacrosanct and of such prime importance as a football game.

However, in spite of the turmoil it had created, the vessel refused to move by so much as the fraction of an inch. Many began to surmise that the occupants had been overcome by the conditions of their transit through space; or perhaps they had died, unable to endure the gravity and atmospheric pressure of the earth. It was decided to leave the vessel unapproached until morning of the next day, when the committee of investigation would visit it. During that afternoon and night, scientists from many states were speeding toward California by airplane and rocket-ship, to be on hand in time for this event.

It was felt advisable to limit the number of this committee. Among the fortunate savants who had been selected, was John Gaillard, assistant astronomer at the Mt. Wilson observatory. Gaillard represented the more radical and freely speculative trend of scientific thought, and had become well known for his theories concerning the inhabitability of the inferior planets, particularly Mars and Venus. He had long championed the idea of intelligent and highly organized life on these worlds, and had even published more than one treatise dealing with the subject, in which he had elaborated his theories with much specific detail. His excitement at the news of the strange vessel was intense. He was one of those who had sighted the gleaming and unclassifiable speck far out in space, beyond the orbit of the moon, in the late hours of the previous night; and he had felt even then a premonition of its true character. Others of the party were free and open-minded in their attitude; but no one was more deeply and vitally interested than Gaillard.

Godfrey Stilton, professor of astronomy at the University of California, also on the committee, might have been chosen as the very antithesis of Gaillard in his views and tendencies. Narrow, dogmatic, skeptical of all that could not be proved by line and rule, scornful of all that lay beyond the bourn of a strait empiricism, he was loath to admit the ultra-terrene origin of the vessel, or even the possibility of organic life on any other world than the earth. Several of his confreres belonged to the same intellectual type.

Apart from these two men and their fellow-scientists, the party included three newspaper reporters, as well as the local chief of police, William Polson, and the Mayor of Berkeley, James Gresham, since it was felt that the forces of government should be represented. The entire committee comprised forty men; and a number of expert machinists, equipped with acetylene torches and cutting tools, were held in reserve outside the stadium, in case it should be found necessary to open the vessel by force.

At nine A.M. the investigators entered the stadium and approached the glittering, multi-angled object. Many were conscious of the thrill that attends some unforeknowable danger; but more were animated by the keenest curiosity and by feelings of extreme wonderment. Gaillard, in especial, felt himself in the presence of ultramundane mystery and marvelled as he neared the coppery-golden bulk: his feeling amounted almost to an actual vertigo, such as would be experienced by one who gazes athwart unfathomable gulfs upon the arcanic secrets and the wit-transcending wonders of a foreign sphere. It seemed to him that he stood upon the verge between the determinate and the incommensurable, betwixt the finite and the infinite.

Others of the group, in lesser degree, were possessed by similar emotions. And even the hard-headed, unimaginative Stilton was disturbed by a queer uneasiness; which, being minded as he was, he assigned to the weather—or a "touch of liver."

The strange ship reposed in utter stillness, as before. The fears of those who half-expected some deadly ambush were allayed as they drew near; and the hopes of those who looked for a more amicable manifestation of living occupancy were ungratified. The party gathered before the main port, which, like all the others, was made in the form of a great diamond. It was several feet above their heads, in a vertical angle or plane of the hull; and they stood staring through its mauve transparency on the unknown, intricate mechanisms beyond, that were colored as if by the rich panes of some cathedral window.

All were in doubt as to what should be done; for it seemed evident that the occupants of the vessel, if alive and conscious, were in no hurry to reveal themselves to human scrutiny. The delegation resolved to wait a few minutes before calling on the services of the assembled mechanics with their acetylene torches; and while waiting they walked about and inspected the metal of the walls, which seemed to be an alloy of copper and red gold, tempered to a preternatural hardness by some process unfamiliar to telluric metallurgy. There was no sign of jointure in the myriad planes and facets; and the whole enormous shell, apart from its lucid ports, might well have been wrought from a single sheet of the rich alloy.

Gaillard stood peering upward at the main port, while his companions sauntered about the vessel talking and debating among themselves. Somehow, he felt an intuition that something strange and miraculous was about to happen; and when the great port began to open slowly, without visible agency, dividing into two valves that slid away at the sides, the thrill which he experienced was not altogether one of surprise. Nor was he surprised when a sort of metal escalator, consisting of narrow stairs that were little more than rungs, descended step by step from the opening and came down to the ground at his very feet.

The port had opened and the escalator had unfolded in silence, with no faintest creak or clang; but others beside Gaillard had perceived the occurrence, and all hastened in great excitement and gathered before the steps.

Contrary to their not unnatural expectations, no one emerged from the vessel; and they could see little more of the interior than had been visible through the shut valves. They looked for some exotic ambassador from Mars, some gorgeous and bizarre plenipotentiary from Venus to descend the queer steps; and the silence and solitude and mechanical adroitness of it all were uncanny. It seemed that the great ship was a living entity, and possessed a brain and nerves of its own, hidden in the metal-sheathed interior.

The open portal and stairs offered an obvious invitation; and after some hesitancy, the scientists made up their minds to enter. Some were still fearful of a trap; and five of the forty men warily decided to remain without; but all the others were more powerfully drawn by curiosity and investigative ardor; and one by one they climbed the stairs and filed into the vessel.

They found the interior even more provocative of wonder than the outer walls had been. It was quite roomy and was divided into several compartments of ample size, two of which, at the vessel's center, were lined with low couches covered by soft, lustrous, piliated fabrics of opalescent grey. The others, as well as the ante-chamber behind the entrance, were filled with machinery whose motive force and method of operation were alike obscure to the most expert among the investigators. Rare metals and odd alloys, some of them difficult to classify, had been used in the construction of this machinery. Near the entrance there was a sort of tripodal table or instrument-board whose queer rows of levers and buttons were no less mysterious than the ciphers of some telic cryptogram. The entire ship was seemingly deserted, with no trace of human or extraplanetary life.

Wandering through the apartments and marvelling at the unsolved mechanical enigmas which surrounded them, the delegation-members were not aware that the broad valves of the main port had closed behind them with the same stealthiness and silence that had marked their opening. Nor did they hear the warning shouts of the five men who had remained outside.

Their first intimation of anything untoward came from a sudden lurching and lifting of the vessel. Startled, they looked at the window-like ports, and saw through the violet, vitreous panes the whirling and falling away of those innumerable rows of seats which ringed the immense stadium. The alien space-ship, with no visible hand to control it, was rising rapidly in air with a sort of spiral movement. It was bearing away to some unknown world the entire delegation of hardy scientists that had boarded it, together with the Berkeley Mayor and Chief of Police and the three privileged reporters who had thought to obtain an ultrasensational "scoop" for their respective journals!

The situation was wholly without precedent, and was more than astounding; and the reactions of the various men, though quite divergent in some ways, were all marked by amazement and consternation.

Many were too stunned and confounded to realize all the implications or possibilities; others were frankly terrified; and others still were indignant.

"This is an outrage!" thundered Stilton, as soon as he had recovered a little from his primary surprise. There were similar exclamations from others of the same temperament as he, all of whom felt emphatically that something should be done about the situation, and that someone (who, unfortunately, they could not locate or identify) should be made to suffer for such unparalleled audacity.

Gaillard, though he shared in the general amazement, was thrilled to the bottom of his heart by a sense of unearthly and prodigious adventure, by a premonition of interplanetary emprise. He felt a mystic certainty that he and the others had embarked on a voyage to some world untrodden heretofore by man; that the strange vessel had descended to earth and had opened its port to invite them for this very purpose; that an esoteric and remote power was guiding its every movement and was drawing it to an appointed destination. Vast, inchoate images of unbounded space and splendor and interstellar strangeness filled his mind, and unforelimnable pictures rose to dazzle his vision from an ultratelluric bourn.

In some incomprehensible way, he knew that his life-long desire to penetrate the mysteries of distant spheres would soon be gratified; and he (if not his companions) was resigned from the very first to that bizarre abduction and captivity in the soaring space-flier.

Discussing their position with much volubility and vociferousness, the assembled savants rushed to the various ports and stared down at the world they were leaving. In a mere fraction of time, they had risen to a cloud-like altitude. The whole region about San Francisco Bay, as well as the verges of the Pacific ocean, lay stretched below them like an immense relief map; and they could already see the curvature of the horizon, which seemed to reel and dip as they went upward.

It was an awesome and magnificent prospect; but the growing acceleration of the vessel, which had now gained a speed more than equal to that of the rocket-ships which were used at that time for circling the globe in the stratosphere, soon compelled them to relinquish their standing position and seek the refuge of the convenient couches. Conversation also was abandoned, for everyone began to experience an almost intolerable constriction and oppression, which held their bodies as if with clamps of unyielding metal.

However, when they had all laid themselves on the piliated couches, they felt a mysterious relief, whose source they could not ascertain. It seemed that a force emanated from those couches, which alleviated in some way the leaden stress of increased gravity due to the acceleration, and made it possible for the men to endure the terrific speed with which the space-flier was leaving the earth's atmosphere and gravitational zone.

Presently they found themselves able to stand up and walk around once more. Their sensations, on the whole, were almost normal; though, in contradistinction to the initial crushing weight, there was now an odd lightness which compelled them to shorten their steps to avoid colliding with the walls and machinery. Their weight was less than it would have been on earth, but the loss was not enough to produce discomfort or sickness, and was accompanied by a sort of exhilaration.

They perceived that they were breathing a thin, rarefied and bracing air, not dissimilar to that of terrene mountain-tops, though permeated by one or two unfamiliar elements that gave it a touch of nitric sharpness. This air tended to increase the exhilaration and to quicken their respiration and pulses a little.

"This is damnable!" spluttered the indignant Stilton, as soon as he found that the powers of locomotion and breathing were reasonably subject to control. "It is contrary to all law, decency and order. The U. S. Government should do something about it immediately."

"I fear," observed Gaillard, "that we are now beyond the jurisdiction of the U. S., as well as that of all other mundane governments. No plane or rocket-ship could reach the air-strata through which we are passing; and we will penetrate the interstellar ether in a moment or so. Presumably this vessel is returning to the world from which it came; and we are going with it."

"Absurd! preposterous! outrageous!" Stilton's voice was a roar, slightly subdued and attenuated by the fine atmospheric medium. "I've always maintained that space-travel was utterly chimerical. Even earth-scientists haven't been able to invent a space-ship; and it is ridiculous to assume that highly intelligent life, capable of such invention, could exist on other planets."

"How, then," queried Gaillard, "do you account for our situation?"

"The vessel is of human origin, of course. It must be a new and ultra-powerful type of rocket-ship, devised by the Soviets, and under automatic or radio control, which will probably land us in Siberia after travelling in the highest layers of the stratosphere."

Gaillard, smiling with gentle irony, felt that he could safely abandon the argument. Leaving Stilton to stare wrathfully through a port at the receding bulk of the world, on which the whole of North America, together with Alaska and the Hawaiian Islands, had begun to declare their coastal outlines, he joined others of the party in a renewed investigation of the ship.

Some still maintained that living beings must be hidden on board; but a close search of every apartment, corner and cranny resulted as before. Abandoning this objective, the men began to re-examine the machinery, whose motive-power and method of operation they were still unable to fathom. Utterly perplexed and mystified, they watched the instrument-board, on which certain of the keys would move occasionally, as if shifted by an unseen hand. These changes of alignment were always followed by some change in the vessel's speed, or by a slight alteration of its course, possibly to avoid collision with meteoric fragments.

Though nothing definite could be learned about the propelling mechanism, certain negative facts were soon established. The method of propulsion was plainly non-explosive, with no roaring and flaming discharge of rockets. All was silent, gliding, and vibrationless, with nothing to betoken mechanical activity, other than the shifting of the keys and the glowing of certain intricate coils and pistons with a strange blue light. This light, cold as the scintillation of Arctic ice, was not electric in its nature, but suggested rather some unknown form of radio-activity.

After awhile, Stilton joined those who were grouped about the instrument-board. Still muttering his resentment of the unlawful and unscientific indignity to which he had been subjected, he watched the keys for a minute or so, and then, seizing one of them with his fingers, he tried to experiment, with the idea of gaining control of the vessel's movements.

To his amazement and that of his confreres, the key was immovable. Stilton strained till the blue veins stood out on his hand, and sweat poured in rills from his baldish brow. Then, one by one, he tried others of the keys, tugging desperately, but always with the same result. Evidently the board was locked against other control than that of the unknown pilot.

Still persisting in his endeavor, Stilton came to a key of large size and different shape from the rest. Touching it, he screamed in agony, and withdrew his fingers from the strange object with some difficulty. The key was cold, as if it had been steeped in the absolute zero of space. It had actually seemed to sear his fingers with its extreme iciness. After that, he desisted, and made no further effort to interfere with the workings of the vessel.

Gaillard, after watching this interlude, had wandered back to one of the main apartments. Peering out once more from his seat on a couch of supernal softness and resilience, he beheld a breathtaking spectacle. The whole world, a great, glowing, many-tinted globe, was swimming abreast of the flier in the black and starlined gulf. The aw-fulness of the undirectioned deeps, the unthinkable isolation of infini-tude rushed upon him, and he felt sick and giddy for a few instants with the shock of realization, and was swept by an overwhelming panic, limitless and without name.

Then, strangely, the terror passed, in a dawning exultation at the prospect of the novel voyage through unsounded heavens and toward untrodden shores. Oblivious of danger, forgetful of the dread aliena-tion from man's accustomed environment, he gave himself up to a mag-ical conviction of marvellous adventure and unique destiny to come.

Others, however, were less capable of orientating themselves to these bizarre and terrific circumstances. Pale and horror-stricken, with a sense of irredeemable loss, of all-encompassing peril and giddy confu-sion, they watched the receding earth from whose comfortable purlieus they had been removed so inexplicably and with such awful suddenness.

Many were speechless with fear, as they realized more clearly their impotence in the grip of an all-powerful and incognizable force.

Some chattered loudly and incoherently, in an effort to conceal their perturbation. The three reporters lamented their inability to communicate with the journals they represented. James Gresham, the Mayor, and William Polson, the Chief of Police, were non-plussed and altogether at a loss as to what to do or think, in circumstances that seemed to nullify completely their wonted civic importance. And the scientists, as might have been expected, were divided into two main camps. The more radical and adventurous were more or less prone to welcome whatever might be in store, for the sake of new knowledge; while the others accepted their fate with varying degrees of reluctance, of protest and apprehension.

Several hours went by; and the moon, a ball of dazzling desolation in the great abyss, had been left behind with the waning earth. The flier was speeding alone through the cosmic vastness, in a universe whose grandeur was a revelation even to the astronomers, familiar as they were with the magnitudes and multitudes of suns, nebulae and galaxies. The thirty-five men were being estranged from their natal planet and hurled across unthinkable immensity at a speed far beyond that of any solar body or satellite. It was hard to estimate the precise velocity; but some idea of it could be gained from the rapidity with which the sun and the nearer planets, Mars, Mercury and Venus, changed their relative positions. They seemed almost to fly athwart the heavens like so many jugglers' balls.

It was plain that some sort of artificial gravity prevailed in the ship; for the weightlessness that would otherwise have been inevitable in outer space was not experienced at any time. Also, the scientists found that they were being supplied with air from certain oddly-shapen tanks. Evidently, too, there was some kind of hidden heating-system or mode of insulation against the interspatial zero; for the temperature of the vessel's interior remained constant, at about 65° or 70°.

Looking at their watches, some of the party found that it was now noon by terrestrial time; though even the most unimaginative were impressed by the absurdity of the twenty-four hour division of day and night amid the eternal sunlight of the void.

Many began to feel hungry and thirsty, and to voice their appetence aloud. Not long after, as if in response, like the service given by a good table d'hôte, or restaurant, certain panels in the inner metal wall, hitherto unnoticed by the savants, opened noiselessly before their eyes and revealed a series of long buffets, on which were curious wide-mouthed ewers containing water and deep, tureen-like plates filled to the rim with unknown food-stuffs.

Too astonished to comment at much length on this new miracle, the delegation-members proceeded to sample the viands and beverage thus offered. Stilton, still morosely indignant, refused to taste them but was alone in his abstention.

The water was quite drinkable, though slightly alkaline, as if it had come from desert wells; and the food, a sort of reddish paste, concerning whose nature and composition the chemists were doubtful, served to appease the pangs of hunger even if it was not especially seductive to the palate.

After the earth-men had partaken of this refection, the panels closed as silently and unobtrusively as they had opened. The vessel plunged on through space, hour after hour, till it became obvious to Gaillard and his fellow-astronomers that it was either heading directly for the planet Mars or would pass very close to Mars on its way to some further orb.

The red world, with its familiar markings, which they had watched so often through observatory telescopes, and over whose character and causation they had long puzzled, began to loom before them and swelled upon the heavens with thaumaturgic swiftness. Then they perceived a signal deceleration in the speed of the flier, which continued straight on toward the coppery planet, as if its goal were concealed amid the labyrinth of obscure and singular mottlings; and it became impossible to doubt any longer that Mars was their destination.

Gaillard, and those who were more or less akin to him in their interests and proclivities, were stirred by an awesome and sublime expectancy as the vessel neared the alien world. Then it began to float gently down above an exotic landscape in which the well-known "seas" and "canals", enormous with their closeness, could plainly be recognized.

Soon they approached the surface of the ruddy planet, spiraling through its cloudless and mistless atmosphere, while the deceleration slowed to a speed that was little more than that of a falling parachute. Mars surrounded them with its strait, monotonous horizons, nearer than those of earth, and displaying neither mountains nor any salient elevation of hills or mammocks; and soon they hung above it at an altitude of a half-mile or less. Here the vessel seemed to halt and poise, without descending further.

Below them now they saw a desert of low-ridge and yellowish-red sand, intersected by one of the so-called "canals", which ran sinuously away on either side to disappear beyond the horizon.

The scientists studied this terrain in ever-growing amazement and excitement, as the true nature of the veining "canal" was forced upon their perception. It was not water, as many had heretofore presumed, but a mass of pale-green vegetation, of vast and serrate leaves or fronds, all of which seemed to emanate from a single crawling flesh-colored stalk, several hundred feet in diameter and with swollen nodular joints at half-mile intervals! Aside from this anomalous and super-gigantic vine, there was no trace of life, either animal or vegetable, in the whole landscape; and the extent of the crawling stalk, which netted the entire visible terrain but seemed by its form and characteristics to be the mere tendril of some vaster growth, was a thing to stagger the preconceptions of mundane botany

Many of the scientists were almost stupefied with astonishment as they gazed down from the violet ports on this titanic creeper. More than ever, the journalists mourned the staggering head-lines with which they would be unable, under existing circumstances, to endow their respective dailies. Gresham and Polson felt that there was something vaguely illegal about the existence of anything so monstrous in the way of a plant-form; and the scientific disapproval felt by Stilton and his academically minded confreres was most pronounced.

"Outrageous! unheard-of! ludicrous!" muttered Stilton. "This thing defies the most elementary laws of botany. There is no conceivable precedent for it."

Gaillard, who stood beside him, was so wrapt in his contemplation of the novel growth, that he scarcely heard Stilton's comment. The conviction of vast and sublime adventure which had grown upon him ever since the beginning of that bizarre, stupendous voyage, was now confirmed by a clear daylight certitude. He could give no definite form or coherence to the feeling that possessed him; but he was overwhelmed by the intimation of present marvel and future miracle, and the intuition of strange, tremendous revelations to come.

Few of the party cared to speak, or would have been capable of speech. All that had happened to them during the past few hours, and all on which they now gazed, was so far beyond the scope of human action and cognition, that the normal exercise of their faculties was more or less inhibited by the struggle for adjustment to these unique and non-terrestrial conditions.

After they had watched the gargantuan vine for a minute or two, the savants became aware that the vessel was moving again, this time in a lateral direction. Flying very slowly and deliberately, it followed the course of the creeper toward what seemed to be the west of Mars, above which a small and pallid sun was descending through the dingy, burnt-out sky and casting a thin, chilly light athwart the desolate land.

The men were overpoweringly conscious of an intelligent determination behind all that was occurring; and the sense of this remote, unknowable supervision and control was stronger in Gaillard even than in the others. No one could doubt that every movement of the vessel was timed and predestined; and Gaillard felt that the slowness with which it followed the progress of the great stalk was calculated to give the scientific delegation ample opportunity for the study of their new environment; and, in particular, for observation of the growth itself.

In vain, however, did they watch their shifting milieu for aught that could denote the presence of organic forms of a human, non-human or preter-human type, such as might imaginably exist on Mars. Of course, only such entities, it was thought, could have built, despatched, and guided by some kind of automatic or radio control the vessel in which they were held captive.

The flier went on for at least an hour, traversing an immense territory in which, after many miles, the initial sandy desolation yielded place to a sort of swamp. Here, where sluggish waters webbed the marly soil, the winding creeper swelled to incredible proportions, with lush leaves that embowered the marshy ground for almost a mile on either side of the overlooming stalk.

Here, too, the foliage assumed a richer and more vivid greenness, fraught with sublime vital exuberance; and the stem itself displayed an indescribable succulence, together with a shining and glossy luster, a bloom that was weirdly and incongruously suggestive of well-nourished flesh. The thing seemed to palpitate at regular and rhythmic intervals beneath the eyes of the observers, like a living entity; and in places there were queerly shaped nodes or attachments on the stem, whose purpose no one could imagine.

Gaillard called the attention of Stilton to the strange throbbing that was noticeable in the plant; a throbbing which seemed to communicate itself even to the hundred-foot leaves, so that they trembled like plumes.

"Humph!" said Stilton, shaking his head with an air of mingled disbelief and disgust. "That palpitation is altogether impossible. There must be something wrong with our eyes—some disturbance of focus brought on by the velocity of our voyage, perhaps. Either that, or there is some peculiar refractive quality in the atmosphere, which gives the appearance of movement to stable objects."

Gaillard refrained from calling his attention to the fact that this imputed phenomenon of visual disorder or aerial refraction was confined in its application entirely to the plant and did not extend its range to the bordering landscape.

Soon after this, the vessel came to an enormous branching of the plant; and the earth-men discovered that the stalk they had been following was merely one of three that ramified from a vaster stem to intersect the boggy soil at widely divergent angles and vanish athwart opposing horizons. The junction was marked by a mountainous double node that bore a bizarre likeness to human hips. Here the throbbing was stronger and more perceptible than ever; and odd veinings and mottlings of a reddish color were visible on the pale surface of the stem.

The savants became more and more excited by the unexampled magnitude and singular characteristics of this remarkable growth. But revelations of a still more extraordinary nature were in store. After poising a moment above the monstrous joint, the vessel flew on at a higher elevation with increased speed, along the main stem, which extended for an incalculable distance into the occident of Mars, revealing fresh ramifications at variable intervals, and growing ever larger and more luxuriant as it penetrated marshy regions which were doubtless the residual ooze of a sunken sea.

"My God! the thing must surround the entire planet," said one of the reporters in an awed voice.

"It looks that way," Gaillard assented gravely. "We must be travelling almost in a line with the equator; and we have already followed the plant for hundreds of miles. From what we have seen, it would seem that the Martian 'canals' are merely its branchings; and perhaps the areas mapped as 'seas' by astronomers are masses of its foliage."

"I can't understand it," grumbled Stilton. "The dammed thing is utterly contrary to science, and against nature—it oughtn't to exist in any rational or conceivable cosmos."

"Well," said Gaillard, a little tartly, "it does exist; and I don't see how you are going to get away from it. Apparently, too, it is the only vegetable form on the planet; at least, so far, we have failed to find anything else of the sort. After all, why shouldn't the floral life of Mars be concentrated in a single type? And why shouldn't there be just one example of that type? It shows a marvellous economy on the part of nature. There is no reason at all for assuming that the vegetable or even the animal kingdoms on other worlds would exhibit the same fission and multiplicity that are shown on earth."

Stilton, as he listened to this unorthodox argument, glared at Gaillard like a Mohammedan at some errant infidel, but was either too angry or too disgusted for further speech.

The attention of the scientists was now drawn to a greenish area along the line of their flight, covering many square miles. Here, they saw that the main stem had put out a multitude of tendrils, whose foliage hid the underlying soil like a thick forest. Even as Gaillard had postulated, the origin of the sea-like areas on Mars was now explained.

Forty or fifty miles beyond this mass of foliation, they came to another that was even more extensive. The vessel soared to a great height, and they looked down on the realm-wide expanse of leafage. In its middle they discerned a circular node, leagues in extent, and rising like a rounded alp, from which emanated in all directions the planet-circling stems of the weird growth. Not only the size, but also certain features of the immense node, were provocative of utter dumbfoundment in the beholders. It was like the head of some gargantuan cuttlefish; and the stalks that ran away on all sides were suggestive of tentacles. And, strangest of all, the men descried in the center of the head two enormous masses, clear and lucent like water, which combined the size of lakes with the form and appearance of optic organs!

The whole plant palpitated like a breathing bosom; and the awe with which the involuntary explorers surveyed it was incommunicable by human words. All were compelled to recognize that even aside from its unparalleled proportions and habit of growth, the thing was in no sense alliable with any mundane botanic genera. And to Gaillard, as well as to others, the thought occurred that it was a sentient organism, and that the throbbing mass on which they now gazed was the brain or central ganglion of its unknown nervous system. The vast eyes, holding the sunlight like colossal dew-drops, seemed to return their scrutiny with an unreadable and superhuman intelligence; and Gaillard was obsessed by the feeling that preternatural knowledge and wisdom bordering upon omniscience were hidden in those hyaline depths.

The vessel began to descend, and settled vertically down in a sort of valley close to the mountainous head, where the foliation of two departing stems had left a patch of clear land. It was like a forest glade, with impenetrable woods on three sides, and a high crag on the fourth. Here, for the first time during the experience of its occupants, the flier came to rest on the soil of Mars; floating gently down without jar or vibration; and almost immediately after its landing, the valves of the main port unfolded, and the metal stairway descended to the ground, in obvious readiness to disembark the human passengers.

One by one, some with caution and timidity, others with adventuresome eagerness, the men filed out of the vessel and started to inspect their surroundings. They found that the Martian air differed little if at all from that which they had been breathing in the space-flier; and at that hour, with the sun still pouring into the strange valley from the west, the temperature was moderately warm.

It was an outré and fantastic scene; and the details were unlike those of any tellurian landscape. Underfoot was a soft, resilient soil, like a moist loess, wholly devoid of grass, lichens, fungi or any minor plant-forms. The foliage of the mammoth vine, with horizontal fronds of a baroque type, feathery and voluminous, hung about the glade to an altitudinous height like that of ancient evergreens, and quivered in the windless air with the pulsation of the stems.

Close at hand there rose the vast, flesh-colored wall of the central plant-head, which sloped upward like a hill toward the hidden eyes and was no doubt deeply embedded and rooted in the Martian soil. Stepping close to the living mass, the earth-men saw that its surface was netted with millions of wrinkle-like reticulations, and was filled with great pores resembling those of animal skin beneath some extra-powerful microscope. They conducted their inspection in an awe-struck silence; and for some time no one felt able to voice the extraordinary conclusions to which most of them had now been driven.

The emotions of Gaillard were almost religious as he contemplated the scarce-imaginable amplitude of this ultra-terrene life-form, which seemed to him to exhibit attributes nearer to those of divinity than he had found in any other manifestation of the vital principle.

In it, he saw the combined apotheosis of the animal and the vegetable. The thing was so perfect and complete and all-sufficing, so independent of lesser life in its world-enmeshing growth. It poured forth the sense of aeonian longevity, perhaps of immortality. And to what arcanic and cosmic consciousness might it not have attained during the cycles of its development! What super-normal senses and faculties might it not possess! What powers and potentialities beyond the achievement of more limited, more finite forms!

In a lesser degree, many of his companions were aware of similar feelings. Almost, in the presence of this portentous and sublime anomaly, they forgot the unsolved enigma of the space-vessel and their voyage across the heretofore unbridged immensities. But Stilton and his brother-conservatives were highly scandalized by the inexplicable nature of it all; and if they had been religiously minded, they would have expressed their sense of violation and outrage by saying that the monstrous plant, as well as the unexampled events in which they had taken an unwilling part, were tainted with the most grievous heresy and flagrant blasphemy.

Gresham, who had been eyeing his surroundings with a pompous and puzzled solemnity, was the first to break the silence.

"I wonder where the local Government hangs out?" he queried. "Who the hell is in power here anyway? Hey, Mr. Gaillard, you astronomers know a lot about Mars. Ain't there a U. S. Consulate somewhere in this god-forsaken hole?"

Gaillard was compelled to inform him that there was no consular service on Mars; and also that the form of government on that planet, as well as its official location, was still an open problem.

"However," he went on, "I shouldn't be surprised to learn that we are now in the presence of the sole and supreme ruler of the Martian realms."

"Huh! I don't see anyone." grunted Gresham with a troubled frown, as he surveyed the quivering masses of foliage and the alp-like head of the great plant. The import of Gaillard's observation was too far beyond his intellectual orbit.

Gaillard had been inspecting the flesh-tinted wall of the head with supreme and fascinated interest. At some distance, to one side, he perceived certain peculiar outgrowths, either shrunken or vestigial, like drooping and flaccid horns. They were large as a man's body, and might at some time have been much larger. It seemed as if the plant had put them forth for some unknown purpose, and had allowed them to wither when the purpose had been accomplished. They still retained an uncanny suggestion of semi-human parts and members, of strange appendages, half arms and half tentacles, as if they had been modelled from some exemplar of undiscovered Martian animal life.

Just below them, on the ground, Gaillard noticed a litter of queer metallic tools, with rough sheets and formless ingots of the same coppery material from which the space-flier had been constructed.

Somehow, the spot suggested an abandoned ship-yard; though there were no scaffoldings such as would ordinarily be used in the building of a vessel. An odd inkling of the truth arose in Gaillard's mind as he surveyed the metal remnants, but he was too thoroughly bemused and overawed by the wonder of all that had occurred, as well as by all he had ascertained or surmised, to communicate his inferences to the other savants.

In the meanwhile the entire party had been wandering about the glade, which comprised an area of several hundred yards. One of the astronomers, Philip Colton, who had made a side-line of botany, was examining the serried foliage of the super-gigantic creepers with a mingling of utmost interest and perplexity. The fronds or branches were lined with pinnate needles covered by a long, silky pubescence; and each of these needles was four feet in length by three or four inches in thickness, possibly with a hollow and tubular structure. The fronds grew in level array from the main creeper, filling the air like a horizontal forest, and reaching to the very ground in close, imbricated order.

Colton took a jack-knife from his pocket and tried to cut a section from one of the pinnate leaves. At the first touch of the keen blade, the whole frond recoiled violently beyond his reach; and then swinging back, it dealt him a tremendous blow which stretched him on the ground and hurled the knife from his fingers to a considerable distance.

If it had not been for the lesser gravity of Mars, he would have been severely injured by the fall. As it was, he lay bruised and breathless, staring with ludicrous surprise at the great frond, which had resumed its former position among its fellows, and now displayed no other movement than the singular trembling due to the rhythmic palpitation of the stem to which it was attached.

Colton's discomfiture had been noticed by his confreres; and all at once, as if their tongues had been loosed by this happening, a babel of discussion arose among them. It was no longer possible for anyone to doubt the animate or half-animate nature of the growth; and even the outraged and ireful Stilton, who considered that the most sacred laws of scientific probity were being violated, was driven to concede the presence of a biologic riddle not to be explained in terms of orthodox morphology.

Gaillard, who did not care to take any great part in this discussion, preferring his own thoughts and conjectures, continued to watch the throbbing growth. He stood a little apart from the others, and nearer than they to the fleshy and multiporous slope of the huge head; and all at once, as he watched, he saw the sprouting of what appeared to be a new tendril from the surface, at a distance of about four feet above the ground.

The thing grew like something in a slow moving-picture, lengthening out and swelling visibly, with a bulbous knob at the end. This knob soon became a large, faintly convoluted mass, whose outlines puzzled and tantalized Gaillard with their intimation of something he had once seen but could not now remember. There was a bizarre hint of nascent limbs and members, which soon become more definite; and then, with a sort of shock, he saw that the thing resembled a human foetus!

His involuntary exclamation of amazement drew others; and soon the whole delegation was grouped about him, watching the incredible development of the new growth with bated breath. The thing had put forth two well-formed legs, which now rested on the ground, supporting with their five-toed feet the upright body, on which the human head and arms were fully evolved, though they had not yet attained adult size.

The process continued; and simultaneously, a sort of woolly floss began to appear around the trunk, arms and legs, like the rapid spinning of some enormous cocoon. The hands and neck were bare; but the feet were covered with a different material, which took on the appearance of green leather. When the floss thickened and darkened to an iron-grey, and assumed quite modish outlines, it became obvious that the figure was being clothed in garments such as were worn by the earth-men, probably in deference to human ideas of modesty.

The thing was unbelievable; and stranger and more incredible than all else was the resemblance which Gaillard and his companions began to note in the face of the still growing figure. Gaillard felt as if he were looking into a mirror; for in all essential details the face was his own! The garments and shoes were faithful replicas of those worn by himself; and every limb and part of this outré being, even to the fingertips, was proportioned like his!

The scientists saw that the process of growth was apparently complete. The figure stood with shut eyes and a somewhat blank and expressionless look on its features, like that of a man who has not yet awakened from slumber. It was still attached by a thick tendril to the breathing, mountainous node; and this tendril issued from the base of the brain, like an oddly misplaced umbilical cord.

The figure opened its eyes and stared at Gaillard with a long, level, enigmatic gaze that deepened his sense of shock and stupefaction. He sustained this gaze with the weirdest feeling imaginable—the feeling that he was confronted by his alter ego, by a *doppelganger* in which was also the soul or intellect of some alien and vaster entity. In the regard of the cryptic eyes, he felt the same profound and sublime mystery that had looked out from the lake-sized orbs of shining dew or crystal in the plant-head.

The figure raised its right hand and seemed to beckon to him. Gaillard went slowly forward till he and his miraculous double stood face to face. Then the strange being placed its hand on his brow; and it seemed to Gaillard that a mesmeric spell was laid upon him from that moment. Almost without his own volition, for a purpose he was not yet permitted to understand, he began to speak; and the figure, imitating his every tone and cadence, repeated the words after him.

It was not till many minutes had elapsed, that Gaillard realized the true bearing and significance of this remarkable colloquy. Then, with a start of clear consciousness, he knew that he was giving the figure lessons in the English language! He was pouring forth in a fluent, uninterrupted flood the main vocabulary of the tongue, together with its grammatical rules. And somehow, by a miracle of super-intellect, all that he said was being comprehended and remembered by his interlocutor.

Hours must have gone by during this process; and the Martian sun was now dipping toward the serrate walls of foliage. Dazed and exhausted, Gaillard realized that the long lesson was over; for the being removed its hand from his brow and addressed him in scholarly, well-modulated English:

"Thank you. I have learned all that I need to know for the purposes of linguistic communication. If you and your confreres will now attend me, I shall explain all that has mystified you, and declare the reasons for which you have been brought from your own world to the shores of a foreign planet."

Like men in a dream, barely crediting the fantastic evidence of their senses and yet unable to refute or repudiate it, the earth-men listened while Gaillard's amazing double continued:

"The being through whom I speak, made in the likeness of one of your own party, is a mere special organ which I have developed so that I could communicate with you. I, the informing entity, who combine in myself the utmost genius and energy of those two divisions of life which are known to you as the plant and the animal—I, who possess the virtual omniety and immortality of a god, have had no need of articulate speech or formal language at any previous time in my existence. But since I include in myself all potentialities of evolution, together with mental powers that verge upon omniscience, I have had no difficulty whatever in acquiring this new faculty.

"It was I who constructed, with other special organs that I had put forth for this purpose, the space-flier that descended upon your planet and then returned to me a delegation, most of whom, I have surmised, would represent the scientific fraternities of mankind. The building of the flier, and its mode of control, will be made plain when I tell you that I am the master of many cosmic forces beyond the rays and energies known to tellurian savants. These forces I can draw from the air, the soil or the ether at will, or can even summon from remote stars and nebulae.

"The space-vessel was wrought from metal which I had integrated from molecules floating at random through the atmosphere; and I used the solar rays in concentrated form to create the temperature at which these metals were fused into a single sheet. The power used in propelling and guiding the vessel is a sort of super-electric energy whose exact nature I shall not elucidate, other than to say that it is associated with the basic force of gravity, and also with certain radiant properties of the interstellar ether not detectible by any instruments which you possess. I established in the flier the gravitation of Mars, and supplied it with Martian air and water, and also with chemically created food-stuffs, in order to accustom you during your voyage to the conditions that prevail on Mars.

"I am, as you may have already surmised, the sole inhabitant of this world. I could multiply myself if necessary; but so far, for reasons which you will soon apprehend, I have not felt that this would be desirable. Being complete and perfect in myself, I have had no need of companionship with other entities; and long ago, for my own comfort and security, I was compelled to extirpate certain rival plant-forms, and also certain animals who resembled slightly the mankind of your world; and who, in the course of their evolution, were becoming troublesome and even dangerous to me.

"With my two great eyes, which possess an optic magnifying power beyond that of your strongest telescopes, I have studied Earth and the other planets during the Martian nights, and have learned much regarding the conditions that exist upon each. The life of your world, your history, and the state of your civilization have been in many ways an open book to me; and I have also formed an accurate idea of the geological, faunal and floral phenomena of your globe. I understand your imperfections, your social injustice and maladjustment, and the manifold disease and misery to which you are liable, owing to the dissonant, multiple entities into which the expression of your life-principle has been subdivided.

"From all such evils and error, I am exempt. I have attained to well-nigh absolute knowledge and masterdom; and there is no longer anything in the universe for me to fear, aside from the inevitable process of dehydration and dessication which Mars is slowly undergoing, like all other aging planets.

"This process I am unable to retard, except in a limited and partial manner; and I have already been compelled to tap the artesian waters of the planet in many places. I could live upon sunlight and air alone; but water is necessary to maintain the alimental properties of the atmosphere; and without it, my immortality would fail in the course of time; my giant stems would shrink and shrivel; and my vast, innumerable leaves would grow sere for want of the vital humor.

"Your world is still young, with superabundant seas and streams and a moisture-laden air. You have more than is requisite of the element which I lack; and I have brought you here, as representative members of mankind, to propose an exchange which cannot be anything but beneficial to you as well as to myself.

"In return for a modicum of the water of your world, I will offer you the secrets of eternal life and infinite energy, and will teach you to overcome your social imperfections and to master wholly your planetary environment. Because of my great size, my stems and tendrils which girdle the Martian equator and reach even to the poles, it would be impossible for me to leave my natal world; but I will teach you how to colonize the other planets and explore the universe beyond. For these various ends, I suggest the making of an intermundane treaty and a permanent alliance between myself and the peoples of Earth.

"Consider well what I offer you; for the opportunity is without example or parallel. In relation to men, I am like a god in comparison with insects. The benefits which I can confer upon you are inestimable; and in return I ask only that you establish on Earth, under my instruction, certain transmitting stations using a super-potent wavelength, by means of which the essential elements of sea-water, minus the undesirable saline properties, can be teleported to Mars. The amount thus abstracted will make little or no difference in your tide-levels or in the humidity of your air; but for me, it will mean an assurance of everlasting life."

The figure ended its peroration, and stood regarding the earth-men in polite and somewhat inscrutable silence, while it waited for their answer.

As might have been expected, the emotions with which the delegation-members had heard this singular address were far from unanimous in their tenor. All the men were beyond mere surprise or astonishment, for miracle had been piled upon miracle till their brains were benumbed with wonder; and they had reached the point where they took the creation of a human figure and its endowment with human utterance wholly for granted. But the proposal made by the plant-entity through its man-like organ was another matter; and it played up-on varying chords in the minds of the scientists, the reporters, the Mayor, and the Chief of Police.

Gaillard, who felt himself wholly in accord with this proposition, and more and more thoroughly *en rapport* with the Martian entity, wished to accede at once and to pledge his own support and that of his fellows to a furthering of the suggested treaty and plan of exchange. He was forced to point out to the Martian that the delegation, even if single-minded in its consent, was not empowered to represent the peoples of Earth in forming the projected alliance; that the most it could do would be to lay the offer before the Government of the U.S. and of other terrestrial realms.

Half the scientists, after some deliberation, announced themselves as being in favor of the plan and willing to promote it to the utmost of their ability. The three reporters were also willing to do the same; and they promised, perhaps rashly, that the influence of the world-press would be added to that of the renowned savants.

Stilton and the other dogmatists of the party, however, were em-phatically and even rabidly opposed, and declined to consider the Mar-tian's offer for an instant. Any treaty or alliance of the sort, they maintained, would be highly undesirable and improper. It would never do for the nations of Earth to involve themselves in an entanglement of such questionable nature, or to hold commerce of any sort with a being such as the plant-monster, which had no rightful biologic status. It was unthinkable that orthodox and sound-minded scientists should lend their advocacy to anything so dubious. They felt too that there was a savor of deception and trickery about the whole business; and at any rate it was too irregular to be countenanced, or even to be consid-ered with anything but reprehension.

The schism among the savants was rendered final by a hot argu-ment, in which Stilton roundly denounced Gaillard and the other pro-Martians as virtual traitors to humanity, and intellectual Bolshevists whose ideas were dangerous to the integrity of human thought. Gresham and Polson were on the side of mental law and order, being professionally conservative; and thus the party was about evenly divided between those who favored accepting the Martian's offer, and those who spurned it with more or less suspicion and indignation.

During the course of this vehement dispute, the sun had fallen behind the high ramparts of foliage, and an icy chill, such as might well be looked for in a semi-desolate world with attenuating air, had already touched the pale rose twilight. The scientists began to shiver; and their thoughts were distracted from the problem they had been debating by the physical discomfort of which they were increasingly conscious.

They heard the voice of the strange manikin in the dusk:

"I can offer you a choice of shelters for the night and also for the duration of your stay on Mars. You will find the space-flier well-lighted and warmed, with all the facilities which you may require. Also, I can offer you another hospitality. Look beneath my foliage, a little to your right, where I am now preparing a shelter no less commodious and comfortable than the vessel—a shelter which will help to give you an idea of my varied powers and potentialities."

The earth-men saw that the flier was brilliantly illuminated, pouring out a gorgeous amethystine radiance from its violet ports. Then, beneath the foliage close at hand, they perceived another and stranger luminosity which seemed to be emitted, like some sort of radio-active or noctilucent glow, by the great leaves themselves.

Even where they were standing, they felt a balmy warmth that began to temper the frigid air; and stepping toward the source of these phenomena, they found that the crowded leaves had lifted and arched themselves into a roomy alcove. The ground beneath was lined with a fabric-like substance of soft hues, deep and elastic underfoot, like a fine mattress. Ewers filled with liquids and platters of food-stuffs were disposed on low tables; and the air in the alcove was gentle as that of the spring night in a subtropic land.

Gaillard and the other pro-Martians, filled with profound awe and wonder, were ready to avail themselves at once of the shelter of this thaumaturgic hostelry. But the anti-Martians would have none of it, regarding it as the workmanship of the devil. Suffering keenly from the cold, with chattering teeth and shivering limbs, they promenaded the open glade for some time, and at last were driven to seek the hospitable port of the space-flier, thinking it the lesser of two evils by some queer twist of logic.

The others, after eating and drinking from the mysteriously provided tables, laid themselves down on the mattress-like fabrics. They found themselves greatly refreshed by the liquid in the ewers, which was not water but some kind of roseate, aromatic wine. The food, a literal manna, was more agreeably flavored than that of which they had partaken during their voyage in the space-vessel. In the nerve-wrought and highly excited state that was consequent upon their experiences, none of them had expected to sleep. The unfamiliar air, the altered gravity, the unknown radiations of the exotic soil, as well as their unprecedented journey and the miraculous discoveries and revelations of the day, were all profoundly upsetting and conducive to a severe disequilibration of mind and body.

However, Gaillard and his companions fell into a deep and dreamless slumber as soon as they had laid themselves down. Perhaps the liquid and solid refreshments which they had taken many have conduced to this; or perhaps there was some narcotic or mesmeric influence in the air, falling from the vast leaves or proceeding from the brain of the plant-lord.

The anti-Martians did not fare so well in this respect, and their slumber was restless and broken. Most of them had touched the proffered viands in the space-flier very sparingly; and Stilton, in particular, had refused to eat or drink at all. Doubtless, too, their antagonistic frame of mind was such as to make them more resistant to the hypnotic power of the plant, if such were being exerted. At any rate, they did not share in the benefits conferred upon the others.

A little before dawn, when Mars was still shrouded in crepuscular gloom but slightly lightened by the two small moons Phobos and Deimos, Stilton arose from the soft couch on which he had tossed in night-long torment, and began to experiment once more, undeterred by his previous failure and discomfiture, with the mechanical controls of the vessel.

To his surprise, he found that the odd-shaped keys were no longer resistant to his fingers. He could move and arrange them at will; and he soon discovered the principle of their working and was able to levitate and steer the flier.

His confreres had now joined him, summoned by his shout of triumph. All were wide-awake, and jubilant with the wild hope of escaping from Mars and the jurisdiction of the plant-monster. Thrilling with this hope, and fearing every moment that the Martian would re-assert its esoteric control of the mechanism, they rose unhindered from the darkling glade to the alien skies and headed toward the brilliant green orb of Earth, descried among the unfamiliar constellations.

Looking back, they saw the vast eyes of the Martian watching them weirdly from the gloom, like pools of clear and bluish phosphorescence; and they shuddered with the dread of being recalled and re-captured. But, for some inscrutable reason, they were permitted to maintain their earthward course without interference. However, the voyage was fraught with a certain amount of disaster; and Stilton's clumsy pilotage hardly formed an ample substitute for the half-divine knowledge and skill of the Martian. More than once, the vessel collided with meteors; none of which, fortunately, were heavy enough to penetrate its hull. And when, after many hours, they approached the earth, Stilton failed to secure the proper degree of deceleration. The flier fell with terrible precipitancy and was saved from destruction only by dropping into the South Atlantic. The jarred mechanism was rendered unworkable by the fall, and most of the occupants were severely bruised and stunned.

After floating at random for days, the coppery bulk was sighted by a northward-going liner and was towed to port in Lisbon. Here the scientists abandoned it, and made their way back to America, after detailing their adventures to representatives of the world-press, and issuing a solemn warning to all the world-peoples against the subversive designs and infamous proposals of the ultra-planetary monster.

The sensation created by their return and by the news they brought was tremendous. A tide of profound alarm and panic, due in part to the immemorial human aversion toward the unknown, swept immediately upon the nations; and immense, formless, exaggerated fears were bred like shadowy hydras in the dark minds of men.

Stilton and his fellow-conservatives continued to foster these fears, and to create with their pronouncements a globe-wide wave of anti-Martian prejudice, of blind opposition and dogmatic animosity. They enlisted on their side as many of the scientific fraternity as they could; that is to say, all those who were minded like themselves, as well as others overawed or subdued by the pressure of authority. They sought also, with much success, to marshal the political powers of the world in a strong league that would ensure the repudiation of any further offers of alliance from the Martian.

In all this gathering of inimical forces, this regimenting of earthly conservation and insularity and ignorance, the religious factor, as was inevitable, soon asserted itself. The claim to divine knowledge and power made by the Martian, was seized upon by all the various mundane hierarchies, by Christian and Muhammadan, by Buddhist and Parsee and Voodoist alike, as forming a supremely heinous blasphemy. The impiety of such claims, and the menace of a non-anthropomorphic god and type of worship that might be introduced on earth, could not be tolerated for a moment. Khalif and Pope, lama and imaum, parson and mahatma, all made common cause against this ultra-terrestrial invader.

Also, the reigning political powers felt that there might be something Bolshevistic behind the offer of the Martian to promote an Utopian state of society on earth. And the financial, commercial, and man-ufacturing interests likewise thought that it might imply a threat to their welfare or stability. In short, every branch of human life and ac-tivity was well-represented in the anti-Martian movement.

In the interim, on Mars, Gaillard and his companions had awak-ened from their sleep to find that the luminous glow of the arching leaves had given place to the ardent gold of morn. They discovered that they could venture forth with comfort from the alcove; for the air of the glade without had grown swiftly warm beneath the rising sun.

Even before they had noticed the absence of the coppery flier, they were apprised of its departure by the man-organ of the great plant. This being, unlike its human prototypes, was exempt from fatigue; and it had remained standing or reclining all night against the fleshy wall to which it was attached. It now addressed the earth-men thus:

"For reasons of my own, I have made no attempt to prevent the flight of your companions, who, with their blindly hostile attitude, would be worse than useless to me, and whose presence could only hinder the rapport which should exist between you and myself. They will reach the earth, and will try to warn its peoples against me and to poison their minds against my benefic offer. Such an outcome, alas, cannot be avoided, even if I were to bring them back to Mars or divert their flight by means of my control and send them speeding forever through the void beyond the worlds. I perceive that there is much ignorance and dogmatism and blind self-interest to be overcome, before the ex-celling light which I proffer can illumine the darkness of earthly minds.

"After I have kept you here for a few days, and have instructed you thoroughly in the secrets of my transcendent wisdom, and have imbued you with surprising powers that will serve to demonstrate my omnivalent superiority to the nations of Earth, I shall send you back to Earth as my ambassadors; and though you will meet with much oppo-sition from your fellows, my cause will prevail in the end, beneath the infallible support of truth and science."

Gaillard and the others received this communication as well as the many that followed it, with supreme respect and semi-religious reverence. More and more they became convinced that they stood in the presence of a higher and ampler entity than man; that the intellect which thus discoursed to them through the medium of a human form was well-nigh inexhaustible in its range and depth, and possessed many characteristics of infinitude and more than one attribute of deity.

Agnostic though most of them were by nature or training, they began to accord a certain worship to this amazing plant-lord; and they listened with an attitude of complete submission if not of abjection, to the outpourings of cycle-gathered lore, the immortal secrets of cosmic law and life and energy, in which the great being proceeded to instruct them.

The illumination thus accorded them was both simple and esoteric. The plant-lord began by dwelling at some length upon the monistic nature of all phenomena, of matter, light, color, sound, electricity, gravity, and all other forms of irradiation, as well as time and space; which, it said, were only the various perceptual manifestations of a single underlying principle or substance.

The listeners were then taught the evocation and control, by quite rudimentary chemical media, of many forces and rates of energy that had hitherto lain beyond the detection of human senses or instruments. They were taught also the terrific power obtainable by refracting with certain sensitized elements the ultraviolet and infra-red rays of the spectrum; which, in a highly concentrated form, could be used for the disintegration and rebuilding of the molecules of matter.

They learned how to make engines that emitted beams of destruction and transmutation; and how to employ these unknown beams, more potent even than the so-called "cosmic rays," in the renewal of human tissues and the conquest of disease and old age.

Simultaneously with this tuition, the plant-lord carried on the building of a new space-car, in which the earth-men were to return to their own planet and preach the Martian evangel. The construction of this car, whose plates and girders seemed to materialize out of the void air before their very gaze, was a practical lesson in the use of arcanic natural forces. Atoms that would form the requisite alloys were brought together from space by the play of invisible magnetic beams, were fused by concentrated solar heat in a specially refractive zone of atmosphere, and were then moulded into the desired form as readily as the bottle that shapes itself from the pipe of the glass-blower.

Equipped with this new knowledge and potential masterdom, with a cargo of astounding mechanisms and devices made for their use by the plant-lord, the pro-Martians finally embarked on their earthward voyage.

A week after the abduction of the thirty-five earth-men from the stadium at Berkeley, the space-car containing the Martian's proselytes landed at noon in this same stadium. Beneath the infinitely skillful and easy control of the far-off plant-being, it came down without accident, lightly as a bird; and as soon as the news of its arrival had spread, it was surrounded by a great throng, in which the motives of hostility and curiosity were almost equally paramount.

Through the denunciation of the dogmatists led by Stilton, the sa-vants and the three reporters beneath the leadership of Gaillard had been internationally outlawed before their arrival. It was expected that they would return sooner or later through the machinations of the plant-lord; and a special ruling that forbade them to land on terrene soil, under penalty of imprisonment, had been made by all the Gov-ernments.

Ignorant of this, and ignorant also of how wide-spread and viru-lent was the prejudice against them, they opened the vessel's port and stood in readiness to emerge.

Gaillard, going first, paused at the head of the metal stairway, and something seemed to arrest him as he looked down on the milling fac-es of the mob that had gathered with incredible swiftness. He saw en-mity, fear, hatred, suspicion, in many of these faces; and in others a gaping and zany-like inquisitiveness, such as might be shown before the freaks of some travelling circus. A small corps of policemen, elbowing and thrusting the rabble aside with officious rudeness, was pushing toward the front; and cries of derision and hatred, gathering by two and threes and uniting to a rough roar, were now hurled at the occupants of the car.

"Damn the pro-Martians! Down with the dirty traitors! Hang the — — — dogs!"

An overripe tomato, large and dripping, sailed toward Gaillard and splashed on the steps at his feet. Hisses and hoots and cat-calls added to the roaring bedlam; but above it all, he and his comrades heard a quiet voice that spoke within the car; the voice of the Martian, borne across inestimable miles of ether:

"Beware, and defer your landing. Resign yourselves to my guidance, and all will be well."

Gaillard stepped back as he heard this minatory voice, and the valvular port closed quickly behind the folded stairs, just as the policemen who had come to arrest the vessel's occupants broke from the forefront of the throng.

Peering out on those hateful faces, Gaillard and his brother-savants beheld an astounding manifestation of the Martian's power. A wall of violet flame, descending from the remote heavens to the ground, seemed to intervene between the car and the crowd; and the policemen, bruised and breathless but uninjured, were hurled backward as if by a great wave. This flame, whose color changed to blue and green and yellow and scarlet like a sort of aurora, played for hours about the vessel and rendered it impossible for anyone to approach. Retreating to a respectful distance, awe-struck and terrified, the crowd looked on in silence; and the police waited in vain for a chance to fulfill their commission. After awhile, the flame became white and misty, and upon it, as upon the bosom of a cloud, a bizarre and mirage-like scene was imprinted, visible alike to the occupants of the car and to the throng without. This scene was the Martian landscape in which the central brain of the plant-lord was located; and the crowd gasped with astonishment as it met the gaze of the enormous telescopic eyes, and saw the unending stems and league-wide masses of sempervirent foliage.

Other scenes and demonstrations followed, all of which were calculated to impress upon the throng the wonder-working powers and marvellous faculties of this remote being.

Pictures that illustrated the historic life of the Martian, as well as the various arcanic natural energies subject to its dominion, followed each other in rapid succession. The purpose of the desired alliance with Earth, and the benefits which would accrue thereby to humanity, were also depicted. The divine benignity and wisdom of this puissant being, its superior organic nature, and its vital and sciential supremacy, were made plain to the dullest observer.

Many of those who had come to scoff, or had been prepared to receive the pro-Martians and their evangel with scorn and hate and violence, became converted to the alien cause forthwith by these sublime demonstrations.

However, the more dogmatic scientists, the true "die-hards" as represented by Godfrey Stilton, maintained an adamantine obstructionism, in which they were supported by the officers of law and government, as well as by the presbyters of the various religions. The world-wide dissidence of opinion which soon resulted, became the cause of many civil wars or revolutions, and, in one or two cases, ended in actual warfare between nations.

Numerous efforts were made to apprehend or destroy the Martian space-car, which, beneath the guidance of its ultra-planetary master, appeared in many localities all over the world, descending suddenly from the stratosphere to perform incredible scientific miracles before the eyes of astonished multitudes. In all quarters of the globe, the mirage-like pictures were flashed on the screen of cloudy fire, and more and more people went over to the new cause.

Bombing planes pursued the vessel and sought to drop their dead-ly freight upon it, but without success; for whenever the car was en-dangered, the auroral flames intervened, deflecting and hurling back the exploded bombs, often to the detriment of their launchers.

Gaillard and his confreres, with leonine boldness, emerged many times from the car, to display before crowds or selected bodies of sa-vants the marvellous inventions and chemical thaumaturgies with which they had been endowed by the Martian. Everywhere the police sought to arrest them, maddened mobs endeavored to do them violence, armed regiments tried to surround them and cut them off from the car. But with an adroitness that seemed no less than supernatural, they con-trived always to elude capture; and often they discomfited their pursu-ers by astonishing displays or evocations of esoteric force, temporarily paralyzing the civic officers with unseen rays, or creating about them-selves a defensive zone of intolerable heat or trans-arctic cold.

In spite of all these myriad demonstrations, however, the citadels of human ignorance and insularity remained impregnable in many places. Deeply alarmed by this ultra-terrene menace to their stability, the governments and religions of Earth, as well as the more conserva-tive scientific elements, rallied their resources in a most heroic and de-termined effort to stem the incursion. Men of all ages, everywhere, were conscripted for service in the national armies; and even women and children were equipped with the deadliest weapons of the age for use against the pro-Martians, who, with their wives and families, were classed as infamous renegades to be hunted down and killed without ceremony like dangerous beasts.

The internecine warfare that ensued was the most terrible in hu-man history. Class became divided against class and family against fam-ily. New and more lethal gases than any heretofore employed, were devised by chemists, and whole cities or territories were smothered beneath their agonizing pall. Others were blown into skyward-flying fragments by single charges of super-potent explosives; and war was carried on by planes, by rocket-ships, by submarine, by dreadnaughts, by tanks, by every vehicle and engine of death or destruction that the homicidal ingenuity of man had yet created.

The pro-Martians, who had won several victories at first, were now gravely outnumbered; and the tide of battle began to turn against them. Scattered in many lands, they found themselves unable to unite and organize their forces to the same degree as those of their official opponents. Though Gaillard and his devoted confreres went everywhere in the space-vessel, aiding and abetting the radicals, and instructing them in the use of new weapons and cosmic energies, the party suffered great reverses through the sheer brute preponderance of its foes. More and more it became split up into small bands, hunted and harried, and driven to seek refuge in the wilder or less explored sections of the earth.

In North America, however, a large army of the scientific rebels, whose families had been compelled to join them, contrived to hold the antagonists at bay for awhile. Surrounded at last, and faced by overwhelming odds, this army was on the verge of a crushing defeat.

Gaillard, hovering above the black, voluminous clouds of the battle, in which poisonous gases mingled with the fumes of high explosives, felt for the first time the encroachment of actual despair. It seemed to him, and also to his companions, that the Martian had abandoned them, disgusted perhaps with the bestial horror of it all and the hateful, purblind narrowness and fanatic nescience of mankind.

Then, through the smoke-smothered air, a fleet of coppery-golden cars descended, to land on the battle-front among the Martian adherents. There were thousands of these cars; and from all the entrance-ports, which had opened simultaneously, there issued the voice of the plant-lord, summoning its supporters and bidding them enter the vessels.

Saved from annihilation by this act of Martian providence, the entire army obeyed the command; and as soon as the last man, woman and child had gone aboard, the ports closed again, and the fleet of space-cars, wheeling in graceful and derisive spirals above the heads of the baffled conservatives, soared from the battle-clouds like a flock of reddish-golden birds and vanished in the noontide heavens, led by the car containing Gaillard's party.

At the same time, in all portions of the world where the little bands of heroic radicals had been cut off and threatened with capture or destruction, other cars descended in like manner and carried away the pro-Martians and their families even to the last unit. These vessels joined the main fleet in mid-space; and then all continued their course beneath the mysterious piloting of the plant-lord, flying at super-cosmic velocity through the star-surrounded gulf.

Contrary to the anticipations of the mundane exiles, the vessels were not drawn toward Mars; and it soon became evident that their objective was the planet Venus. The voice of the Martian, speaking athwart the eternal ether, made the following announcement:

"In my infinite wisdom, my supreme foreprescience, I have re-moved you from the hopeless struggle to establish on Earth the sover-eign light and truth which I offer. You alone I have found worthy; and the moiety of mankind, who have refused salvation with hatred and contumely, preferring the natal darkness of death and disease and ig-norance in which they were born, must be left henceforward to their inevitable fate.

"You, as my loyal and well-trusted servants, I am sending forth to colonize beneath my tutelage a great continent on the planet Venus, and to found amid the primal exuberance of this new world a super-scientific nation."

The fleet soon approached Venus, and circled the equator for a great distance in the steam-thick atmosphere, through which nothing could be descried other than a hot and over-fuming ocean, close to the boiling-point, which seemed to cover the entire planet. Here, beneath the never-setting sun, intolerable temperatures prevailed everywhere, such as would have parboiled the flesh of a human being exposed directly to the semi-aqueous air. Suffering even in their insulated cars from this terrific heat, the exiles wondered how they were to exist in such a world.

At last, however, their destination came in view and their doubts were resolved. Nearing the nightward side of Venus which is never exposed to daylight, in a latitude where the sun slanted far behind them as over arctic realms, they beheld through thinning vapors an immense tract of land, the sole continent amid the planetary sea. This continent was covered by rich jungles, containing a flora and fauna similar to those of pre-glacial eras on the earth. Calamites and cycads and fern-plants of unbelievable luxuriance revealed themselves to the earth-men; and they saw everywhere the great, brainless reptiles, the megalosaurs, plesiosaurs, labyrinthodons and pterodactyls of Jurassic times.

Beneath the instruction of the Martian, before landing, they slew these reptiles, incinerating them completely with infra-red beams, so that not even their carcasses would remain to taint the air with putrefactive effluvia. When the whole continent had been cleared of its noxious life, the cars descended; and emerging, the colonists found themselves in a terrain of unequalled fertility, whose very soil seemed to pulsate with primordial vigors, and whose air was rich with ozone and oxygen and nitrogen.

Here the temperature, though still sub-tropic, was agreeable and balmy; and through the use of protective fabrics provided by the Martian, the earth-men soon accustomed themselves to the eternal sunlight and intense ultra-violet radiation. With the super-knowledge at their disposal, they were able to combat the unknown, highly pernicious bacteria peculiar to Venus, and even to exterminate such bacteria in the course of time. They became the lords of a salubrious climate, dowered with four mild and equable seasons by the slight annual rotation of the planet; but having one eternal day, like the mythic Isles of the Blest beneath a low and undeparting sun.

Beneath the leadership of Gaillard, who remained in close rapport and continual communication with the plant-lord, the great forests were cleared in many places. Cities of lofty and ethereal architecture, lovely as those of some trans-stellar Eden, builded by the use of force-beams, began to rear their graceful turrets and majestic cumuli of domes above the giant calamites and ferns.

Through the labors of the terrene exiles, a truly Utopian nation was established, giving allegiance to the plant-lord as to some tutelary deity; a nation devoted to cosmic progress, to scientific knowledge, to spiritual tolerance and freedom; a happy, law-abiding nation, blest with millennial longevity, and exempt from sorrow and disease and error.

Here, too, on the shores of the Venusian sea, were builded the great transmitters that sent through interplanetary space, in ceaseless waves of electronic radiation, the water required to replenish the dehydrated air and soil of Mars, and thus to ensure for the plant-being a perpetuity of god-like existence.

In the meanwhile, on earth, unknown to Gaillard and his fellow-exiles, who had made no effort to communicate with the abandoned world, an amazing thing had occurred; a final proof of the virtual omnipotence and all-inclusive sapience of the Martian.

In the great vale of Kashmeer, in Northern India, there descended one day from the clear heavens a mile-long seed, flashing like a huge meteor, and terrifying the superstitious Asian peoples, who saw in its fall the portent of some tremendous disaster. The seed rooted itself in this valley; and before its true nature had been ascertained, the supposed meteorite began to sprout and send forth on all sides a multitude of mammoth tendrils which burst immediately into leaf. It covered both the southward plains and the eternal snows and rock of the Hindu Kush and Himalayas with their gigantic verdure.

Soon the Afghan mountaineers could hear the explosion of its leaf-buds amid their passes, echoing like distant thunder; and, at the same time, it rushed like a Juggernaut upon Central India. Spreading in all directions, and growing with the speed of express-trains, the tendrils

of the mighty vine proceeded to enmesh the Asian realms. Overshadow-
ing vales, peaks, hills, plateaus, deserts, cities and sea-boards with its titan leaves, it invaded Europe and Africa; and then, bridging the Bering
Straits, it entered North America and ran southward, ramifying on all
sides till the whole continent, and also South America even to Tierra
de Fuego, had been buried beneath the masses of insuperable foliage.

Frantic efforts to stay the progress of the plant were made by armies with bombs and cannon, with lethal sprays and gases; but all in
vain. Everywhere humanity was smothered beneath the vast leaves,
like those of some omnipresent upas, which emitted a stupefying and
narcotic odor that conferred upon all who inhaled it a swift euthanasia.

Soon the plant had netted the whole globe; for the seas offered little or no barrier to its full-grown stems and tendrils. When the process
of growth was complete, the anti-Martian moiety of the human race
had joined the uncouth monsters of pre-historic time in that limbo of
oblivion to which all superseded and outdated genera have gone. But,
through the divine clemency of the plant-lord, the final death that
overtook the "die-hards" was no less easy than irresistible.

Stilton and a few of his associates contrived to evade the general
doom for awhile by fleeing in a rocket-ship to the Antarctic plateau.
Here, as they were congratulating themselves on their escape, they saw
far-off on the horizon the rearing of the swift stems, beneath whose
foliage the ice and snow appeared to melt away in rushing torrents.
These torrents soon became a diluvial sea, in which the last dogmatists
were drowned. Only in this way did they elude the euthanasia of the
great leaves, which had overtaken all their fellows.

THE SONG OF A COMET

Pale plummet of the stark immensities,
From perished heavens cast, I fall and flare
Through gulfs by stellar orbits girdled round;
And spaces bare
Of sparkless night between the galaxies—
By path of sun nor circling planet bound.
No star allots my lone and cyclic gyre;
I mark the systems vanish one by one;
Among the swarming worlds I lunge,
And sudden plunge
Close to the zones of solar fire;
Or 'mid the mighty wrack of stars undone,
Flash, and with momentary rays
Compel the dark to yield
Their aimless forms, whose once far-potent blaze
In ashes chill is now inurned.
Upon the shadowy heavens half-revealed,
I show their planets turned,
Whose strange ephemerae,
On adamantine tablets deeply written,
In cities long unlitten,
Have left their history
And lore beyond redemption or surmise.
Adown contiguous skies,
I pass the thickening brume
Of systems yet unshaped, that hang immense

Along mysterious shores of gloom;
Or see—unimplicated in their doom—
The final and disastrous gyre
Of blinded suns that meet,
And from their mingled heat
And battle-clouds intense,
Overspread the deeps with fire.

Upon the lion's track,
Or far beyond the abysms of the Lyre,
I thread, through mazes of the zodiac,
Mine orbit placed amid
The multiple and irised stars, or hid,
Unsolved and intricate,
In many a planet-swinging sun's estate.
At times I steal in solitary flight
Along the rim of the exterior night
That rounds the universe;
And then return,
Past outer footholds of sidereal light,
To see the systems gather and disperse;
And learn
What vast and multifarious marvels wait
In the dim void that has no ultimate;
What wraiths of suns extinguished long ago
On alien welkins burn;
What flaming blossoms grow
From the black battlefields of cosmic wars;
What stellar hells, or ampler spheres sublime,
Enisled in diverse time,
Are wrought from sharded moons and meteors;
And haply I discern

What paler fires, to mine own self akin,

Still haunt the night's eternal corridors,

Or in the toils of great Arcturus spin.

Then, restless still, I rise

Through vaults of mightier gloom, to watch the dark

Snatch at the flame of failing suns;

Or mark

That midden of the stagnant nadir skies

Where many a fated orbit runs.

An arrow sped from some forgotten bow,

Through change of firmaments and systems sent,

And finding bourn nor bars,

I fly, nor know

For what remoter mark my flight is meant.

The Immeasurable Horror

I do not mean to boast when I say that cowardice has never been among my failings. It would be needless to boast, in view of my honorable record as an ether-ace in six interplanetary expeditions. But I tell you that I would not return to Venus for any consideration—not for all the platinum and radium in its mountain-sides, nor all the medicinal saps and pollens and vegetable ambergris of its forests. There will always be men to imperil their lives and their sanity in the Venusian trading posts, and fools who will still try to circumnavigate a world of unearthly dangers. But I have done my share, and I know that Venus was not designed for human nerves or human brains. The loathsome multiform fecundity of its overheated jungles ought to be enough for any one—not to mention the way in which so many posts with their buildings of neo-manganese steel have been wholly blotted out between the departure of one space-freighter and the arrival of the next. No, Venus was not meant for man. If you still doubt me, listen to my story.

I was with the first Venusian expedition, under the leadership of Admiral Carfax, in 1977. We were able to make no more than a mere landing, and were then compelled to return earthward because of our shortage of oxygen, due to a serious miscalculation regarding our needs. It was unsafe, we found, to breathe the thick, vapor-laden air of Venus for more than short intervals; and we couldn't afford to make an overdraught on our tanks. In 1979 we went back, more fully equipped for all contingencies this time, and landed on a high plateau near the equator. This plateau, being comparatively free from the noxious flora and fauna of the abysmal steaming jungles, was to form the base of our explorations.

I felt signally honored when Admiral Carfax put me in charge of the planetary coaster whose various parts had been brought forth from the bowels of the huge ether-ship and fitted together for local use. I, Richard Harmon, was only an engineer, a third assistant pilot of the space-vessel, with no claim whatever to scientific renown; and the four men entrusted to my guidance were all experts of international fame. They were John Ashley, botanist, Aristide Rocher, geologist, Robert Manville, biologist and zoologist, and Hugo Markheim, head of the Interplanetary Survey. Carfax and the remaining sixteen of our party were to stay with the ether-ship till we returned and made our report. We were to follow the equator, landing often for close observations, and make, if feasible, a complete circuit of the planet. In our absence, a second coaster was to be fitted together, in preparation for a longitudinal voyage around the poles.

The coaster was of that type which is now commonly used for flying at all levels within the terrestrial atmosphere. It was made of neonin-tempered aluminum, it was roomy and comfortable, with ports of synthetic crystal tougher than steel, and could be hermetically closed. There were the usual engines run by explosive atomic power, and a supplementary set of the old electro-solar turbines in case of emergency. The vessel was fitted with heating and refrigerating systems, and was armed with electronic machine-guns having a forty-mile range; and we carried for hand-weapons a plentiful supply of infra-red grenades, of heat-tubes and zero-tubes, not knowing what hostile forms of life we might encounter. These weapons were the deadliest ever devised by man; and a child could have wiped out whole armies with them. But I could smile now at their inadequacy. . . .

The plateau on which we had landed was far up in a range which we named the Purple Mountains because they were covered from base to summit with enormous two-foot lichens of a rich Tyrian hue. There were similarly covered areas in the plateau, where the soil was too thin for the sustenance of more elaborate plant-forms. Here, among the multitudinous geysers, and the horned, fantastic peaks that were intermittently visible through a steam-charged atmosphere, we had established ourselves in a lichen-field. Even here we had to wear our refrigerating suits and carry oxygen whenever we stepped out of the ether-ship; for otherwise the heat would have parboiled us in a few minutes, and the ultra-terrestrial gases in the air would have speedily overpowered us. It was a weird business, putting the coaster together under such circumstances. With our huge inflated suits and masks of green vitrolium, we must have looked like a crew of demons toiling in the fumes of Gehenna.

I shall never forget the hour when the five of us who had been chosen for that first voyage of discovery said good-bye to Admiral Carfax and the others and stepped into the coaster. Somehow, there was a greater thrill about it than that which attended the beginning of our trip through sidereal space. The 23,000 miles of our proposed circuit would of course be a mere bagatelle: but what marvels and prodigies of unimagined life or landscape might we not find! If we had only known the truth! . . . but indeed it was fortunate that we could not know . . . .

Flying very slowly, as near to the ground as was practicable, we left the plateau and descended through a long jungle-invaded pass to the equatorial plains. Sometimes, even when we almost grazed the jungle-tops, we were caught in voluminous rolling masses of cloud; and sometimes there were spaces where we could see dimly ahead for a few miles, or could even discern the white-hot glaring of the dropsical sun that hung perpetually at zenith.

We could get only a vague idea of the vegetation beneath us. It was a blurred mass of bluish and whitish greens, of etiolated mauves and saffrons tinged with jade. But we could see that many of them had the character of calamites and giant grasses rather than trees. For a long while we sought vainly an open space in which to alight and begin our investigations.

After we had flown on for an hour or two above the serried jungle, we crossed a great river that couldn't have been so very far below the boiling point, to judge from the columns of steam that coiled upward from it. Here we could measure the height of the jungle, for the shores were lined with titanic reeds marked off in ten yard segments, that rose for a hundred yards in air, and were overshadowed by the palm-ferns behind them. But even here there was no place for us to descend. We crossed other rivers, some of which would have made the Amazon look like a summer creek; and we must have gone on for another hour above that fuming, everlasting forest ere we came to a clear spot of land.

We wondered about that clearing, even at first sight. It was a winding mile-wide swath in the jungle, whose end and beginning were both lost in the vapors. The purplish soil seemed to have been freshly cleared, and was clean and smooth as if a whole legion of steam-rollers had gone over it. We were immensely excited, thinking that it must be the work of intelligent beings—of whom, so far, we had found no slightest trace.

I brought the coaster gently down in the clearing, close to the jungle's edge; and donning our refrigerating suits and arming ourselves with heat-tubes, we unscrewed the seven-inch crystal of the man-hole and emerged.

The curiosity we felt concerning that clearing was drowned in our wonder before the bordering forest. I doubt if I can give you any real idea of what it was like. The most exuberant tropical jungle on earth would have been a corn-patch in comparison. The sheer fertility of it was stupendous, terrifying, horrifying—everything was overgrown, overcrowded with a fulsome rankness that pushed and swelled and mounted even as you watched it. Life was everywhere, seething, bursting, pullulating, rotting. I tell you, we could actually see it grow and decay, like a slow moving picture. And the variety of it was a botanist's nightmare. Ashley cursed like a longshoreman when he tried to classify some of the things we found. And Manville had his problems too, for all sorts of novel insects and animals were flopping, crawling, crashing and flying through the monstrous woods.

I'm almost afraid to describe some of those plants. The overlooming palm-ferns with their poddy fronds of unwholesome mauve were bad enough. But the smaller things that grew beneath them, or sprouted from their boles and joints! Half of them were unspeakably parasitic; and many were plainly sarcophagous. There were bell-shaped flowers the size of wine-barrels that dripped a paralyzing fluid on anything that passed beneath them; and the carcasses of flying lizards and strange legless mammals were rotting in a circle about each of them, with the tips of new flowers starting from the putrefaction in which they had been seeded. There were vegetable webs in which squirming things had been caught—webs that were like a tangle of green, hairy ropes. There were broad, low-lying masses of fungoid white and yellow, that yielded like a bog to suck in the unwary creatures that had trodden upon them. And there were orchids of madly grotesque types that rooted themselves only in the bodies of living animals; so that many of the fauna we saw were adorned with floral parasites.

Even though we were all armed with heat-tubes, we didn't care to go very far in those woods. New plants were shooting up all around us; and nearly everything, both animal and vegetable, seemed to have alimentary designs upon us. We had to turn our heat-tubes on the various tendrils and branches that coiled about us; and our suits were heavily dusted with the white pollen of carnivorous flowers—a pollen that was anaesthetic to the helpless monsters on which it fell. Once a veritable behemoth with a dinosaur-like head and forelegs, loomed above us suddenly from the ferns it had trampled down, but fled with screams of deafening thunder when we levelled our heat-rays upon it till its armored hide began to sizzle. Long-legged serpents larger than anacondas were stalking about; and they were so vicious, and came in such increasing numbers, that we found it hard to discourage them. So we retreated toward the coaster.

When we came again to the clearing, where the soil had been perfectly bare a few minutes before, we saw that the tips of new trees and plants were already beginning to cover it. At their rate of growth, the coaster would have been lost to sight among them in an hour or two. We had almost forgotten the enigma of that clearing; but now the problem presented itself with renewed force.

"Harmon, that swath must have been made within the last hour!" exclaimed Manville to me as we climbed back into the vessel behind the others.

"If we follow it," I rejoined, "we'll soon find who, or what, is making it. Are you fellows game for a little side-trip?" I had closed the man-hole and was now addressing all four of my companions.

There was no demur from any one, though the following of the swath would mean a diagonal divagation from our set course. All of us were tense with excitement and curiosity. No one could venture a surmise that seemed at all credible, concerning the agency that had left a mile-wide trail. And also we were undecided as to the direction of its progress.

I set the engines running, and with that familiar roar of disintegrating carbon atoms in the cylinders beneath us, we soared to the level of the fern-tops and I steered the coaster along the swath in the direction toward which its nose happened to be pointing. However, we soon found that we were on the wrong track; for the new growth below us became disproportionately taller and thicker, as the mighty jungle sought to refill the gap that had been cloven through its center. So I turned the coaster, and we went back in the opposite direction.

I don't believe we uttered half a dozen words among us as we followed the swath, and saw the dwindling of the plant-tops below till that bare purplish soil reappeared. We had no idea what we would find; and we were now too excited even for conjecture. I will readily admit that I, for one, felt a little nervous: the things we had already seen in the forest, together with that formidable recent clearing which no earthly machinery could have made, were enough to unsettle the equilibrium of the human system. As I have said before, I am no coward; and I have faced a variety of ultra-terrene perils without flinching. But already I began to suspect that we were among things which no earth-being was ever meant to face or even imagine. The hideous fertility of that jungle had almost sickened me. What, then, could be the agency that had cleared that jungle away more cleanly than a harvester running through a grain-field?

I watched the vapor-laden scene ahead in the reflector beside me; and the others all had their faces glued to the crystalline ports. Nothing untoward could be seen as yet; but I began to notice a slight, unaccountable increase of our speed. I had not increased the power—we had been running slowly, at no more than one hundred fifty miles per hour; and now we were gaining, as if we were borne in the sweep of some tremendous air-current or the pull of a magnetic force.

The vapors had closed in before us; now they eddied to each side, leaving the landscape visible for many miles. I think we all saw the Thing simultaneously; but no one spoke for a full thirty seconds. Then Manville muttered, very softly: "My God!"

In front, no more than a half-mile distant, the swath was filled from side to side with a moving mass of livid angleworm pink that rose above the jungle-tops. It was like a sheer cliff before us as we flew toward it. We could see that it was moving away from us, was creeping onward through the forest. The mass gave the impression of a jellyfish consistency. It rose and fell, expanding and contracting in a slow rhythmic manner, with a noticeable deepening of color at each contraction.

"Life!" murmured Manville, "Life, in an unknown form, on a scale that would not be possible in our world."

The coaster was now rushing toward the worm-colored mass at more than two hundred miles an hour. A moment more, and we would have plunged into that palpitating wall. I turned the wheel sharply, and we veered to the left and rose with an odd sluggishness above the jungle, where we could look down. That sluggishness worried me, after our former headlong speed. It was as if we were fighting some new gravitational force of an unexampled potency.

We all had a feeling of actual nausea as we gazed down. There were leagues and leagues of that living substance; and the farther end was lost in the fuming vapors. It was moving faster than a man could run, with that horribly regular expansion and contraction, as if it were breathing. There were no visible limbs or appendages, no organs of any distinguishable kind; but we knew that the thing was alive and aware.

"Fly closer," whispered Manville. Horror and scientific fascination contended in his voice.

I steered diagonally downward, and felt an increase of the strange pull against which we were fighting. I had to reverse the gears and turn on more power to prevent the vessel from plunging headlong. We hung above the pink mass at a hundred yard elevation and watched it. It flowed beneath us like an unnatural river, in a flat, glistening tide.

"*Voyez!*" cried Rocher, who preferred to speak in his native tongue, though he knew English as well as any of us.

Two flying monsters, large as pterodactyls, were now circling above the mass not far below us. It seemed as if they, like the vessel, were struggling against a powerful downward attraction. Through the air-tight sound-valves we could hear the thunderous beating of their immense wings as they strove to rise and were drawn gradually toward the pink surface. As they neared it, the mass rose up in a mighty wave, and in the deep mouth-like hollow that formed at the wave's bottom a colorless fluid began to exude and collect in a pool. Then the wave curved over, caught the struggling monsters, and lapsed again to a level, slowly palpitating surface above its prey.

We waited a little; and I realized that the onward flowing of the mass had ceased. Except for that queer throbbing, it was now entirely quiescent. But somehow there was a deadly menace in its tranquility, as if the thing were watching or meditating. Apparently it had no eyes, no ears, no sense-organs of any sort; but I began to get the idea that in some unknowable manner, through senses beyond our apprehension, it was aware of our presence and was considering us attentively.

Now, all at once, I saw that the mass was no longer quiescent. It had begun to rise toward us, very stealthily and gradually, in a pyramidal ridge; and at the ridge's foot, even as before, a clear, transparent pool was gathering.

The coaster wavered and threatened to fall. The magnetic pull, whatever it was, had grown stronger than ever. I turned on fresh power; we rose with a painful, dragging slowness, and the ridge below shot abruptly into a pillar that loomed beside us and toppled over toward the vessel.

Before it could reach us, Manville had seized the switch that operated one of the machine-guns, had aimed it at the pillar and released a stream of disintegrative bolts that caused the overhanging menace to vanish like a melting arm of cloud. Below us the pyramidal base of the truncated pillar writhed and shuddered convulsively, and sank back once more into a level surface. The coaster soared dizzily, as if freed from a retarding weight; and reaching what I thought would be a safe elevation, we flew along the rim of the mass in an effort to determine its extent. And as we flew, the thing began to glide along beneath us at its former rate of progress.

I don't know how many miles of it there were, winding on through the monstrous jungle like a glacier of angleworm flesh. I tell you, the thing made me feel as if my solar plexus had gone wrong. There was neither head nor tail to that damnable mass, and nothing anywhere that we could identify as special organs: it was a weltering sea of life, of protoplasmic cells organized on a scale that staggered all preconceptions of biology. Manville was nearly out of his senses with excitement; and the rest of us were so profoundly shocked and overwhelmed, that we began to wonder if the thing were real, or were merely an hallucination of nerves disordered by novel and terrific planetary forces.

Well, we came to the end of it at last, where the pink wave was eating its way through the jungle. Everything in its path was being crushed down and absorbed—the four hundred foot ferns, the giant grasses, the grotesque carnivorous plants and their victims, the flying, waddling, creeping and striding monsters of all types. And the thing made so little sound—there was a low murmur like that of gently moving water, and the snap or swish of trees as they went down, but nothing more.

"I guess we might as well go on," observed Manville regretfully. "I'd like to analyze a section of that stuff; but we've seen what it can do; and I can't ask you to take any chances with the coaster."

"No," I agreed, "there's nothing to be done about it. So, if you gentlemen are all willing, we might as well resume our course."

I set the vessel back toward the equator, at a goodly speed.

"Christ! that stuff is following us!" cried Manville a minute later. He had been watching from a rear port.

Intent on steering forthrightly, it had not occurred to me to keep an eye on the thing. Now I looked into the rear reflector. The pink mass had changed its course, and was crawling along behind us, evidently at an increased rate of progression, for otherwise we would have been out of sight by now.

We all felt pretty creepy, I assure you. But it seemed ridiculous to imagine that the thing could overtake us. Even at our moderate speed, we were gaining upon it momently; and, if need be, we could treble our rate or soar to higher atmospheric levels. But even at that the whole business made a very disagreeable impression.

Before long we plunged into a belt of thick vapors and lost sight of our pursuer. We seemed to be traversing a sort of swamp, for we caught glimpses of titan reeds and mammoth aquatic plants amid winding stretches of voluminously steaming water. We heard the bellow of unknown leviathans, and saw the dim craning of their hideous heads on interminable necks as we passed. And once the coaster was covered with boiling spray from a marsh-geyser or volcano, and we flew blindly till we were out of it again. Then we crossed a lake of burning oil or mineral pitch, with flames that were half a mile in height; and the temperature rose uncomfortably in spite of our refrigerating system. Then there were more marshes, involved in rolling steam. And after an hour or two we emerged from the vapors, and another zone of prodigiously luxuriant jungle began to reveal its fronded tops below us.

Flying over that jungle was like moving in a hashish eternity. There was no end to it and no change—it simply went on and on through a world without limits or horizons. And the white, vaporous glare of the swollen sun, ever at zenith, became a corroding torture to nerves and brain. We all felt a terrific fatigue, more from the nervous tax than anything else. Manville and Rocher went to sleep, Markheim nodded at his post, and I began to watch for a place where I could bring the coaster safely down and take a nap myself. The vessel would have kept its own course, if I had set the gears; but I didn't want to miss anything, or take any chance of collision with a high mountain range.

Well, it seemed there was no place to land in that interminable bristling wilderness of cyclopean growths. We flew on, and I grew sleepier and sleepier. Then, through the swirling mists ahead, I saw the vague looming of low mountains. There were bare, needle-sharp peaks and long, gentle scaurs of a blackish stone, almost entirely covered with red and yellow lichens taller than heather. It all looked very peaceful and desolate. I brought the coaster down on a level shelf of one of the scaurs, and fell asleep almost before the heavy thudding of the engines had died.

I don't know what it was that awakened me. But I sat up with a start, with a preternaturally distinct awareness that something was wrong. I glanced around at my companions, who were all slumbering quietly. And then I peered into the reflectors, where the entire land-scape about us was depicted.

I was unable to believe it for a moment—that worm-colored glaci-er that had crawled up the scarp beneath us, and was now hanging over the vessel like a sheer, immeasurable, flowing precipice. It had reached out in mighty arms on either side, as if to surround us. It seemed to blot out the misty heavens as it hung there, pulsing and darkening and all a-slaver with rills of a hueless liquid from the mouths that had formed in its front. I lost a few precious seconds ere I could start the atomic engines; and as the vessel rose, the top of that loath-some cliff lengthened out and fell over like the crest of a breaking bil-low. It caught us with a buffeting shock, it enveloped us, we went down tossing and pitching as into a sea-trough; and our interior grew dark and blind till I switched on the lights.

The vessel was now lurching nose downward, as that unbelievable wave sucked it in. My companions were awake, and I shouted half-incoherent orders to them as I turned on the full power of our cylin-ders and also set the electro-solar turbines going. The sides and ceiling of the coaster seemed to bend inward with the pressure as we sought to wrench ourselves free. My companions had flown to the machine-guns, they pumped them incessantly, and bolts of electronic force tore like a broadside of lightning into the mass that had engulfed us. We tried literally to blast ourselves out, with each gun revolving at the wid-est possible radius. I don't know how it was ever done; but at last the pressure above us began to give, there was a glimmering of light through our rear ports; and pitching dizzily, we broke loose. But even as the light returned, something dripped on my bare arms from the ceiling—a thin rill of water-clear fluid that seared like vitriol and al-most laid me out with the sheer agony as it ate into my flesh. I heard someone scream and fall, and turning my head, saw Manville writhing on the floor beneath a steady drip of the same fluid. The roof and walls of the coaster were rent in several places, and some of the rifts were widening momently. That execrable liquid, which doubtless served as both saliva and digestive juice, had been eating the adamantine-tempered metal like acid, and we had not escaped any too soon.

The next few minutes were worse than a whole herd of nightmares. Even with our double engine-power, even with the machine-guns still tearing at the mass beside us, it was a struggle to get away, to combat the malign extra-gravitational magnetism of that hellish life-substance. And all the while, Venusian air was pouring in through the rents and our atmosphere was becoming unbreathable. Also, the refrigerating system was half-useless now, and we sweltered in a steaming inferno, till each of us donned his air-tight insulative suit in turn, while the others held to the guns and the steering. Manville had ceased to writhe, and we saw that he was dead. We would not have dared to look at him overlong, even if there had been time; for half his face and body were eaten away by the corroding liquid.

We soared gradually, till we could look down on the horror that had so nearly devoured us. There it was, mile on mile of it stretching up the mountain-side, with the farther end somewhere in the jungle below. It seemed impossible, in view of the distance we had traversed, that the thing was the same life-mass we had met earlier in the day. But whatever it was, it must have smelt us out somehow; and seemingly it didn't mind scaling a mountain to get us. Or perhaps it was in the habit of climbing mountains. Anyway, it was hard to discourage, for our gun-fire seemed to make mere pin-holes in it that closed up again when the gunner's aim shifted. And when we started to drop grenades upon it from our hard-won elevation, it merely throbbed and heaved a little more vehemently, and darkened to a cancerous red as if it were getting angry. And when we flew off on the way we had come, toward the jungle and the swamp beyond, the damnable thing started to flow backward beneath us along the lichen-mantled slope. Evidently it was determined to have us.

I reeled in the seat with the pain of my seared arms as I held our course. We were in no condition to continue the circuit of Venus; and there was nothing for it but a return to the Purple Mountains.

We flew at top speed; but that flowing mass of life—protoplasm, organism, or whatever it was—fairly raced us. At last we got ahead of it, where it slithered in mile-wide devastation through the jungle—but not very far ahead at that. It hung on interminably, and we all grew sick with watching it.

Suddenly we saw that the thing had ceased to follow us, and was veering off at a sharp angle.

"What do you make of that?" cried Markheim. We were all so amazed by the cessation of pursuit, that I halted the vessel and we hung in mid-air, wondering what had happened.

Then we saw. Another endless mass, of a vermin-like grey, was crawling through the jungle to meet the pink mass. The two seemed to rise up in sheer columns, like warring serpents, as they neared each other. Then they came together; and we could see that they were battling, were devouring each other, were gaining and losing alternately as they flowed back and forth in a huge area from which all vegetation was speedily blotted. At length the pink mass appeared to have won a decisive victory: it poured on and on, without cease, ingesting the other, driving it back. And we watched no longer, but resumed our flight toward the Purple Mountains.

I have no very distinct recollection of that flight: it is all a blur of incalescent vapors, of boundless, fuming forests, of blazing bitumen lakes and volcano-spouting marshes. I lived in a reeling eternity of pain, sickness, vertigo; and toward the last, a raging delirium in which I was no longer aware of my surroundings; except by fits and starts. I don't know how I held on, how I kept the course: my subliminal mind must have done it, I suppose. The others were all pretty sick, too, and could not have helped me. I seemed to be fighting an immeasurable, formless monster in that delirium; and after a dozen aeons of inconclusive combat, I came out of it long enough to see that the Purple

Mountains were jutting their horns from the vapors just ahead. Dimly I steered along the jungle-taken pass and across the plateau; and the glaring heavens turned to a sea of blackness, a sea that fell and bore me down to oblivion as I landed the coaster beside the glimmering bulk of the ether-ship.

Somehow, very tortuously and vaguely, I floated out of that sea of blackness. I seemed to take hours in regaining full awareness; and the process was painful and confusing, as if my brain were unwilling to function. When I finally came to myself, I was lying in my bunk on the ether ship, and Admiral Carfax and the three doctors of the expedition were beside me, together with Markheim and Rocher. They told me I had been unconscious for fifty hours. My collapse, they thought, had been partly due to unnatural nerve-strain and shock. But my arms were both in a terrible state from the ravages of the vitriolic animal fluid that had dripped upon them. It had been necessary to amputate my left arm at the elbow; and only the most skillful care had saved the other from a like fate. My companions, though ill to the point of nausea had retained consciousness, and had told the story of our unbelievable adventures.

"I don't see how you drove the coaster," said Carfax. This, from our reticent and praise-sparing chief, was an actual brevet.

My right arm was a long time in healing—indeed, it never became quite normal again, never regained the muscular strength and nervous quickness required for aviation or space-flying. And I wasn't so sorry, either: my nerves were pretty badly shaken; and I was content to let others do their share, when the holes in the acid-eaten coaster had been caulked with metal melted by our heat-tubes, and another exploring party was sent out along the equator.

We waited for a hundred hours on the plateau in the Purple Mountains; but the coaster didn't return. Radio communications with it had ceased after the first nine hours. The second coaster was put together, and went out with Admiral Carfax himself in charge. Markheim and Rocher also insisted on going along. We kept in touch with the vessel till it began to approach the enormous tundras in which the sun-lit hemisphere of Venus terminates, and beyond which are the frozen realms of perpetual twilight and darkness. The radio reports were full of incredible things, and I won't tell you how many of those moving life-masses were sighted, eating their way through the hideously fertile jungles or crawling out of the steam-enveloped Venusian seas that gave them birth. Nothing, however, was found of the first coaster. Then the reports ceased; and a black horror settled upon us who had remained in the ether-ship.

The huge space-vessel was ill-adapted to horizontal flight within atmospheric levels. But we set out anyway, and tried to find the coasters, though we all knew that there could no longer be anything to find. I won't detail our trip; we all saw enough to turn our stomachs permanently; and those horrors of immeasurable life were sweet and charming in comparison with some of the things that our searchlights revealed on the dark side of the planet . . . . Anyhow, we gave it up at last, and came back to earth. And I, for one, have been well satisfied to remain on Terra Firma. Others can do the exploring and work the Venusian mines and plantations. I know too well the fate of those lost parties and their vessels. And I know what has happened to the warehouses of neo-manganese steel that have utterly disappeared and have been replaced by a half-grown jungle.

SADASTOR

Listen, for this is the tale that was told to a fair lamia by the demon Charnadis as they sat together on the top of Mophi, above the sources of the Nile, in those years when the sphinx was young. Now the lamia was vexed, for her beauty was grown an evil legend in both Thebais and Elephantine; so that men were become fearful of her lips and cautious of her embrace, and she had no lover for almost a fortnight. She lashed her serpentine tail on the ground, and moaned softly, and wept those mythical tears which a serpent weeps. And the demon told this tale for her comforting:

Long, long ago, in the red cycles of my youth (said Charnadis), I was like all young demons, and was prone to use the agility of my wings in fantastic flights; to hover and poise like a gier-eagle above Tartarus and the pits of Python; or to lift the broad blackness of my vans on the orbit of stars. I have followed the moon from evening twilight to morning twilight; and I have gazed on the secrets of that Medusean face which she averts eternally from the earth. I have read through filming ice the ithyphallic runes on columns yet extant in her deserts; and I know the hieroglyphs which solve forgotten riddles, or hint aeonian histories, on the walls of her cities taken by ineluctable snow. I have flown through the triple ring of Saturn, and have mated with lovely basilisks, on isles towering league-high from stupendous oceans where each wave is like the rise and fall of Himalayas. I have dared the clouds of Jupiter, and the black and freezing abysses of Neptune, which are crowned with eternal starlight; and I have sailed beyond to incommensurable suns, compared with which the sun that

152

thou knowest is a corpse-candle in a stinted vault. There, in tremendous planets, I have furled my flight on the terraced mountains, large as fallen asteroids, where, with a thousand names and a thousand images, undreamt-of Evil is served and worshipt in unsurmisable ways. Or, perched in the flesh-colored lips of columnar blossoms, whose perfume was an ecstasy of incommunicable dreams, I have mocked the wiving monsters, and have lured their females, that sang and fawned at the base of my hiding-place.

Now, in my indefatigable questing among the remoter galaxies, I came one day to that forgotten and dying planet which in the language of its unrecorded peoples was called Sadastor. Immense and drear and grey beneath a waning sun, far-fissured with enormous chasms, and covered from pole to pole with the never-ebbing tides of the desert sand, it hung in space without moon or satellite, an abomination and a token of doom to fairer and younger worlds. Checking the speed of my interstellar flight, I followed its equator with a poised and level wing, above the peaks of cyclopean volcanoes, and bare, terrific ridges of elder hills, and deserts pale with the ghastliness of salt, that were manifestly the beds of former oceans.

In the very center of one of these ocean-beds, beyond sight of the mountains that formed its primeval shoreline, and leagues below their level, I found a vast and winding valley that plunged even deeplier into the abysses of this dreadful world. It was walled with perpendicular cliffs and buttresses and pinnacles of a rusty-red stone, that were fretted into a million bizarrely sinister forms by the sinking of the olden seas. I flew slowly among these cliffs as they wound ever downward in tortuous spirals for mile on mile of utter and irredeemable desolation, and the light grew dimmer above me as ledge on ledge and battlement on battlement of that strange red stone upreared themselves between my wings and the heavens. Here, when I rounded a sudden turn of the precipice, in the profoundest depth where the rays of the sun fell only for a brief while at noon, and the rocks were purple with everlasting shadow, I found a pool of dark-green water—the last remnant of the former ocean, ebbing still amid steep, insuperable walls. And from this pool there cried a voice, in accents that were subtly sweet as the mortal wine of the mandragora, and faint as the murmuring of shells. And the voice said:

"Pause and remain, I pray, and tell me who thou art, who comest thus to the accursed solitude wherein I die."

Then, pausing on the brink of the pool, I peered into its gulf of shadow, and saw the pallid glimmering of a female form that upreared itself from the waters. And the form was that of a siren, with hair the color of ocean-kelp, and berylline eyes, and a dolphin-shapen tail. And I said to her:

"I am the demon Charnadis. But who art thou, who lingerest thus in this ultimate pit of abomination, in the depth of a dying world?"

She answered: "I am a siren, and my name is Lyspial. Of the seas wherein I swam and sported at leisure many centuries ago, and whose gallant mariners I drew to an enchanted death on the shores of my disastrous isle, there remains only this fallen pool. Alas! For the pool dwindles daily, and when it is wholly gone I too must perish."

She began to weep, and her briny tears fell down and were added to the briny waters.

Fain would I have comforted her, and I said:

"Weep not, for I will lift thee upon my wings and bear thee to some newer world, where the sky-blue waters of abounding seas are shattered to intricate webs of wannest foam, on low shores that are green and aureate with pristine spring. There, perchance for aeons, thou shalt have thine abode, and galleys with painted oars and great barges purpureal-sailed shall be drawn upon thy rocks in the red light of sunsets domed with storm, and shall mingle the crash of their figured prows with the sweet sorcery of thy mortal singing."

But still she wept, and would not be comforted, crying:

"Thou art kind, but this would avail me not, for I was born of the waters of this world, and with its waters I must die. Alas! my lovely seas, that ran in unbroken sapphire from shores of perennial blossoms to shores of everlasting snow! Alas! the sea-winds, with their mingled perfumes of brine and weed, and scents of ocean flowers and flowers of the land, and far-blown exotic balsams! Alas! the quinquiremes of cycle-ended wars, and the heavy-laden argosies with sails and cordage of byssus, that plied between barbaric isles with their cargoes of topaz or garnet-colored wines and jade and ivory idols, in the antique summers that now are less than legend! Alas! the dead captains, the beautiful dead sailors that were borne by the ebbing tide to my couches of amber seaweed, in my caverns underneath a cedared promontory! Alas! the kisses that I laid on their cold and hueless lips, on their sealed marmorean eyelids!"

And sorrow and pity seized me at her words, for I knew that she spoke the lamentable truth, that her doom was in the lessening of the bitter waters. So, after many proffered condolences, no less vague than vain, I bade her a melancholy farewell and flew heavily away between the spiral cliffs where I had come, and clomb the somber skies till the world Sadastor was only a darkling mote far down in space. But the tragic shadow of the siren's fate, and her sorrow, lay grievously upon me for hours, and only in the kisses of a beautiful fierce vampire, in a far-off and young and exuberant world, was I able to forget it. And I tell thee now the tale thereof, that haply thou mayest be consoled by the contemplation of a plight that was infinitely more dolorous and irremediable than thine own.

THE IMMORTALS OF MERCURY

I

Cliff Howard's first sensation, as he came back to consciousness, was one of well-nigh insufferable heat. It seemed to beat upon him from all sides in a furnace-like blast and to lie upon his face, limbs and body with the heaviness of molten metal. Then, before he had opened his eyes, he became aware of the furious light that smote upon his lids, turning them to a flame-red curtain. His eyeballs ached with the muffled radiation; every nerve of his being cringed from the pouring sea of incalescence; and there was a dull throbbing in his scalp, which might have been either headache induced by the heat, or the pain of a somewhat recent blow.

He recalled, very dimly, that there had been an expedition— somewhere—in which he had taken part; but his efforts to remember the details were momentarily distracted by new and inexplicable sensations. He felt now that he was moving swiftly, borne on something that pitched and bounded against a high wind that seared his face like the breath of hell.

He opened his eyes, and was almost blinded when he found himself staring at a whitish heaven where blown columns of steam went by like spectral genii. Just below the rim of his vision, there was something vast and incandescent, toward which, instinctively, he feared to turn. Suddenly he knew what it was, and began to realize his situation. Memory came to him in a tumbling torment of images; and with it, a growing wonder and alarm.

He recalled the ramble he had taken, alone, amid the weird and

156

scrubby jungles of the twilight zone of Mercury—that narrow belt, warm and vaporous, lying between the broiling deserts on which an enormous sun glares perpetually, and the heaped and mountainous glaciers of the planet's nightward side.

He had not gone far from the rocket-ship—a mile at most, toward the sulphurous, fuming afterglow of the sun, now wholly hidden by the planet's libration. Johnson, the head of that first scientific expedition to Mercury, had warned him against these solitary excursions; but Howard, a professional botanist, had been eager to hasten his investigations of the unknown world, in which they had now sojourned for a week of terrestrial time.

Contrary to expectation, they had found a low, thin, breathable atmosphere, fed by the melting of ice in the variable twilight belt—an air that was drawn continually in high winds toward the sun; and the wearing of special equipment was unnecessary. Howard had not anticipated any danger; for the shy, animal-like natives had shown no hostility and had fled from the earth-men whenever approached. The other life-forms, as far as had been determined, were of low, insensitive types, often semi-vegetative, and easily avoided when poisonous or carnivorous.

Even the huge, ugly, salamander-like reptiles who seemed to roam at will from the twilight zone to the scalding deserts beneath an eternal day, were seemingly quite inoffensive.

Howard had been examining a queer, unfamiliar growth resembling a large truffle, which he had found in an open space, among the pale, poddy, wind-bowed shrubs. The growth, when he touched it, had displayed signs of sluggish animation and had started to conceal itself, burrowing into the boggy soil. He was prodding the thing with the sponge-like branch of a dead shrub, and was wondering how to classify it, when, looking up, he had found himself surrounded by the Mercutian savages. They had stolen upon him noiselessly from the semi-fungoid thickets; but he was not alarmed at first, thinking merely that they had begun to overcome their shyness and show their barbaric curiosity.

They were gnarled and dwarfish creatures, who walked partially erect at most times; but ran upon all fours when frightened. The earthmen had named them the Dlukus, because of the clucking sounds resembling this word which they often made. Their skins were heavily scaled, like those of reptiles; and their small, protruding eyes appeared to be covered at all times with a sort of thin film. Anything ghastlier or more repulsive than these beings could hardly have been found on the inner planets. But when they closed in upon Howard, walking with a forward crouch and clucking incessantly, he had taken their approach for a sort of overture and had neglected to draw his *tonanite* pistol. He saw that they were carrying rough pieces of some blackish mineral, and had surmised, from the way in which their webbed hands were held toward him, that they were bringing him a gift or peace-offering.

Their savage faces were inscrutable; and they had drawn very close before he was disillusioned as to their intent. Then, without warning, in a cool, orderly manner, they had begun to assail him with the fragments of the mineral they carried. He had fought them; but his resistance had been cut short by a violent blow from behind, which had sent him reeling into oblivion.

All this he remembered clearly enough; but there must have been an indefinite blank, following his lapse into insensibility. What, he wondered, had happened during this interim, and where was he going? Was he a captive among the Dlukus? The glaring light and scorching heat could mean only one thing—that he had been carried into the sunward lands of Mercury. That incandescent thing toward which he dared not look was the sun itself, looming in a vast arc above the horizon.

He tried to sit up, but succeeded merely in raising his head a little. He saw that there were leathery thongs about his chest, arms and legs, binding him tightly to some mobile surface that seemed to heave and pant beneath him. Slewing his head to one side, he found that this surface was horny, rounded and reticulated. It was like something he had seen.

Then, with a start of horror, he recognized it. He was bound, Mazeppa-like, to the back of one of those salamandrine monsters to which the earth-scientists had given the name of "heat-lizards." These creatures were large crocodiles, but possessed longer legs than any terrestrial saurian. Their thick hides were apparently, to an amazing extent, non-conductors of heat, and served to insulate them against temperatures that would have parboiled any other known form of life.

The exact range of their habitat had not yet been learned; but they had been seen from the rocket-ship, during a brief sunward dash, in deserts where water was perpetually at the boiling point; where rills and rivers, flowing from the twilight zone, wasted themselves in heavy vapors from terrible cauldrons of naked rock.

Howard's consternation, as he realized his plight and his probable fate, was mingled with a passing surprise. He felt sure that the Dlukus had bound him to the monster's back, and wondered that beings so low in the evolutionary scale should have been intelligent enough to know the use of thongs. Their act showed a certain power of calculation, as well as a devilish cruelty. It was obvious that they had abandoned him deliberately to an awful doom.

However, he had little time for reflection. The heat-lizard, with an indescribable darting and running motion, went swiftly onward into the dreadful hell of writhing steam and heated rock. The great ball of intolerable whiteness seemed to rise higher momently and to pour its beams upon Howard like the flood of an opened furnace. The horny mail of the monster was like a hot gridiron beneath him, scorching through his clothes; and his wrists and neck and ankles were seared by the tough leather cords as he struggled madly and uselessly against them.

Turning his head from side to side, he saw dimly the horned rocks that leaned toward him from curtains of hellish mist. His head swam deliriously, and the very blood appeared to simmer in his veins. He lapsed at intervals into deadly faintness: a black shroud seemed to fall upon him, but his vague senses were still oppressed by the crushing, searing radiation. He seemed to descend into bottomless gulfs, pursued by unpitying cataracts of fire and seas of molten heat. The darkness of his swoon was turned to immitigable light.

At times, Howard came back to full consciousness, and was forced to grit his teeth to avoid screaming with agony. His eyelids seemed to scorch his eyes, as he blinked in the blinding refraction; and he saw his surroundings in broken glimpses, through turning wheels of fire and blots of torrid color, like scenes from a mad kaleidoscope.

The heat-lizard was following a tortuous stream that ran in hissing rapids, among twisted crags and chasm-riven scarps. Rising in sheets and columns, the steam of the angry water was blown at intervals toward the earth-man, scalding his bare face and hands. The thongs cut into his flesh intolerably, when the monster leapt across mighty fissures that had been made by the cracking of the super-heated stone.

Howard's brain seemed to broil in his head, and his blood was a fiery torrent in his roasted body. He fought for breath—and the breath seared his lungs. The vapors eddied about him in deepening swirls, and he heard a muffled roaring whose cause he could not determine. He became aware that the heat-lizard had paused; and moving his head a little, saw that it was standing on the rocky verge of a great gulf, into which the waters fell to an unknown depth, amid curtains of steam.

His heart and his senses failed him, as he struggled like a dying man to draw breath from the suffocating air. The precipice and the monster seemed to pitch and reel beneath him, the vapors swayed vertiginously, and he thought that he was plunging with his weird steed into the unfathomably shrouded gulf.

Then, from the burning mist, the hooded forms of white and shining devils appeared to rise up and seize him, as if to receive him into their unknown hell. He saw their strange, unhuman faces; he felt the touch of their fingers, with a queer and preternatural coolness, on his seared flesh; and then all was darkness. . . .

II

Howard awoke under circumstances that were novel and inexplicable. Instantly, with great clearness, he remembered all that had occurred prior to his final lapse, but could find no clue to his present situation.

He was lying on his back in a green radiance—a soft and soothing light that reminded him of the verdant grass and emerald seawater of the far-off Earth. The light was all about him, it seemed to flow beneath and above him, laving his body with cool ripples that left a sense of supreme well-being.

He saw that he was quite naked; and he had the feeling of immense buoyancy, as if he had been rendered weightless. Wondering, he saw that his skin was entirely free of burns, and realized that he felt no pain, no ill-effects of any kind, such as would have seemed inevitable after his dread ordeal in the Mercutian desert.

For awhile, he did not associate the green luminosity with any idea of spatial limitation; for he seemed to be floating in a vast abyss. Then, suddenly, he perceived his error. Putting out his hands, he touched on either side the wall of a narrow vault, and saw that its roof was only a few feet above him. The floor lay at an equal distance beneath; and he himself, without visible support, was reclining in mid-air. The green light, streaming mysteriously from all the sides of the vault, had given him the illusion of unbounded space.

Abruptly, at his feet, the end of the vault seemed to disappear in a white glory like pure sunlight. Long, sinuous, six-fingered hands reached out from the glow, grasped him about the ankles, and drew him gently from the green-lit space in which he floated. Weight seemed to return to him as his limbs and body entered the dazzling whiteness; and a moment later, he found himself standing erect in a large chamber, lined with some sort of pale, shimmering metal. Beside him, a strange, unearthly being was closing the panel-like door through which he had been drawn from the emerald-litten vault; and beyond this being, there were two others of the same type, one of whom was holding Howard's garments in his arms.

In growing astonishment, Howard gazed at these incredible entities. Each of them was about the height of a tall man, and the physical conformation was vaguely similar to that of mankind, but was marked by an almost god-like beauty and grace of contour, such as could hardly have been found in the most perfect of antique marbles.

Nostrils, ears, lips, hands, and all other features and members, were carved with well-nigh fantastic delicacy; and the skin of these beings, none of whom wore any sort of raiment, was white and translucent, and seemed to shine with an internal radiance. In place of hair, the full, intellectual heads were crowned with a mass of heavy flesh-like filaments, hued with changing iridescence, and tossing and curling with a weird, restless life, like the serpent locks of Medusa. The feet were like those of men, except for long, horny spurs that protruded from the heels.

The three entities returned the earth-man's gaze with unreadable eyes, brilliant as diamonds and cold as far-off stars. Then, to complete his amazement, the being who had just closed the door of the vault began to address him in high, flute-sweet tones, which baffled his ears at first, but after a little, became recognizable as flawless English.

"We trust," said the being, "that you have recovered wholly from your late experience. It was fortunate that we were watching you through our televisors when you were seized by the savages and were bound to the back of the *groko*—that creature known to you as the 'heat-lizard.' These beasts are often tamed by the savages, who, being ignorant of the use of artificial heat, make a strange use of the *groko's* proclivities for ranging the terrible sunward deserts. Captives caught from rival tribes—and sometimes even their own kin—are tied to the monsters, who carry them through oven-like temperatures till the victims are thoroughly roasted—or, as you would say, done to a turn. Then the *grokos* return to their masters—who proceed to feast on cooked meat.

"Luckily we were able to rescue you in time; for the *groko*, in its wanderings, approached one of our cavern-exits in the great desert. Your body was covered with enormous burns when we found you; and you would assuredly have died from the effects, if we had not exposed you to the healing ray in the green vault. This ray, like many others, is unknown to your scientists; and it has, among other things, the peculiar power of nullifying gravity. Hence your sensation of weightlessness under its influence."

"Where am I? And who are you?" cried Howard.

"You are in the interior of Mercury," said the being. "I am Agvur, a savant, and a high noble of the ruling race of this world." He went on in a tone of half-disdainful explanation, as if lecturing to a child: "We call ourselves the Oumnis; and we are an old people, wise and erudite in all the secrets of nature. To protect ourselves from the intense radiations of the sun, which of course are more powerful on Mercury than on the further planets, we dwell in caverns lined with a metallic substance of our own composition. This substance, even in thin sheets, excludes all the harmful rays, some of which can pierce all other forms of matter to any depth. When we emerge to the outer world, we wear suits of this metal, whose name in our language is *mouffa*.

"Being thus insulated at all times, we are practically immortal, as well as exempt from disease; for all death and decay, in the course of nature, are caused by certain solar rays whose frequency is beyond detection of your instruments. The metal does not exclude the radiations that are beneficial and necessary to life; and by means of an apparatus similar in its principle to radio, our underworld is illumined with transmitted sunlight."

Howard began to express his thanks to Agvur. His brain was giddy with wonder, and his thoughts whirled in a maze of astounding speculations.

Agvur, with a swift and graceful gesture, seemed to wave aside his expression of gratitude. The being who bore Howard's garments came forward, and helped him, in a deft, valet-like fashion, to put them on.

Howard wanted to ask a hundred questions; for the very existence of intelligent, highly evolved beings such as the Oumnis on Mercury had been unsuspected by earth-scientists. Above all, he was curious regarding the mastery of human language displayed by Agvur. His question, as if divined by a sort of telepathy, was forestalled by the Mercutian.

"We are possessed of many delicate instruments," said Agvur, "which enable us to see and hear—and even to pick up other sense-impressions—at immense distances. We have long studied the nearer planets, Venus, Earth and Mars, and have often amused ourselves by listening to human conversations. Our brain-development, which is vastly superior to yours, has made it a simple matter for us to learn your speech; and of course the science, history and sociology of your world is an open book to us. We watched the approach of your ether-ship from space; and all the movements of your party since landing have been observed by us."

"How far am I from the rocket-ship?" asked Howard. "I trust you can help me to get back."

"You are now a full mile beneath the surface of Mercury," said Agvur, "and the part of the twilight zone in which your vessel lies is about five miles away and could readily be reached by an incline lead-ing upward to a small exit in a natural cavern within sight of the ship. Doubtless some of the members of your party have seen the cavern and have assumed that it was a mere animal-den. When your vessel landed, we took care to block the exit with a few loose boulders and fragments of detritus, easily removable.

"As to rejoining your comrades—well, I fear that it will scarcely be practicable. You must be our guest—perhaps indefinitely." There was a kind of brusqueness in his tone as he concluded:

"We do not want our existence known to terrestrial explorers. From what we have seen of your world, and your dealings with the

peoples of Mars and Venus, whose territories you have begun to arro-
gate, we think it would be unwise to expose ourselves to human curiosity and rapacity. We are few in number, and we prefer to remain in
peace—undisturbed."

Before Howard could frame any sort of protest, there came a singular interruption. Loud and imperious, with clarion-like notes, a voice
rang out in the empty air between Agvur and the earth-man. Howard
was ungovernably startled; and the three Mercutians all seemed to
stiffen with rapt attention. The voice went on for nearly a minute,
speaking rapidly, with accents of arrogant command. Howard could
make nothing of the words, whose very phonetic elements were
strange and unfamiliar. But a chill ran through him at something which
he sensed in the formidable voice—a something that told of relentless,
implacable power.

The voice ended on a high, harsh note, and the listening Mercutians made a queer gesture with their heads and hands, as if to indicate
submission to a superior will.

"Our temporal ruler and chief scientist, Ounavodo," said Agvur,
"has just spoken from his hall in the lower levels. After hours of deliberation, he has reached a decision regarding your fate. In a sense, I re-
gret the decision, which seems a trifle harsh to me; but the mandates
of the Shol, as we call our ancient ruler, are to be obeyed without question. I must ask you to follow me; and I shall explain as we go along.
The order must be executed without delay."

In perplexity not unmingled with consternation, Howard was led
by Agvur to a sort of inclined hall or tunnel, on which the chamber
opened. The tunnel was seemingly interminable, and was lit by brilliant
and apparently sourceless light—the transmitted sun-rays of which the
Mercutian had spoken. Like the chamber, it was lined with a pale metallic substance.

An odd machine, shaped like a small open boat, and mounted on
little wheels or castors, stood before the door, on the easy monoto-

nous grade. Agvur stationed himself in its hollow prow, motioning Howard to follow. When the other Oumnis had placed themselves behind Howard, Agvur pulled a sort of curving lever, and the machine began to glide rapidly, in perfect silence, down the interminable hall.

"This tunnel," said Agvur, "runs upward to the exit near your vessel; and it leads down to the heart of our underworld realms. If the worst happens—as I fear it may—you will see only the antechambers of our labyrinth of caverns, in which we have dwelt, immune to disease and old age, for so many centuries. I am sorry; for I had hoped to take you to my own laboratories, in the nether levels. There you might have served me . . . in certain biologic tests.

"Ounavodo," he went on, in calm explanatory tones, "has ordered the fusing and casting of a certain quantity of the *mouffa*-alloy, to be used in the making of new garments. This alloy, invented aeons ago by our metallurgists, is a compound of no less than six elements, and is made in two grades, one for the lining of our caverns, and the other exclusively for raiment.

"Both, for their perfection, require a seventh ingredient—a small admixture of living, protoplasmic matter, added to the molten metal in the furnace. Only thus—for a reason that is still mysterious to our savants—can the *mouffa* acquire its full power of insulation against the deadly solar rays.

"The *mouffa* used in comparatively heavy sheets for cavern-lining needs only the substance of inferior life-forms, such as the *grokos*, the half-animal savages of the twilight zone, and various creatures which we catch or breed in our underworld tunnels. But the higher grade of *mouffa*, employed in light, flexible sheets for suiting, requires the protoplasm of superior life.

"Regretfully, at long intervals, we have been compelled to sacrifice one of our own scanty number in the making of new metal to replace that which has become outworn. Whenever possible, we select those who in some manner have offended against our laws; but such infringements are rare, and commonly the victim has been chosen by a sort of divination.

"After studying you closely in his televisic mirror, Ounavodo has decided that you are sufficiently high in the evolutionary scale to provide the protoplasmic element in the next lot of *mouffa*. At least, he thinks that the test is worth trying, in the interests of science."

"However, in order that you should not feel that you are being discriminated against or treated unjustly, you will merely take your chance of being chosen from among many others. The method of selection will be revealed to you in due time."

While Agvur was speaking, the vehicle had sped swiftly down the endless incline, passing several other barge-shaped cars driven by the white, naked Immortals, whose serpentine locks flowed behind them on the air. Occasionally there were openings in the tunnel wall, leading no doubt to side-caverns; and after a mile or two, they came to a triple branching, where caverns ran upward at reverse angles from the main passage. Horrified and shaken as he was by Agvur's disclosure, Howard took careful note of the route they were following.

He made no reply to the Mercutian. He felt his helplessness in the hands of an alien, extra-human race, equipped, it would seem, with scientific knowledge and power to which humanity had not yet attained. Thinking with desperate quickness, he decided that it would be better to pretend resignation to the will of his captors. His hand stole instinctively to the pocket in which he had carried the little *tonanite* pistol with its twelve charges of deadly heat-producing explosive; and he was dismayed, though hardly surprised, to find that the weapon was gone.

His movement was noted by Agvur; and a strange sardonic smile flickered across the unhumanly intellectual face of the savant. In his desperation, Howard thought of leaping from the car; but to do this would have meant death or serious injury at the high speed of their descent.

He became aware that the incline had ended in a large level cavern with numerous side-openings where multitudes of Oumnis were passing in and out. Here they left the boat-like vehicle; and Howard was led by Agvur through one of the side-exits, into another vast chamber, where perhaps fifty of the white people were standing in silent, semi-circular rows.

These beings were all fronting toward the opposite wall; but many of them turned to watch the earth-man with expressions of unreadable curiosity or disdain, as Agvur drew him forward to the first of the waiting ranks and motioned him to take his place at the end.

Now, for the first time, Howard saw the singular object which the Oumnis were facing. Apparently it was some sort of rootless plant-growth, with a swollen, yellowish bole or body like that of a barrel-cactus. From this body, tall as a man, leafless branches of vivid arsenic green, fringed with a white hispidity, trailed in limp, sinuous masses on the cavern-floor.

Agvur spoke in a piercing whisper: "The plant is called the Roccalim, and we employ it to choose, from a given quota, the person who shall be cast into the furnace of molten *mouffa*. You will perceive that, including yourself, there are about fifty candidates for this honor—all of whom, for one reason or another, in varying degrees, have incurred the displeasure of Ounavodo, or have given rise to doubt regarding their social usefulness. One by one, you are to walk about the Roccalim in a complete circle, approaching well within reach of the sensitive, mobile branches; and the plant will indicate the destined victim by touching him with the tips of these branches."

Howard felt, as Agvur spoke, the chill of a sinister menace; but in the weirdness of the ceremony that followed, he almost lost his apprehension of personal peril.

One by one, from the further end of the row in which he was standing, the silent Oumnis went forward and circled the strange plant, walking slowly within a few feet of the inert branches of poisonous green that resembled sleepy, half-coiled serpents. The Roccalim preserved a torpid stillness, without the least sign of animation, as Oumni after Oumni finished his perilous circuit and retired to the further side of the room, there to stand and watch the perambulations of the others.

About twenty of the white Immortals had undergone this ordeal, when Howard's turn came. Resolutely, with a sense of unreality and grotesquery rather than actual danger, he stepped forward and began his circuit of the living plant. The Oumnis looked on like alabaster statues; and all was utterly still and silent, except for a muffled, mysterious throbbing as of underworld machinery at a distance.

Howard moved on in an arc, watching the green branches with a growing tenseness. He had gone half the required distance when he felt, rather than saw, a flash of swift, intense light that appeared to stab downward from the cavern roof and strike the lumpish yellow bole of the Roccalim. The light faded in the merest fraction of time, leaving Howard in doubt as to whether he had really seen it.

Then, as he went on, he perceived with startled horror that the trailing tentacular boughs had begun to twitch and quiver, and were lifting slowly from the floor and waving toward him. On and on they came, rising and straightening, like a mass of ropy kelp that flows in an ocean-stream. They reached him, they slithered with reptilian ease about his body, and touched his face with their venomous-looking tips, clammy and inquisitive.

Howard drew back, wrenching himself away from the waving mass, and found Agvur at his elbow. The face of the Mercutian was touched with an unearthly gloating; and his iridescent locks floated upward, quivering with weird restlessness, like the Roccalim branches.

At that moment, it came to Howard that his fate had been predetermined from the beginning; that the swift, evanescent flash of light, proceeding from an unknown source, had perhaps served in some manner to irritate the living plant and provoke the action of its tentacular limbs.

Swift anger flared in the earth-man, but he repressed it. He must be cautious, must watch for an opportunity—even the slimmest—of escape. By giving the impression that he was resigned, he might throw his captors off their guard.

He saw that a number of new Mercutians, equipped with long glittering tubes like blow-pipes, had entered the cavern and were surrounding him. The companions of his late ordeal had begun to disperse in various directions.

"I am sorry," said Agvur, "that the choice should have fallen upon you. But your death will be swift—and the time is near at hand. The fusing must be completed, and the metal must be poured off and cast in thin, malleable sheets, before the next term of darkness and slumber, which will occur in little more than an hour. During this term—three hours out of every thirty-six—the transmitted sunlight is excluded from all our chambers and passages; and most of our machinery, which derives its power from light, is rendered inactive."

III

In mingled horror and dumbfoundment, Howard was taken through an opposite entrance of the Roccalim's cavern and along a sort of hall which appeared to run parallel with the one in which the incline had ended. Agvur walked at his side; and the Oumni guards were grouped before and behind him. He surmised that the glittering, hollow tubes they carried were weapons of some novel type.

As they went on, the mysterious throbbing noise drew steadily nearer. Howard saw that the far end of the corridor was illumined with a fiery red light. The air was touched with queer metallic odors; and the temperature, which had heretofore been one of unobtrusive warmth, seemed to rise slightly.

At one side, through an open door in the passage wall, as they neared the source of the red light, Howard saw a large room whose further end was filled with lofty banks of shining cylinder-shaped mechanisms. In front of these mechanisms, a solitary Mercutian stood watching an immense pivot-mounted ball which appeared to be filled nearly to the top with liquid blackness, leaving a crescent of bright crystal. Near the ball, there was a sort of inclined switchboard, from which arose many rods and levers, made of some transparent material.

"The lighting apparatus of all our caverns is controlled from that room," said Agvur, with a sort of casual boastfulness. "When the ball has turned entirely black, the sunlight will be turned off for the three-hour period, which gives us all the sleep and rest we require."

A moment more, and the party reached the end of the passage. Howard stood blinking and breathless with wonder when he saw the source of the dazzling red light.

He was on the threshold of a cavern so enormous that its roof was lost in luminosity and gave the effect of a natural sky. Titanic machines of multiform types, some squat and ungainly and others like prodigious bulbs or huge inverted funnels, crowded the cavern-floor; and in the center, towering above the rest was a double, terrace-like platform of sable stone, thirty feet in height, with many pipes of dark metal that ramified from its two tiers to the floor, like the legs of some colossal spider. From the middle of the summit, the ruddy light arose in a great pillar. Gleaming strangely against the fiery glow, the forms of Oumnis moved like midges.

Just within the entrance of the Cyclopean room, there stood a sort of rack, from which hung a dozen suits of the *mouffa*-metal. Their construction was very simple, and they closed and opened at the breast, with odd dove-tailings. The head was a loose, roomy hood; and the metal had somehow been rendered transparent in a crescent-like strip across the eyes.

The suits were donned by Agvur and the guards; and Howard noticed that they were extremely light and flexible. He himself, at the same time, was ordered to disrobe.

"The *mouffa* mixture, during the process of fusing, gives off some dangerous radiations," said Agvur. "These will hardly matter in your case; and the suits of finished metal will protect my companions and me against them, even as against the deadly solar rays."

Howard had now removed all his clothes, which he left lying near the rack. Still pretending his resignation, but thinking desperately all the while and observing closely the details of his situation, he was led along the crowded floor, amid the sinister throbbing and muttering of the strange engines. Steep, winding stairs gave access to the terraced mass of dark stone. The earth-man saw as he went upward, that the lower tier was fitted with broad, shallow moulds, in which doubtless the metal would run off from the furnace to cool in sheets.

Howard felt an almost overpowering heat when he stood on the upper platform; and the red glare blinded him. The furnace itself, he now saw, was a circular crater, fifteen feet across, in the black stone. It was filled nearly to the rim with the molten metal, which eddied with a slow maelstrom-like movement, agitated by some unknown means, and glowing unbearably. The black stone must have been a non-conductor of heat, for it was cool beneath Howard's bare soles.

On the broad space about the furnace, a dozen Oumnis, all sheathed in the glittering *mouffa*, were standing. One of them was turning a small, complicated-looking wheel, mounted obliquely on a miniature pillar; and as if he were regulating the temperature of the furnace, the metal glowed more brightly and eddied with new swiftness in its black crater.

Apart from this wheel, and several rods that protruded from long, notched grooves in the stone, there was no visible machinery on the platform. The stone itself was seemingly all one block, except for a slab, ten feet long and two feet wide, which ran to the crater's verge. Howard was directed to stand on this slab, at the end opposite to the furnace.

"In another minute," said Agvur, "the slab will begin to move, will tilt, and precipitate you into the molten *mouffa*. If you wish, we can administer to you a powerful narcotic, so that your death will be wholly free of fear or pain."

Overcome by an unreal horror, Howard nodded his head in mechanical assent, snatching hopelessly at the momentary reprieve. Perhaps . . . even yet . . . there might be a chance; though he could have laughed at himself for the impossible notion.

Peering again toward the awful furnace, he was startled to see an inexplicable thing. Foot by foot, from the solid stone of the crater's further lip, there rose the figure of a Mercutian, till it stood with haughty features, very tall and pale and wholly naked upon the platform. Then, as Howard gasped with incredulous awe, the figure seemed to step in a stately manner from the verge, and hang suspended in air above the glowing cauldron.

"It is the Shol, Ounavodo," said Agvur in reverent tones, "though he is now many miles away in the nether caverns, he has projected his televisual image to attend the ceremony."

One of the Mercutian guards had come forward, bearing in his hands a heavy, shallow bowl of some bronze-like substance, filled with a hueless liquid. This he proffered to the earth-man.

"The narcotic acts immediately," said Agvur, as if in reassurance.

Giving a quick, unobtrusive glance about him, Howard accepted the bowl and raised it to his lips. The narcotic was odorless as well as colorless, and had the consistency of a thick, sluggish oil.

"Be quick," admonished Agvur. "The slab responds to a timing mechanism; and already it starts to move."

Howard saw that the slab was gliding slowly, bearing him as on a great protruding tongue toward the furnace. It began to tilt a little beneath his feet.

Tensing all his muscles, he leapt from the slab and hurled the heavy bowl in the face of Agvur, who stood close by. The Mercutian staggered, and before he could regain his balance, Howard sprang upon him, and lifting him bodily, flung him across the rising, sliding slab, which bore Agvur along in its accelerated movement. Stunned by the fall, and unable to recover himself, he rolled from the tilting stone into the white-hot maelstrom and disappeared with a splash. The liquid seethed and eddied with a swifter motion than before.

For a moment, the assembled Oumnis stood like metal statues; and the televisual image of the Shol, standing inscrutable and watchful above the furnace, had not stirred. Leaping at the foremost guards, Howard flung them aside as they started to lift their tubular weapons. He gained the platform's railless verge, but saw that several Oumnis had run to intercept him before he could reach the stairs. It was a twelve-foot drop to the second platform, and he feared to leap with bare feet. The strange curving pipes which ran from the upper platform to the main cavern-floor, offered his only possible means of escape.

These pipes were of darkish metal, perfectly smooth and jointless, and were about ten inches thick. Straddling the nearest one, where it entered the black stone just below the verge, Howard began to slide as quickly as he could toward the floor.

His captors had followed him to the platform-edge; and facing them as he slid, the earth-man saw two of the Immortals aim their weapons at him. From the hollow tubes, there issued glowing balls of yellow fire which came flying toward Howard. One of them fell short, striking the side of the great pipe, and causing it to melt away like so much solder. He saw the dripping of the molten metal as he ducked to avoid the second ball.

Others of the Oumnis were levelling their weapons; and a rain of the terrible fire-globes fell about Howard as he slid along the pipe's lower portion, where it curved sharply toward the floor. One of the balls brushed his right arm and left an agonizing burn.

He reached the floor, and saw that a dozen Immortals were descending the platform-stairs in great bounds. The main cavern, fortunately, was deserted. The earth-man leapt for the shelter of a huge rhomboidal machine, and heard the hiss and drip of liquid metal as the fire-balls struck behind him.

Threading his way among the looming mechanisms, and interposing their bulks as much as possible between himself and his pursuers, Howard made for the entrance through which he had been conducted to the furnace by Agvur. There were other exits from the immense cavern; but these would have led him deeper into the unknown labyrinth. He had no clearly formulated plan, and his ultimate escape was more than problematical; but his instincts bade him to go on as long as he could before being recaptured.

He heard the mysterious pounding of the untended mechanisms all about him; but there was no sound from his pursuers, who came on in grim silence, with incredible leaps, gaining visibly upon him.

Then, startlingly, as he rounded one of the machines, he found himself confronted by the televisual phantom of the Shol, standing in an attitude of menace, and waving him back with imperious gestures. He felt the awful burning gaze of eyes that were hypnotic with age-old wisdom and immemorial power; and he seemed to hurl himself against an unseen barrier, as he sprang at the formidable image. He felt a slight electric shock that jarred his entire body; but apparently the phantom was capable of little more than visual manifestation. It seemed to melt away; and then it was hovering above and a little before him, pointing out his line of flight to the pursuing Oumnis.

Passing a huge squat cylinder, he came to the rack on which the suits of *mouffa* had hung. Two of them still remained. Disregarding his own garments, which lay in a heap nearby, he snatched one of the metal suits from its place and rolled the thin, marvellously flexible stuff into a bundle as he continued his flight. Perhaps, somewhere, he would have a chance to put it on; and thus disguised, might hope to prolong his freedom—or even to find his way from this tremendous underworld.

There was a broad open space between the rack and the cavern exit. Howard's pursuers emerged from the medley of towering mechanisms before he could reach the doorway, and he was forced to dodge another fusillade of the fire-balls, which splattered in white-hot fury all around him. Before him, the menacing phantom of the Shol still hovered.

Now he had gained the corridor beyond the exit. He meant to retrace the route by which he had come with Agvur, if possible. But as he neared the door through which he had seen the watcher of the darkening globe, and the light-controlling mechanisms, he perceived that a number of Mercutians, armed with fire-tubes, were coming to intercept his flight in the corridor. Doubtless they had been summoned through some sort of teleaudition by the furnace-tenders.

Looking back, he saw that his former guards were closing upon him. In a few moments, he would be surrounded and trapped. With no conscious idea, other than the impulse to flee, he darted through the open door of the cavern of light-machines.

The solitary watcher still stood beside the massive ball with his back toward the earth-man. The crystal crescent on the dark globe had narrowed to a thin horn, like the bow of a dying moon.

A mad, audacious inspiration came to Howard, as he recalled what Agvur had told him about the control of the lighting-system. Quickly and silently he stole toward the watcher of the ball.

Again the vengeful image of the Shol stood before him, as if to drive him back; and as he neared the unsuspecting watcher, it rose in air and poised above the ball, warning the Oumni with a loud, harsh cry. The watcher turned, snatching up a heavy metal rod that lay on the floor, and leapt to meet Howard, raising his weapon for a ferocious blow.

Before the rod could descend, the earth-man's fist had caught the Mercutian full in the face, driving him back upon the slanting dial of regulative levers beside the pivot-mounted ball. There was a shivering crash as he fell among the curving crystalline rods; and at the same instant, utter overwhelming darkness rushed upon the room and blotted out the banks of gleaming mechanism, the fallen Oumni, and the phantom of Shol.

IV

Standing uncertain and bewildered, the earth-man heard a low moaning from the injured Mercutian, and a loud wail of consternation from the corridor without, where the two groups of his pursuers had found themselves overtaken by darkness. The wailing ceased abruptly; and except for the moaning near at hand, which still went on, there was absolute silence. Howard realized that he no longer heard the mutter of the strange engines in the furnace-room. Doubtless their operation had in some manner been connected with the lighting system, and had ceased with darkness.

Howard still retained the suit of *mouffa*. Groping about, he found the metal rod that had dropped from the hand of the watcher. It would make a highly serviceable weapon. Grasping it firmly, he started in what he surmised to be the direction of the door. He went slowly and cautiously, knowing that his pursuers would have gathered to await him, or might even be creeping toward him.

Listening intently, he heard a faint metallic rustle. Some of the Oumnis, clothed in *mouffa*, were coming to seek him in the darkness. His own bare feet were soundless; and stepping to one side, he heard the rustling pass. With redoubled caution, he stole on toward the door, stretching one hand before him.

Suddenly his fingers touched a smooth surface, which he knew to be the wall. He had missed the door in his groping. Listening again, he seemed to hear a faint sound on the left, as if he were being followed; and moving in the opposite direction, along the wall, he encountered empty space and saw a dim glimmer of seemingly sourceless light.

His eyes were growing accustomed to the darkness, and he made out a mass of dubious shadows against the glimmering. He had found the door, which was lined with waiting Oumnis.

Lifting his bar, he rushed upon the shadows, striking blow after blow, and stumbling over the bodies that fell before his onslaught.

There were shrill cries about him, and he broke from chill, *mouffa-*sheathed fingers that sought to clutch him in the gloom. Then, somehow, he had broken through, and was in the corridor.

The glimmering, he saw, came from the cavern of machines, where the hidden furnace still burned. Into the dying glow that lit the entrance, there came hurrying figures, each of which appeared to have an enormous Cyclopean eye of icy green. Howard realized that more Mercutians, bearing artificial lights, were coming to join the pursuit.

Keeping close to the corridor wall, he ran as fast as he dared in the solid blackness, toward the cavern of the Roccalim. He heard a stealthy metallic rustling, as the foremost Oumnis followed; and glancing back, saw them dimly outlined against the remote glow. They came on in a cautious, lagging manner, as if they were waiting for the new contingent with the green lights. After a little, he saw that the two parties had united and were following him steadily.

Fingering the wall at intervals as he ran, Howard reached the entrance of the large chamber in whose center stood the Roccalim. The lights were gaining upon him rapidly. Calculating in his mind, as well as he could, the direction of the opposite doorway, giving on the main tunnel that led to the incline, he started toward it. As he went on, he veered a little, thinking to avoid the monstrous plant-growth. It was like plunging into a blind abyss; and he seemed to wander for an immense distance, feeling sure that he would reach the opposite wall at any moment.

Suddenly his feet tripped on an unknown obstruction, and he fell at full length, landing on what seemed to be a tangle of great hairy ropes that pricked his bare skin in a thousand places. Instantly, he knew that he had collided with the Roccalim.

The mass of python-like branches lay inert beneath him, without a quiver of animation. Doubtless, in the absence of light, the queer, semi-animal growth was torpid.

Pulling himself from the spiny couch on which he had fallen,

Howard looked back and perceived the thronging of green lights, cold and malignant as the eyes of boreal dragons. His pursuers were entering the cavern, and would overtake him in a few instants.

Still clutching the *mouffa* garments and the metal bar, he groped across the tangle of branches, pricking his feet painfully at every step. Suddenly he plunged through to the floor, and found that he was standing in an open space where the heavy creepers, descending from the bole, had parted on either side. Crouching down, as the lights approached him, he found a low, hollow place into which he could crawl beneath the branches, close to the cactus-like stem.

The creepers were thick enough to conceal him from casual scrutiny. Lying there, with their prickly weight upon him, he saw through narrow rifts the passing of the green lights toward the outer cavern. Apparently none of the Mercutians had thought of pausing to examine the mass of Roccalim branches.

Emerging from his fantastic hiding-place, after all the Oumnis had gone past, Howard followed them boldly. He saw the vanishing of their icy lamps as they entered the outside tunnel. Moving again in utter darkness, he found the exit. There he recovered the running pencils of light, cast by the hurrying lamps as their bearers went toward the incline.

Following, Howard stumbled against an unseen object, which was either the vehicle used by Agvur, or another of the same type. Probably, in the shutting-off of power, these vehicles were now useless: otherwise, some of them might have been employed by the earth-man's pursuers. Hunters and hunted were on an equal footing; and realizing this, Howard felt for the first time an actual thrill of hope.

Going on, with the lights moving steadily before him, he started up the interminable incline which led—perhaps—to freedom. The tunnel was deserted, except for the hunters and their human quarry; and it seemed as if the multitude of Oumnis seen by Howard on his arrival with Agvur had all retired with the falling of darkness. Perhaps they had to for the usual three-hour term of night and repose.

The light-bearers appeared to disregard all the side passages that ran from the main tunnel. It occurred to Howard that they were hastening toward the surface exits, with the idea of cutting off his possible escape. Afterward they would hunt him down at leisure.

The incline ran straight ahead; and there was little danger of losing sight of the lights. Howard paused an instant to slip on the suit of *mouf-fa*, hoping that it might serve to deceive or baffle his hunters later on. The raiment was easily donned, and fitted him quite loosely; but the unfamiliar intricate method of fastening eluded his untaught fingers. He could not remember quite how it had been done; so he went on with the strange garment open at the breast. The queer elongated heels, made to accommodate the spurs of the Immortals, flapped behind him.

He kept as much as possible the same relative distance between himself and the Oumnis. Glancing back, after awhile, he was horrified to see, far down, the tiny green eyes of another group of lights following him. Evidently others had rallied to the pursuit.

It was a long, interminably tedious climb—mile after mile of that monotonous tunnel whose gloom was relieved only by the sinister points of green light. The Mercutians went on at a tireless pace, unhuman and implacable; and only by ceaseless exertion, half walking, half running, could the earth-man maintain his position midway between the companies of lamps.

He panted heavily, and a faintness came upon him at times, in which the lights seemed to blur. A great weariness clogged his limbs and his brain. How long it was since he had eaten, he could not know. He was not aware of hunger or thirst; but he seemed to fight an ever-growing weakness. The corridor became a black eternity, haunted by the green eyes of cosmic demons.

Hour after hour he went on, through a cycle of sunless night. He lost the sense of time, and his movements became a sort of automation. His limbs were numb and dead, and it was only his relentless will that lived and drove him on. Almost, at times, he forgot where he was going—forgot everything but the blind, primitive impulse of flight. He was a nameless thing, fleeing from anonymous terror.

At last, through the crushing numbness of his fatigue, there dawned the realization that he was gaining a little on the group of lights ahead. Possibly their bearers had paused in doubt or debate. Then, suddenly, he saw that the lights were spreading out, were diverging and vanishing on either hand, till only four of them remained.

Dimly puzzled, he went on, and came to that triple division of the tunnel which he remembered passing with Agvur. He saw now that the party of Oumnis had divided into three contingents, following all the branches. Doubtless each tunnel led to a separate exit.

Recalling what Agvur had said, he kept to the middle passage. This, if Agvur had spoken truly, would lead to an exit in the twilight zone, not far from the rocket-ship. The other tunnels would lead he knew not where—perhaps to the terrible deserts of heat and the piled, chaotic glaciers of the nightward hemisphere. The one he was following, with luck, would enable him to rejoin his comrades.

A sort of second wind came to Howard now—as if hope had revived his swooning faculties. More clearly than before, he became conscious of the utter silence and profound mystery of this underworld empire, of which he had seen—was to see—so little. His hope quickened when he looked back and saw that the lights behind him had diminished in number, as if the second party had likewise separated to follow all three of the tunnels. It was obvious that there was no general pursuit. In all likelihood the smashing of the transmission levers had deranged all the machineries of the Immortals, even to their system of communication. Howard's escape, doubtless, was known only to those who had been present or near at the time. He had brought chaos and demoralization upon this super-scientific people.

V

Mile after mile of that monotone of gloom. Then, with a start of bewilderment, the earth-man realized that the four lights in front had all disappeared. Looking back, he saw that the lamps which followed him had similarly vanished. About, before and behind there was nothing but a solid, tomb-like wall of darkness.

Howard felt a strange disconcertment, together with the leaden, crushing return of his weariness. He went on with doubtful, slackening steps, following the right hand wall with cautious fingers. After awhile he turned a sharp corner; but he did not recover the lost lights. There was a drafty darkness in the air, and odor of stone and mineral, such as he had not met heretofore in the *mouffa*-lined caverns. He began to wonder if he had somehow gone astray: there might have been other branchings of the tunnel, which he had missed in his groping. In a blind surge of alarm, he started to run, and crashed headlong against the angular wall of another turn in the passage.

Half-stunned, he picked himself up. He hardly knew, henceforth, whether he was maintaining the original course of his flight or was doubling on his own steps. For aught that he could tell, he might be lost beyond all redirection in a cross-labyrinth of caverns. He stumbled and staggered along, colliding many times with the tunnel-sides, which seemed to have closed in upon him and to have grown rough with flinty projections.

The draft in his face grew stronger, with a smell of water. Presently the blindfold darkness before him melted into a chill, bluish glimmering, which revealed the rugate walls and boulder-flanged roof of the natural passage he was following.

He came out in a huge, chamber-like cave of some marble-pallid stone with twisted columnar forms. The glimmering, he saw, was a kind of phosphorescence emitted by certain vegetable growths, probably of a thallophytic nature, which rose in thick clusters from the floor, attaining the height of a tall man. They were flabby and fulsome-looking, with abortive branches, and pendulous fruit-shaped nodes of etiolated purple along their puffy, whitish-blue stems. The phosphorescence, which issued equally from all portions of these plants, served to light the gloom for some distance around, and brought out dimly the columnated character of the cavern's further walls.

Howard saw, as he passed among them, that the plants were rootless. It seemed that they would topple at a touch; but happening to stumble against one of the clumps, he found that they supported his weight with resilient solidity. No doubt they were attached firmly by some sort of suction to the smooth stone.

In the middle of the cave, behind a lofty fringing of these luminous fungi, he discovered a pool of water, fed by a thin trickle that descended through the gloom from a high vault that the phosphorescence could not illumine. Impelled by a sudden, furious thirst, he slid back the *mouf-fa*-hood and drank recklessly, though the fluid was sharp and bitter with strange minerals. Then, with the ravening hunger of one who has not eaten for days, he began to eye the pear-shaped nodes of the tall thallophytes. He broke one of them from its parent stem, tore off the glimmering rind, and found that it was filled with a mealy pulp. A savorous, peppery odor tempted him to taste the pulp. It was not unpleasant, and forgetting all caution (possibly he had become a little mad from his extra-human ordeals) he devoured the stuff in hasty mouthfuls.

The node must have contained a narcotic principle; for almost immediately he was overpowered by an insuperable drowsiness. He fell back and lay where he had fallen, in a deep sodden sopor without dreams, for a length of time which, as far as he could know, might have been the interim of death between two lives. He awoke with violent nausea, a racking headache, and a feeling of hopeless, irredeemable confusion.

He drank again from the bitter pool, and then began to hunt with cloudy senses and feeble, uncertain steps for another exit than the tunnel by which he had entered. His mind was dull and heavily drugged, as if from the lingering of the unknown narcotic, and he could formulate no conscious plan of action but was led only by an animal-like impulse of flight.

He discovered a second opening, low, and fanged with broken-off pillar formations, in the opposite wall of the cavern. It was filled with Stygian darkness; and before entering it, he tore a lumpy branch from one of the phosphorescent fungi, to serve him in lieu of other light.

His subsequent wanderings were nightmarish and interminable. He seemed to have gotten into some tremendous maze of natural caverns, varying greatly in size, and intersecting each other in a bewildering honeycomb fashion: an underworld that lay beyond the metal-insulated realm of the Oumnis.

There were long, tediously winding tunnels that went down into Cimmerian depth, or climbed at acclivitous angles. There were strait cubby-holes, dripping with unknown liquid ores, through which he crawled like a lizard on his belly; and Dantean gulfs that he skirted on slippery, perilous, broken ledges, hearing far below him the sullen sigh or the weirdly booming roar of sub-Mercutian waters.

For awhile, his way led mainly downward, as if he were plunging to the bowels of the planet. The air became warmer and more humid. He came at last to the sheer brink of an incommensurable abyss, where noctilucent fungi, vaster than any he had yet seen, grew tall as giant trees along the precipice that he followed for miles.

They were like fantastic monolithic tapers; but their luminosity failed to reveal the giddy depth above and beneath.

He met none of the Oumnis in this inexhaustible world of night and silence. But after he had rounded the great gulf, and had started to re-ascend in smaller caverns, he began to encounter, at intervals, certain blind, white, repulsive creatures the size of an overgrown rat, but without even the rudiments of tail or legs. In his demoralized condition of mind and body, he felt a primitive fear of these things, rather than the mere repugnance which their aspect would normally have aroused. However, they were non-aggressive and shrank sluggishly away from him. Once, he trod inadvertently on one of the creatures and leapt away, howling with fright, when it squirmed nauseously beneath his heel. Finding he had crushed its head, he took courage and began to belabor the flopping abnormality with the metal rod which he still carried. He mashed it into an oozy pulp—a pulp that still quivered with life; and then, overcome by bestial, atavistic hunger, and forgetting all the painfully acquired prejudices of civilized man, he knelt down and devoured the pulp with shameless greed. Afterward, replete, he stretched himself out and slept for many hours.

VI

He awoke with renewed physical strength, but with nerves and mind that were still partially shattered by his experiences. Like a savage who awakens in some primordial cave, he felt the irrational terror of darkness and mystery. His memories were dazed and broken, and he could recall the Oumnis only as a vague and almost supernatural source of fear, from which he had fled.

The fungus-bough, which had served him in lieu of a torch or lantern, was lying beside him in the darkness. With the bough in one hand and the metal rod in the other, he resumed his wanderings. He met more of the white, legless creatures; but he had conquered his fear of them now, and looked upon them only as a possible source of food. He proceeded to kill and eat one of them anon, relishing the worm-soft flesh as an aborigine would have relished a meal of grubs or white ants.

He had lost all notion of the passing of time or its measurement. He was a thing that clambered endlessly on Tartarean cavern-slopes or along the brink of lightless rivers and pools and chasms, killing when he was hungry, sleeping when his weariness became too urgent. Perhaps he went on for days; perhaps for many weeks, in a blind, instinctive search for light and outer air.

The flora and fauna of the caverns changed. He dragged himself through passages that were wholly lined with bristling, glowing thallophytes, some of which were tough and sharp as if fibred with iron. He came to tepid lakes whose waters were infested by long, agile, hydra-bodied creatures, divided into tapeworm segments, that rose to dispute his way but were powerless to harm his *mouffa*-covered limbs with their toothless, pulpy mouths. For awhile, he seemed to be passing through a zone of unnatural warmth, due, no doubt, to the presence of hidden volcanic activity. There were hot geysers, and gulfs from which sultry vapors rose, filling the air with queer, metallic-smelling gases that seemed to burn corrosively in his nostrils and lungs. Some remnant of his former scientific knowledge caused him to recoil from such neighborhoods and retrace his footsteps into caverns free of these gases.

Fleeing from one of the mephitic-laden caves, he found himself in a mile-wide chamber, lined with fungi of uncommon exuberance, amid whose luminiferous growths he met with one of his most terrible adventures. A vast and semi-ophidian monster, white as the other life-forms he had met, and equally legless but owning a single, Cyclopean, phosphoric eye, leapt upon him from the unearthly vegetation and hurled him to the ground with the ram-like impact of its blunt, shapeless head. He lay half-stunned, while the monster began to ingest him in its enormous maw, starting with his feet. Seemingly the metal which he wore was no barrier to its appetite. The creature had swallowed him nearly to the hips, when he recovered his senses and realized his frightful predicament.

Smitten with hideous terror, howling and gibbering like a caveman, he lifted the metal rod, which his clutching fingers had somehow retained, and struck frantically at the awful head into whose mouth he was being drawn by inches. The blows made little or no impression on the great rubbery mass; and soon he was waist-deep in the monstrous maw. In his dire need, a trace of reasoning-power returned to him; and using the rod like a rapier he thrust it into the immense, glaring eye, burying it to his hand, and probably penetrating whatever rudimentary semblance of brain the animal possessed. A pale and egg-like fluid oozed from the broken eye, and the slobbering lips tightened intolerably upon Howard, almost crushing him in what proved to be the death-spasm. The white, swollen barrel-thick body tossed for many minutes; and during its convulsions, Howard was knocked insensible. When he came to again, the creature was lying comparatively still; and the sack-like mouth had begun to relax, so that he was able to extricate himself from the dreadful gorge.

The shock of this experience completed his mental demoralization and drove him even further into primitive brutehood. At times, his brain was almost a blank; and he knew nothing, remembered nothing but the blind horror of those infra-planetary caverns and the dumb instinct that still impelled him to seek escape.

Several times, as he continued his way through the thickets of fungi, he was forced to flee or hide from other monsters of the same type as the one that had so nearly ingested him. Then he entered a region of steep acclivities that took him ever upward. The air became chill and the caverns were seemingly void of vegetable or animal life. He wondered dully as to the reason of the growing cold; but his broken mind could suggest no explanation.

Before entering this realm, he had supplied himself with another fragment of luminiferous fungus to light his way. He was groping through a mountain-like wilderness of chasms and riven scarps and dolomites, when, at some distance above, he saw with inexpressible fright a glimmering as of two cold green eyes that moved among the crags. He had virtually forgotten the Oumnis and their lamps; but something—half intuition, half memory—warned him of direr peril than any he had hitherto met in the darkness.

He dropped his luminous torch and concealed himself behind one of the dolomitic formations. From his hiding-place, he saw the passing of two of the Immortals, clad in silvery *mouffa*, who descended the scarp and vanished in the craggy gulfs below. Whether or not they were hunting for him, he could not know; but when they had gone from sight, he resumed his climb, hurrying at breakneck speed and feeling that he must get as far away as possible from the bearers of those icy green lights.

The dolomites dwindled in size, and the steep chamber narrowed like the neck of a bottle and closed in upon him presently from all sides, till it was only a narrow, winding passage. The floor of the passage became fairly level. Anon, as he followed it, he was startled and blinded by a glare of light directly ahead—a light that was brilliant as pure sunshine. He cowered and stepped back, shielding his eyes with his hands till they became somewhat tempered to the glare. Then, stealthily, with a mingling of confused fears and dim, unworded hopes, he crept toward the light and came out in an endless metal hall, apparently deserted but filled as far as eye could see with the apparently sourceless brilliance.

The mouth of the rough natural passage from which he had emerged was fitted with a sort of valve, which had been left open, doubtless by the Immortals he had seen among the nether crags. The boat-shaped vehicle they had used was standing in the hall. This vehicle, and the hall itself, were familiar to him, and he began to recollect, in a partial way, the ordeals he had undergone among the Oumnis before his flight into outer darkness.

The hall was slightly inclined; and he seemed to remember that the upward grade would presumably lead to a lost world of freedom. Apprehensively and furtively, he began to follow it, loping like an animal.

After he had gone for perhaps a mile, the floor became perfectly level, but the hall itself started to turn in a sort of arc. He was unable to see very far ahead. Then, so abruptly that he could not check his headlong flight, he came in view of three Oumnis, clothed in metal, who were all standing with their backs to him. A boat-vehicle was near at hand. One of the Immortals was tugging at a huge, capstan-like bar that protruded from the wall of the passage; and as if in response to the bar, a sort of gleaming metal valve was descending slowly from the roof. Inch by inch, it came down like a mighty curtain; and soon it would close the entire passage and render impossible the earth-man's egress.

Somehow, it did not occur to Howard that the tunnel beyond the valve might lead to other realms than the outer air for which he longed so desperately. As if by a miracle, something of his former courage and resourcefulness had returned to him; and he did not turn and flee incontinently at sight of the Immortals, as he would have done a short time before. He felt that now or never was his opportunity to escape from the sub-Mercutian levels.

Leaping forward on the unsuspecting Oumnis, all of whom were intent on the closing of the valve, he struck at the foremost with his metal bar. The Mercutian toppled and went down with a clattering of *mouffa* on the floor. The one who was operating the lever continued his task, and Howard had no time to strike him down, for the remaining Immortal, with tigerish agility, had sprung back and was levelling the deadly fire-tube which he carried.

Howard saw that the great valve was still descending—was barely two feet above the cavern floor. He made a flying dive for the opening, sprawling on all fours and then crawling prone on his stomach beneath the terrible curtain of metal.

Struggling to rise, he found himself impeded and held back. He was in utter darkness now; but getting to his knees and groping about, he determined the cause of his retardation. The fallen valve had caught the loose elongated heel of the *mouffa* on his right foot. He had all the sensations of a trapped animal as he sought to wrench himself free. The tough *mouffa* held, weighed down by the enormous valve; and it seemed that there was no escape.

Then, amid his desperation, he somehow remembered that the

mouffa-armor was open at the breast. Awkwardly and painfully, he managed to crawl forth from it, leaving it there like a discarded lizard-skin.

Getting to his feet, he raced on in the darkness. He was without light, for he had dropped the phosphorescent bough in his dive under the closing valve. The cavern was rough and flinty to his naked feet; and he felt an icy wind, bleak as the breath of glaciers, that blew upon him as he went. The floor sloped upward, and in places it was broken into stair-like formations against which he stumbled and fell, bruising himself severely. Then he cut his head cruelly on a sharp stone that projected from the low roof. The wet, warm blood flowed down across his brow and into his eyes.

The passage steepened and the air took on a terrible frigidity. There was no sign of pursuit from the Oumnis; but fearing they would raise the valve and follow him, the earth-man hastened on. He was puzzled by the growing Arctic cold, but the suppositional reason seemed to elude him. His naked limbs and torso were studded with goose-flesh; and he began to shiver with violent ague, in spite of the high speed at which he ran and climbed.

Now the cavern-stairs were more regular and defined. They seemed to mount forever in the darkness; and growing accustomed to them he was able to grope his way from step to step with no more than an occasional fall or stumble. His feet were cut and bleeding; but the cold had begun to numb them and he felt little pain.

He saw a dim, circular patch of light far above him, and gasping with the icy air, which appeared to grow thinner and more irrespirable, he rushed toward it. Hundreds, thousands of those black, glaciated steps he seemed to climb before he neared the light. He came out beneath a sable heaven crowded with chill, pulseless, glaring stars, in a sort of valley-bottom among drear unending scarps and pinnacles, still and silent as a frozen dream of death. They gleamed in the starlight with reflections of myriad-angled ice; and the valley-bottom itself was lit by patches of a leprous whiteness. One of these patches fringed the mouth of the incline on whose topmost step the earth-man was standing.

He fought agonizingly for breath in the tenuous infra-zero air and his body stiffened momently with a permeating rigor as he stood and peered in numb bewilderment at the icy, mountainous chaos of the landscape in which he had emerged. It was like a dead crater in a world of unspeakable and perpetual desolation, where life could never have been.

The flowing blood had congealed upon his brow and cheeks. With glazing eyes, he saw, in a nearby cliff, the continuation of the cavern-steps. Hewn for some unimaginable purpose by the Immortals, they ran upward in the ice toward the higher summits.

It was not the familiar twilight zone of Mercury in which he had come forth—it was the bleak, nightward side, eternally averted from the sun, and blasted with the frightful cold of cosmic space. He felt the pinnacles and chasms close him in, relentless and rigid, like some hyperborean hell. Then the realization of his plight became something very remote and recessive, a dim thought that floated above his ebbing consciousness. He fell forward on the snow with limbs already stiff and unbending; and the mercy of the final numbness grew complete.

THE MAZE OF THE ENCHANTER

With no other light than that of the four diminutive moons of Xiccarph, each in a different phase but all decrescent, Tiglari had crossed the bottomless swamp of Soorm, wherein no reptile dwelt and no dragon descended—but where the pitch-black ooze was alive with continual heavings and writhings. He had carefully avoided the high causey of white corundum that spanned the fen, and had threaded his way with infinite peril from isle to sedgy isle that shuddered gelatinously beneath him. When he reached the solid shore and the shelter of the palm-tall rushes, he was equally careful to avoid the pale porphyry stairs that wound heavenward through dizzy, nadir-cleaving chasms and along glassy scarps to the ever-mysterious and terrible house of Maal Dweb. The causey and the stairs were guarded by those that he did not wish to meet: the silent, colossal iron servitors of Maal Dweb, whose arms ended in long crescent blades of tempered steel which were raised in implacable scything against any who came thither without their master's permission.

Tiglari's naked body was smeared from crown to heel with the juice of a jungle plant repugnant to all the fauna of Xiccarph. By virtue of this he hoped to pass unharmed the ferocious ape-like creatures that roamed at will through the cliff-hung gardens and halls of the Tyrant. He carried a coil of woven root-fiber, wonderfully strong and light, and weighted with a brazen ball at one end, for use in climbing the mountain. At his side, in a sheath of chimera-skin, he wore a needle-sharp knife that had been dipt in the mortal poison of winged vipers.

Many, before Tiglari, with the same noble dream of tyrannicide, had attempted to cross the pitchy fen and scale the forbidding scarps.

But none had returned; and the fate of such as had actually won to the mountain palace of Maal Dweb was a much-disputed problem; since no man had ever again beheld them, living or dead. But Tiglari, the jungle hunter, skilled in the slaying of fierce and crafty beasts, was undeterred by the more than hideous probabilities before him.

The escalade of the mountain would have been a highly dangerous feat by the full light of the three suns of Xiccarph. With eyes that were keen as those of some night-flying pterodactyl, Tiglari hurled his weighted coil about projecting coigns and fang-like salients. Hand over hand, he went up with simian ease from foothold to precarious foothold; and at length he attained a narrow buttress beneath the final cliff. From this vantage, it was an easy matter to fling his rope around the crooked bole of a tree that leaned gulfward with scimitar-like foliage from the gardens of Maal Dweb.

Evading the sharp and semi-metallic leaves that seemed to slash downward as the tree bent limberly with his dangling weight, he stood, stooping warily, on the fearsome and widely fabled mesa. Here, it was rumored, with no human aid, the half-demoniac sorcerer and scientist had carved the more lofty pinnacles of the old mountain into walls, cupolas and turrets, and had levelled a great space about them. This space he had covered immediately with loamy soil, produced by magic; and therein he had planted curious baneful trees from outlying worlds beyond the suns of Xiccarph, together with flowers that might have been those of some teeming and exuberant hell.

Little enough was actually known of these gardens; but the flora that grew on the northern, southern and western sides of the palace was popularly believed to be less deadly than that which faced the dawning of the triple suns. Much of this latter vegetation, according to myth, had been trained and topiarized in the form of an almost infinite labyrinth, balefully ingenious, from which egress was impossible: a maze that concealed in its windings the most fatal and atrocious traps, the most unpredictable dooms, invented by the malign Daedalus.

Mindful of this labyrinth, Tiglari had approached the palace on the side that fronted the three-fold sunset.

Breathless, with arms that ached from the long, arduous climb, he crouched in the garden shadows. About him he saw the heavy-hooded blossoms that leaned from a winy gloom in venomous languor, or fawned toward him with open corollas that exhaled a narcotic perfume or diffused a pollen of madness. Anomalous, multiform, with silhouettes that curdled the blood or touched the brain with nightmare, the trees of Maal Dweb appeared to gather and conspire against him beyond the flowers. Some arose with the sinuous towering of plumed pythons, of aigretted dragons. Others crouched with radiating limbs that were like the hairy members of colossal arachnidans. They seemed to close in upon Tiglari with a stealthy motion. They waved their frightful darts of thorn, their scythe-like leaves. They blotted the four moons with webs of arabesque menace. They reared from interminably coiling roots behind mammoth foliages that resembled an army of interlocking shields.

With endless caution and calculation, the hunter made his way forward, seeking a rift in the armed phalanx of vegetable monstrosities. His faculties, ever alert, were abnormally quickened by a grievous fear, intensified by a mighty hatred. The fear was not for himself, but for the girl Athlé, his beloved and the fairest of his tribe, who had gone up alone that very evening by the causey of corundum and the porphyry stairs at the summons of Maal Dweb. His hatred was that of a brave man and an outraged lover for the all-powerful, all-dreaded tyrant whom no man had ever seen, and from whose abode no woman came back; who spoke with an iron voice that was audible at will in the far cities or the outmost jungles; who punished the rebellious and the disobedient with a doom of falling fire that was swifter than the thunderstone.

Maal Dweb had taken ever the fairest from among the maidens of the planet Xiccarph; and no palace of the walled towns, or savage outland cave, was exempt from his unknown scrutiny. He had chosen no less than fifty girls during the three decades of his tyranny; and these, forsaking their lovers and kinsfolk voluntarily, lest the wrath of Maal Dweb should descend upon them, had gone one by one to the mountain citadel and were lost behind its cryptic walls. There, as the odalisques of the aging sorcerer, they were supposed to dwell in halls that multiplied their beauty with a thousand mirrors; and were said to have for servants women of brass and men of iron that mimicked in all ways the motion and speech of living people.

Tiglari had poured before Athlé the uncouth adoration of his heart and the barbaric spoils of the chase, but having many rivals, was still unsure of her favor. Cool as a river lily, and no less impartial, she had accepted his worship and that of the others, among whom the warrior Mocair was perhaps the most formidable. Returning at eve from the hunt, Tiglari had found the tribe in lamentation; and learning that Athlé had departed to the harem of Maal Dweb, was swift to follow. He had not announced his intention to his fellow tribesmen, since the ears of Maal Dweb were everywhere; and he did not know whether Mocair or any of the others had preceded him in his desperate errantry. Mocair, however, had been absent; and it was not unlikely that he had already dared the obscure and hideous perils of the mountain.

The thought of this was enough to drive Tiglari forward with a rash disregard of the poisonous, reptile flowers and clutching foliations. He came anon to a gap in the horrible grove, and saw the saffron lights from the lower windows of Maal Dweb, and a dark thronging of domes and turrets that assailed the constellations above. The lights were vigilant as the eyes of sleepless dragons, and appeared to regard him with an evil, unblinking awareness. But Tiglari leapt toward them, across the gap, and heard the clash of sabered leaves that met behind him.

Before him was an open lawn, covered with a queer grass that squirmed like innumerable worms beneath his bare feet. He did not care to linger upon that lawn, but ran onward with light, skimming paces. There were no footmarks in the grass; but nearing the portico of the palace, he saw a coil of thin rope that someone had flung aside, and knew that Mocair had preceded him.

There were paths of mottled marble about the palace, and fountains and waterfalls that played with a gurgling as of blood from the throats of carven monsters. The open portals were unguarded, and the whole building was still as a mausoleum lit by windless lamps. No shadows moved behind the brilliant yellow windows; and darkness slept unbroken among the high towers and cupolas. Tiglari, however, mistrusted sorely this appearance of quietude and slumber, and followed the bordering paths for some distance before daring to approach nearer to the palace.

Certain large and shadowy animals, which he took for the apish monsters of Maal Dweb, went by him in the gloom. They were hairy and uncouth, with sloping heads. Some of them ran in four-footed fashion, while others maintained the half-erect posture of anthropoids. They did not offer to molest Tiglari; but, whining dismally like dogs, they slunk away as if to avoid him. By this token, he knew that they were veritable beasts, and could not abide the odor with which he had smeared his limbs and torso.

At length, he came to a lampless portico with crowded columns. Here, with the silent gliding of a jungle snake, he entered the mysterious and ever-dreadful house of Maal Dweb. Behind the dark pillars, a door stood open; and beyond the door were the dim and seemingly endless reaches of an empty hall.

Tiglari went in with redoubled caution, and began to follow the arrased wall. The palace was full of unknown perfumes, languorous and somnolent: a subtle reek as of censers in hidden alcoves of love. He did not like the perfumes; and the silence troubled him more and more as he went deeper into the palace. It seemed to him that the darkness was thick with unheard breathings, was alive with invisible and sinister movements.

Slowly, like the opening of great yellow eyes, the yellow flames arose in mighty lamps of copper that hung along the hall. Tiglari hid himself behind a heavy-figured arras; but peeping out with eerie trepidation, he saw that the hall was still deserted. Finally, he dared to resume his progress. All about him, the imperial hangings, broidered with purple men and azure women on a field of bright blood, appeared to stir with uneasy life in a wind that he could not feel; and the lamps regarded him with unwavering splendid eyes. But there was no sign of the presence of Maal Dweb; and the metal servitors and human odalisques of the tyrant were nowhere to be seen.

The doors on either side of the hall, with cunningly mated valves of ebony and ivory, were all closed. At the far end, Tiglari saw a rift of flaming light in a somber double arras. Parting the arras very softly, he peered into a huge, brightly illumined chamber that seemed at first sight to be the harem of Maal Dweb, peopled with all the girls that the enchanter had summoned to his mountain dwelling over a course of decades. In fact, it seemed that there were many hundreds, leaning or recumbent on ornate couches, or standing in attitudes of languor or terror. Tiglari discerned in the throng the women of Ommu-Zain, whose flesh is whiter than desert salt; the slim girls of Uthmai, who are moulded from breathing, palpitating jet; the queenly amber girls of equatorial Xala; and the small women of Ilap, who have the tones of newly greening bronze. But among them all, he could not find the lilied beauty of Athlé.

Greatly did he marvel at the number of the women and the utter stillness with which they maintained their various postures. There was no lifting nor falling of eyelids, no dropping of hands, no curving nor opening of lips. They were like images of living, subtly painted marble, or goddesses that slept in some enchanted hall of eternity.

Tiglari, the intrepid hunter, was awed and frightened. Here, surely, was proof of the fabled sorceries of Maal Dweb. These women—if indeed they were women and not mere statues—had been made the thralls of a death-like spell of immortal slumber. It was as if some invisible medium of adamantine silence had filled the room, had formed about its occupants: a silence wherein, it seemed, no mortal being could draw breath.

However, if Tiglari were to continue his search for Maal Dweb and Athlé, it was necessary for him to traverse the enchanted chamber. Feeling that a marble sleep might descend upon him at the very crossing of the sill, he went in with holden breath and furtive pard-like paces. About him the women preserved their eternal stillness, their various airs and attitudes. Each, it appeared, had been overcome by the spell at the instant of some particular emotion, whether of fear, wonder, curiosity, vanity, weariness, anger or voluptuousness. Their number was fewer than he had supposed, and the room itself was smaller, but metal mirrors, panelling the walls, had created an illusion of multitude and immensity.

At the further end, he came to a second double arras, slightly parted, and revealing only shadow beyond. Peering through, he beheld a twilight chamber, illuminated dimly by two censers that gave forth a particolored glow and a red fume as of vaporing blood. The censers were set on lofty tripods in the far corners, facing each other. Between them, beneath a canopy of some dark and smouldering stuff with fringes braided like women's hair, was a couch of nocturnal purples with a valance of silver birds that fought against golden snakes. On the couch, in sober garments, a man reclined as if weary or asleep. The face of the man was a pale mask of mystery lying amid ambiguous shadows; but it did not occur to Tiglari that this being was any other than the redoubtable and tyrannic sorcerer whom he had come to slay. He knew that this was Maal Dweb, whom no man had seen in the flesh, but whose power was manifest to all; the occult, omniscient ruler of Xiccarph; the overlord of kings; the suzerain of the three suns and of all their moons and planets.

Like ghostly sentinels, the symbols of the grandeur of Maal Dweb, the images of his frightful empire, rose up to confront Tiglari. But the thought of Athlé was a red mist that blotted all. He forgot his eerie terrors, his awe of the ensorcelled palace. The rage of the bereaved lover, the bloodthirst of the cunning hunter, awoke within him to guide his agile, stealthy paces, to make firm his powerful thews. The chamber was empty, except for the still and languid figure on the couch. Tiglari neared the unconscious sorcerer; and his hand grew tight on the hilt of the needle-like knife that was dipt in viper-venom.

The man before him lay with closed eyes and a cryptic weariness on his mouth and eyelids. He seemed to meditate rather than sleep, like one who wanders in a maze of distant memories or profound reveries. About him the walls were draped with funereal hangings, darkly and vaguely figured. Above him the twin censers wrought a cloudy glow, and diffused throughout the room their drowsy myrrh, which made the senses of Tiglari swim with a strange dimness.

Crouching tiger-wise beside the valance of birds and serpents, he made ready for the stroke. Then, mastering the subtle vertigo of the perfumes, he rose up; and his arm, with the darting movement of some heavy but supple adder, struck fiercely at the tyrant's heart.

It was as if he had tried to pierce a wall of adamant. In mid-air, before and above the recumbent enchanter, the knife clashed on some impenetrable substance that Tiglari could not see; and the point broke off and tinkled on the floor at his feet. Uncomprehending, baffled, he peered at the being whom he had sought to slay. Maal Dweb had not stirred nor opened his eyes. There was neither frown nor smile on his features; but their look of enigmatic weariness was somehow touched with a faint and cruel amusement.

Hesitantly, Tiglari put out his hand to verify a certain curious notion that had occurred to him. Even as he had suspected, there was no couch or canopy between the fuming censers—only a vertical, unbroken, highly-polished surface, in which the whole scene was apparently reflected. He had tried to kill a mirrored image. But, to his further mystification, he himself was not visible in the mirror.

He whirled about, thinking Maal Dweb must be somewhere in the room. Even as he turned, the funereal draperies rushed back with an evil, silken whispering from the walls, as if drawn by unseen hands. The chamber leapt into sudden glaring light, the walls appeared to recede illimitably; and naked giants, whose umber-brown limbs and torsos glistened as if smeared with ointment, stood in menacing postures on every side. Their eyes glowered like those of jungle creatures; and each of them held an enormous knife, from which the point had been broken.

This, thought Tiglari, was a fearsome thaumaturgy; and he crouched down beneath the tripods, wary as a trapped animal, to await the assault of the giants. But these beings, crouching simultaneously, mimicked his every movement. By degrees it came to him that what he saw was his own reflection, multiplied and monstrously amplified in the mirrors of Maal Dweb.

He turned again. The tasseled canopy, the couch of night-dark purples with its figured valance, the reclining dreamer in plain vestments, all had vanished. Of that which he had beheld, only the smoking censers remained, rearing before a glassy wall that gave back like the others the reflection of Tiglari himself.

Bafflement and terror united now in the savage brain of the hunter. He felt that Maal Dweb, the all-seeing, all-potent magician, was playing a game and was deluding him with elaborate mockeries. Rashly indeed had Tiglari pitted his simple brawn and forest craft against a being of such supernatural power and demoniac artifice. He dared not stir; he scarcely ventured to breathe. The monstrous reflections appeared to watch him like ogres who guard a captive pygmy. The light, which emanated as if from hidden lamps in the mirrors, took on a more pitiless and alarming luster, and centered itself upon him with a silent horror. The vast, illusive reaches of the room appeared to deepen; and far away in their shadows, he saw the gathering of vapors with human faces that melted and re-formed incessantly and were never twice the same.

Ever the eerie radiance brightened; ever the mist of faces, like a hell-born fume, dissolved and re-limned itself behind the immobile giants, in the lengthening vistas. An unheard laughter, malevolent, scornful, seemed to lurk beyond the stillness. How long Tiglari waited, he could not tell; the bright and frozen horror of that room was a thing apart from time.

Now, in the litten air, a voice began to speak: a voice that was toneless, deliberate—and disembodied. It was faintly contemptuous; a little weary; slightly cruel. It was impossible to align or locate: near as the beating of Tiglari's heart, and yet infinitely far.

"What do you seek, Tiglari?" said the voice. "Do you think to enter with impunity the palace of Maal Dweb? Others—many others, with the same intentions—have come before you: but all have paid a certain price for their temerity."

"I seek the maiden Athlé," said Tiglari. "What have you done with her?" The words were strange to him, their very sound was remote, as if another than himself had spoken.

"Athlé is very beautiful," replied the voice. "It is the will of Maal Dweb to make a certain use of her loveliness. The use is not one that should concern a hunter of wild beasts . . . You are unwise, Tiglari."

"Where is Athlé?" persisted the hunter.

"Athlé has gone to find her fate in the labyrinth of Maal Dweb. Not long ago, the warrior Mocair, who had followed her to my palace, went out at my suggestion to pursue his search amid the threadless windings of that never to be exhausted maze. Go now, Tiglari, and seek her also . . . There are many mysteries in my labyrinth; and among them all, mayhap, there is one which you are destined to solve."

The hunter saw that a door had opened in the mirror-panelled wall. In the depth of the mirrors, two of the metal slaves of Maal Dweb had appeared. Taller than living men, and gleaming from head to foot with implacable lusters as of burnished swords, they came forward upon Tiglari. The right arm of each was handed with a crescent sickle. Hasti-

ly, with no backward glance, the hunter went out through the open
door. Behind him he heard the surly clash of its meeting valves.

The short night of the planet Xiccarph was not yet over; and the
four moons had all gone down. But before him he saw the beginning
of the fabled maze, illuminated clearly by glowing globular fruits that
hung lantern-wise from baroque arches and arcades of foliage. Guided
by their still, uncanny luminescence, he entered the labyrinth.

At first, it was a place of elfin fantasies and whims. There were
quaintly turned estrades, pillared with slim and antic trees, latticed with
the drolly peering faces of extravagant orchids, that led the seeker to
hidden, surprising bowers of goblinry. It was as if those outer meanderings had been planned merely to entice and bemuse and beguile.

Then, by vague degrees, as the hunter went on, it seemed that the
designer's mood had darkened, had become more ominous and baleful. The trees that lined the path, with twisted, intertwining boles, were
Laocoöns of struggle and torture, lit by enormous fungi that seemed to
lift unholy tapers. The path itself ran downward, or climbed with evilly
tilted steps through caverns of imbricated leafage that shone with the
brazen glistening of dragon-scales. At every turn the way divided before Tiglari; the devious branchings multiplied; and skillful though he
was in jungle-craft, it would have been wholly impossible for him to
retrace his wanderings. He kept on, hoping that chance would somehow lead him to Athlé; and many times he called her name aloud, but
was answered only by remote, derisive echoes, or by the dolorous
howling of some unseen beast that had become lost in the maze of
Maal Dweb.

He came to eerie pools, alight with coiling and wreathing witch-
fires, in dim arboreal grottoes. Greenish, bloated hands as of dead men
appeared to lift from the changing films of phosphorescence; and once
he thought that he beheld the drowning face of Athlé. He plunged into
the shallow pool—but found only fetid slime, and a swollen, nauseous
thing that squirmed slowly beneath his touch.

Now he was mounting through arbors of malignant hydra growths that coiled and uncoiled about him tumultuously. The way lightened more and more; the night-shining fruits and blossoms were pale and sickly as the dying tapers of a witches' revel. The earliest of the three suns had risen; and its gamboge-yellow beams were filtering in through the plaited horrors of frilled and venomous vines.

Far off, and seeming to fall from some hidden height in the labyrinth before him, he heard a chorus of brazen voices that were like articulate bells or gongs. He could not distinguish the words; but the accents were those of a solemn and portentous announcement. They were fraught with mystic finality, with hieratic doom. They ceased; and there was no sound other than the hiss and rustle of swaying plants.

Tiglari went on. The tortuous maze became wilder and more anomalous. There were tiered growths, like obscene sculptures or architectural forms, that seemed to be of stone and metal. Others were like carnal nightmares of rooted flesh, that wallowed and fought and coupled in noisome ooze. Foul things with chancrous blossoms flaunted themselves on infernal obelisks. Living parasitic mosses of crimson crawled on vegetable monsters that swelled and bloated behind the columns of accursed pavilions.

It seemed now that the hunter's every step was predestined and dictated. He was no longer free to choose his way; for many of the paths were overgrown by things that he did not care to face; and others were blocked by horrid portcullises of cacti, or ended in pools whose waters teemed with leeches larger than tunnies. The second and third suns of Xiccarph arose; but their beams of emerald and carmine served but to heighten the terrors of the web that had closed in about Tiglari.

By stairs where floral serpents crept, and gradients lined with tossing, clashing aloes, he climbed slowly on. Rarely could he see the labyrinthine reaches below, or the levels toward which he was tending. Somewhere on the blind path, he met one of the ape-like animals of

Maal Dweb: a dark, savage creature, sleek and glistening like a wet ot-
ter, as if it had bathed in one of the hidden pools. It passed him with a
hoarse growl, recoiling as the others had done from his repulsively
smeared body . . . But nowhere could he find the maiden Athlé or the
warrior Mocair, who had preceded him into the maze.

Now he had reached a curious little pavement of somber onyx, oblong, and wholly surrounded, except on the side of his approach, by
enormous flowers with fluted bronze-like stems and great leaning balls
that seemed to be the mottled heads of bestial chimeras, yawning to
disclose their carmine throats. Through the gap in this singular hedge,
he stepped forward on the pavement and stood staring irresolutely at
the serried blooms: for here the way seemed to end.

The onyx beneath his feet was wet with some unknown, sticky fluid. He was dazed with the wonder, strangeness, and intricate, coiling
horror through which he had passed; but a dim warning of peril stirred
within him. He turned toward the gap through which he had entered,
but his impulse of retreat was all too late. From the base of each of the
tall flower stems, a long tendril like a wire of bronze uncoiled with
lightning rapidity, and closed about his ankles. He stood trapped and
helpless at the center of a taut net. Then, while he struggled ineffectu-
ally, the huge stems began to lean and tilt toward him, till the carmine
mouths of the blossoms were close about his knees like a circle of
fawning monsters.

Nearer they came, almost touching him. From their thick lips a
clear, hueless liquid, dripping slowly at first, and then running in little
rills, descended on his feet and ankles and shanks. Indescribably, his
flesh crawled beneath it; then there was a peculiar passing numbness;
then a furious stinging like the bites of innumerable insects. Between
the crowding heads of the flowers he saw that his legs had undergone
a mysterious and horrifying change; their natural hairiness had thickened, had assumed a dark and shaggy pile like the fur of apes; the
shanks themselves had somehow shortened; and the feet had grown

longer, with uncouth finger-like toes such as were possessed by the animals of Maal Dweb!

In a frenzy of nameless alarm and fear, he drew his broken-tipped knife and began to slash at the flowers. It was as if he had struck at monstrous bells of ringing iron, had assailed the armored heads of dragons. The blade snapped at the hilt. Then the blossoms, lifting hideously, were leaning about his waist, were laving his hips and thighs in their thin, evil slaver.

Across the bizarre nightmare in which his brain and body were drowning impotently, he heard the startled cry of a woman. Through the open gap in the hedge, he beheld a strange scene which the hitherto impenetrable maze, parting as if by magic, had revealed. Fifty feet away, on the same level as the onyx pavement, there stood an elliptic dais or low altar of moonwhite stone at whose center the maiden Athlé, emerging from the labyrinth on a raised walk of porphyry, had paused in an attitude of wonder. Before her, in the claws of an immense marble lizard that reared above the dais, a great circular mirror of steely metal was held upright, with the monster's head hidden from view behind it. Athlé, as if fascinated by some celestial vision, was peering into the steely disk. She presented her wide-eyed profile to Tiglari; and the mirror itself was seen obliquely, with the foreshortened body of the lizard reaching away at a sharp angle and mingling obscenely with the half-reptilian maze. Midway between the onyx pavement and the ellipse of pale stone, a row of six slender brazen columns, topped with graven heads like demoniac Termini, rose at broad intervals and faced alternately the hunter and the girl.

Tiglari would have called out to Athlé; but at that moment she took a single step toward the mirror, as if drawn by something that she saw in its depths; and the dull disk seemed to brighten with some internal, incandescent flame. The eyes of the hunter were temporarily blinded by the spiky rays that leapt forth from it for an instant, enveloping and transfixing the maiden. When the dimness cleared away in swirling blots of sultry color, he saw that Athlé, in a pose of statuesque rigidity, was still regarding the mirror with startled eyes. She had not moved; the wonder was frozen on her face: and it came to Tiglari that she was like the women who slept an enchanted slumber in the palace of Maal Dweb. Even as this thought occurred to him, he heard the ringing chorus of metallic voices, that seemed to emanate from the graven demon heads upon the columns.

"The maiden Athlé," announced the voices in solemn and portentous tones, "has beheld herself in the mirror of Eternity, and has passed forever beyond the changes and corruptions of Time."

Tiglari felt that he was sinking into some enormous, obscurely terrible fen of dreams. He could comprehend nothing of what had befallen Athlé; and his own fate was an equally dark and dread enigma; beyond the solution of a simple hunter.

Now the leaning blossoms had lifted about his shoulders, were laving his arms, his body. Beneath their abhorrent alchemy the transformation continued. A long fur sprang up on the thickening torso; the arms lengthened; they became simian; the hands took on a likeness to the feet. From the neck downward, Tiglari differed in no wise from the apes of the garden.

In helpless abject horror, he waited for the completion of the metamorphosis. Then, slowly, he became aware that a man in sober garments, with eyes and mouth replete with the weariness of strange things, was standing before him. Behind the man, as if attending him, were two of the sickle-handed automatons of iron.

In a somewhat languid voice, the man uttered an unknown word that vibrated in the air with prolonged, mysterious aftertones. The circle of craning flowers drew back from Tiglari, resuming their former upright positions in a weird hedge; and the wiry tendrils were withdrawn from his ankles, leaving him free. Hardly able to comprehend his release, he heard a sound of brazen voices, and knew dimly that the demon heads of the columns had spoken, saying:

"The hunter Tiglari has been laved in the nectar of the blossoms of primordial life, and has become in all ways, from the neck downward, even as the beasts that he hunted."

When the solemn chorus ceased, the weary man in sober raiment came nearer and addressed him:

"I, Maal Dweb, had intended to deal with you precisely as I dealt with Mocair and many others. Mocair was the beast that you met in the labyrinth, with new-made fur that was still sleek and wet from the liquor of the flowers; and you saw some of his predecessors about the palace. However, I find that my whims are not always the same. You, Tiglari, unlike the others, shall at least remain a man from the neck upward; and you are free to resume your wanderings in the labyrinth, and escape from it if you can. I do not wish to see you again, and my clemency arises from another reason than esteem for your kind. Go now: the maze has many windings which you are yet to traverse."

A dreadful awe was upon Tiglari; his native fierceness, his savage volition, were tamed by the enchanter's languid will. With one backward look of fearful concern and wonder at the frozen shape of Athlé, he withdrew obediently, slouching like a great ape. His fur glistening wetly to the three suns, he vanished amid the meanderings of the labyrinth.

Maal Dweb, attended by his metal slaves, went over to the figure of Athlé, which still regarded the steely mirror with astonished eyes.

"Mong Lut," he said, addressing by name the nearer of the two automatons that followed at his heels, "it has been, as you know, my caprice to eternalize the frail beauty of women. Athlé, like the others whom I have summoned to the mountain and have sent out to explore the ingenious secrets of my maze, has looked upon that mirror whose sudden radiance turns the flesh to a stone that is fairer than marble and no less eternal . . . Also, as you know, it has been my whim to turn men into beasts with the copious fluid of certain artificial flowers, so that their outer semblance should conform strictly to their inner nature. Is it not well, Mong Lut, that I should have done these things? Am I not Maal Dweb, in whom all knowledge and all power reside?"

"Yea, master," echoed the automaton in an iron voice, "you are Maal Dweb, the all-wise, the all-powerful, and it is well that you should have done these things."

"However," continued Maal Dweb, "the repetition of even the most remarkable thaumaturgies can grow monotonous after a certain number of times. I do not think that I shall deal again in this fashion with any woman, nor deal thus with any man. Is it not well, Mong Lut, that I should vary my sorceries in future? Am I not Maal Dweb, the all-resourceful?"

"Indeed, you are Maal Dweb," agreed the automaton, "and it would be well for you to diversify your enchantments."

Maal Dweb, in his manner, was not ill pleased with the answers that the automaton had given. He cared little for converse, other than the iron echoing of his metal servitors, who assented always to all that he said, and who spared him the tedium of arguments. And it may have been that there were times when he wearied a little even of this, and preferred the silence of the petrified women, or the muteness of the beasts that could no longer call themselves men.

THE FLOWER-WOMEN

Athlé," said Maal Dweb, "I suffer from the frightful curse of omnipotence. In all Xiccarph, and in the five outer planets of the triple suns, there is no one, there is nothing, to dispute my domination. Therefore, my ennui has become intolerable."

The girlish eyes of Athlé regarded the enchanter with a gaze of undying astonishment, which, however, was not due to his strange avowal. She was the last of the fifty-one women that Maal Dweb had turned into statues in order to preserve their frail, corruptible beauty from the worm-like gnawing of Time. Since, through a laudable desire to avoid monotony, he had resolved never to repeat again this particular sorcery, the magician had cherished Athlé with the affection which an artist feels for the final masterpiece of a series. He had placed her on a little dais, beside the ivory chair in his chamber of meditation. Often he addressed to her his queries or monologues; and the fact that she did not reply nor even hear was to him a signal and unfailing recommendation.

"There is but one remedy for this boredom of mine," he went on,—"the abnegation, at least for a while, of that all too certain power from which it springs. Therefore, I, Maal Dweb, the ruler of six worlds and all their moons, shall go forth alone, unheralded, and without other equipment than that which any fledgling sorcerer might possess. In this way, perhaps, I shall recover the lost charm of incertitude, the foregone enchantment of peril. Adventures that I have not foreseen will be mine; and the future will wear the alluring veil of the mysterious. It remains, however, to select the field of my adventurings."

Maal Dweb arose from his curiously carven chair and waved back the four automatons of iron, having the likeness of armed men, that sprang to attend him. He passed along the halls of his palace, where painted hangings told in vermilion and purple the dread legends of his power. Through ebon valves that opened noiselessly at the uttering of a high-pitched word, he entered the chamber in which was his planetarium.

The room was walled, floored and vaulted with a dark crystal, full of tiny, numberless fires, that gave the illusion of unbounded space with all its stars. In mid-air, without chains or other palpable support, there hung an array of various globes that represented the three suns, the six planets and thirteen moons of the system ruled by Maal Dweb. The miniature suns, amber, emerald, and carmine, bathed their intricately circling worlds with an illumination that reproduced at all times the diurnal conditions of the system itself; and the pigmy satellites maintained always their corresponding orbits and relative positions.

The sorcerer went forward, walking as if on some unfathomable gulf of night, with stars and galaxies beneath him. The poising worlds were level with his shoulders as he passed among them. Disregarding the globes that corresponded to Mornoth, Xiccarph, Ulassa, Nouph and Rhul, he came to Votalp, the outermost, which was then in aphelion on the farther side of the room.

Votalp, a large and moonless world, revolved imperceptibly as he studied it. For one hemisphere, he saw, the yellow sun was at that time in total eclipse behind the sun of carmine; but in spite of this, and its greater distance from the solar triad, Votalp was lit with sufficient clearness. It was mottled with strange hues like a great cloudy opal; and the mottlings were microscopic oceans, isles, mountains, jungles and deserts. Peering closer, as if into a crystal, the enchanter saw the mimic planet swell and deepen. Fantastic sceneries leapt into momentary salience, taking on the definitude and perspective of actual landscapes, and then faded back amid the iridescent blur. Glimpses of teeming, multifarious life, incredible tableaux and monstrous happenings, were beheld by Maal Dweb as he looked down like some celestial spy.

It seemed, however that he found little to divert or inveigle him in these outré doings and exotic wonders. Vision after vision rose before him, summoned and dismissed at will, as if he were turning the pages of a too familiar volume, and he saw nothing over which he cared to linger. The wars of gigantic wyverns; the matings of half-vegetable monsters; the queer algâe that had filled a certain ocean with their living, moving labyrinths; the remarkable spawn of certain polar glaciers—all these elicited no gleam nor sparkle in his dulled eyes of blackish emerald.

At length, on that portion of the planet which was turning into the double dawn from its moonless night, he perceived an occurrence that drew and held his attention. He began to calculate, for the first time, the precise latitude and longitude of the surrounding milieu.

"There," he said to himself, "is a situation not without interest. In fact, the whole affair is quaint and curious enough to warrant my intervention. I shall visit Votalp."

He withdrew from the planetarium and made a few preparations for his meditated journey. Having changed his robe of magisterial sable and scarlet for a hodden mantle, and having removed from his person every charm and talisman, with the exception of two phylacteries acquired in the years of his novitiate, he went forth into the garden of his mountain-builded palace. He left no instructions with the many retainers who served with him: for these retainers were automatons of iron and brass, who would fulfill their various duties without injunction till he returned.

Traversing the curious labyrinth which he alone could solve, he came to the verge of the sheer mesa, where python-like lianas drooped into awful space, and metallic palms deployed their armaments of foliage against the far-flown horizons of the world Xiccarph. Empires and cities, lying supine beneath his magical dominion, were unrolled before him; but, giving them hardly a glance, he walked along the estrade of black psammite at the very brink, till he reached a narrow promontory around which there hung at all times a deep and hueless cloud, obscuring the prospect of the lands below and beyond.

The secret of this cloud, affording access to multiple dimensions and deeply folded realms of space conterminate with far worlds, was known only to Maal Dweb. He had built a silver drawbridge on the promontory; and by lowering its airy span into the cloud, he could pass at will to the further zones of Xiccarph, or could cross the very void between the planets.

Now, after making certain highly recondite calculations, he manipulated the machinery of the light drawbridge so that its other end would fall upon the particular terrain that he desired to visit in Votalp. Then, assuring himself that his calculations and adjustments were flawless, he followed the silver span into the dim, bewildering chaos of the cloud. Here, as he groped in a grey blindness, it seemed that his body and members were drawn out over infinite gulfs, and were bent through impossible angles. A single misstep would have plunged him into spatial regions from which all his cunning sorcery could have contrived no manner of return or release; but he had often trod these hidden ways, and he did not lose his equilibrium. The transit appeared to involve whole centuries of time; but finally he emerged from the cloud and came to the further end of the drawbridge.

Before him was the scene that had lured his interest in Votalp. It was a semi-tropic valley, level and open in the foreground, and rising steeply at the other extreme, with all its multiform fantasies of vegetation, toward the cliffs and chasms of sable mountains horned with blood-red stone. The time was still early dawn, but the amber sun, freeing itself slowly from the occultation of the sun of carmine, had begun to lighten the deep hues and shadows of the valley with strange copper and orange. The emerald sun was still below the horizon.

The terminus of the silver bridge had fallen on a mossy knoll, behind which the hueless cloud had gathered, even as about the promontory in Xiccarph. Maal Dweb descended the knoll, feeling no concern whatever for the bridge. It would remain as he had left it, till the time of his return; and if, in the interim, any creatures from Votalp should cross the gulf and invade his mountain citadel, they would meet a fearful doom in the snares and windings of the labyrinth; or, failing this, would be exterminated by his iron servitors.

As he went down the knoll into the valley, the enchanter heard an eerie, plaintive singing, like the voices of sirens who bewail some irremediable misfortune. The singing came from a sisterhood of unusual creatures, half-woman and half-flower, that grew on the valley bottom beside a sleepy stream of purple water. There were several scores of these lovely and charming monsters, whose feminine bodies of pink and pearl reclined amid the vermilion velvet couches of billowing petals to which they were attached. These petals were borne on single, mattress-like leaves and heavy, short, well-rooted stems. The flowers were disposed in irregular circles, clustering thickly toward the center, and with open intervals in the outer rows.

Maal Dweb approached the flower-women with a certain caution; for he knew that they were vampires. Their arms ended in long tendrils, pale as ivory, swifter and more supple than the coils of darting serpents, with which they were wont to secure the unwary victims drawn by their singing. Of course, knowing in his wisdom the inexorable laws of nature, he felt no disapproval of such vampirism; but, on the other hand, he did not care to be its object.

He circled about the strange family at a little distance, his movements hidden from their observation by boulders overgrown with luxuriant lichens of red and yellow. Soon he neared the straggling outer line of plants that were upstream from the knoll on which he had landed; and here, in confirmation of the vision beheld in the mimic world in his planetarium, he found that the turf was upheaved and broken where five of the blossoms, growing apart from their companions, had been disrooted and removed bodily. He had seen in his vision the rape of the fifth flower, and he knew that the others were now lamenting her.

Suddenly, as if they had forgotten their sorrow, the wailing of the flower-women turned to a wild and sweet and voluptuous singing, like that of the Lorelei. By this token, the enchanter knew that his presence had been detected. Inured though he was to such bewitchments, Maal Dweb found himself far from insensible to the perilous luring of the voices. Contrary to his intention, half-forgetful of the danger, he found himself emerging from the lee of the lichen-crested rocks. By insidious degrees, the melody began to fire his blood with a strange intoxication; it sang in his brain like some bewildering wine. Step by step, with a temporary loss of prudence for which, later, he was quite unable to account, he approached the canorous blossoms.

Now, pausing at an interval that he deemed safe in his bemusement, he beheld plainly the half-human features of the vampires, leaning toward him with fantastic invitation. Their weirdly slanted eyes, like oblong opals of dew and venom, the snaky coiling of their bronze-green hair, the bright, baneful scarlet of their lips, that thirsted subtly even as they sang, awoke within him the knowledge of his peril. Too late, he sought to defy the captiously woven spell. Unwinding with a movement swift as light, the long pale tendrils of one of the creatures wrapped him round, and he was drawn, resisting vainly, toward her couch.

At the moment of his capture, the whole sisterhood had ceased their singing. They began to utter little cries of triumph, shrill and sibilant. Murmurs of expectation, like the purrings of hungry flame, arose from the nearest, who hoped to share in the good fortune of the sorcerer's captress.

Maal Dweb, however, was now able to utilize his faculties. Without alarm or fear, he contemplated the lovely monster, who had drawn him to the verge of her velvet bed, and was fawning upon him with sinisterly parted lips.

Using a somewhat primary power of divination, he apprised himself of certain matters concerning the vampire. Having learnt the true, occult name which this creature shared with all others of her kind, he then spoke the name aloud in a firm but gentle tone; and winning thus, by an elemental law of magic, the power of mastery over his captress and her sisters, he felt the instant relaxation of the tendrils. The flower-woman, with fear and wonder in her strange eyes, drew back like a startled lamia; but Maal Dweb, employing the half-articulate sounds of her own language, began to soothe and reassure her. In a little while, he was on friendly terms with the whole sisterhood. These simple and naive beings forgot their vampiric intentions, their surprise and wonderment, and seemed to accept the magician very much as they accepted the three suns and the meteoric conditions of the planet Votalp.

Conversing with them, he soon verified the information obtained through the mimic globe. As a rule, their emotions and memories were short-lived, their nature being closer to that of plants or animals than of humankind; but the loss of five sisters, occurring on successive mornings, had filled them with grief and terror that they could not forget. The missing flowers had been carried away bodily. The depredators were certain reptilian beings, colossal in size and winged like pterodactyls, who came down from their new-built citadel among the red and sable mountains at the valley's upper extreme. These beings, known as the Ispazars, seven in number, had become formidable sorcerers, developing an intellection beyond that of their kind, together with many esoteric faculties. Preserving the cold and evilly cryptic nature of reptiles, they had made themselves the masters of an abhuman science. But, until the present, Maal Dweb had ignored them and had not thought it worth while to interfere with their evolution.

Now, through an errant whim, in his search for adventure, he had decided to pit himself against the Ispazars, employing no other weapons of sorcery than his own wit and will, his remembered learning, his clairvoyance, and the two simple amulets that he wore on his person.

"Be comforted," he said to the flower-women, "for verily I shall deal with these miscreants in a fitting manner." At this; they broke into a shrill babble, repeating tales the bird-people of the valley had borne to them, regarding the fortress of the Ispazars, whose walls rose sheer-ly from a hidden peak unscaled by man, and were void of portal or window save in the highmost ramparts, where the flying reptiles went in and out. And they told him other tales, concerning the ferocity and cruelty of the Ispazars. . . .

Smiling as if at the chatter of children, he diverted their thoughts to other matters, and told them many stories of odd and curious mar-vels, and queer happenings in alien worlds. In the meanwhile he per-fected his plan for obtaining entrance to the citadel of the reptilian wizards.

The day went by in such divertissements; and one by one the three suns of the system fell beyond the valley's rim. The flower-women grew inattentive, they began to nod and drowse in the richly darkening twilight; and Maal Dweb proceeded with certain preparations that formed an essential part of his scheme.

Through his power of second-sight, he had determined the identity of the victim whom the winged reptiles would carry away in their next raid, on the morrow. This creature, as it happened, was the one who had sought to ensnare him. Like the others, she was now preparing to fold herself for the night in her couch of voluminous petals. Confiding part of his plan to her, Maal Dweb manipulated in a singular fashion one of the amulets which he wore, and by virtue of this manipulation, reduced himself to the proportions of a pigmy. In this state, with the assistance of the drowsy siren, he was able to conceal himself in a hol-low space among the petals; and thus embowered, like a bee in a rose, he slept securely through the short, moonless night of Votalp.

The dawn awakened him, glowing as if through lucent curtains of ruby and purple. He heard the flower-women murmuring sleepily to one another as they opened their blossoms to the early suns. Their murmurs, however, soon changed into shrill cries of agitation and fear; and above the cries, there came a vibrant drumming as of great drag-on-wings. He peered from his hiding-place, and saw in the double dawn the descent of the Ispazars, from whose webbed vans a darkness fell on the valley. Nearer they drew, and he saw their cold and scarlet eyes beneath scaly brows, their long and undulant bodies, their lizard limbs with prehensile claws; and he heard the deep, articulate hissing of their voices. Then the petals closed about him blindly, shuddering and constrictive, as the flower-woman recoiled from the swooping monsters. All was confusion, terror, tumult; but he knew, from his observation of the previous rape, that two of the Ispazars had encircled the flower's stem with their python-like tails, and were pulling it from the ground as a human sorcerer might pull a mandrake plant.

He felt the convulsive agony of the disrooted blossom, he heard the lamentable shrieking of her sisters. Then there came a heavier beating of the drum-loud wings, and the feeling of giddy ascension and flight.

Through all this, Maal Dweb had maintained the utmost presence of mind; and he did not betray himself to the Ispazars. After many minutes, there was a slackening of the headlong flight, and he knew that the reptiles were nearing their citadel. A moment more, and the ruddy gloom of the shut petals darkened and purpled about him, as if they had passed from the sunlight into a place of deep shadow. The thrumming of wings ceased abruptly; the living flower was dropped as if from a height on some hard surface, and Maal Dweb was nearly hurled from his hiding place by the violence of her fall. Moaning faintly, twitching a little, she lay where her captors had flung her. The enchanter heard the hissing voices of the reptile wizards, the rough, sharp slithering of their scaly tails on a stone floor, as they withdrew.

Whispering words of comfort to the dying blossom, he felt the petals relax about him. He crept forth very cautiously, and found himself in an immense, gloomily concamerated hall, whose windows were like the mouths of a deep cavern. The place was a sort of alchemy, a den of alien sorceries and abhorrent pharmaceutics. Everywhere, in the gloom, there were vats, cupels, furnaces, alembics, and matrasses of unhuman form, bulking and towering colossally to the pigmy eyes of Maal Dweb. Close at hand, a monstrous cauldron fumed like a crater of black metal, its curving sides ascending far above the magician's head. None of the Ispazars was in sight; but, knowing that they might return at any moment, he hastened to make ready against them, feeling, for the first time in many years, the thrill of peril and expectation.

Manipulating the second amulet, he regained his normal proportions. The room, though still spacious, was no longer a hall of giants, and the cauldron beside him sank and lessened till its rim rose only to his shoulder. He saw now that the cauldron was filled with an unholy mixture of ingredients, among which were finely shredded portions of the missing flower-women, together with the gall of chimeras and the ambergris of leviathans. Heated by unseen fires, it boiled tumultuously, foaming with black, pitchy bubbles, and putting forth a nauseous vapor.

With the shrewd eye of a past-master of all chemic lore, Maal Dweb proceeded to estimate the various contents of the cauldron, and was then able to divine the purpose for which the brewage was intended. The conclusion to which he was driven appalled him slightly, and served to heighten his respect for the power and science of the reptile sorcerers. He saw, indeed, that it would be highly advisable to arrest their evolution.

After brief reflection, it occurred to him that, in accordance with chemical laws, the adding of certain simple components to the brewage would bring about an eventuation neither desired nor anticipated by the Ispazars. On high tables about the walls of the alchemy, there were jars, flasks and vials containing curious drugs and powerful elements, some of which were drawn from the more arcanic kingdoms of nature. Disregarding the moon-powder, the coals of star-fire, the jellies made from the brains of gorgons, the ichor of salamanders, the dust of lethal fungi, the marrow of sphinxes, and other equally quaint and pernicious matters, the magician soon found the essences that he required. It was the work of an instant to pour them into the seething cauldron; and having done this, he awaited with composure the return of the reptiles.

The flower-woman, in the meanwhile, had ceased to moan and twitch. Maal Dweb knew that she was dead; since beings of this genus were unable to survive long when uprooted with such violence from their natal soil. She had folded herself to the face in her straitened petals, as if in a red and blackening shroud. He regarded her briefly, not without commiseration; and at that moment he heard the voices of the seven Ispazars, who had now re-entered the alchemy.

They came toward him among the crowded vessels, walking erect in the fashion of men on their short lizard legs, their ribbed and sable wings retracted behind them, and their eyes glaring redly in the gloom. Two of them were armed with long, sinuous-bladed knives; and others were equipped with enormous adamantine pestles, to be employed, no doubt, in bruising the flesh of the floral vampire.

When they saw the enchanter; they were both startled and angered. Their necks and torsos began to swell like the hoods of cobras, and a great hissing rose among them, like the noise of jetted steam. Their aspect would have struck terror to the heart of any common man; but Maal Dweb confronted them calmly, repeating aloud, in low, even tones, a word of sovereign protective power. The Ispazars hurled themselves toward him, some running along the floor with an undulant slithering motion, and others rising on rapid-beating vans to attack him from above. All, however, dashed themselves vainly on the sphere of unseen force he had drawn about him, through the utterance of the word of power. It was a strange thing to see them clawing vengefully at the void air, or striking futile blows with their weapons, which rang as if on a brazen wall.

Now, perceiving that the man before them was a sorcerer, the reptile magicians began to make use of their own abhuman sorcery. They called from the air great bolts of livid flame, python-shapen, which leaped and writhed incessantly, warring with the sphere of protective power, driving it back as a shield is driven by press of numbers in battle, but never breaking it down entirely. Also, they chanted evil, sibilant runes, that were designed to charm away the magician's memory, and cause him to forget his magic. Sore was the travail of Maal Dweb, as he fought the serpent fires and runes; and blood mingled with the sweat of his brow from that endeavor. But still, as the bolts struck nearer and the singing loudened, he kept uttering the unforgotten word; and the word still protected him.

Now, above the snaky chanting, he heard the deep hiss of the cauldron, boiling more turbulently than before because of those matters which he had added to its contents. And he saw, between the ever-writhing bolts, that a more voluminous vapor, dark as the steam of a primal fen, was mounting from the cauldron and was spreading throughout the alchemy.

Soon the Ispazars were immersed in the fumes, as in a cloud of darkness; and dimly they began to coil and twist, convulsed with a strange agony. The python flames died out on the air; and the hissings of the Ispazars became inarticulate as those of common serpents. Then, falling to the floor, while the black mist gathered and thickened above them, they crawled to and fro on their bellies in the fashion of true reptiles; and, emerging at times from the vapor, they seemed to shrink and dwindle as if hell-fire had consumed them.

All this was even as Maal Dweb had planned. He knew that the Ispazars had forgotten their sorcery and science; and a swift devolution, flinging them back to the lowest state of serpent-hood, had come upon them through the action of the vapor. But, before the completion of the change, he admitted one of the seven Ispazars to the sphere that now served to protect him from the fumes. The creature fawned at his feet like a tame dragon, acknowledging him for its master. Presently the cloud of vapor began to lift, and he saw the other Ispazars, who were now little larger than fen-snakes. Their wings had withered into useless frills, and they crept and hissed on the floor of the alchemy, amid the alembics and crucibles and athanors of their lost science.

Maal Dweb regarded them for a little, not without pride in his own sorcery. The struggle had been difficult, even dangerous; and he reflected that his boredom had been thoroughly overcome, at least for the nonce. From a practical viewpoint, he had done well; for, in ridding the flower-women of their persecutors, he had also eradicated a possible future menace to his own dominion over the worlds of the three suns.

Turning to that Ispazar which he had spared for a necessary purpose, he seated himself firmly astride its back, behind the thick jointing of the vans. He spoke a magic word that was understood by the monster. Bearing him between its wings, it rose and flew obediently through one of the high windows; and, leaving behind it for ever the citadel that was not to be scaled by man, nor by any wingless creature, it carried the magician over the red horns of the sable mountains, across the valley where dwelt the sisterhood of floral vampires, and descended on the mossy knoll, at the end of that silver bridge whereby he had entered Votalp. There Maal Dweb dismounted; and, followed by the crawling Ispazar, he began his return journey to Xiccarph through the hueless cloud, above the multi-dimensional deeps.

Midway in that peculiar transit, he heard a sharp, sudden clapping of wings. It ceased with remarkable abruptness, and was not repeated. Looking back, he found that the Ispazar had fallen from the bridge, and was vanishing brokenly amid irreconcilable angles, in the gulf from which there was no return.

THE STAR-TREADER

A voice cried to me in a dawn of dreams,
Saying, "Make haste: the webs of death and birth
Are brushed away, and all the threads of earth
Wear to the breaking; spaceward gleams
Thine ancient pathway of the suns,
Whose flame is part of thee;
And the deep gulfs abide coevally
Whose darkness runs
Through all thy spirit's mystery.
Go forth, and tread unharmed the blaze
Of stars wherethrough thou camest in old days;
Pierce without fear each vast
Whose hugeness crushed thee not within the past.
A hand strikes off the chains of Time,
A hand swings back the door of years;
Now fall earth's bonds of gladness and of tears,
And opens the strait dream to space sublime."

II

Who rides a dream, what hand shall stay!
What eye shall note or measure mete
His passage on a purpose fleet,
The thread and weaving of his way!
It caught me from the clasping world,
And swept beyond the brink of Sense,

My soul was flung, and poised, and whirled
Like to a planet chained and hurled
With solar lightning strong and tense.
Swift as communicated rays
That leap from severed suns a gloom
Within whose waste no suns illume,
The winged dream fulfilled its ways.
Through years reversed and lit again
I followed that unending chain
Wherein the suns are links of light;
Retraced through lineal, ordered spheres
The twisting of the threads of years
In weavings wrought of noon and night;
Through stars and deeps I watched the dream unroll,
Those folds that form the raiment of the soul.

III

Enkindling dawns of memory,
Each sun had radiance to relume
A sealed, disused, and darkened room
Within the soul's immensity.
Their alien ciphers shown and lit,
I understood what each had writ
Upon my spirit's scroll;
Again I wore mine ancient lives,
And knew the freedom and the gyves
That formed and marked my soul.

IV

I delved in each forgotten mind,
The units that had builded me,

Whose deepnesses before were blind
And formless as infinity—
Knowing again each former world—
From planet unto planet whirled
Through gulfs that mightily divide
Like to an intervital sleep.
One world I found, where souls abide
Like winds that rest upon a rose;
Thereto they creep
To loose all burden of old woes.
And one there was, a garden-close
Whose blooms are grown of ancient sin
And death the sap that wells and flows:
The spirits weep that dwelt therein.
And one I knew, where chords of pain
With stridors fill the Senses' lyre;
And one, where Beauty's olden chain
Is forged anew with stranger loveliness,
In flame-soft links of never-quenched desire
And ineluctable duress.

V

Where no terrestrial dreams had trod
My vision entered undismayed,
And Life her hidden realms displayed
To me as to a curious god.
Where colored suns of systems triplicate
Bestow on planets weird, ineffable,
Green light that orbs them like an outer sea,
And large auroral noons that alternate
With skies like sunset held without abate,

Life's touch renewed incomprehensibly
The strains of mirth and grief's harmonious spell.
Dead passions like to stars relit
Shone in the gloom of ways forgot;
Where crownless gods in darkness sit
The day was full on altars hot.
I heard—enisled in those melodic seas—
The central music of the Pleiades,
And to Alcyone my soul
Swayed with the stars that own her song's control.
Unchallenged, glad, I trod, a revenant
In worlds Edenic longly lost;
Or dwelt in spheres that sing to those,
Through space no light has crossed,
Diverse as Hell's mad antiphone uptossed
To Heaven's angelic chant.

VI

What vasts the dream went out to find!
I seemed beyond the world's recall
In gulfs where darkness is a wall
To render strong Antares blind!
In unimagined spheres I found
The sequence of my being's round—
Some life where firstling meed of Song,
The strange imperishable leaf,
Was placed on brows that starry Grief
Had crowned, and Pain anointed long;
Some avatar where Love
Sang like the last great star at morn
Ere the pale orb of Death filled all its sky;

Some life in fresher years unworn
Upon a world whereof
Peace was a robe like to the calms that lie
On pools aglow with latter spring:
There Time's pellucid surface took
Clear image of all things, nor shook
Till the black cleaving of Oblivion's wing;
Some earlier awakening
In pristine years, when giant strife
Of forces darkly whirled
First forged the thing called Life—
Hot from the furnace of the suns—
Upon the anvil of a world.

VII

Thus knew I those anterior ones
Whose lives in mine were blent;
Till, lo! my dream, that held a night
Where Rigel sends no message of his might,
Was emptied of the trodden stars,
And dwindled to the sun's extent—
The brain's familiar prison-bars,
And raiment of the sorrow and the mirth
Wrought by the shuttles intricate of earth.

THE DEMON OF THE FLOWER

Lying one summer night below the stars, when the Milky Way was spanning the sapphire zenith, and the wind had fallen asleep in the high, somber pines, I heard this tale as a whispering borne from strange worlds beyond the Scorpion:

Not as the plants and flowers of earth, growing peacefully beneath a simple sun, were the blossoms of the planet Lophai. Coiling and uncoiling in double dawns; tossing tumultuously to enormous suns of jade green and balas-ruby orange; swaying and weltering in auroracurtained nights and rich twilights, they resembled fields of rooted serpents that dance eternally to an otherworld music.

Many were small and furtive, and crept in the fashion of vipers on the low ground. Others were tall as pythons, rearing proudly to the jewelled light in hieratic postures. Some were like abdominous wyverns with long, slender throats and coronals of scroll-shaped antennae. And some bore the far-off likeness of pygmy cockadrills with high, carmine-tinted combs.

The flowers grew with single or double stems that burgeoned into hydra heads; or triple or quadruple stems that joined again to put forth a single blossom. They were frilled and festooned with varicolored leaves, that suggested the wings of flying lizards, the pennons of faery lances, the phylacteries of an alien sacerdotalism. They bloomed with petals that issued like flaming tongues from ebon mouths; or curled in scarlet wattles as of wild dragons turned to plants by a wizard spell; or floated on the air in deep reticulations as of fleshy nets of madder and rose; or hung aloft like bucklers gold and lazuli, gashed and perforated by weapons of exotic war.

They were armed with venomous darts, with deadly fangs; and many possessed the power of fatal constriction. All were weirdly alive and sentient, were malignly restless and alert, save in the irregular, infrequent winters when Lophai hung at its twofold aphelion. Then they ceased their perennial tossing in a brief torpor, and folded their monstrous petals beneath the rays that fall obliquely from remote poles.

The flowers were the lords of Lophai, and all other life existed only by their sufferance. The people of the world had been their inferiors from unrecorded cycles; and even in the oldest myths there was no suggestion that any other order of things had ever prevailed. And the plants themselves, together with the fauna and mankind of Lophai, gave immemorial obeisance to that supreme and terrible flower known as the Voorqual, in which a tutelary demon, more ancient than the twin suns, was believed to have made its immortal avatar.

The Voorqual was served by a human priesthood, chosen from amid the royalty and aristocracy of Lophai. In the heart of the chief city, Lospar, in an equatorial realm, it had grown from antiquity on the summit of a high pyramid of sable terraces that overloomed the town like the hanging gardens of some greater Babylon, crowded with the lesser but deadly floral forms. At the center of the broad apex, the Voorqual stood alone in a basin level with the surrounding platform of black mineral. The basin was filled with a compost in which the dust of royal mummies formed an essential ingredient.

The tall, demonian flower sprang from a bulb so old, so encrusted with the growth of centuries that it resembled an urn of stone. Above this, there rose the gnarled and mighty stalk that had displayed in earlier times the bifurcation of a mandrake, but whose halves had now grown together into a scaly, furrowed thing like the tail of some mythic sea-monster. The stalk was variegated with hues of greening bronze, of antique copper, with the sere yellows and burnt madders of tropic autumn, the livid blues and deathly purples of carnal corruption. It ended in a crown of stiff, blackish leaves, banded and spotted with poisonous, metallic white, and edged with sharp serrations as of savage weapons. From below the crown, there issued a long, sinuous arm, scaled like the main stem, and serpentining downward and outward to terminate in the huge upright bowl of a bizarre blossom—as if the arm, in sardonic fashion, should hold out a hellish beggar's cup.

Abhorrent and monstrous was the bowl—which, like the leaves, was legended to renew itself at intervals of a thousand years. It smouldered at the base with sullen ruby steeped in sepulchral shadow; it lightened into zones of sultry dragon's blood, into belts of the rose of infernal sunset, on the fluted, swelling sides; and it flamed at the rim to a yellowish nacarat red, like the ichor of salamandrine devils. To one who dared to peer within, the deep grail was lined with funereal violet, blackening toward the bottom, pitted with myriad pores, and striated with turgescent veins of sulphurous green.

Swaying slowly, in a weird, lethal hypnotic rhythm, with a deep and solemn sibilation, the Voorqual dominated the city of Lospar and the world Lophai. Below, on the tiers of the pyramid, the thronged ophidian plants kept time to this rhythm in their tossing and hissing. And far beyond Lospar, to the poles of the planet and in all its longitudes, the fields of living blossoms obeyed the sovereign tempo of the Voorqual.

Boundless was the power exercised by this being over the people who, for want of a better name, I have called the humankind of Lophai. Many and frightful were the legends that had gathered through aeons about the Voorqual. And dire was the sacrifice demanded each year at the summer solstice by the demon; the filling of its proffered cup with the life-blood of a priest or priestess, chosen from amid the assembled hierophants who passed before the Voorqual till the poised cup, inverted and empty, descended like a devil's miter on the hapless head of one of their number.

Lunithi, king of the realms about Lospar, and high-priest of the Voorqual, was the last if not the first of his race to rebel against this singular and sinister domination. There were doubtful myths of some primordial ruler who had dared to refuse the required sacrifice; and whose people, in consequence, had been decimated by a mortal war with the serpentine plants which, obeying the angry demon, had uprooted themselves everywhere from the soil and had marched on the cities of Lophai, slaying or vampirizing all who fell in their way. Lunithi, from childhood, had obeyed implicitly and without question the will of the floral overlord; had offered the stated worship, had performed the necessary rites. To withhold them would have been blasphemy. He had not dreamt of rebellion till, at the time of the annual choosing of the victim, and thirty suns before the date of his nuptials with Nala, priestess of the Voorqual, he saw the hesitant, inverted grail come down in deathly crimson on the fair head of his betrothed.

A mute and sorrowful consternation, a sullen, recalcitrant dismay which he sought to smother even in his own heart, was experienced by Lunithi. Nala, dazed and resigned, in a mystic inertia of despair, accepted her doom without question; but a blasphemous doubt formed itself surreptitiously in the mind of the king. Scarcely he dared admit the thought to full consciousness, lest the demon should know by means of its telepathic powers and visit him some baleful retribution.

Trembling with his own impiety, he asked himself if there was not some way in which he could save Nala from the sacrificial knife, could cheat the demon of its ghastly tribute. To do this, and escape with impunity to himself and his subjects, he knew infallibly that he must strike at the very life of the monster, which was believed to be deathless and invulnerable. It seemed impious even to wonder concerning the truth of this unanimous belief, which had long assumed the force of a religious tenet among the peoples of Lophai.

Amid such reflections as these, Lunithi remembered an old myth concerning the existence of a neutral and independent being known as the Occlith: a demon coeval with the Voorqual, and allied neither to man nor to the flower creatures. This being was said to dwell beyond the desert of Aphom, in the otherwise unpeopled mountains of white stone that are never visited by snow and which lie above the habitat of the ophidian blossoms. In latter days, at least, no man had seen the Occlith, for the journey through Aphom was a thing not lightly to be undertaken. But this entity was supposed to be immortal; and it lived apart and alone, meditating upon all things and interfering never with their processes. However, it was said to have given, in earlier times, valuable advice concerning affairs of state to a certain king who had gone forth from Lospar to its lair among the white crags.

In his grief and desperation, Lunithi resolved to seek the Occlith and to question it anent the possibility of slaying the Voorqual. If, by any mortal means, the demon could be destroyed, he would remove from Lophai the long-established tyranny whose shadow fell upon all things from the sable pyramid.

It was necessary for him to proceed with utmost caution, to confide in no one, to veil his very thoughts at all times from the occult scrutiny of the Voorqual. In the interim of five days between the choosing of the victim and the consummation of the sacrifice, he must carry out his mad plan.

Unattended, and disguised as a simple herder, Lunithi left his palace during the brief night of universal three-hour slumber, and stole forth toward the desert through fields comparatively free of the serpentine growths. In the dawn of the balas-ruby sun, he had reached the pathless waste, and was toiling painfully over its knife-sharp ridges of dark stone, like the waves of a mounting ocean petrified in storm.

Soon the rays of the green sun were added to those of the other, and Aphom became a painted inferno through which Lunithi dragged his way, crawling from scarp to glassy scarp and resting at whiles in the colored shadows. There was no water anywhere; but swift mirages gleamed and faded; and the sifting sand appeared to run like rills in the bottom of deep, flaming valleys.

At setting of the first sun, Lunithi came within sight of the pale mountains beyond Aphom, towering like a precipice of frozen foam above the desert's darker sea. They were tinged with evanescent lights of azure and jade and orange in the going of the yellow-red orb and the westward slanting of its binary. Then the lights melted into tourmaline and beryl, and the green sun was regnant over all, till it too went down, leaving a twilight whose colors were those of shoaling seawater. In the gloom, Lunithi reached the foot of the lower crags; and there, exhausted, he slept till the second dawn.

Rising, he began his escalade of the white mountains, which rose bleak and terrible before him against the hidden suns, with cliffs that were sheer as the terraces of Titans. Like the king who had gone before in the ancient myth, he found the precarious way that led upward through narrow, broken chasms. And at last he came to the vaster fissure, riving the heart of the white range, by which it was possible to reach the legendary lair of the Occlith.

The beetling walls of the chasm rose higher and higher above him, shutting out the double daylight but creating with their pallor a wan and deathly glimmer to illumine his way through the dusk. The fissure was such as might have been cloven by the sword of a macrocosmic giant. It led downward, steepening ever, like a wound that pierced the heart of Lophai.

Lunithi, like all of his race, was able to exist for prolonged periods without other nutriment than sunlight and water. He had brought with him a metal flask, filled with the aqueous element of Lophai, from which he drank sparingly as he descended along the chasm; for, like Aphom itself, the white mountains were waterless; and he feared to touch the rills and pools of unknown fluids upon which he came at intervals in the gloom. There were sanguine-colored springs that bubbled from the walls, to vanish in fathomless rifts; and sluggish brooklets of mercurial metal, green or blue or amber, that wound beside him like liquescent serpents and then disappeared mysteriously in dark caverns. Acrid metallic vapors rose from clefts in the chasm-floor; and Lunithi felt himself among strange alchemies and chemistries of nature. In this fantastic world of stone, which the plants of Lophai could never invade, he seemed to have gone beyond the Satanic tyranny of the Voorqual.

At last he came to a clear, hueless pool, that almost filled the entire width of the chasm, leaving on one side a narrow, insecure ledge along which he was forced to scramble. A fragment of the marble stone, loosened by his passing, fell into the pool as he gained the opposite edge; and the clear liquid foamed and hissed like a thousand vipers. Wondering as to its properties, and fearful of the virulent hissing, which did not subside for some time, Lunithi hurried on, and came after an interval to the end of the fissure.

Here he emerged in the huge crater-like pit that was the home of the Occlith. Fluted and columned walls went up to an overwhelming height on all sides; and the sun of orange ruby, now at zenith, was pouring down a vertical cataract of gorgeous fires and shadows.

Addorsed against the further wall of the pit, Lunithi beheld that fabulous being known as the Occlith, which had the likeness of a high cruciform pillar of blue mineral, shining with its own esoteric luster. Going forward, he prostrated himself before the pillar; and then, in accents that quavered with a deep awe, he ventured to ask the desired oracle.

For awhile the Occlith maintained its aeonian silence. Peering timidly, the king perceived the twin lights of mystic silver that brightened and faded with a slow, regular pulsation in the arms of the blue cross. Then, from the lofty, shining thing, by means of no visible organ, there issued a voice that was like the tinkling of mineral fragments lightly clashed together, but which somehow shaped itself into articulate words.

"It is possible," said the Occlith, "to slay the plant known as the Voorqual, in which an elder demon has its habitation. Though the flower has attained millennial age, it is not necessarily immortal: for all things have their proper term of existence and decay; and nothing has been created without its corresponding agency of death.... I do not advise you to slay the plant . . . but I can furnish you with the information which you desire. In the mountain chasm through which you came to seek me, there flows a hueless spring of mineral poison, deadly to all the ophidian plant-life of this world...."

The Occlith went on, and told Lunithi the manner in which the poison should be prepared and administered. The chill, toneless, tinkling voice concluded:

"I have answered your question. If there is anything more that you wish to learn, it would be well to ask me now."

Prostrating himself again, Lunithi gave thanks to the Occlith; and, considering that he had learned all that was requisite in regard to the Voorqual, he did not avail himself of the opportunity to question further the strange entity of living stone. And the Occlith, cryptic and aloof in its termless, impenetrable meditation, apparently saw fit to vouchsafe nothing more except in answer to a direct query.

Withdrawing from the marble-walled abyss, Lunithi returned in haste along the narrow chasm; till, reaching the clear pool of which the Occlith had spoken, he paused to empty his water-flask and fill it with the angry, hissing liquid. Then he resumed his journey.

At the end of two days, after incredible fatigues and torments in the blazing hell of Aphom, he reached Lospar in the time of darkness and slumber, as when he had departed. Since his absence had been unannounced, it was supposed by everyone that he had retired to the underground adyta below the pyramid of the Voorqual for purposes of prolonged meditation, as was sometimes his wont.

In fearful hope and trepidation, dreading the miscarriage of his plan, and shrinking still from its audacious impiety, Lunithi awaited the night preceding that double dawn of summer solstice when, in a secret room of the black pyramid, the monstrous offering was to be prepared. Nala would be slain by a fellow-priest or priestess, chosen by lot, and her life-blood would drip from the channeled altar into a great cup; and the cup would then be borne with solemn rites to the Voor-qual and its contents poured into the evilly supplicative bowl of the sanguinated blossom.

He saw little of Nala during that brief interim. She was more with-drawn than ever, and seemed to have consecrated herself wholly to the coming doom. To no one—and least of all to his beloved—did Lu-nithi dare to hint a possible prevention of the sacrifice.

There came the dreaded eve, with its swiftly changing twilight of jewelled hues and its darkness hung with auroral flames. Lunithi stole across the sleeping city and entered the pyramid whose massive black-ness towered amid the frail and open architecture of buildings that were little more than canopies and lattices of stone. With infinite cau-tion, hiding his real intention in the nethermost crypts of his mind, he made the preparations prescribed by the Occlith. Into the huge sacrifi-cial cup of black metal, in a room eternally lit with stored sunlight, he emptied the seething, sibilant poison he had brought with him from the white mountains. Then, opening with surgical adroitness a vein in one of his arms, he added a certain amount of his own life-fluid to the lethal potion. The blood appeared to quiet that angry venom, above whose foaming crystal it floated like a magic oil, without mingling; so that the entire cup, to all appearance, was filled with the liquid most acceptable to the Satanic blossom.

Bearing in his hands the black grail, Lunithi mounted a coiling stairway that led to the Voorqual's presence. His heart quailing within him, his senses swooning in chill gulfs of superstitious terror, he emerged on the lofty sable summit above the shadowy town.

In a luminous azure gloom, against the weird and iridescent streamers of light that foreran the double dawn, he saw the dreamy swaying of the monstrous plant, and heard its somnolent hissing that was answered drowsily by innumerable blossoms on the terraces be-low. A nightmare oppression, black and tangible, seemed to flow from the pyramid and to lie in stagnant shadow on all the lands of Lophai.

Aghast at his own temerity, and deeming that his shrouded thoughts would surely be understood as he drew nearer, or that the Voorqual would be suspicious of an offering brought before the customary hour, Lunithi made obeisance to his floral overlord. The Voorqual vouchsafed no sign that it had deigned to perceive his presence; but the great flower-cup, with its flaring crimsons dulled to garnet and purple in the twilight, was held forward as if in readiness to receive the hideous gift.

Breathless, and fainting with religious fear, in a moment of suspense that seemed eternal, Lunithi poured the blood-mantled poison into the yawning cup. The venom boiled and hissed like a wizard's brew as the thirsty flower drank it up; and Lunithi saw the coiling arm draw back in sudden doubt and tilt its demonian grail quickly, as if to repudiate the sacrificial draft.

It was too late; for the poison had been absorbed by the blossom's porous lining. The tilting motion changed in mid-air to an agonized writhing of the serpentine arm; and then the Voorqual's huge, scaly stalk and serrate leaf-crown began to toss in a frenetic dance of death, waving darkly against the auroral curtains of morn. Its deep, solemn hissing sharpened to an insupportable note, fraught with the pain of a dying devil; and looking down from the platform edge on which he crouched to avoid the swaying growth, Lunithi saw that the lesser plants on all the black terraces beneath were tossing in mad unison with their master. Like noises in an evil dream, he heard the chorus of their tortured sibilations.

He dared not look again at the Voorqual, till he became aware of a strange, unnatural silence, and saw that the blossoms below had ceased to writhe and were drooping limply on their stems. Then, incredulous, he knew that the Voorqual was dead.

Turning, in mingled horror and triumph, he beheld the flaccid stalk that had fallen prone on its bed of unholy compost. He saw the sudden withering of the stiff, sworded leaves, of the gross and hellish flower. Even the stony bulb appeared to collapse and crumble before his eyes. The entire stem, with its evil colors fading swiftly, shrank and fell in upon itself like a sere and empty serpent-skin.

At the same time, in some obscure manner, Lunithi was still aware of a presence that brooded above the pyramid. Even in the death of the Voorqual, it seemed to him that he was not alone. Then, as he stood and waited, fearing he knew not what, he felt the passing of a cold and unseen thing in the azure gloom—a thing that flowed across his body like the coils of some enormous python, without sound, in dark and clammy undulations. A moment more and it was gone; and Lunithi no longer felt the brooding presence.

He turned to go; and it seemed that the dying night was ominous of an unconceived terror that gathered before him as he went down the long volutes of somber stairs. Slowly he descended; and a weird despair was upon him. He had slain the Voorqual, had seen it wither in death; so Nala should be saved from the morrow's sacrifice. Yet he could not believe the thing he had done; the lifting of the ancient doom was still no more than an idle myth.

The twilight had begun to brighten as he passed through the slumbering city. According to custom of Lophai, no one would be abroad for another hour. Then the priests of the Voorqual would gather for the annual rite of blood-offering.

Midway between the pyramid and his own palace, Lunithi was more than startled to meet the maiden Nala. Pale and ghostly, she glided by him with a swift and swaying movement almost serpentine, which differed strangely from her habitual languor. Lunithi dared not accost her when he saw her shut, unheeding eyes, like those of a somnambulist; and he was deeply awed and troubled by the serpentine ease, the unnatural surety of her motion. It reminded him of something which he feared to remember. In a turmoil of fantastic doubt and apprehension, he followed her.

Threading the exotic maze of Lospar with the fleet and sinuous glide of a homing serpent, Nala entered the sacred pyramid. Lunithi, less swift than the maiden, had fallen behind; and he knew not where she had gone in the myriad vaults and interior chambers; but a strange and fearsome intuition drew his steps without delay to the platform of the summit.

He knew not what he should find; but his heart was drugged with an esoteric hopelessness; and he was aware of no surprise when he came forth in the many-colored dawn and beheld the thing which awaited him.

The maiden Nala—or that which he knew to be Nala—was standing in the basin of evil soil, above the withered remains of the Voorqual. She had undergone—was still undergoing—a monstrous and diabolic transformation. Her frail, slight body had assumed a long and dragon-like form, and the tender skin was marked off in incipient scales that darkened momentarily with a mottling of baleful hues. Her head was no longer recognizable as such, and the human lineaments were flaring into a weird semi-circle of pointed leaf-buds. Her lower limbs had joined together, had rooted themselves in the ground. One of her arms was becoming a part of the ophidian bole; and the other was lengthening into a scaly stem that bore the dark-red bud of a sinister blossom.

More and more the monstrosity took on the similitude of the Voorqual; and Lunithi, crushed by the ancient awe and dark, terrible faith of his ancestors, could feel no longer any doubt of its true identity. Soon there was no trace of Nala in the thing before him, which began to sway with a dreamy, python-like rhythm, and to utter a deep and measured sibilation, to which the plants on the lower tiers responded. He knew then that the Voorqual had returned to claim its sacrifice and preside forever above the city Lospar and the world Lophai.

THE FLOWER-DEVIL

In a basin of porphyry, at the summit of a pillar of serpentine, the thing has existed from primeval time, in the garden of the kings that rule an equatorial realm of the planet Saturn. With black foliage, fine and intricate as the web of some enormous spider; with petals of livid rose, and purple like the purple of putrefying flesh; and a stem rising like a swart and hairy wrist from a bulb so old, so encrusted with the growth of centuries that it resembles an urn of stone, the monstrous flower holds dominion over all the garden. In this flower, from the years of the oldest legend, an evil demon has dwelt—a demon whose name and whose nativity are known to the superior magicians and mysteriarchs of the kingdom, but to none other. Over the half-animate flowers, the ophidian orchids that coil and sting, the bat-like lilies that open their ribbèd petals by night, and fasten with tiny yellow teeth on the bodies of sleeping dragon-flies; the carnivorous cacti that yawn with green lips beneath their beards of poisonous yellow prickles; the plants that palpitate like hearts, the blossoms that pant with a breath of venomous perfume—over all these, the Flower-Devil is supreme, in its malign immortality, and evil, perverse intelligence—inciting them to strange maleficence, fantastic mischief, even to acts of rebellion against the gardeners, who proceed about their duties with wariness and trepidation, since more than one of them has been bitten, even unto death, by some vicious and venefic flower. In places, the garden has run wild from lack of care on the part of the fearful gardeners, and has become a monstrous tangle of serpentine creepers, and hydra-headed plants, convolved and inter-writhing in lethal hate or venomous love, and horrible as a rout of wrangling vipers and pythons.

And, like his innumerable ancestors before him, the king dares not destroy the Flower, for fear that the devil, driven from its habitation, might seek a new home, and enter into the brain or body of one of the king's subjects—or even the heart of his fairest and gentlest, and most beloved queen!

THE MONSTER OF THE PROPHECY

FOREWORD

The disappearance of an unknown and presumably minor poet, no matter how insoluble or obscure the circumstances, would not ordinarily resolve itself into a theme of much popular interest and discussion. But the case whose inner details I am now about to relate, was far from ordinary even in its mundane sequel: the publication of Theophilus Alvor's "Ode to Antares" in *The Contemporary Muse*, the praise it elicited from certain influential critics, and the unavailing efforts of the editor and these critics to find Alvor or to learn what had become of him, ended by turning the matter into a seven days' newspaper sensation, during which the front page head-lines waxed and waned in their typographical proportions, and many divergent theories were advanced by reporters, editorial writers and the police, as well as by Alvor's new-won admirers and his land-lady. Also, among other results, a publisher was found for the three volumes of hitherto unmarketable verse and the no less unmarketable collection of prose tales which the poet had left in his lodgings; and a modest but growing fame was assured for him even after the newspapers had turned their attention to fresher mysteries.

Very little was ascertainable by anyone concerning what could have happened to Alvor, and this little afforded room for almost any amount of permissible conjecture. The poet was a new-comer in Brooklyn and had made no friends and few acquaintances there; and his land-lady was the only person who could bring forward anything of the least illuminative value or significance. She testified that Alvor had been unable to pay his room-rent for two weeks prior to his disappearance, and that he was in a state of obvious depression at the time and had looked increasingly pale, dilapidated and ill-fed. She herself, out of a certain motherly kindness aroused by his refinement and forlorn aspect, had forborne to press him for her money and had even given him several meals at her own table. The most popular and plausible theory advanced was that of suicide; but none of the divers anonymous bodies found in Brooklyn or dragged from East River at that time could be identified as Alvor; also, it could not be learned that anyone resembling him had purchased a revolver or a bottle of poison. Other theories propounded were, that he had stowed away on some trans-oceanic vessel, had been shanghaied, or had simply walked out of Brooklyn or ridden away on a freight train to try his fortune elsewhere. Rumors sprang up that he had been seen in remote places, in New Orleans, Mobile, Chicago, San Francisco, and even Mexico City; and there were those who purported to have authentic information that he had gone to Peru, with the idea of collecting material for a long narrative poem dealing with the Incas. None of these reports, however, was verifiable, and since the poet himself never returned to enjoy the profits of his spreading fame, and no word came from him, his disappearance remained an unsolvable mystery.

Indeed, in all the world there was no one who could have thrown the least light on this mystery. The truth of what had happened to Theophilus Alvor was known only to the people of a far-off planet, whose communications with the races of this earth are infrequent and obscure.

I

A dismal, fog-dank afternoon was turning into a murky twilight when Theophilus Alvor paused on Brooklyn Bridge to peer down at the dim river with a shudder of sinister surmise. He was wondering how it would feel to cast himself into the chill, turbid waters, and whether he could summon up the necessary courage for an act which, he had persuaded himself, was now becoming inevitable as well as laudable. He felt that he was too weary, sick and disheartened to go on with the evil dream of existence.

From any human stand-point, there was doubtless abundant reason for Alvor's depression. Young, and full of unquenched visions and desires, he had come to the city from an up-state village three months before, hoping to find a publisher for his writings; but his old-fashioned classic verses, in spite (or because) of their high imaginative fire, had been unanimously rejected both by magazines and book-firms. His last literary hope, a little volume of fanciful tales in prose, which he had written since his arrival in Brooklyn, had now been returned with disconcerting promptness by a firm which he had deemed the likeliest of all conceivable sponsors. Though Alvor had lived frugally and had chosen lodgings so humble as almost to constitute the proverbial poetic garret, the small sum of his savings was now exhausted. He was not only quite penniless, but his clothes were so worn as to be no longer presentable in editorial offices, and the soles of his shoes were becoming rapidly nonexistent from the tramping he had done. He had not eaten for days, and his last meal, like the several preceding ones, had been at the expense of his soft-hearted Irish landlady. After hours of aimless and desolate wandering through the fog-muffled streets, he was at this moment miles from his lodgings; and he had about made up his mind that he would not return to them.

For more reasons than one, Alvor would have preferred another death than that of drowning. The foul and icy waters were not inviting from an aesthetic view-point; and in spite of all he had heard to the contrary, he did not believe that such a death could be anything but disagreeable and painful. By choice he would have selected a sovereign Oriental opiate, whose insidious slumber would have led through a realm of gorgeous dreams to the gentle night of an ultimate oblivion; or, failing this, a deadly poison of merciful swiftness. But such Lethean media are not readily obtainable by a man with an empty purse.

Damning his own lack of forethought in not reserving enough money for such an eventuation, Alvor shuddered on the twilight bridge, and looked at the dismal waters, and then at the no less dismal fog through which the troubled lights of the city had begun to break. And then, through the instinctive habit of a country-bred person who is also imaginative and beauty-seeking, he looked at the heavens above the city to see if any stars were visible. He thought of his recent "Ode to Antares," which, unlike his earlier productions, was written in *vers libre* and had a strong modernistic irony mingled with its planturous lyricism. He had hoped for its acceptance by *The Contemporary Muse*, but had heard nothing after many weeks, and surmised with a mordant pessimism that it had long been relegated to the editorial waste-basket. Now, with a sense of irony far more bitter than that which he had put into his ode, he looked for the ruddy spark of Antares itself, but was unable to find it in the sodden sky. His gaze and his thoughts returned to the river.

"There is no need for that, my young friend," said a voice at his elbow. Alvor was startled not only by the words and by the clairvoyance they betrayed, but also by something that was unanalyzably strange in the tones of the voice that uttered them. The tones were those of a man of culture, they were well-modulated, they were both refined and authoritative; but in them there was a quality which, for lack of more precise words or imagery, he could think of only as metallic and unhuman. While his mind wrestled with swift-born unseizable fantasies, he turned to look at the stranger who had accosted him.

The man was neither uncommonly nor disproportionately tall; and he was modishly dressed, with a long overcoat and top hat. His features were not unusual, from what could be seen of them in the dusk, except for his full-lidded and burning eyes, like those of some nyctalopic animal. But from him there emanated a palpable sense of things that were inconceivably strange and outré and remote—a sense that was more patent, more insistent than any impression of mere form and odor and sound could have been, and which was well-nigh tactual in its intensity. Even at that meeting in the twilight, Alvor was conscious of wonder and fear and awe before this stranger about whom there was nothing ostensibly remarkable except his metallic voice and his fiery eyes.

"I repeat," continued the man, "that there is no necessity for you to drown yourself in that river. A vastly different fate can be yours, if you choose . . . In the meanwhile, I shall be honored and delighted if you will accompany me to my house, which is not far away."

In a state of astonishment preclusive of all analytical thought, or even of any clear cognizance of where he was going or what was happening, Alvor followed the stranger with a docility that would have surprised even himself if he had not been beyond all comparatively minor elements of surprise. A mutual silence was maintained while they traversed several blocks in the swirling fog. Then the stranger paused before a dark mansion.

"I live here," he said, as he mounted the steps and unlocked the door. "Will you deign to enter?" He turned on the lights with the last word, as he mounted the steps and waited for Alvor to precede him. Entering, Alvor saw that he was in the hall of an old house which must in its time have had considerable pretensions to aristocratic dignity, for the paneling, carpet and furniture were all antique and were both rare and luxurious.

Alvor was conducted by his host to a library with furniture of the same well-nigh fabulous period as the hall. The place was crowded to the very ceiling with numberless books. Motioning the poet to be seated, the stranger poured out a small glassful of golden liquor and gave it to his guest. It was Benedictine, and the mellow warmth of the flavorous drink was truly magical. The poet's weakness and weariness fell off like a dissolving fog, and the mental confusion in which he had accompanied his benefactor began to clear away.

"Rest here," commanded his host, and left the room. Alvor resigned himself to the luxury of an ample arm-chair, while his brain occupied itself with countless conjectures. He could make up his mind to nothing, but the wildest thoughts occurred to him every instant, and he felt that there was an element of unique mystery about the whole proceeding. His first impressions of the stranger were momently intensified, though for no tangible reason.

His host returned in a few minutes.

"Will you come to the dining-room?" he suggested. "I know that you are hungry and I have ordered some food for you. Afterward, we will talk."

An excellent meal for two had been brought in from a neighboring restaurant. Alvor, who was faint with inanition, ate with no attempt to conceal his ravening appetite, but noticed that the stranger made scarcely even a pretense of touching his own food. With a manner preoccupied and distrait, the man sat opposite Alvor, giving no more ostensible heed to his guest than the ordinary courtesies of a host required.

"We will talk now," said the stranger, when Alvor had finished. The poet, whose energies and mental faculties were now fully revived, became bold enough to survey his host with a frank attempt at appraisal. On his part, the stranger looked at the thin Dantean features and slight frame of the poet with a cool unreadable air which seemed to indicate that he knew all that was essential to know about Alvor. Meeting his luminous gaze, Alvor was almost overcome by sensations no less novel than powerful. He saw a man of indefinite age, whose lineaments and complexion were Caucasian, but whose nationality he was unable to determine. The eyes had lost something of their weird luminosity beneath the electric light, but nevertheless, they were most remarkable, and from them there poured a sense of unearthly knowledge and power and strangeness not to be formulated by human thought or conveyed in human speech. Under his scrutiny, vague, dazzling, intricate, unshapable images rose on the dim borders of the poet's mind and fell back into oblivion ere he could envisage them.

Apparently without rime or reason, some lines of his "Ode to Antares" returned to him, and he found that he was repeating them over and over beneath his breath:

> "Star of strange hope,
> Pharos beyond our desperate mire,
> Lord of unscalable gulfs,
> Lamp of unknowable life."

The hopeless, half-satiric yearning for another sphere which he had expressed in this poem, haunted his thoughts with a weird insistence.

"Of course, you have no idea who or what I am," said the stranger, "though your poetic intuitions are groping darkly toward the secret of my identity. On my part, there is no need for me to ask you anything, since I have already learned all that there is to learn about your life, your personality, and the dismal predicament from which I am now able to offer you a means of escape. Your name is Theophilus Alvor, and you are a poet whose classic style and romantic genius are not likely to win adequate recognition in this age and land. With an inspiration more prophetic than you dream, you have written, among other masterpieces, a quite admirable 'Ode to Antares'."

"How do you know all this?" cried Alvor.

"To those who have the sensory apparatus with which to perceive them, thoughts are no less audible than spoken words. I can hear your thoughts, so you will readily understand that there is nothing surprising in my possession of more or less knowledge concerning you."

"But who are you?" exclaimed Alvor. "I have heard of people who could read the minds of others; but I did not believe that there was any human being who actually possessed such powers."

"I am not a human being," rejoined the stranger, "even though I have found it convenient to don the semblance of one for awhile, just as you or another of your race might wear a masquerade costume. Permit me to introduce myself: my name, as nearly as can be conveyed in the phonetics of your world, is Vizaphmal, and I have come from a planet of the far-off mighty sun that is known to you as Antares. In my own world, I am a scientist, though the more ignorant classes look upon me as a wizard. In the course of profound experiments and researches, I have invented a device which enables me at will to visit other planets, no matter how remote in space. I have sojourned for varying intervals in more than one solar system; and I have found your world and its inhabitants so quaint and curious and monstrous that I have lingered here a little longer than I intended, because of my taste for the bizarre—a taste which is ineradicable, though no doubt reprehensible. It is now time for me to return: urgent duties call me, and I cannot tarry. But there are reasons why I should like to take with me to my world a member of your race; and when I saw you on the bridge tonight, it occurred to me that you might be willing to undertake such an adventure. You are, I believe, utterly weary of the sphere in which you find yourself, since a little while ago you were ready to depart from it into the unknown dimension that you call death. I can offer you something much more agreeable and diversified than death, with a scope of sensation, a potentiality of experience beyond anything of which you have had even the faintest intimation in the poetic reveries looked upon as extravagant by your fellows."

Again and again, while listening to this long and singular address, Alvor seemed to catch in the tones of the voice that uttered it a supervening resonance, a vibration of overtones beyond the compass of a mortal throat. Though perfectly clear and correct in all details of enunciation, there was a hint of vowels and consonants not to be found in any terrestrial alphabet. Once more, as if in reply to an evocation, dim, splendid increate images arose in processional on the borderland of his brain and passed uncomprehended to the gulf from whence they issued. However, the logical part of his mind refused to accept entirely these intimations of the supermundane; and he was now seized by the idea that the man before him was some new type of lunatic. Of course,

Alvor was far from sharing the vulgar prejudice against lunacy, and his feelings while he received this idea were those of imaginative interest or even envy, rather than horror.

"Your thought is natural enough, considering the limitations of your experience," observed the stranger calmly. "However, I can easily convince you of its error by revealing myself to you in my true shape."

He made the gesture of one who throws off a garment. Alvor was blinded by an insufferable blaze of light, whose white glare, emanating in huge beams from an orb-like center, filled the entire room and seemed to pass illimitably beyond through dissolving walls. When his eyes became accustomed to the light, he saw before him a being who had no conceivable likeness to his host. This being was more than seven feet in height, and had no less than five intricately jointed arms and three legs that were equally elaborate. His head, on a long, swan-like neck, was equipped not only with visual, auditory, nasal and oral organs of unfamiliar types, but had several appendages whose use was not readily to be determined. His three eyes, obliquely set and with oval pupils, rayed forth a green phosphorescence; the mouth, or what appeared to be such, was very small and had the lines of a downward-curving crescent; the nose was rudimentary, though with finely wrought nostrils; in lieu of eye-brows, he had a triple series of semi-circular markings on his forehead, each of a different hue; and above his intellectually shapen head, above the tiny drooping ears with their complex lobes, there towered a gorgeous comb of crimson, not dissimilar in form to the crest on the helmet of a Grecian warrior. The head, the limbs and the whole body were mottled with interchanging lunes and moons of opalescent colors, never the same for a moment in their unresting flux and reflux.

Alvor had the sensation of standing on the rim of prodigious gulfs, on a new earth beneath new heavens; and the vistas of illimitable horizons, fraught with the multitudinous terror and manifold beauty of an imagery no human eye had ever seen, hovered and wavered and flashed upon him with the same unstable fluorescence as the lunar variegations of the body at which he stared with such stupefaction. Then, in a little while, the strange light seemed to withdraw upon itself, retracting all its beams to a common center, and faded in a whirl of darkness. When this darkness had cleared away, he saw once more the form of his host, in conventional garb, with a slight ironic smile about his lips.

"Do you believe me now?" Vizaphmal queried.

"Yes, I believe you."

"Are you willing to accept my offer?"

The poet was unable to answer for a short interval. Vast inchoate symbols, broken pictures of a novel allurement and a no less novel horror crowded upon his mind and confused his impulses. Then he remembered his sordid lodgings, his empty pockets, his pile of unsalable manuscripts, and the foul river into which he had been ready to cast himself an hour ago.

"I accept it," he quavered. A thousand questions were forming in Alvor's mind, but he dared not ask them. Divining these questions, the stranger spoke as follows:

"You wonder how it is possible for me to assume a human shape. I assure you, it is merely a matter of taking thought. My mental images are infinitely clearer and stronger than those of any earth-being, and by conceiving myself as a man, I can appear to you and your fellows as such. Though I have been among you no more than a few months, I have had no trouble in learning your language, in adapting myself to your ways, and in comprehending all I have desired to comprehend through the same excelling faculty.

"You wonder also as to the modus operandi of my arrival on earth. This I shall now show and explain to you, if you will follow me."

He led the way to an upper story of the old mansion. Here, in a sort of attic, beneath a large sky-light in the southward-sloping roof, there stood a curious mechanism, wrought of a dark metal which Alvor could not identify. It was a tall, complicated framework with many transverse bars and two stout upright rods terminating at each end in a single heavy disk. These disks seemed to form the main portions of the top and bottom.

"Put your hand between the bars," commanded Alvor's host.

Alvor tried to obey this command, but his fingers met with an adamantine obstruction, and he realized that the intervals of the bars were filled with an unknown material clearer than glass or crystal.

"You behold here," said Vizaphmal, "an invention which, I flatter myself, is quite unique anywhere this side of the galactic suns. The two substances of which it is made are both alloys of metals rare even in my world, and totally undiscoverable in yours. The disks at top and bottom are a vibratory device with a twofold use; and no other material than that of which they are wrought would have the same properties, the same achievable rates of vibrations."

"But I do not understand," exclaimed Alvor. "What is the purpose of this thing?"

"As I have hinted, there are two purposes. When you and I have locked ourselves within the frame-work, as we shall do anon, a few revolutions of the lower disk will have the effect of isolating us from our present environment, and we shall find ourselves in the midst of what is known to you as space, or ether. The vibrations of the upper disk, which we shall then employ, are of such potency as to annihilate space itself in any direction desired. Space, like everything else in the atomic universe, is subject to laws of integration and dissolution. It was merely a matter of finding the vibrational power that would effect this dissolution; and, by untiring research, by ceaseless experimentation, I located and isolated the rare metallic elements which, in a state of union, are capable of this power."

All this appeared amazingly lucid to Alvor. The idea of such a mechanism overwhelmed him; but he was prepared to believe anything, and nothing in the universe would have seemed impossible to him after that vision of the parti-colored entity with five arms and three legs.

While the poet was pondering all he had seen and heard, Vizaphmal touched a tiny knob, and one side of the framework swung open. He then turned off the electric light in the garret, and simultaneously with its extinction, a ruddy glow was visible in the interior of the machine, serving to illumine all the parts, but leaving the room around it in darkness. Standing beside his invention, Vizaphmal looked at the sky-light, and Alvor followed his gaze. The fog had cleared away and many stars were out, including the red gleam of Antares, now high in the south. The stranger was evidently making certain preliminary calculations, for he moved the machine a little after peering at the star, and adjusted a number of fine wires in the interior, as if he were tuning some stringed instrument. Either the metals that composed the framework were of phenomenal lightness, or else Vizaphmal was endued with preternatural strength, for when he moved it about in the course of his alignment he gave no sign of any strain or effort.

At last he turned to Alvor.

"Everything is now in readiness," he announced. "If you are still prepared to accompany me, we will take our departure."

Alvor was conscious of an unexpected coolness and fortitude as he answered: "I am at your service." The unparalleled occurrences and disclosures of the evening, the well-nigh undreamable prospect of a plunge across untold immensitude, such as no man had been privileged to dare before, had really benumbed his imagination, and he was unable at the moment to conceive the true awesomeness of what he had undertaken.

Vizaphmal indicated the place where Alvor was to stand in the machine. The poet entered, and assumed a position between one of the upright rods and the side, opposite Vizaphmal. He found that a layer of the transparent material was interposed between his feet and the large disk in which the two rods were based. No sooner had he stationed himself, when, with a celerity and an utter silence that were uncanny, the frame-work closed upon itself with hermetic tightness, till the jointure where it had opened was no longer detectable.

"We are now in a sealed compartment," explained the Antarean, "into which nothing can penetrate. Both the dark metal and the crystalline are substances that refuse the passage of heat and cold, of air and ether, or of any known cosmic ray, with the one exception of light itself, which is admitted by the clear metal."

When he ceased, Alvor realized that they were walled about with an insulating silence utter and absolute as that of some intersidereal void. The traffic in the streets without, the rumbling and roaring and jarring of the great city, so loud a minute before, might have been a million miles away in some other world for all that he could hear or feel of its vibration.

In the red glow that pervaded the machine, emanating from a source he could not discover, the poet gazed at his companion. Vizaphmal had now resumed his Antarean form, as if all necessity for a human disguise were at an end, and he towered above Alvor, glorious with inter-merging zones of fluctuant colors, where hues the poet had not seen in any spectrum were simultaneous or intermittent with flaming blues and coruscating emeralds and amethysts and fulgurant purples and vermillions and saffrons. Lifting one of his five arms, which terminated in two finger-like appendages with many joints all capable of bending in any direction, the Antarean touched a thin wire that was stretched overhead between the two rods. He plucked at this wire like a musician at a lute-string, and from it there emanated a single clear note higher in pitch than anything Alvor had ever heard. Its sheer unearthly acuity caused a shudder of anguish to run through the poet, and he could scarcely have borne a prolongation of the sound, which, however, ceased in a moment and was followed by a much more endurable humming and singing noise which seemed to arise at his feet. Looking down, he saw that the large disk at the bottom of the medial rods had begun to revolve. This revolution was slow at first, but rapidly increased in its rate, till he could no longer see the movement; and the singing sound became agonizingly sweet and high till it pierced his senses like a knife.

Vizaphmal touched a second wire, and the revolution of the disk was brought abruptly to an end. Alvor felt an unspeakable relief at the cessation of the torturing music.

"We are now in etheric space," the Antarean declared. "Look out, if you so desire."

Alvor peered through the interstices of the dark metal, and saw around and above and below them the unlimited blackness of cosmic night and the teeming of uncountable trillions of stars. He had a sensation of frightful and deadly vertigo, and staggered like a drunken man as he tried to keep himself from falling against the side of the machine.

Vizaphmal plucked at a third wire, but this time Alvor was not aware of any sound. Something that was like an electric shock, and also like the crushing impact of a heavy blow, descended upon his head and shook him to the soles of his feet. Then he felt as if his tissues were being stabbed by innumerable needles of fire, and then that he was being torn apart in a thousand thousand fragments, bone by bone, muscle by muscle, vein by vein, and nerve by nerve, on some invisible rack. He swooned and fell huddled in a corner of the machine, but his unconsciousness was not altogether complete. He seemed to be drowning beneath an infinite sea of darkness, beneath the accumulation of shoreless gulfs, and above this sea, so far away that he lost it again and again, there thrilled a supernal melody, sweet as the singing of sirens or the fabled music of the spheres, together with an insupportable dissonance like the shattering of all the battlements of time. He thought that all his nerves had been elongated to an enormous distance, where the outlying parts of himself were being tortured in the oubliettes of fantastic inquisitions by the use of instruments of percussion, diabolically vibrant, that were somehow identified with certain of his own body-cells. Once he thought that he saw Vizaphmal, standing a million leagues remote on the shore of an alien planet, with a sky of soaring many-

colored flame behind him and the night of all the universe rippling gently at his feet like a submissive ocean. Then he lost the vision, and the
intervals of the far unearthly music became more prolonged, and at last
he could not hear it at all, nor could he feel any longer the torturing of
his remote nerve-ends. The gulf deepened above him, and he sank
through eons of darkness and emptiness to the very nadir of oblivion.

II

Alvor's return to consciousness was even more slow and gradual than
his descent into Lethe had been. Still lying at the bottom of a shoreless
and boundless night, he became aware of an unidentifiable odor with
which in some way the sense of ardent warmth was associated. This
odor changed incessantly, as if it were composed of many diverse ingredients, each of which predominated in turn. Myrrh-like and mystic
in the beginning as the fumes of an antique altar, it assumed the heavy
languor of unimaginable flowers, the sharp sting of vaporizing chemi-
cals unknown to science, the smell of exotic water and exotic earth,
and then a medley of other elements that conveyed no suggestion of
anything whatever, except of evolutionary realms and ranges that were
beyond all human experience or calculation. For awhile he lived and
was awake only in his sensory response to this potpourri of odors;
then the awareness of his own corporeal being came back to him
through tactual sensations of an unusual order, which he did not at
first recognize as being within himself, but which seemed to be those
of a foreign entity in some other dimension, with whom he was connected across unbridgeable gulfs by a nexus of gossamer tenuity. This
entity, he thought, was reclining on a material of great softness, into
which he sank with a supreme and leaden indolence and a feeling of
sheer bodily weight that held him utterly motionless. Then, floating
along the ebon cycles of the void, this being came with ineffable slowness toward Alvor, and at last, by no perceptible transition, by no

breach of physical logic or mental congruity, was incorporate with him. Then a tiny light, like a star burning all alone in the center of infinitude, began to dawn far-off; and it drew nearer and nearer and grew larger and larger till it turned the black void to a dazzling luminescence, to a many-tinted glory that smote full upon Alvor.

He found that he was lying with wide-open eyes on a huge couch, in a sort of pavilion consisting of a low and elliptical dome supported on double rows of diagonally fluted pillars. He was quite naked, though a sheet of some thin and pale yellow fabric had been thrown across his lower limbs. He saw at a glance, even though his brain-centers were still half-benumbed as by the action of some opiate, that this fabric was not the product of any terrestrial loom. Beneath his body, the couch was covered with grey and purple stuffs, but whether they were made of feathers, fur or cloth he was quite uncertain, for they suggested all three of these materials. They were very thick and resilient, and accounted for the sense of extreme softness underneath him that marked his return from the swoon. The couch itself stood higher above the floor than an ordinary bed, and was also longer, and in his half-narcotized condition this troubled Alvor even more than other aspects of his situation which were far less normal and explicable.

Amazement grew upon him as he looked about with reviving faculties, for all that he saw and smelt and touched was totally foreign and unaccountable. The floor of the pavilion was wrought in a geometric marquetry of ovals, rhomboids and equilaterals, in white, black and yellow metals that no earthly mine had ever disclosed; and the pillars were of the same three metals, regularly alternating. The dome alone was entirely of yellow. Not far from the couch, there stood on a squat tripod a dark and wide-mouthed vessel from which poured an opalescent vapor. Someone standing behind it, invisible through the cloud of gorgeous fumes, was fanning the vapor toward Alvor. He recognized it as the source of the myrrh-like odor that had first troubled his re-animating senses. It was quite agreeable, but was borne away from him again and again by gusts of hot wind which brought into the pavilion a mixture of perfumes that were both sweet and acrid and were altogether novel. Looking between the pillars, he saw the monstrous heads of towering blossoms with pagoda-like tiers of sultry, sullen petals, and beyond them a terraced landscape of low hills of mauve and nacarat soil, extending toward a horizon incredibly remote, till they rose and rose against the heavens. Above all this was a whitish sky, filled with a blinding radiation of intense light from a sun that was now hidden by the dome. Alvor's eyes began to ache, the odors disturbed and oppressed him, and he was possessed by a terrible dubiety and perplexity, amid which he remembered vaguely his meeting with Vizaphmal, and the events preceding his swoon. He was unbearably nervous, and for some time all his ideas and sensations took on the painful disorder and irrational fears of incipient delirium.

A figure stepped from behind the veering vapors and approached the couch. It was Vizaphmal, who bore in one of his five hands the large thin circular fan of bluish metal he had been using. He was holding in another hand a tubular cup, half-full of an erubescent liquid.

"Drink this," he ordered, as he put the cup to Alvor's lips. The liquid was so bitter and fiery that Alvor could swallow it only in sips, between periods of gasping and coughing. But once he had gotten it down, his brain cleared with celerity and all his sensations were soon comparatively normal.

"Where am I?" he asked. His voice sounded very strange and unfamiliar to him, and its effect bordered upon ventriloquism—which, as he afterward learned, was due to certain peculiarities of the atmospheric medium.

"You are on my country estate, in Ulphalor, a kingdom which occupies the whole northern hemisphere of Satabbor, the inmost planet of Sanarda, that sun which is called Antares in your world. You have been unconscious for three of our days, a result which I anticipated, knowing the profound shock your nervous system would receive from the experience through which you have passed. However, I do not think you will suffer any permanent illness or inconvenience; and I have just now administered to you a sovereign drug which will aid in the adjustment of your nerves and your corporeal functions to the novel conditions under which you are to live henceforward. I employed the opalescent vapor to arouse you from your swoon, when I deemed that it had become safe and wise to do this. The vapor is produced by the burning of an aromatic sea-weed, and is magisterial in its restorative effect."

Alvor tried to grasp the full meaning of this information, but his brain was still unable to receive anything more than a mélange of impressions that were totally new and obscure and outlandish. As he pondered the words of Vizaphmal, he saw that rays of bright light had fallen between the columns and were creeping across the floor. Then the rim of a vast ember-colored sun descended below the rim of the dome and he felt an overwhelming, but somehow not insupportable, warmth. His eyes no longer ached, not even in the direct beams of this luminary; nor did the perfumes irritate him, as they had done for awhile.

"I think," said Vizaphmal, "that you may now arise. It is afternoon, and there is much for you to learn, and much to be done."

Alvor threw off the thin covering of yellow cloth, and sat up, with his legs hanging over the edge of the high couch.

"But my clothing?" he queried.

"You will need none in our climate. No one has ever worn anything of the sort in Satabbor."

Alvor digested this idea, and though he was slightly disconcerted, he made up his mind that he would accustom himself to whatever should be required of him. Anyway, the lack of his usual habiliments was far from disagreeable in the dry, sultry air of this new world.

He slid from the couch to the floor, which was nearly five feet below him, and took several steps. He was not weak or dizzy, as he had half-expected, but all his movements were characterized by the same sense of extreme bodily weight of which he had been dimly aware while still in a semi-conscious condition.

"The world in which you now dwell is somewhat larger than your own," explained Vizaphmal, "and the force of gravity is proportionately greater. Your weight has been increased by no less than a third; but I think you will soon become habituated to this, as well as to the other novelties of your situation."

Motioning the poet to follow him, he led the way through that portion of the pavilion which had been behind Alvor's head as he lay on the couch. A spiral bridge of ascending stairs ran from this pavilion to a much larger pile where numerous wings and annexes of the same aerial architecture of domes and columns flared from a central edifice with a circular wall and many thin spires. Below the bridge, about the pavilion, and around the whole edifice above, were gardens of trees and flowers that caused Alvor to recall the things he had seen during his one experiment with hashish. The foliation of the trees was either very fine and hair-like, or else it consisted of huge, semi-globular and discoid forms depending from horizontal branches and suggesting a novel union of fruit and leaf. Almost all colors, even green, were shown in the bark and foliage of these trees. The flowers were mainly similar to those Alvor had seen from the pavilion, but there were others of a short, puffy-stemmed variety, with no trace of leaves, and with malignant purple-black heads full of crimson mouths, which swayed a little even when there was no wind. There were oval pools and meandering streams of a dark water with irisated glints all through this garden, which, with the columnar edifice, occupied the middle of a small plateau.

As Alvor followed his guide along the bridge, a perspective of hills and plains all marked out in geometric diamonds and squares and triangles, with a large lake or inland sea in their midst, was revealed momently. Far in the distance, more than a hundred leagues away, were the gleaming domes and towers of some baroque city, toward which the enormous orb of the sun was now declining. When he looked at this sun and saw the whole extent of its diameter for the first time, he felt an overpowering thrill of imaginative awe and wonder and exultation at the thought that it was identical with the red star to which he had addressed in another world the half-lyric, half-ironic lines of his ode.

At the end of the spiral bridge, they came to a second and more spacious pavilion, in which stood a high table with many seats attached to it by means of curving rods. Table and chairs were of the same material, a light, greyish metal. As they entered this pavilion, two strange beings appeared and bowed before Vizaphmal. They were like the scientist in their organic structure, but were not so tall, and their coloring was very drab and dark, with no hint of opalescence. By certain bizarre indications, Alvor surmised that the two beings were of different sexes.

"You are right," said Vizaphmal, reading his thoughts. "These persons are a male and female of the two inferior sexes called Abbars, who constitute the workers, as well as the breeders, of our world. There are two superior sexes, who are sterile, and who form the intellectual, esthetic and ruling classes, to whom I belong. We call ourselves the Alphads. The Abbars are more numerous, but we hold them in close subjection; and even though they are our parents as well as our slaves, the ideas of filial piety which prevail in your world would be regarded as truly singular by us. We supervise their breeding, so that the due proportion of Abbars and Alphads may be maintained, and the character of the progeny is determined by the injection of certain serums at the time of conceiving. We ourselves, though sterile, are capable of what you call love, and our amorous delights are more complex than yours in their nature."

He now turned and addressed the two Abbars. The phonetic forms and combinations that issued from his lips were unbelievably different from those of the scholarly English in which he had spoken to Alvor. There were strange gutturals and linguals and oddly prolonged vowels which Alvor, for all his subsequent attempts to learn the language, could never quite approximate and which argued a basic divergence in the structure of the vocal organs of Vizaphmal from that of his own.

Bowing till their heads almost touched the floor, the two Abbars disappeared among the columns in a wing of the building and soon returned, carrying long trays on which were unknown foods and beverages in utensils of unearthly forms.

"Be seated," said Vizaphmal. The meal that followed was far from unpleasant, and the food-stuffs were quite palatable, though Alvor was not sure whether they were meats or vegetables. He learned that they were really both, for his host explained that they were the prepared fruits of plants which were half-animal in their cellular composition and characteristics. These plants grew wild, and were hunted with the same care that would be required in hunting dangerous beasts, on account of their mobile branches and the poisonous darts with which they were armed. The two beverages were a pale, colorless wine with an acrid flavor, made from a root, and a dusky, sweetish liquid, the natural water of this world. Alvor noticed that the water had a saline after-taste.

"The time has now come," announced Vizaphmal at the end of the meal, "to explain frankly the reason why I have brought you here. We will now adjourn to that portion of my home which you would term a laboratory, or workshop, and which also includes my library."

They passed through several pavilions and winding colonnades, and reached the circular wall at the core of the edifice. Here a high narrow door, engraved with heteroclitic ciphers, gave admission to a huge room without windows, lit by a yellow glow whose cause was not ascertainable.

"The walls and ceiling are lined with a radio-active substance," said Vizaphmal, "which affords this illumination. The vibrations of this substance are also highly stimulating to all the processes of thought."

Alvor looked about him at the room, which was filled with alembics and cupels and retorts and sundry other scientific mechanisms, all of unfamiliar types and materials. He could not even surmise their use.

Beyond them, in a corner, he saw the apparatus of intersecting bars, with the two heavy disks, in which he and Vizaphmal had made their passage through etheric space. Around the walls there were a number of deep shelves, laden with great rolls like the volumes of the ancients.

Vizaphmal selected one of these rolls, and started to unfurl it. It was four feet wide, was grey in color, and was closely written with many columns of dark violet and maroon characters that ran horizontally instead of up and down.

"It will be necessary," said Vizaphmal, "to tell you a few facts regarding the history, religion and intellectual temper of our world, before I read to you the singular prophecy contained in one of the columns of this ancient chronicle.

"We are a very old people, and the beginnings, or even the first maturity of our civilization, antedate the appearance of the lowliest forms of life on your earth. Religious sentiment and the veneration of the past have always been dominant factors among us, and have shaped our history to an amazing extent. Even today, the whole mass of the Abbars and the majority of the Alphads are immersed in superstition, and the veriest details of quotidian life are regulated by sacerdotal law. A few scientists and thinkers, like myself, are above all such puerilities; but, strictly between you and me, the Alphads, for all their superior and highly aristocratic traits, are mainly the victims of arrested development in this regard. They have cultivated the epicurean and aesthetic side of life to a high degree, they are accomplished artists, sybarites and able administrators or politicians; but, intellectually, they have not freed themselves from the chains of a sterile pantheism and an all too prolific priesthood.

"Several cycles ago, in what might be called an early period of our history, the worship of all our sundry deities was at its height. There was at this time a veritable eruption, a universal plague of prophets, who termed themselves the voices of the gods, even as similarly minded persons have done in your world. Each of these prophets made his own especial job-lot of predictions, often quite minutely worked out and elaborate, and sometimes far from lacking in imaginative quality. A number of these prophecies have since been fulfilled to the letter, which, as you may well surmise, has helped enormously in confirming the hold of religion. However, between ourselves, I suspect that their fulfillment has had behind it more or less of a shrewd instrumentality, supplied by those who could profit therefrom in one way or another.

"There was one vates, Abbolechiolor by name, who was even more fertile-minded and long-winded than his fellows. I shall now translate to you, from the volumen I have just unrolled, a prediction that he made in the year 299 of the cycle of Sargholoth, the third of the seven epochs into which our known history has been sub-divided. It runs thus:

"'When, for the second time following this prediction, the two outmost moons of Satabbor shall be simultaneously darkened in a total eclipse by the third and innermost moon, and when the dim night of this occultation shall have worn away in the dawn, a mighty wizard shall appear in the city of Sarpoulom, before the palace of the kings of Ulphalor, accompanied by a most unique and unheard-of monster with two arms, two legs, two eyes and a white skin. And he that then rules in Ulphalor shall be deposed ere noon of this day, and the wizard shall be enthroned in his place, to reign as long as the white monster shall abide with him.'"

Vizaphmal paused, as if to give Alvor a chance to cogitate the matters that had been presented to him. Then, while his three eyes assumed a look of quizzical sharpness and shrewdness, he continued:

"Since the promulgation of this prophecy, there has already been one total eclipse of our two outer moons by the inner one. And, according to all the calculations of our astronomers, in which I can find no possible flaw, a second similar eclipse is now about to take place—in fact, it is due this very night. If Abbolechiolor was truly inspired, tomorrow morn is the time when the prophecy will be fulfilled. However, I decided somewhile ago that its fulfillment should not be left to chance; and one of my purposes in designing the mechanism with which I visited your world, was to find a monster who would meet the specifications of Abbolechiolor. No creature of this anomalous kind has ever been known, or even fabled, to exist in Satabbor; and I made a thorough search of many remote and outlying planets without being able to obtain what I required. In some of these worlds, there were monsters of very uncommon types, with an almost unlimited number of visual organs and limbs; but the variety to which you belong, with only two eyes, two arms and two legs, must indeed be rare throughout the infra-galactic universe, since I have not discovered it in any other planet than your own.

"I am sure that you now conceive the project I have long nurtured. You and I will appear at dawn in Sarpoulom, the capital of Ulphalor, whose domes and towers you saw this afternoon far off on the plain. Because of the celebrated prophecy, and the publicly known calculations regarding the imminence of a second two-fold eclipse, a great crowd will doubtless be gathered before the palace of the kings to await whatever shall occur. Akkiel, the present king, is by no means popular, and your advent in company with me, who am widely famed as a wizard, will be the signal for his dethronement. I shall then be ruler in his place, even as Abbolechiolor has so thoughtfully predicted. The holding of supreme temporal power in Ulphalor is not undesirable, even for one who is wise and learned and above most of the vanities of life, as I am. When this honor has devolved upon my unworthy shoulders, I shall be able to offer you, as a reward for your miraculous aid, an existence of rare and sybaritic luxury, of rich and varied sensation, such as you can hardly have imagined. It is true, no doubt, that you will be doomed to a certain loneliness among us: you will always be looked upon as a monster, a portentous anomaly; but such, I believe, was your lot in the world where I found you and where you were about to cast yourself into a most unpleasant river. There, as you have learned, all poets are regarded as no less anomalous than double-headed snakes or five-legged calves."

Alvor had listened to this speech in manifold and ever-increasing amazement. Toward the end, when there was no longer any doubt concerning Vizaphmal's intention, he felt the sting of a bitter and curious irony at the thought of the role he was destined to play. However, he could do no less than admit the cogency of Vizaphmal's final argument.

"I trust," said Vizaphmal, "that I have not injured your feelings by my frankness, or by the position in which I am about to place you."

"Oh, no, not at all," Alvor hastened to assure him.

"In that case, we shall soon begin our journey to Sarpoulom, which will take all night. Of course, we could make the trip in the flash of an instant with my space-annihilator, or in a few minutes with one of the air-machines that have long been employed among us. But I intend to use a very old-fashioned mode of conveyance for the occasion, so that we will arrive in the proper style, at the proper time, and also that you may enjoy our scenery and view the double eclipse at leisure."

When they emerged from the windowless room, the colonnades and pavilions without were full of a rosy light, though the sun was still an hour above the horizon. This, Alvor learned, was the usual prelude of a Satabborian sunset. He and Vizaphmal watched while the whole landscape before them became steeped in the ruddy glow, which deepened through shades of cinnabar and ruby to a rich garnet by the time Antares had begun to sink from sight. When the huge orb had disappeared, the intervening lands took on a fiery amethyst, and tall auroral flames of a hundred hues shot upward to the zenith from the sunken sun. Alvor was spell-bound by the glory of the spectacle.

Turning from this magnificent display at an unfamiliar sound, he saw that a singular vehicle had been brought by the Abbars to the steps of the pavilion in which they stood. It was more like a chariot than anything else, and was drawn by three animals undreamt of in human fable or heraldry. These animals were black and hairless, their bodies were extremely long, each of them had eight legs and a forked tail, and their whole aspect, including their flat, venomous, triangular heads, was uncomfortably serpentine. A series of green and scarlet wattles hung from their throats and bellies, and semi-translucent membranes, erigible at will, were attached to their sides.

"You behold," Vizaphmal informed Alvor, "the traditional conveyance that has been used since time immemorial by all orthodox wizards in Ulphalor. These creatures are called *orpods*, and they are among the swiftest of our mammalian serpents."

He and Alvor seated themselves in the vehicle. Then the three *orpods*, who had no reins in all their complicated harness, started off at a word of command on a spiral road that ran from Vizaphmal's home to the plain beneath. As they went, they erected the membranes at their sides and soon attained an amazing speed.

Now, for the first time, Alvor saw the three moons of Satabbor, which had risen opposite the afterglow. They were all large, especially the innermost one, a perceptible warmth was shed by their pink rays, and their combined illumination was nearly as clear and bright as that of a terrestrial day.

The land through which Vizaphmal and the poet now passed was uninhabited, in spite of its nearness to Sarpoulom, and they met no one. Alvor learned that the terraces he had seen upon awaking were not the work of intelligent beings, as he had thought, but were a natural formation of the hills. Vizaphmal had chosen this location for his home because of the solitude and privacy, so desirable for the scientific experiments to which he had devoted himself.

After they had traversed many leagues, they began to pass occasional houses, of a like structure to that of Vizaphmal's. Then the road meandered along the rim of cultivated fields, which Alvor recognized as the source of the geometric division he had seen from afar during the day. He was told that these fields were given mainly to the growing of root-vegetables, of a gigantic truffle and a kind of succulent cactus, which formed the chief foods of the Abbars. The Alphads ate by choice only the meat of animals and the fruits of wild, half-animal plants, such as those with which Alvor had been served.

By midnight the three moons had drawn very close together and the second moon had begun to occlude the outermost. Then the inner moon came slowly across the others, till in an hour's time the eclipse was complete. The diminution of light was very marked, and the whole effect was now similar to that of a moonlit night on earth.

"It will be morning in a little more than two hours," said Vizaphmal, "since our nights are extremely short at this time of year. The eclipse will be over before then. But there is no need for us to hurry."

He spoke to the *orpods*, who folded their membranes and settled to a sort of trot.

Sarpoulom was now visible in the heart of the plain, and its outlines were rendered more distinct as the two hidden moons began to draw forth from the adumbration of the other. When to this triple light the ruby rays of earliest morn were added, the city loomed upon the travelers with fantastic many-storied piles of that same open type of metal architecture which the home of Vizaphmal had displayed. This architecture, Alvor found, was general throughout the land, though an older type with closed walls was occasionally to be met with, and was used altogether in the building of prisons and the inquisitions maintained by the priesthood of the various deities.

It was an incredible vision that Alvor saw—a vision of high domes upborne on slender elongated columns, tier above tier, of airy colonnades and bridges and hanging gardens loftier than Babylon or than Babel, all tinged by the ever-changing red that accompanied and followed the Satabborian dawn, even as it had preceded the sunset. Into this vision, along streets that were paven with the same metal as that of the buildings, Alvor and Vizaphmal were drawn by the three *orpods*.

The poet was overcome by the sense of an unimaginably old and alien and diverse life which descended upon him from these buildings. He was surprised to find that the streets were nearly deserted and that little sign of activity was manifest anywhere. A few Abbars, now and then, scuttled away in alleys or entrances at the approach of the *orpods*, and two beings of a coloration similar to that of Vizaphmal, one of whom Alvor took to be a female, issued from a colonnade and stood staring at the travelers in evident stupefaction.

When they had followed a sort of winding avenue for more than a mile, Alvor saw between and above the edifices in front of them the domes and upper tiers of a building that surpassed all the others in its extent.

"You now behold the palace of the kings of Ulphalor," his companion told him.

In a little while they emerged upon a great square that surrounded the palace. This square was crowded with the people of the city, who, as Vizaphmal had surmised, were all gathered to await the fulfillment or non-fulfillment of the prophecy of Abbolechiolor. The open galleries and arcades of the huge edifice, which rose to a height of ten stories, were also laden with watching figures. Abbars were the most plentiful element in this throng, but there were also multitudes of the gayly-colored Alphads among them.

At sight of Alvor and his companion, a perceptible movement, a sort of communal shuddering which soon grew convulsive, ran through the whole assemblage in the square and along the galleries of the edifice above. Loud cries of a peculiar shrillness and harshness arose, there was a strident sound of beaten metal in the heart of the palace, like the gongs of an alarm, and mysterious lights glowed out and were extinguished in the higher stories. Clangors of unknown machines, the moan and roar and shriek of strange instruments, were audible above the clamor of the crowd, which grew more tumultuous and agitated in its motion. A way was opened for the car drawn by the three *orpods*, and

Vizaphmal and Alvor soon reached the entrance of the palace.

There was an unreality about it all to Alvor, and the discomfiture he had felt in drawing upon himself the weird phosphoric gaze of ten thousand eyes, all of whom were now intent with a fearsome uncanny curiosity on every detail of his physique, was like the discomfiture of some absurd and terrible dream. The movement of the crowd had ceased, while the car was passing along the unhuman lane that had been made for it, and there was an interval of silence. Then, once more, there was babble and debate, and cries that had the accent of martial orders or summonses were caught up and repeated. The throng began to move, with a new and more concentric swirling, and the foremost ranks of Abbars and Alphads swelled like a dark and tinted wave into the colonnades of the palace. They climbed the pillars with a dreadful swift agility to the stories above, they thronged the courts and pavilions and arcades, and though a weak resistance was apparently put up by those within, there was nothing that could stem them.

Through all this clangor and clamor and tumult, Vizaphmal stood in the car with an imperturbable mien beside the poet. Soon a number of Alphads, evidently a delegation, issued from the palace and made obeisance to the wizard, whom they addressed in humble and supplicative tones.

"A revolution has been precipitated by our advent," explained Vizaphmal, "and Akkiel the king has fled. The chamberlains of the court and the high priests of all our local deities are now offering me the throne of Ulphalor. Thus the prophecy is being fulfilled to the letter. You must agree with me that the great Abbolechiolor was happily inspired."

III

The ceremony of Vizaphmal's enthronement was held almost immediately, in a huge hall at the core of the palace, open like all the rest of the structure, and with columns of colossal size. The throne was a great globe of azure metal, with a seat hollowed out near the top, accessible by means of a serpentine flight of stairs. Alvor, at an order issued by the wizard, was allowed to stand at the base of this globe with some of the Alphads.

The enthronement itself was quite simple. The wizard mounted the stairs, amid the silence of a multitude that had thronged the hall, and seated himself in the hollow of the great globe. Then a very tall and distinguished-looking Alphad also climbed the steps, carrying a heavy rod, one half of which was green, and the other a swart, sullen crimson, and placed this rod in the hands of Vizaphmal. Later, Alvor was told that the crimson end of this rod could emit a death-dealing ray, and the green a vibration that cured almost all the kinds of illness to which the Satabborians were subject. Thus it was more than symbolical of the twofold power of life and death with which the king had been invested.

The ceremony was now at an end, and the gathering quickly dispersed. Alvor, at the command of Vizaphmal, was installed in a suite of open apartments on the third story of the palace, at the end of many labyrinthine stairs. A dozen Abbars, who were made his personal retainers, soon came in, each carrying a different food or drink. The foods were beyond belief in their strangeness, for they included the eggs of a moth-like insect large as a plover, and the apples of a fungoid tree that grew in the craters of dead volcanoes. They were served in ewers of a white and shining mineral, upborne on legs of fantastic length, and wrought with a cunning artistry. Likewise he was given, in shallow bowls, a liquor made from the blood-like juice of living plants, and a wine in which the narcotic pollen of some night-blooming flower had been dissolved.

The days and weeks that now followed were, for the poet, an experience beyond the visionary resources of any terrestrial drug. Step by step, he was initiated, as much as possible for one so radically alien, into the complexities and singularities of life in a new world. Gradually his nerves and his mind, by the aid of the erubescent liquid which Vizaphmal continued to administer to him at intervals, became habituated to the strong light and heat, the intense radiative properties of a soil and atmosphere with unearthly chemical constituents, the strange foods and beverages, and the people themselves with their queer anatomy and queerer customs. Tutors were engaged to teach him the language, and, in spite of the difficulties presented by certain unmanageable consonants, certain weird ululative vowels, he learned enough of it to make his simpler ideas and wants understood.

He saw Vizaphmal every day, and the new king seemed to cherish a real gratitude toward him for his indispensable aid in the fulfillment of the prophecy. Vizaphmal took pains to instruct him in regard to all that it was necessary to know, and kept him well-informed as to the progress of public events in Ulphalor. He was told, among other things, that no news had been heard concerning the whereabouts of Akkiel, the late ruler. Also, Vizaphmal had reason to be aware of more or less opposition toward himself on the part of the various priest-hoods, who, in spite of his life-long discretion, had somehow learned of his free-thinking propensities.

For all the attention, kindness and service that he received, and the unique luxury with which he was surrounded, Alvor felt that these people, even as the wizard had forewarned him, looked upon him merely as a kind of unnatural curiosity or anomaly. He was no less monstrous to them than they were to him, and the gulf created by the laws of a diverse biology, by an alien trend of evolution, seemed impossible to bridge in any manner. He was questioned by many of them, and, in especial, by more than one delegation of noted scientists, who desired to know as much as he could tell them about himself. But the queries were so patronizing, so rude and narrow-minded and scornful and smug, that he was soon wont to feign a total ignorance of the language on such occasions. Indeed, there was a gulf; and he was rendered even more acutely conscious of it whenever he met any of the female Abbars or Alphads of the court, who eyed him with disdainful inquisitiveness, and among whom a sort of tittering usually arose when he passed. His naked members, so limited in number, were obviously as great a source of astonishment to them as their own somewhat intricate and puzzling charms were to him. All of them were quite nude; indeed, nothing, not even a string of jewels or a single gem, was ever worn by any of the Satabborians. The female Alphads, like the males, were extremely tall and were gorgeous with epidermic hues that would have outdone the plumage of any peacock; and their anatomical structure was most peculiar . . . Alvor began to feel the loneliness of which Vizaphmal had spoken, and he was overcome at times by a great nostalgia for his own world, by a planetary homesickness. He became atrociously nervous, even if not actually ill.

While he was still in this condition, Vizaphmal took him on a tour of Ulphalor that had become necessary for political reasons. More or less incredulity concerning the real existence of such a monstrosity as Alvor had been expressed by the folk of outlying provinces, of the polar realms and the antipodes, and the new ruler felt that a visual demonstration of the two-armed, two-legged and two-eyed phenomenon would be far from inadvisable, to establish beyond dispute the legitimacy of his own claim to the throne. In the course of this tour, they visited many unique cities, and the rural and urban centers of industries peculiar to Satabbor; and Alvor saw the mines from which the countless minerals and metals used in Ulphalor were extracted by the toil of millions of Abbars. These metals were found in a pure state, and were of inexhaustible extent. Also he saw the huge oceans, which, with certain inland seas and lakes that were fed from underground sources, formed the sole water-supply of the aging planet, where no rain had even been rumored to fall for centuries. The sea-water, after undergoing a treatment that purged it of a number of undesirable elements, was carried all through the land by a system of conduits. Moreover, he saw the marshlands at the north pole, with their vicious tangle of animate vegetation, into which no one had ever tried to penetrate.

They met many outland peoples in the course of this tour; but the general characteristics were the same throughout Ulphalor, except in one or two races of the lowest aborigines, among whom there were no Alphads. Everywhere the poet was eyed with the same cruel and ignorant curiosity that had been shown in Sarpoulom. However, he became gradually inured to this, and the varying spectacles of bizarre interest and the unheard-of scenes that he saw daily, helped to divert him a little from his nostalgia for the lost earth.

When he and Vizaphmal returned to Sarpoulom, after an absence of many weeks, they found that much discontent and revolutionary sentiment had been sown among the multitude by the hierarchies of the Satabborian gods and goddesses, particularly by the priesthood of Cunthamosi, the Cosmic Mother, a female deity in high favor among the two reproductive sexes, from whom the lower ranks of her hierophants were recruited. Cunthamosi was worshipped as the source of all things; her maternal organs were believed to have given birth to the sun, the moon, the world, the stars, the planets and even the meteors which often fell in Satabbor. But it was argued by her priests that such a monstrosity as Alvor could not possibly have issued from her womb, and that therefore his very existence was a kind of blasphemy, and that the rule of the heretic wizard, Vizaphmal, based on the advent of this abnormality, was likewise a flagrant insult to the Cosmic Mother. They did not deny the apparently miraculous fulfillment of the prophecy of Abbolechiolor, but it was maintained that this fulfillment was no assurance of the perpetuity of Vizaphmal's reign, and no proof that his reign was countenanced by any of the gods.

"I can not conceal from you," said Vizaphmal to Alvor, "that the position in which we both stand is now slightly parlous. I intend to bring the space-annihilator from my country home to the court, since it is not impossible that I may have need of it, and that some foreign sphere will soon become more salubrious for me than my native one."

However, it would seem that this able scientist, alert wizard and competent king had not altogether grasped the full imminence of the danger that threatened his reign; or else he spoke, as was sometimes his wont, with sardonic moderation. He showed no further concern, beyond setting a strong guard about Alvor to attend him at all times, lest an attempt should be made to kidnap the poet in consideration of the last clause of the prophecy.

Three days after the return to Sarpoulom, while Alvor was standing in one of his private balconies looking out over the roofs of the town, with his guards chattering idly in the rooms behind, he saw that the streets were dark with a horde of people, mainly Abbars, who were streaming silently toward the palace. A few Alphads, distinguishable even at a distance by their gaudy hues, were at the head of this throng. Alarmed at the spectacle, and remembering what the king had told him, he went to find Vizaphmal and climbed the eternal tortuous series of complicated stairs that led to the king's personal suite. Others among the inmates of the court had seen the advancing crowd, and there was agitation, terror and frantic hurry everywhere. Mounting the last flight of steps to the king's threshold, Alvor was astounded to find that many of the Abbars, who had gained ingress from the other side of the palace and had scaled the successive rows of columns and stairs with ape-like celerity, were already pouring into the room. Vizaphmal himself was standing before the open frame-work of the space-annihilator, which had now been installed beside his couch. The rod of royal investiture was in his hand, and he was leveling the crimson head at the foremost of the invading Abbars. As this creature leapt toward him, waving an atrocious weapon lined by a score of hooked blades, Vizaphmal tightened his hold on the rod, thus pressing a secret spring, and a thin rose-colored ray of light was emitted from the end, causing the Abbar to crumple and fall. Others, in no wise deterred, ran forward to succeed him, and the king turned his lethal beam upon them with the calm air of one who is conducting a scientific experiment, till the floor was piled with dead Abbars. Still others took their place, and some began to cast their hooked weapons at the king. None of these touched him, but he seemed to weary of the sport, and stepping within the frame-work, he closed it upon himself. A moment more, and then there was a roar as of a thousand thunders, and the mechanism and Vizaphmal were no longer to be seen. Never, at any future time, was the poet to learn what had become of him, nor in what stranger world than Satabbor he was now indulging his scientific fancies and curiosities.

Alvor had no time to feel, as he might conceivably have done, that he had been basely deserted by the king. All the nether and upper stories of the great edifice were now a-swarm with the invading crowd, who were no longer silent, but were uttering shrill, ferocious cries as they bore down the opposition of the courtiers and slaves. The whole place was inundated by an ever-mounting sea, in which there were now myriads of Alphads as well as of Abbars; and no escape was possible. In a few instants, Alvor himself was seized by a group of the Abbars, who seemed to have been enraged rather than terrified or discomfited by the vanishing of Vizaphmal. He recognized them as priests of Cunthamosi by an odd oval and vertical marking of red pigments on their swart bodies. They bound him viciously with cords made from the intestines of a dragon-like animal, and carried him away from the palace, along streets that were lined by a staring and gibbering mob, to a building on the southern outskirts of Sarpoulom, which Vizaphmal had once pointed out to him as the Inquisition of the Cosmic Mother.

This edifice, unlike most of the buildings in Sarpoulom, was walled on all sides and was constructed entirely of enormous grey bricks, made from the local soil, and bigger and harder than blocks of granite. In a long five-sided chamber illumined only by narrow slits in the roof, Alvor found himself arraigned before a jury of the priests, presided over by a swollen and pontifical-looking Alphad, the Grand Inquisitor.

The place was filled with ingenious and grotesque implements of torture, and the very walls were hung to the ceiling with contrivances that would have put Torquemada to shame. Some of them were very small, and were designed for the treatment of special and separate nerves; and others were intended to harrow the entire epidermic area of the body at a single twist of their screw-like mechanism.

Alvor could understand little of the charges being preferred against him, but gathered that they were the same, or included the same, of which Vizaphmal had spoken—to wit, that he, Alvor, was a monstrosity that could never have been conceived or brought forth by Cunthamosi, and whose very existence, past, present and future, was a dire affront to this divinity. The entire scene—the dark and lurid room with its array of hellish instruments, the diabolic faces of the inquisitors, and the high unhuman drone of their voices as they intoned the charges and brought judgment against Alvor—was laden with a horror beyond the horror of dreams.

Presently the Grand Inquisitor focussed the malign gleam of his three unblinking orbs upon the poet, and began to pronounce an interminable sentence, pausing a little at quite regular intervals which seemed to mark the clauses of the punishment that was to be inflicted. These clauses were well-nigh innumerable, but Alvor could comprehend almost nothing of what was said; and doubtless it was as well that he did not comprehend.

When the voice of the swollen Alphad had ceased, the poet was led away through endless corridors and down a stairway that seemed to descend into the bowels of Satabbor. These corridors, and also the stairway, were luminous with a self-emitted light that resembled the phosphorescence of decaying matter in tombs and catacombs. As Alvor went downward with his guards, who were all Abbars of the lowest type, he could hear somewhere in sealed unknowable vaults the moan and shriek of beings who endured the ordeals imposed by the inquisitors of Cunthamosi.

They came to the final step of the stairway, where, in a vast vault, an abyss whose bottom was not discernible yawned in the center of the floor. On its edge there stood a fantastic sort of windlass on which was wound an immense coil of blackish rope.

The end of this rope was now tied about Alvor's ankles, and he was lowered head downward into the gulf by the inquisitors. The sides were not luminous like those of the stairway, and he could see nothing. But, as he descended into the gulf, the terrible discomfort of his position was increased by sensations of an ulterior origin. He felt that he was passing through a kind of hairy material with numberless filaments that clung to his head and body and limbs like minute tentacles, and whose contact gave rise to an immediate itching. The substance impeded him more and more, till at last he was held immovably suspended as in a net, and all the while the separate hairs seemed to be biting into his flesh with a million microscopic teeth, till the initial itching was followed by a burning and a deep convulsive throbbing more exquisitely painful than the flames of an *auto da fe*. The poet learned long afterward that the material into which he had been lowered was a subterranean organism, half-vegetable, half-animal, which grew from the side of the gulf, with long mobile feelers that were extremely poisonous to the touch. But at the time, not the least of the horrors he underwent was the uncertainty as to its precise nature.

After he had hung for quite a while in this agonizing web, and had become almost unconscious from the pain and the unnatural position, Alvor felt that he was being drawn upward. A thousand of the fine thread-like tentacles clung to him and his whole body was encircled with a mesh of insufferable pangs as he broke loose from them. He swooned with the intensity of this pain, and when he recovered, he was lying on the floor at the edge of the gulf, and one of the priests was prodding him with a many-pointed weapon.

Alvor gazed for a moment at the cruel visages of his tormenters, in the luminous glow from the sides of the vault, and wondered dimly what infernal torture was next to follow, in the carrying-out of the interminable sentence that had been pronounced. He surmised, of course, that the one he had just undergone was mild in comparison to the many that would succeed it. But he never knew, for at that instant there came a crashing sound like the fall and shattering of the universe; the walls, the floor and the stairway rocked to and fro in a veritable convulsion, and the vault above was riven in sunder, letting through a rain of fragments of all sizes, some of which struck several of the inquisitors and swept them into the gulf. Others of the priests leapt over the edge in their terror, and the two who remained were in no condition to continue their official duties. Both of them were lying beside Alvor with broken heads from which, in lieu of blood, there issued a glutinous light-green liquid.

Alvor could not imagine what had happened, but knew only that he himself was unhurt, as far as the results of the cataclysm were concerned. His mental state was not one to admit of scientific surmise: he was sick and dizzy from the ordeal he had suffered, and his whole body was swollen, was blood-red and violently burning from the touch of the organisms in the gulf. He had, however, enough strength and presence of mind to grope with his bound hands for the weapon that had been dropped by one of the inquisitors. By much patience, by untiring ingenuity, he was able to cut the thongs about his wrists and ankles on the sharp blade of one of the five points.

Carrying this weapon, which he knew that he might need, he began the ascent of the subterranean stairway. The steps were half-blocked by fallen masses of stone, and some of the landings and stairs, as well as the sides of the wall, were cloven with enormous rents; and his egress was by no means an easy matter. When he reached the top, he found that the whole edifice was a pile of shattered walls, with a great pit in its center from which a cloud of vapors issued. An immense meteor had fallen, and had struck the Inquisition of the Cosmic Mother.

Alvor was in no condition to appreciate the irony of this event, but at least he was able to comprehend his chance of freedom. The only inquisitors now visible were lying with squashed bodies whose heads or feet protruded from beneath the large squares of overthrown brick, and Alvor lost no time in quitting the vicinity.

It was now night, and only one of the three moons had arisen. Alvor struck off through the level arid country to the south of Sarpoulom, where no one dwelt, with the idea of crossing the boundaries of Ulphalor into one of the independent kingdoms that lay below the equator. He remembered Vizaphmal telling him once that the people of these kingdoms were more enlightened and less priest-ridden than those of Ulphalor.

All night he wandered, in a sort of daze that was at times delirium. The pain of his swollen limbs increased, and he grew feverish. The moonlit plain seemed to shift and waver before him, but was interminable as the landscape of a hashish-dream. Presently the other two moons arose, and in the over-taxed condition of his mind and nerves, he was never quite sure as to their actual number. Usually, there appeared to be more than three, and this troubled him prodigiously. He tried to resolve the problem for hours, as he staggered on, and at last, a little before dawn, he became altogether delirious.

He was unable afterward to recall anything about his subsequent journey. Something impelled him to go on even when his thews were dead and his brain an utter blank: he knew nothing of the waste and terrible lands through which he roamed in the hour-long ruby-red of morn and beneath a furnace-like sun; nor did he know when he crossed the equator at sunset and entered Omanorion, the realm of the empress Ambiala, still carrying in his hand the five-pointed weapon of one of the dead inquisitors.

IV

It was night when Alvor awoke, but he had no means of surmising that it was not the same night in which he had fled from the Inquisition of the Cosmic Mother; and that many Satabborian days had gone by since he had fallen totally exhausted and unconscious within the boundary-line of Omanorion. The warm, rosy beams of the three moons were full in his face, but he could not know whether they were ascending or declining. Anyhow, he was lying on a very comfortable couch that was not quite so disconcertingly long and high as the one upon which he had first awakened in Ulphalor. He was in an open pavilion, and this pavilion was also a bower of multitudinous blossoms which leaned toward him with faces that were both grotesque and weirdly beautiful, from vines that had scaled the columns, or from the many curious metal pots that stood upon the floor. The air that he breathed was a medley of perfumes more exotic than frangipane; they were extravagantly sweet and spicy, but somehow he did not find them oppressive. Rather, they served to augment the deep, delightful languor of all his sensations.

As he opened his eyes and turned a little on the couch, a female Alphad, not so tall as those of Ulphalor and really quite of his own stature, came out from behind the flower-pots and addressed him. Her language was not that of the Ulphalorians, it was softer and less utterly unhuman, and though he could not understand a word, he was immediately aware of a sympathetic note or undertone which, so far, he had never heard on the lips of anyone in this world, not even Vizaphmal.

He replied in the language of Ulphalor, and found that he was understood. He and the female Alphad now carried on as much of a conversation as Alvor's linguistic abilities would permit. He learned that he was talking to the empress Ambiala, the sole and supreme ruler of Omanorion, a quite extensive realm contiguous to Ulphalor. She told him that some of her servitors, while out hunting the wild, ferocious, half-animal fruits of the region, had found him lying unconscious near a thicket of the deadly plants that bore these fruits, and had brought him to her palace in Lompior, the chief city of Omanorion. There, while he still lay in a week-long stupor, he had been treated with medicaments that had now almost cured the painful swellings resultant from his plunge among the hair-like organisms in the Inquisition.

With genuine courtesy, the empress forbore to question the poet regarding himself, nor did she express any surprise at his anatomical peculiarities. However, her whole manner gave evidence of an eager and even fascinated interest, for she did not take her eyes away from him at any time. He was a little embarrassed by her intent scrutiny, and to cover this embarrassment, as well as to afford her the explanations due to so kind a hostess, he tried to tell her as much as he could of his own history and adventures. It was doubtful if she understood more than half of what he said, but even this half obviously lent him an increasingly portentous attraction in her eyes. All of her three orbs grew round with wonder at the tale related by this fantastic Ulysses, and whenever he stopped she would beg him to go on. The garnet and ruby and cinnabar gradations of the dawn found Alvor still talking and the empress Ambiala still listening.

In the full light of Antares, Alvor saw that his hostess was, from a Satabborian viewpoint, a really beautiful and exquisite creature. The iridescence of her coloring was very soft and subtle, her arms and legs, though of the usual number, were all voluptuously rounded, and the features of her face were capable of a wide range of expression. Her usual look, however, was one of a sad and wistful yearning. This look Alvor came to understand, when, with a growing knowledge of her language, he learned that she too was a poet, that she had always been troubled by vague desires for the exotic and the far-off, and that she was thoroughly bored with everything in Omanorion, and especially with the male Alphads of that region, none of whom could rightfully boast of having been her lover even for a day. Alvor's biological difference from these males was evidently the secret of his initial fascination for her.

The poet's life in the palace of Ambiala, where he found that he was looked upon as a permanent guest, was from the beginning much more agreeable than his existence in Ulphalor had been. For one thing, there was Ambiala herself, who impressed him as being infinitely more intelligent than the females of Sarpoulom, and whose attitude was so thoughtful and sympathetic and admiring, in contra-distinction to the attitude of those aforesaid females. Also, the servitors of the palace and the people of Lompior, though they doubtless regarded Alvor as a quite singular sort of being, were at least more tolerant than the Ulphalorians; and he met with no manner of rudeness among them at any time. Moreover, if there were any priesthoods in Omanorion, they were not of the uncompromising type he had met north of the equator, and it would seem that nothing was to be feared from them. No one ever spoke of religion to Alvor in this ideal realm, and somehow he never actually learned whether or not Omanorion possessed any gods or goddesses. Remembering his ordeal in the Inquisition of the Cosmic Mother, he was quite willing not to broach the subject, anyway.

Alvor made rapid progress in the language of Omanorion, since the empress herself was his teacher. He soon learned more and more about her ideas and tastes, about her romantic love for the triple moonlight, and the odd flowers that she cultivated with so much care and so much delectation. These blossoms were rare anywhere in Satabbor: some of them were anemones that came from the tops of almost inaccessible mountains many leagues in height, and others were forms inconceivably more bizarre than orchids, mainly from terrific jungles near the southern pole. He was soon privileged to hear her play on a certain musical instrument of the country, in which were combined the characters of the flute and the lute. And at last, one day, when he knew enough of the tongue to appreciate a few of its subtleties, she read to him from a scroll of vegetable vellum one of her poems, an ode to a star known as Atana by the people of Omanorion. This ode was truly exquisite, was replete with poetic fancies of a high order, and expressed a half-ironic yearning, sadly conscious of its own impossibility, for the ultra-sidereal realms of Atana. Ending, she added:

"I have always loved Atana, because it is so little and so far away."

On questioning her, Alvor learned, to his overwhelming amazement, that Atana was identical with a minute star called Arot in Ulphalor, which Vizaphmal had once pointed out to him as the sun of his own earth. This star was visible only in the rare interlunar dark, and it was considered a test of good eyesight to see it even then.

When the poet had communicated this bit of astronomical information to Ambiala, that the star Atana was his own native sun, and had also told her of his "Ode to Antares," a most affecting scene occurred, for the empress encircled him with her five arms and cried out:

"Do you not feel, as I do, that we were destined for each other?"

Though he was a little discomposed by Ambiala's display of affection, Alvor could do no less than assent. The two beings, so dissimilar in external ways, were absolutely overcome by the rapport revealed in this comparing of poetic notes; and a real understanding, rare even with persons of the same evolutionary type, was established between them henceforward. Also, Alvor soon developed a new appreciation of the outward charms of Ambiala, which, to tell the truth, had not altogether inveigled him theretofore. He reflected that after all her five arms and three legs and three eyes were merely a superabundance of anatomical features upon which human love was wont to set a by no means lowly value. As for her opalescent coloring, it was, he thought, much more lovely than the agglomeration of outlandish hues with which the human female figure had been adorned in many modernistic paintings.

When it became known in Lompior that Alvor was the lover of Ambiala, no surprise or censure was expressed by any one. Doubtless the people, especially the male Alphads who had vainly wooed the empress, thought that her tastes were queer, not to say eccentric. But anyway, no comment was made: it was her own amour after all, and no one else could carry it on for her. It would seem, from this, that the people of Omanorion had mastered the ultra-civilized art of minding their own business.

THE GOD OF THE ASTEROID

Man's conquest of the interplanetary gulfs has been fraught with many tragedies. Vessel after vessel, like a venturous mote, has disappeared in the infinite—and has not returned. Inevitably, for the most part, the lost explorers have left no record of their fate. Their ships have flared as unknown meteors through the atmosphere of the further planets, to fall like shapeless metal cinders on a never-visited terrain; or have become the dead, frozen satellites of other worlds or moons. A few, perhaps, among the unreturning fliers, have succeeded in landing somewhere, and their crews have perished immediately, or survived for a little while amid the inconceivably hostile environment of a cosmos not designed for men.

In later years, with the progress of exploration, more than one of the early derelicts has been descried, following its solitary orbit; and the wrecks of others have been found on ultra-terrene shores. Occasionally—not often—it has been possible to reconstruct the details of the lone, remote disaster. Sometimes, in a fused and twisted hull, a log or record has been preserved intact. Among others, there is the case of the *Selenite*, the first known rocket-ship to dare the zone of the asteroids.

At the time of its disappearance, fifty years ago, in 1980, a dozen voyages had been made to Mars, and a rocket-base had been established in Syrtis Major, with a small permanent colony of terrestrials, all of whom were trained scientists as well as men of uncommon hardihood and physical stamina.

The effects of the Martian climate, and the utter alienation from familiar conditions, as might have been expected, were extremely trying and even disastrous. There was an unremitting struggle with deadly or pestiferous bacteria new to science, a perpetual assailment by dangerous radiations of soil and air and sun. The lessened gravity played its part also, in contributing to curious and profound disturbances of metabolism. The worst effects were nervous and mental. Queer, irrational animosities, manias or phobias never classified by alienists, began to develop among the personnel at the rocket-base.

Violent quarrels broke out between men who were normally controlled and urbane. The party, numbering fifteen in all, soon divided into several cliques, one against the others; and this morbid antagonism led at times to actual fighting and even bloodshed.

One of the cliques consisted of three men, Roger Colt, Phil Gershom and Edmond Beverly. These three, through banding together in a curious fashion, became intolerably antisocial toward all the others. It would seem that they must have gone close to the borderline of insanity, and were subject to actual delusions. At any rate, they conceived the idea that Mars, with its fifteen earth-men, was entirely too crowded. Voicing this idea in a most offensive and belligerent manner, they also began to hint their intention of faring even further afield in space.

Their hints were not taken seriously by the others, since a crew of three was insufficient for the proper manning of even the lightest rocket-vessel used at that time. Colt, Gershom, and Beverly had no difficulty at all in stealing the *Selenite*, the smaller of the two ships then reposing at the Syrtis Major base. Their fellow-colonists were aroused one night by the cannon-like roar of the discharging tubes, and emerged from their huts of sheet-iron in time to see the vessel departing in a fiery streak toward Jupiter.

No attempt was made to follow it; but the incident helped to sober the remaining twelve and to calm their unnatural animosities. It was believed, from certain remarks that the malcontents had let drop, that their particular objective was Ganymede or Europa, both of which were thought to possess an atmosphere suitable for human respiration. It seemed very doubtful, however, that they could pass the perilous belt of the asteroids. Apart from the difficulty of steering a course amid these innumerable, far-strewn bodies, the *Selenite* was not fuelled or provisioned for a voyage of such length. Gershom, Colt and Beverly, in their mad haste to quit the company of the others, had forgotten to calculate the actual necessities of their proposed voyage, and had wholly overlooked its dangers.

After that departing flash on the Martian skies, the *Selenite* was not seen again; and its fate remained a mystery for thirty years. Then, on tiny, remote Phocea, its dented wreck was found by the Holdane expedition to the asteroids.

Phocea, at the time of the expedition's visit, was in aphelion. Like others of the planetoids, it was discovered to possess a rare atmosphere, too thin for human breathing. Both hemispheres were covered with thin snow; and lying amid this snow, the *Selenite* was sighted by the explorers as they circled about the little world.

Much interest prevailed, for the shape of the partially bare mound was plainly recognizable and not to be confused with the surrounding rocks. Holdane ordered a landing, and several men in space-suits proceeded to examine the wreck. They soon identified it as the long-missing *Selenite*.

Peering in through one of the thick, unbreakable neo-crystal ports, they met the eyeless gaze of a human skeleton, which had fallen forward against the slanting, overhanging wall. It seemed to grin a sardonic welcome. The vessel's hull was partly buried in the stony soil, and had been crumpled and even slightly fused, though not broken, by its plunge. The manhole lid was so thoroughly jammed and soldered that it was impossible to effect an entrance without the use of a cutting-torch.

Enormous, withered, cryptogamous plants with the habit of vines, that crumbled at a touch, were clinging to the hull and the adjacent rocks. In the light snow beneath the skeleton-guarded port, a number of sharded bodies were lying, which proved to be those of tall insect forms, like giant *phasmidae*. From the posture and arrangement of their lank, pipy members, longer than those of a man, it seemed that they had walked erect. They were unimaginably grotesque, and their composition, due to the almost non-existent gravity, was fantastically porous and insubstantial. Many more bodies, of a similar type, were afterwards found on other portions of the planetoid; but no living thing was discovered. All life, it was plain, had perished in the transarctic winter of Phocea's aphelion.

When the *Selenite* had been entered, the party learned, from a sort of log or notebook found on the floor, that the skeleton was all that remained of Edmond Beverly. There was no trace of his two companions; but the log, on examination, proved to contain a record of their fate as well as the subsequent adventures of Beverly almost to the very moment of his own death from a doubtful, unexplained cause.

The tale was a strange and tragic one. Beverly, it would seem, had written it day by day, after the departure from Syrtis Major, in an effort to retain a semblance of morale and mental coherence amid the black alienation and disorientation of infinitude. I transcribe it herewith, omitting only the earlier passages, which were full of unimportant details and personal animadversions. The first entries were all dated, and Beverly had made an heroic attempt to measure and mark off the seasonless night of the void in terms of earthly time. But after the disastrous landing on Phocea, he had abandoned this; and the actual length of time covered by his entries can only be conjectured.

THE LOG

Sept. 10th. Mars is only a pale-red star through our rear ports; and according to my calculations we will soon approach the orbit of the nearest asteroids. Jupiter and its system of moons are seemingly as far off as ever, like beacons on the unattainable shore of immensity. More even than at first, I feel that dreadful, suffocating illusion, which accompanies ether-travel, of being perfectly stationary in a static void.

Gershom, however, complains of a disturbance of equilibrium, with much vertigo and a frequent sense of falling, as if the vessel were sinking beneath him through bottomless space at a headlong speed. The causation of such symptoms is rather obscure, since the artificial gravity regulators are in good working-order. Colt and I have not suffered from any similar disturbance. It seems to me that the sense of falling would be almost a relief from this illusion of nightmare immobility; but Gershom appears to be greatly distressed by it, and says that his hallucination is growing stronger, with fewer and briefer intervals of normality. He fears that it will become continuous.

Sept. 11th. Colt has made an estimate of our fuel and provisions and thinks that with careful husbandry we will be able to reach Europa. I have been checking up on his calculations, and find that he is altogether too sanguine. According to my estimate, the fuel will give out while we are still midway in the belt of asteroids; though the food, water and compressed air would possibly take us most of the way to Europa. This discovery I must conceal from the others. It is too late to turn back. I wonder if we have all been mad, to start out on this errant voyage into cosmical immensity with no real preparation or thought of consequences. Colt, it would seem, has lost even the power of mathematical calculation: his figures are full of the most egregious errors.

Gershom has been unable to sleep, and is not even fit to take his turn at the watch. The hallucination of falling obsesses him perpetually, and he cries out in terror, thinking that the vessel is about to crash on some dark, unknown planet to which it is being drawn by an irresistible gravitation. Eating, drinking and locomotion are very difficult for him, and he complains that he cannot even draw a full breath— that the air is snatched away from him in his precipitate descent. His condition is indeed painful and pitiable.

Sept. 12th. Gershom is worse—bromide of potassium and even a heavy dose of morphine from the *Selenite's* medicine lockers, have not relieved him or enabled him to sleep. He has the look of a drowning man and seems to be on the point of strangulation. It is hard for him to speak.

Colt has become very morose and sullen, and snarls at me when I address him. I think that Gershom's plight has preyed sorely upon his nerves—as it has on mine. But my burden is heavier than Colt's: for I know the inevitable doom of our insane and ill-starred expedition. Sometimes I wish it were all over. . . . The hells of the human mind are vaster than space, darker than the night between the worlds . . .and all three of us have spent several eternities in hell. Our attempt to flee has only plunged us into a black and shoreless limbo, through which we are fated to carry still our own private perdition.

I, too, like Gershom, have been unable to sleep. But, unlike him, I am tormented by the illusion of eternal immobility. In spite of the daily calculations that assure me of our progress through the gulf, I cannot convince myself that we have moved at all. It seems to me that we hang suspended like Mohammed's coffin, remote from earth and equally remote from the stars, in an incommensurable vastness without bourn or direction. I cannot describe the awfulness of the feeling.

Sept. 13th. During my watch, Colt opened the medicine locker and managed to shoot himself full of morphine. When his turn came, he was in a stupor and I could do nothing to rouse him. Gershom had gotten steadily worse and seemed to be enduring a thousand deaths . . . so there was nothing for me to do but keep on with the watch as long as I could. I locked the controls anyway, so that the vessel would continue its course without human guidance if I should fall asleep.

I don't know how long I kept awake—nor how long I slept. I was aroused by a queer hissing whose nature and cause I could not identify at first. I looked around and saw that Colt was in his hammock, still lying in a drug-induced sopor. Then I saw that Gershom was gone, and began to realize that the hissing came from the air-lock. The inner door of the lock was closed securely—but evidently someone had opened the outer manhole, and the sound was being made by the escaping air. It grew fainter and ceased as I listened.

I knew then what had happened—Gershom, unable to endure his strange hallucination any longer, had actually flung himself into space from the *Selenite*! Going to the rear ports, I saw his body, with a pale, slightly bloated face and open, bulging eyes. It was following us like a satellite, keeping an even distance of ten or twelve feet from the lee of the vessel's stern. I could have gone out in a space suit to retrieve the body; but I felt sure that Gershom was already dead, and the effort seemed more than useless. Since there was no leakage of air from the interior, I did not even try to close the manhole.

I hope and pray that Gershom is at peace. He will float forever in cosmic space—and in that further void where the torment of human consciousness can never follow.

Sept. 15th. We have kept our course somehow, though Colt is too demoralized and drug-sodden to be of much assistance. I pity him when the limited supply of morphine gives out.

Gershom's body is still following us, held by the slight power of the vessel's gravitational attraction. It seems to terrify Colt in his more lucid moments; and he complains that we are being haunted by the dead man. It's bad enough for me, too, and I wonder how much my nerves and mind will stand. Sometimes I think that I am beginning to develop the delusion that tortured Gershom and drove him to his death. An awful dizziness assails me, and I fear that I shall start to fall. But somehow I regain my equilibrium.

Sept. 16th. Colt used up all the morphine, and began to show signs of intense depression and uncontrollable nervousness. His fear of the satellite corpse appeared to grow upon him like an obsession; and I could do nothing to reassure him. His terror was deepened by an eerie, superstitious belief.

"I tell you, I hear Gershom calling us," he cried. "He wants company, out there in the black, frozen emptiness; and he won't leave the vessel till one of us goes out to join him. You've got to go, Beverly— it's either you or me—otherwise he'll follow the *Selenite* forever."

I tried to reason with him, but in vain. He turned upon me in a sudden shift of maniacal rage.

"Damn you, I'll throw you out, if you won't go any other way!" he shrieked.

Clawing and mouthing like a mad beast, he leapt toward me where I sat before the *Selenite's* control-board. I was almost overborne by his onset, for he fought with a wild and frantic strength. . . . I don't like to write down all that happened, for the mere recollection makes me sick. . . . Finally he got me by the throat, with a sharp-nailed clutch that I could not loosen, and began to choke me to death. In self-defense, I had to shoot him with an automatic which I carried in my pocket. Reeling dizzily, gasping for breath, I found myself staring down at his prostrate body, from which a crimson puddle was widening on the floor.

Somehow, I managed to put on a space-suit. Dragging Colt by the ankles, I got him to the inner door of the air-lock. When I opened the door, the escaping air hurled me toward the open manhole together with the corpse; and it was hard to regain my footing and avoid being carried through into space. Colt's body, turning transversely in its movement, was jammed across the manhole; and I had to thrust it out with my hands. Then I closed the lid after it. When I returned to the ship's interior, I saw it floating, pale and bloated, beside the corpse of Gershom.

Sept. 17th. I am alone—and yet most horribly I am pursued and companioned by the dead men. I have sought to concentrate my faculties on the hopeless problem of survival, on the exigencies of space navigation; but it is all useless. Ever I am aware of those stiff and swollen bodies, swimming in the awful silence of the void, with the white, airless sun like a leprosy of light on their upturned faces. I try to keep my eyes on the control-board—on the astronomic charts—on the log I am writing—on the stars toward which I am travelling. But a frightful and irresistible magnetism makes me turn at intervals, mechanically, helplessly, to the rearward ports. There are no words for what I feel and think—and words are as lost things along with the worlds I have left so far behind. I sink in a chaos of vertiginous horror, beyond all possibility of return.

Sept. 18th. I am entering the zone of the asteroids—those desert rocks, fragmentary and amorphous, that whirl in far-scattered array between Mars and Jupiter. Today the *Selenite* passed very close to one of them—a small body like a broken-off mountain, which heaved suddenly from the gulf with knife-sharp pinnacles and black gullies that seemed to cleave its very heart. The *Selenite* would have crashed full upon it in a few instants, if I had not reversed the power and steered in an abrupt diagonal to the right. As it was, I passed near enough for the bodies of Colt and Gershom to be caught by the gravitational pull of the planet-oid; and when I looked back at the receding rock, after the vessel was out of danger, they had disappeared from sight. Finally I located them with the telescopic reflector, and saw that they were revolving in space, like infinitesimal moons, about that awful, naked asteroid. Perhaps they will float thus forever, or will drift gradually down in lessening circles, to find a tomb in one of those bleak, bottomless ravines.

Sept. 19th. I have passed several more of the asteroids—irregular fragments, little larger than meteoric stones; and all my skill of space-manship has been taxed severely to avert collision. Because of the need for unrelaxing vigilance, I have been compelled to keep awake at all times. But sooner or later, sleep will overpower me, and the *Selenite* will crash to destruction.

After all, it matters little: the end is inevitable, and must come soon enough in any case. The store of concentrated food, the tanks of compressed oxygen, might keep me alive for many months, since there is no one but myself to consume them. But the fuel is almost gone, as I know from my former calculations. At any moment, the propulsion may cease. Then the vessel will drift idly and helplessly in this cosmic limbo, and be drawn to its doom on some asteroidal reef.

Sep. 21st (?). Everything I have expected has happened, and yet by some miracle of chance—or mischance—I am still alive.

The fuel gave out yesterday (at least I think it was yesterday). But I was too close to the nadir of physical and mental exhaustion to realize clearly that the rocket-explosions had ceased. I was dead for want of sleep, and had gotten into a state beyond hope or despair. Dimly I remember setting the vessel's controls through automatic force of habit; and then I lashed myself in my hammock and fell asleep instantly.

I have no means of guessing how long I slept. Vaguely, in the gulf beyond dreams, I heard a crash as of far-off thunder, and felt a violent vibration that jarred me into dull wakefulness. A sensation of unnatural, sweltering heat began to oppress me as I struggled toward consciousness; but when I had opened my heavy eyes, I was unable to determine for some little time what had really happened.

Twisting my head so that I could peer out through one of the ports, I was startled to see, on a purple-black sky, an icy, glittering horizon of saw-edged rocks.

For an instant, I thought that the vessel was about to strike on some looming planetoid. Then, overwhelmingly, I realized *that the crash had already occurred*—that I had been awakened from my coma-like slumber by the falling of the *Selenite* upon one of those barren cosmic islets.

I was wide-awake now, and I hastened to unlash myself from the hammock. I found that the floor was pitched sharply, as if the *Selenite* had landed on a slope or had buried its nose in the alien terrain. Feeling a queer, disconcerting lightness, and barely able to re-establish my feet on the floor at each step, I made my way to the nearest port. It was plain that the artificial gravity-system of the flier had been thrown out of commission by the crash, and that I was now subject only to the feeble gravitation of the asteroid. It seemed to me that I was light and incorporeal as a cloud—that I was no more than the airy specter of my former self.

The floor and walls were strangely hot; and it came to me that the heating must have been caused by the passage of the vessel through some sort of atmosphere. The asteroid, then, was not wholly airless, as such bodies are commonly supposed to be; and probably it was one of the larger fragments, with a diameter of many miles—perhaps hundreds. But even this realization failed to prepare me for the weird and surprising scene upon which I gazed through the port.

The horizon of serrate peaks, like a miniature mountain-range, lay at a distance of several hundred yards. Above it, the small, intensely brilliant sun, like a fiery moon in its magnitude, was sinking with visible rapidity in the dark sky that revealed the major stars and planets.

The *Selenite* had plunged into a shallow valley, and had half-buried its prow and bottom in a soil that was formed by decomposing rock, mainly basaltic. All about were fretted ridges, guttering pillars and pinnacles; and over these, amazingly, there clambered frail, pipy, leafless vines with broad, yellow-green tendrils flat and thin as paper. Insubstantial-looking lichens, taller than a man, and having the form of flat antlers, grew in single rows and thickets along the valley beside rills of water like molten moonstone.

Between the thickets, I saw the approach of certain living creatures who rose from behind the middle rocks with the suddenness and lightness of leaping insects. They seemed to skim the ground with long, flying steps that were both easy and abrupt.

There were five of these beings, who, no doubt, had been attracted by the fall of the *Selenite* from space and were coming to inspect it. In a few moments, they neared the vessel and paused before it with the same effortless ease that had marked all their movements.

What they really were, I do not know; but for want of other analogies, I must liken them to insects. Standing perfectly erect, they towered seven feet in air. Their eyes, like faceted opals, at the end of curving protractile stalks, rose level with the port. Their unbelievably thin limbs, their stem-like bodies, comparable to those of the *phasmidae*, or "walking-sticks", were covered with grey-green shards. Their heads, triangular in shape, were flanked with immense, perforated membranes, and were fitted with mandibular mouths that seemed to grin eternally.

I think that they saw me with those weird, inexpressive eyes; for they drew nearer, pressing against the very port, till I could have touched them with my hand if the port had been open. Perhaps they too were surprised: for the thin eye-stalks seemed to lengthen as they stared; and there was a queer waving of their sharded arms, a quivering of their horny mouths, as if they were holding converse with each other. After a while they went away, vanishing swiftly beyond the near horizon.

Since then, I have examined the *Selenite* as fully as possible, to ascertain the extent of the damage. I think that the outer hull has been crumpled or even fused in places: for when I approached the manhole, clad in a space-suit, with the idea of emerging, I found that I could not open the lid. My exit from the flier has been rendered impossible, since I have no tools with which to cut the heavy metal or shatter the tough, neo-crystal ports. I am sealed in the *Selenite* as in a prison; and the prison, in due time, must also become my tomb.

Later. I shall no longer try to date this record. It is impossible, under the circumstances, to retain even an approximate sense of earthly time. The chronometers have ceased running, and their machinery has been hopelessly jarred by the vessel's fall. The diurnal periods of this planetoid are, it would seem, no more than an hour or two in duration; and the nights are equally short. Darkness swept upon the landscape like a black wing after I had finished writing my last entry; and since then, so many of these ephemeral days and nights have shuttled by, that I have now ceased to count them. My very sense of duration is becoming oddly confused. Now that I have grown somewhat used to my situation, the brief days drag with immeasurable tedium.

The beings whom I call the walking-sticks have returned to the *Selenite*, coming daily, and bringing scores and hundreds of others. It would seem that they correspond in some measure to humanity, being the dominant life-form of this little world. In most ways, they are incomprehensibly alien; but certain of their actions bear a remote kinship to those of men, and suggest similar impulses and instincts.

Evidently they are curious. They crowd around the *Selenite* in great numbers, inspecting it with their stalk-borne eyes, touching the hull and ports with their attenuated members. I believe they are trying to establish some sort of communication with me. I cannot be sure that they emit vocal sounds, since the hull of the flier is sound-proof; but I am sure that the stiff, semaphoric gestures which they repeat in a certain order before the port as soon as they catch sight of me, are fraught with conscious and definite meaning.

Also, I surmise an actual veneration in their attitude, such as would be accorded by savages to some mysterious visitant from the heavens. Each day, when they gather before the ship, they bring curious spongy fruits and porous vegetable forms which they leave like a sacrificial offering on the ground. By their gestures, they seem to implore me to accept these offerings.

Oddly enough, the fruits and vegetables always disappear during the night. They are eaten by large, luminous, flying creatures with filmy wings, that seem to be wholly nocturnal in their habits. Doubtless, however, the walking-sticks believe that I, the strange ultra-stellar god, have accepted the sacrifice.

It is all strange, unreal, immaterial. The loss of normal gravity makes me feel like a phantom; and I seem to live in a phantom world. My thoughts, my memories, my despair—all are no more than mists that waver on the verge of oblivion. And yet, by some fantastic irony, I am worshipped as a god!

Innumerable days have gone by since I made the last entry in this log. The seasons of the asteroid have changed: the days have grown briefer, the nights longer; and a bleak wintriness pervades the valley. The frail, flat vines are withering on the rocks, and the tall lichen-thickets have assumed funereal autumn hues of madder and mauve. The sun revolves in a low arc above the saw-toothed horizon, and its orb is small and pale as if it were receding into the black gulf among the stars.

The people of the asteroid appear less often, they seem fewer in number, and their sacrificial gifts are rare and scant. No longer do they bring sponge-like fruits, but only pale and porous fungi that seem to have been gathered in caverns.

They move slowly, as if the winter cold were beginning to numb them. Yesterday, three of them fell, after depositing their gifts, and lay still before the flier. They have not moved, and I feel sure that they are dead. The luminous night-flying creatures have ceased to come, and the sacrifices remain undisturbed beside their bearers.

The awfulness of my fate has closed upon me today. No more of the walking-sticks have appeared. I think that they have all died—the ephemerae of this tiny world that is bearing me with it into the Arctic limbo of the solar system. Doubtless their life-time corresponds only to its summer—to its perihelion.

Thin clouds have gathered in the dark air, and snow is falling like fine powder. I feel an unspeakable desolation—a dreariness that I cannot write. The heating-apparatus of the *Selenite* is still in good working-order; so the cold cannot reach me. But the black frost of space has fallen upon my spirit. Strange—I did not feel so utterly bereft and alone while the insect people came daily. Now that they come no more, I seem to have been overtaken by the ultimate horror of solitude, by the chill terror of an alienation beyond life. I can write no longer, for my brain and my heart fail me.

Still, it would seem, I live, after an eternity of darkness and madness in the flier, of death and winter in the world outside. During that time, I have not written in the log; and I know not what obscure impulse prompts me to resume a practice so irrational and futile.

I think it is the sun, passing in a higher and longer arc above the dead landscape, that has called me back from the utterness of despair. The snow has melted from the rocks, forming little rills and pools of water; and strange plant-buds are protruding from the sandy soil. They lift and swell visibly as I watch them. I am beyond hope, beyond life, in a weird vacuum; but I see these things as a condemned captive sees the stirring of spring from his cell. They rouse in me an emotion whose very name I had forgotten.

My food-supply is getting low, and the reserve of compressed air is even lower. I am afraid to calculate how much longer it will last. I have tried to break the neo-crystal ports with a large monkey-wrench for hammer; but the blows, owing partly to my own weightlessness, are futile as the tapping of a feather. Anyway, in all likelihood, the outside air would be too thin for human respiration.

The walking-stick people have re-appeared before the flier. I feel sure, from their lesser height, their brighter coloring, and the immature development of certain members, that they all represent a new generation. None of my former visitors have survived the winter; but somehow, the new ones seem to regard the *Selenite* and me with the same curiosity and reverence that were shown by their elders. They, too, have begun to bring gifts of unsubstantial-looking fruit; and they strew filmy blossoms below the port . . . I wonder how they propagate themselves, and how knowledge is transmitted from one generation to another. . . .

The flat, lichenous vines are mounting on the rocks, are clamber-
ing over the hull of the *Selenite*. The young walking-sticks gather daily
to worship me—they make those enigmatic signs which I have never
understood, and they move in swift gyrations about the vessel, as in
the measures of a hieratic dance . . . . I, the lost and doomed, have
been the god of two generations. No doubt they will still worship me
when I am dead. I think the air is almost gone—I am more light-
headed than usual today, and there is a queer constriction in my throat
and chest. . . .

Perhaps I am a little delirious, and have begun to imagine things;
but I have just perceived an odd phenomenon, hitherto unnoted. I
don't know what it is. A thin, columnar mist, moving and writhing like
a serpent, with opal colors that change momently, has appeared among
the rocks and is approaching the vessel. It seems like a live thing—like
a vaporous entity; and somehow, it is poisonous and inimical. It glides
forward, rearing above the throng of *phasmidae*, who have all prostrated
themselves as if in fear. I see it more clearly now: it is half-transparent,
with a web of grey threads among its changing colors; and it is putting
forth a long, wavering tentacle.

It is some rare life-form, unknown to earthly science; and I cannot
even surmise its nature and attributes. Perhaps it is the only one of its
kind on the asteroid. No doubt it has just discovered the presence of
the *Selenite*, and has been drawn by curiosity, like the walking-stick
people. The tentacle has touched the hull—it has reached the port behind which I stand, pencilling these words. The grey threads in the tentacle glow as if with sudden fire. My God—*it is coming through the neo-
crystal lens*—

PHOENIX

Rodis and Hilar had climbed from their natal caverns to the top chamber of the high observatory tower. Pressed close together, for warmth as well as love, they stood at an eastern window looking forth on hills and valleys dim with perennial starlight. They had come up to watch the rising of the sun: that sun which they had never seen except as an orb of blackness, occluding the zodiacal stars in its course from horizon to horizon.

Thus their ancestors had seen it for millenniums. By some freak of cosmic law, unforeseen, and inexplicable to astronomers and physicists, the sun's cooling had been comparatively sudden, and the earth had not suffered the long-drawn complete desiccation of such planets as Mercury and Mars. Rivers, lakes, seas, had frozen solid; and the air itself had congealed, all in a term of years historic rather than geologic. Millions of the earth's inhabitants had perished, trapped by the glacial ice, the centigrade cold. The rest, armed with all the resources of science, had found time to entrench themselves against the cosmic night in a world of ramified caverns, dug by atomic excavators far below the surface.

Here, by the light of artificial orbs, and the heat drawn from the planet's still-molten depths, life went on much as it had done in the outer world. Trees, fruits, grasses, grains, vegetables, were grown in isotope-stimulated soil or hydroponic gardens, affording food, renewing a breathable atmosphere. Domestic animals were kept; and birds flew; and insects crawled or fluttered. The rays considered necessary for life and health were afforded by the sunbright lamps that shone eternally in all the caverns.

Little of the old science was lost; but, on the other hand, there was now little advance. Existence had become the conserving of a fire menaced by inexorable night. Generation by generation a mysterious sterility had lessened the numbers of the race from millions to a few thousands. As time went on, a similar sterility began to affect animals; and even plants no longer flourished with their first abundance. No biologist could determine the cause with certainty.

Perhaps man, as well as other terrestrial life-forms, was past his prime, and had begun to undergo collectively the inevitable senility that comes to the individual. Or perhaps, having been a surface-dweller throughout most of his evolution, he was inadaptable to the cribbed and prisoned life, the caverned light and air; and was dying slowly from the deprivation of things he had almost forgotten.

Indeed, the world that had once flourished beneath a living sun was little more than a legend now, a tradition preserved by art and literature and history. Its beetling Babelian cities, its fecund hills and plains, were swathed impenetrably in snow and ice and solidified air. No living man had gazed upon it, except from the night-bound towers maintained as observatories.

Still, however, the dreams of men were often lit by primordial memories, in which the sun shone on rippling waters and waving trees and grass. And their waking hours were sometimes touched by an undying nostalgia for the lost earth. . . .

Alarmed by the prospect of racial extinction, the most able and brilliant savants had conceived a project that was seemingly no less desperate than fantastic. The plan, if executed, might lead to failure or even to the planet's destruction. But all the necessary steps had now been taken toward its launching.

It was of this plan that Rodis and Hilar spoke, standing clasped in each other's arms, as they waited for the rising of the dead sun.

"And you must go?" said Rodis, with averted eyes and voice that quavered a little.

"Of course. It is a duty and an honor. I am regarded as the foremost of the younger atomicists. The actual placing and timing of the bombs will devolve largely upon me."

"But—are you sure of success? There are so many risks, Hilar." The girl shuddered, clasping her lover with convulsive tightness.

"We are not sure of anything," Hilar admitted. "But, granting that our calculations are correct, the multiple charges of fissionable materials, including more than half the solar elements, should start chain-reactions that will restore the sun to its former incandescence. Of course, the explosion may be too sudden and too violent, involving the nearer planets in the formation of a nova. But we do not believe that this will happen—since an explosion of such magnitude would require instant disruption of all the sun's elements. Such disruption should not occur without a starter for each separate atomic structure. Science has never been able to break down all the known elements. If it had been, the earth itself would undoubtedly have suffered destruction in the old atomic wars."

Hilar paused, and his eyes dilated, kindling with a visionary fire.

"How glorious," he went on, "to use for a purpose of cosmic renovation the deadly projectiles designed by our forefathers only to blast and destroy. Stored in sealed caverns, they have not been used since man abandoned the earth's surface so many millenniums ago. Nor have the old space-ships been used either . . . . An interstellar drive was never perfected; and our voyagings were always limited to the other worlds of our own system—none of which was inhabited, or inhabitable. Since the sun's cooling and darkening, there has been no object in visiting any of them. But the ships too were stored away. And the newest and speediest one, powered with anti-gravity magnets, has been made ready for our voyage to the sun."

Rodis listened silently, with an awe that seemed to have subdued her misgivings, while Hilar continued to speak of the tremendous project upon which he, with six other chosen technicians, was about to embark. In the meanwhile, the black sun rose slowly into heavens thronged with the cold ironic blazing of innumerable stars, among which no planet shone. It blotted out the sting of the Scorpion, poised at that hour above the eastern hills. It was smaller but nearer than the igneous orb of history and legend. In its center, like a Cyclopean eye, there burned a single spot of dusky red fire, believed to mark the eruption of some immense volcano amid the measureless and cinder-blackened landscape.

To one standing in the ice-bound valley below the observatory, it would have seemed that the tower's litten window was a yellow eye that stared back from the dead earth to that crimson eye of the dead sun.

"Soon," said Hilar, "you will climb to this chamber—and see the morning that none has seen for a century of centuries. The thick ice will thaw from the peaks and valleys, running in streams to re-molten lakes and oceans. The liquefied air will rise in clouds and vapors, touched with the spectrum-tinted splendor of the light. Again, across earth, will blow the winds of the four quarters; and grass and flowers will grow, and trees burgeon from tiny saplings. And man, the dweller in closed caves and abysses, will return to his proper heritage."

"How wonderful it all sounds," murmured Rodis. "But. . . you will come back to me?"

"I will come back to you. . . in the sunlight," said Hilar.

II

The space-vessel *Phosphor* lay in a huge cavern beneath that region which had once been known as the Atlas Mountains. The cavern's mile-thick roof had been partly blasted away by atomic disintegrators. A great circular shaft slanted upward to the surface, forming a mouth in the mountain-side through which the stars of the Zodiac were visible. The prow of the *Phosphor* pointed at the stars.

All was now ready for its launching. A score of dignitaries and savants, looking like strange ungainly monsters in suits and helmets worn against the spatial cold that had invaded the cavern, were present for the occasion. Hilar and his six companions had already gone aboard the *Phosphor* and had closed its air-locks.

Inscrutable and silent behind their metalloid helmets, the watchers waited. There was no ceremony, no speaking or waving of farewells; nothing to indicate that a world's destiny impended on the mission of the vessel.

Like mouths of fire-belching dragons the stern-rockets flared, and the *Phosphor*, like a wingless bird, soared upward through the great shaft and vanished.

Hilar, gazing through a rear port, saw for a few moments the lamp-bright window of that tower in which he had stood so recently with Rodis. The window was a golden spark that swirled downward in abysses of devouring night—and was extinguished. Behind it, he knew, his beloved stood watching the *Phosphor*'s departure. It was a symbol, he mused . . . a symbol of life, of memory . . . of the suns themselves . . . of all things that flash briefly and fall into oblivion.

But such thoughts, he felt, should be dismissed. They were unworthy of one whom his fellows had appointed as a light-bringer, a Prometheus who should rekindle the dead sun and re-lumine the dark world.

There were no days, only hours of eternal starlight, to measure the time in which they sped outward through the void. The rockets, used for initial propulsion, no longer flamed astern; and the vessel flew in darkness, except for the gleaming Argus eyes of its ports, drawn now by the mighty gravitational drag of the blind sun.

Test-flights had been considered unnecessary for the *Phosphor*. All its machinery was in perfect condition; and the mechanics involved were simple and easily mastered. None of its crew had ever been in extraterrestrial space before; but all were well-trained in astronomy, mathematics, and the various techniques essential to a voyage between worlds. There were two navigators; one rocket-engineer; and two engineers who would operate the powerful generators, charged with a negative magnetism reverse to that of gravity, with which they hoped to approach, circumnavigate, and eventually depart in safety from an orb enormously heavier than the system's ten planets merged into one. Hilar and his assistant, Han Joas, completed the personnel. Their sole task was the timing, landing, and distribution of the bombs.

All were descendants of a mixed race with Latin, Semitic, Hamitic, and negroid ancestry: a race that had dwelt, before the sun's cooling, in countries south of the Mediterranean, where the former deserts had been rendered fertile by a vast irrigation-system of lakes and canals.

This mixture, after so many centuries of cavern life, had produced a characteristically slender, well-knit type, of short or medium stature and pale olive complexion. The features were often of negroid softness; the general physique marked by a delicacy verging upon decadence.

To an extent surprising, in view of the vast intermediate eras of historic and geographic change, this people had preserved many pre-atomic traditions and even something of the old classic Mediterranean cultures. Their language bore distinct traces of Latin, Greek, Spanish and Arabic.

Remnants of other peoples, those of sub-equatorial Asia and America, had survived the universal glaciation by burrowing underground. Radio communication had been maintained with these peoples till within fairly recent times, and had then ceased. It was believed that they had died out, or had retrograded into savagery, losing the civilization to which they had once attained.

Hour after hour, intervaled only by sleep and eating, the *Phosphor* sped onward through the black unvarying void. To Hilar, it seemed at times that they flew merely through a darker and vaster cavern whose remote walls were spangled by the stars as if by radiant orbs. He had thought to feel the overwhelming vertigo of unbottomed and undirectioned space. Instead, there was a weird sense of circumscription by the ambient night and emptiness, together with a sense of cyclic repetition, as if all that was happening had happened many times before and must recur often through endless future kalpas.

Had he and his companions gone forth in former cycles to the relighting of former perished suns? Would they go forth again, to rekindle suns that would flame and die in some posterior universe? Had there always been, would there always be, a Rodis who awaited his return?

Of these thoughts he spoke only to Han Joas, who shared something of his innate mysticism and his trend toward cosmic speculation. But mostly the two talked of the mysteries of the atom and its typhonic powers, and discussed the problems with which they would shortly be confronted.

The ship carried several hundred disruption-bombs, many of untried potency: the unused heritage of ancient wars that had left chasm scars and lethal radio-active areas, some a thousand miles or more in extent, for the planetary glaciers to cover. There were bombs of iron, calcium, sodium, helium, hydrogen, sulphur, potassium, magnesium, copper, chromium, strontium, barium, zinc: elements that had all been anciently revealed in the solar spectrum. Even at the apex of their madness, the warring nations had wisely refrained from employing more than a few such bombs at any one time. Chain-reactions had sometimes been started; but, fortunately, had died out.

Hilar and Han Joas hoped to distribute the bombs at intervals over the sun's entire circumference; preferably in large deposits of the same elements as those of which they were composed. The vessel was equipped with radar apparatus by which the various elements could be detected and located. The bombs would be timed to explode with as much simultaneity as possible. If all went well, the *Phosphor* would have fulfilled its mission and traveled most of the return distance to earth before the explosions occurred.

It had been conjectured that the sun's interior was composed of still-molten magma, covered by a relatively thin crust: a seething flux of matter that manifested itself in volcanic activities. Only one of the volcanoes was visible from earth to the naked eye; but numerous others had been revealed to telescopic study. Now, as the *Phosphor* drew near to its destination, the others flamed out on the huge, slowly rotating orb that had darkened a fourth of the ecliptic and had blotted Libra, Scorpio and Sagittarius wholly from view.

For a long time it had seemed to hang above the voyagers. Now, suddenly, as if through some prodigious legerdemain, it lay beneath them: a monstrous, ever-broadening disk of ebon, eyed with fiery craters, veined and spotted and blotched with unknown pallid radioactives. It was like the buckler of some macrocosmic giant of the night, who had entrenched himself in the abyss lying between the worlds.

The *Phosphor* plunged toward it like a steel splinter drawn by some tremendous lodestone.

Each member of the crew had been trained beforehand for the part he was to play; and everything had been timed with the utmost precision. Sybal and Samac, the engineers of the anti-gravity magnets, began to manipulate the switches that would build up resistance to the solar drag. The generators, bulking to the height of three men, with induction-coils that suggested some colossal Laocoön, could draw from cosmic space a negative force capable of counteracting many earth-gravities. In past ages they had defied easily the pull of Jupiter; and the ship had even coasted as near to the blazing sun as its insulation and refrigeration systems would safely permit. Therefore it seemed reasonable to expect that the voyagers could accomplish their purpose of approaching closely to the darkened globe, of circling it, and pulling away when the disruption-charges had all been planted.

A dull, subsonic vibration, felt rather than heard, began to emanate from the magnets. It shook the vessel, ached in the voyagers' tissues. Intently, with anxiety unbetrayed by their impassive features, they watched the slow, gradual building-up of power shown by gauge-dials on which giant needles crept like horologic hands, registering the reversed gravities one after one, till a drag equivalent to that of fifteen Earths had been neutralized. The clamp of the solar gravitation, drawing them on with projectile-like velocity, crushing them to their seats with relentless increase of weight, was loosened. The needles crept on . . . more slowly now . . . to sixteen . . . to seventeen . . . and stopped. The *Phosphor*'s fall had been retarded but not arrested. And the switches stood at their last notch.

Sybal spoke, in answer to the unuttered questions of his companions.

"Something is wrong. Perhaps there has been some unforeseen deterioration of the coils, in whose composition strange and complex alloys were used. Some of the elements may have been unstable—or have developed instability through age. Or perhaps there is some interfering force, born of the sun's decay. At any rate, it is impossible to build more power toward the twenty-seven antigravities we will require close to the solar surface."

Samac added: "The decelerative jets will increase our resistance to nineteen anti-gravities. It will still be far from enough, even at our present distance."

"How much time have we?" inquired Hilar, turning to the navigators, Calaf and Caramod.

The two conferred and calculated.

"By using the decelerative jets, it will be two hours before we reach the sun," announced Calaf finally.

As if his announcement had been an order, Eibano, the jet-engineer, promptly jerked the levers that fired to full power the reversing rockets banked in the *Phosphor*'s nose and sides. There was a slight further deceleration of their descent, a further lightening of the grievous weight that oppressed them. But the *Phosphor* still plunged irreversibly sunward.

Hilar and Han Joas exchanged a glance of understanding and

agreement. They rose stiffly from their seats, and moved heavily toward the magazine, occupying fully half the ship's interior, in which the hundreds of disruption-bombs were racked. It was unnecessary to announce their purpose; and no one spoke either in approval or demur.

Hilar opened the magazine's door; and he and Han Joas paused on the threshold, looking back. They saw for the last time the faces of their fellow-voyagers, expressing no other emotion than resignation, vignetted, as it were, on the verge of destruction. Then they entered the magazine, closing its door behind them.

They set to work methodically, moving back to back along a narrow aisle between the racks in which the immense ovoid bombs were piled in strict order according to their respective elements. Because of various coordinated dials and switches involved, it was a matter of minutes to prepare a single bomb for the explosion. Therefore Hilar and Han Joas, in the time at their disposal, could do no more than set the timing and detonating mechanism of one bomb of each element. A great chronometer, ticking at the magazine's farther end, enabled them to accomplish this task with precision. The bombs were thus timed to explode simultaneously, detonating the others through chain-reaction, at the moment when the *Phosphor* should touch the sun's surface.

The solar pull, strengthening as the *Phosphor* fell to its doom, had now made their movements slow and difficult. It would, they feared, immobilize them before they could finish preparing a second series of bombs for detonation. Laboriously, beneath the burden of a weight already trebled, they made their way to seats that faced a reflector in which the external cosmos was imaged.

It was an awesome and stupendous scene on which they gazed. The sun's globe had broadened vastly, filling the nether heavens. Half-seen, a dim unhorizoned landscape, fitfully lit by the crimson far-sundered flares of volcanoes, by bluish zones and patches of strange radio-active minerals, it deepened beneath them abysmally disclosing mountains that would have made the Himalayas seem like hillocks, revealing chasms that might have engulfed asteroids and planets.

At the center of this Cyclopean landscape burned the great volcano that had been called Hephaestus by astronomers. It was the same volcano watched by Hilar and Rodis from the observatory window. Tongues of flame a hundred miles in length arose and licked skyward from a crater that seemed the mouth of some ultramundane hell.

Hilar and Han Joas no longer heard the chronometer's portentous ticking, and had no eyes for the watching of its ominous hands. Such watching was needless now: there was nothing more to be done, and nothing before them but eternity. They measured their descent by the broadening of the dim solar plain, the leaping into salience of new mountains, the deepening of new chasms and gulfs in the globe that had now lost all semblance of a sphere.

It was plain now that the *Phosphor* would fall directly into the flaming and yawning crater of Hephaestus. Faster and faster it plunged, heavier grew the piled chains of gravity that giants could not have lifted. . . .

At the very last, the reflector on which Hilar and Han Joas peered was filled entirely by the tongued volcanic fires that enveloped the *Phosphor*.

Then, without eyes to see or ears to apprehend, they were part of the pyre from which the sun, like a Phoenix, was reborn.

III

Rodis, climbing to the tower, after a period of fitful sleep and troublous dreams, saw from its window the rising of the rekindled orb.

It dazzled her, though its glory was half-dimmed by rainbow-colored mists that fumed from the icy mountain-tops. It was a sight filled with marvel and with portent. Thin rills of downward-threading water had already begun to fret the glacial armor on slopes and scarps; and later they would swell to cataracts, laying bare the buried soil and stone. Vapors, that seemed to flow and fluctuate on renascent winds, swam sunward from lakes of congealed air at the valley's bottom. It was a visible resumption of the elemental life and activity so long suspended in hibernal night. Even through the tower's insulating walls, Rodis felt the solar warmth that later would awaken the seeds and spores of plants that had lain dormant for cycles.

Her heart was stirred to wonder by the spectacle. But beneath the wonder was a great numbness and a sadness like unmelting ice. Hilar, she knew, would never return to her—except as a ray of the light, a spark of the vital heat, that he had helped to relumine. For the nonce, there was irony rather than comfort in the memory of his promise: "I will come back to you—in the sunlight."

ACKNOWLEDGMENTS

"The Demon of the Flower." *Astounding Stories* 12, No. 4 (December 1933): 131–38. In *Lost Worlds* (Arkham House, 1944). Text taken from *A Vintage from Atlantis* (Night Shade Books, 2007).

"The Dweller in the Gulf." *Wonder Stories* 4, No. 10 (March 1933): 768–75 (as "The Dweller in Martian Depths"). In *The Abominations of Yondo* (Arkham House, 1960). Text taken from *The Maze of the Enchanter* (Night Shade Books, 2009).

"The Flower-Devil." In *Ebony and Crystal* (The Auburn Journal, 1922). Text taken from *Poems in Prose* (Arkham House, 1965).

"The Flower-Women." *Weird Tales* 25, No. 5 (May 1935): 624–32. In *Out of Space and Time* (Arkham House, 1942). Text taken from *The Maze of the Enchanter* (Night Shade Books, 2009).

"The God of the Asteroid." *Wonder Stories* 4, No. 5 (October 1932): 435–39, 469. In *Tales of Science and Sorcery* (Arkham House, 1964). Text taken from *A Vintage from Atlantis* (Night Shade Books, 2007).

"The Immeasurable Horror." *Weird Tales* 18, No. 2 (September 1931): 233–42. In *Other Dimensions* (Arkham House, 1970). Text taken from *The End of the Story* (Night Shade Books, 2006).

"The Immortals of Mercury." In *The Immortals of Mercury* (New York: Stellar Publishing Corp., 1932). In *Tales of Science and Sorcery* (Arkham House, 1964). Text taken from *A Vintage from Atlantis* (Night Shade Books, 2007).

"The Maze of the Enchanter." In *The Double Shadow and Other Fantasies* ([Auburn Journal Print], 1933). *Weird Tales* 32, No. 4 (October 1938): 475–83 (as "The Maze of Mâal Dweb"). Text taken from *The Maze of the Enchanter* (Night Shade Books, 2009).

"The Monster of the Prophecy." *Weird Tales* 19, No. 1 (January 1932): 8–31. In *Out of Space and Time* (Arkham House, 1942). Text taken from *The End of the Story* (Night Shade Books, 2006).

"Phoenix." In August Derleth, ed. *Time to Come: Science-Fiction Stories of Tomorrow* (Farrar, Straus & Young, 1954), 285–98. In *Other Dimensions* (Arkham House, 1970). Text taken from *The Last Hieroglyph* (Night Shade Books, 2010).

"Sadastor." *Weird Tales* 16, No. 1 (July 1930): 133–35. In *Out of Space and Time* (Arkham House, 1942). Text taken from *The End of the Story* (Night Shade Books, 2006).

"Seedling of Mars." *Wonder Stories Quarterly* 3, No. 1 (Fall 1931): 110–25, 136 (as "The Planet Entity"). In *Tales of Science and Sorcery* (Arkham House, 1964). Text taken from *A Vintage from Atlantis* (Night Shade Books, 2007).

"The Song of a Comet." In *The Star-Treader and Other Poems* (A. M. Robertson, 1912). Text taken from *The Complete Poetry and Translations*, Volume 1 (Hippocampus Press, 2008).

"The Star-Treader." In *The Star-Treader and Other Poems* (A. M. Robertson, 1912). Text taken from *The Complete Poetry and Translations*, Volume 1 (Hippocampus Press, 2008).

"To the Daemon." *Acolyte* 2, No. 1 (Fall 1943): 3. Text taken from *Poems in Prose* (Arkham House, 1965).

"The Vaults of Yoh-Vombis." *Weird Tales* 19, No. 5 (May 1932): 599–610. In *Out of Space and Time* (Arkham House, 1942). Text taken from *A Vintage from Atlantis* (Night Shade Books, 2007).

"Vulthoom." *Weird Tales* 26, No. 3 (September 1935): 336–52. In *Genius Loci* (Arkham House, 1948). Text taken from *The Maze of the Enchanter* (Night Shade Books, 2009).

www.ingramcontent.com/pod-product-compliance
Lightning Source LLC
Chambersburg PA
CBHW060950030726
47503CB00003B/804